Praise for Thom Racina's electrifying novels

Secret Weekend

"Brimming with harrowing situations, romance and mysterious characters, *Secret Weekend* is a suspense lover's dream. Thom Racina has packed many surprises into this page-turner with a special shocker saved for the end."—*Romantic Times*

"*Secret Weekend* starts as a breezy read that quickly turns into a pulse-pounding suspense thriller. . . . Thom Racina has written an exciting winner."
—Harriet Klausner

Hidden Agenda

"A fast-paced thriller . . . a smart, up-to-date read."
—*San Francisco Examiner*

"Colorful . . . fiendish . good entertainment . . . could be a heck of a m
Publishers Weekly

"A timely story . . . filled with recognizable people."
—*Library Journal*

"A wild romp through my news terrain. . . . I had a great time with it!"
—Kelly Lange, NBC news anchor, Los Angeles, author of *Trophy Wife*

"*Hidden Agenda* is a thrilling and savvy ride through the worlds of broadcasting, politics, and religion. Real names make it feel chillingly nonfictional, and the ending is a triumph of integrity over hypocrisy. It's unique, and I was spellbound."
—Sally Sussman, head writer, *Days of Our Lives*, NBC-TV

"The power of television news taken to its logical extreme. Thom Racina's ingenious story gives the reader a peek into the media's well-hidden backstage."
—Bill O'Reilly, anchorman, Fox News, author of *Those Who Trespass*

"One of the great 'what if?' stories of the last five years. Racina has done it again, kept me awake for twenty-four hours straight! Clever and controversial. . . ."

—Bill Hersey, writer/producer PBS, NBC

"Great read, wonderful characters and plot, boffo finish . . . I loved this book."

—Bob Healy, The Music Network

Snow Angel

"Fast moving . . . Racina spins a highly cinematic tale set against dramatic backdrops . . . a memorable villain who generates considerable suspense." —*Publishers Weekly*

"A chilling cliff-hanger chase." —*Booklist*

"A tale of obsessive love run nastily amok."

—*Kirkus Reviews*

"Powerful, compelling . . . a highly charged thriller with a surprise ending." —*Tulsa World*

ALSO BY THOM RACINA

Secret Weekend

Hidden Agenda

Snow Angel

The Madman's Diary

Thom Racina

A SIGNET BOOK

SIGNET
Published by New American Library, a division of
Penguin Putnam Inc., 375 Hudson Street,
New York, New York 10014, U.S.A.
Penguin Books Ltd, 27 Wrights Lane,
London W8 5TZ, England
Penguin Books Australia Ltd, Ringwood,
Victoria, Australia
Penguin Books Canada Ltd, 10 Alcorn Avenue,
Toronto, Ontario, Canada M4V 3B2
Penguin Books (N.Z.) Ltd, 182–190 Wairau Road,
Auckland 10, New Zealand

Penguin Books Ltd, Registered Offices:
Harmondsworth, Middlesex, England

First published by Signet, an imprint of New American Library,
a division of Penguin Putnam Inc.

First Printing, April 2001
10 9 8 7 6 5 4 3

Printed in the United States of America

PUBLISHER'S NOTE
This is a work of fiction. Names, characters, places, and incidents either are the product of the author's imagination or are used fictitiously, and any resemblance to actual persons, living or dead, business establishments, events, or locales is entirely coincidental.

For Robert Raucina, my brother Bob,
with love and thanks for Josh Cain
and the terrific tram idea

Thanks to:

Jane Dystel, my wonderful agent; Joseph Pittman, my terrific editor; Louise Burke, Carolyn Nichols, Hillary Schupf, and Amy Longhouse, my support group at NAL; Carla Fight and all my friends in the TWA Ambassador Clubs; my pals in the California desert; and the Indians there who have left us a legacy to be cherished and honored.

The Madman's Diary

Prologue

Had he known he was going to die that night, the man would never have left his house the mess that it was. Fastidious in his public persona, cutting-edge precise in his work, he secretly was a complete slob. Newspapers, clothing, the packaging from his new cell phone, a half-drunk martini, an uncapped olive jar, the plastic wrapper from the newest *Architectural Digest* and a pile of unopened mail that had accompanied it (mostly envelopes announcing that he had been pre-approved for enormous lines of credit), a beaten Rockport walking shoe he had meant to relace, and three battered and chewed toothpicks that had valiantly assisted in praying loose the piece of last night's popcorn hiding between the back molars—that was just the debris on the coffee table. The floor was strewn with various letters, books, newspapers, more shoes and clothing, his prized wooden tennis racquet, an opened bag of Doritos that the dog had gotten at, and the paper-and-plastic model of his high-rise that was now going up in Santa Monica. No matter. Rosa would be there in the morning.

That's why God created maids. "I love squalor," he once told Paul Goldberger of *The New York Times,* "because it's the antithesis of my art." He could tell Paul didn't believe him.

He stopped at the front door before he departed, checked himself in the mirror, and pronounced the image, if he had to say so himself, as dashing as a movie star. Cary Grant, perhaps. He retied his bow tie three times until it met with his approval. His dog, the aging border collie Cody, nodded *his* approval, though Norman was aware that Cody's eyes were going. Love abounding for his master, Cody attempted to jump up on him, but the old architect would have none of it. God forbid dog saliva might end up on his freshly pressed tuxedo slacks. But he did bend down and kiss the old boy on the head, promising to return the next afternoon. Cody whined the kind of mournful sound he usually made when he saw Norman packing his suitcase, which startled the man. "No, I'm not traveling, silly," he assured the animal. "I'll only be gone the night."

Cody, it could be argued, knew better.

When he left the steel-and-glass Bauhaus structure that his old friend Philip Johnson had urged him to erect "to give the neighbors something to carp about" (on a Beverly Hills street lined with heavy Mediterranean mansions), it was still sunny and bright. The keys were already in the ignition of his new Jaguar S Type—British Racing Green, washed and waxed to perfection, yet the soft buttery interior a reflection of the inside of his home: In-N-Out Burger wrappers, yellowing newspapers, maps (he was forever getting lost), Evian bottles, tennis gear, clothing. He never offered to drive anyone anywhere. Except for the one time just a month ago when Judy Sussman, the creative beauty who was designing the interior of the restaurant in his new building, had her own car blocked by a truck and he was forced to let her into his. "Instant death if you reveal this secret," he warned her as she cleared a place for herself among the junk. She smiled, unwrapped a stick of gum, and blithely tossed the wrapper over her shoulder.

Maneuvering the freeway turned out to be relatively painless for Friday at five in the afternoon. Perhaps all the usual morons had left their mundane jobs at three to jump-start what promised to be a beautiful weekend. He made it to the Marina Freeway in only half an hour, and to the club not long after. As he stepped out of the car, the snappy young valet, a handsome boy who no doubt had visions of becoming the next Matt Damon, gushingly greeted him. "Cool car, dude," the kid said with a slouching nod, handing him the ticket. Norman didn't believe him for a second, thinking the boy's idea of elegance was probably one of those souped-up Camaro things or an awful Prowler. *Dude* indeed. He watched the boy get into the Jag, and enjoyed the startled expression on the kid's face when he realized he was about to park an elegant garbage truck.

Before entering the double doors of the once classy, now slightly frayed yacht club, the famous architect looked around. The air was salty with the sea, and cooler than it had been at home. So many times he had told himself he was going to sell the house and move nearer the water, Santa Monica or Venice or perhaps Malibu despite all those awful movie people, build something there that would *really* upset the neighbors.

He glanced at the palm trees swaying, heard the horn of what sounded like a tugboat but was in reality a fabulous Italian yacht, then let his eyes rest on the sheer beauty of a huge wall of magenta bougainvillea, planted to hide an offending chain-link fence around the self-park lot. He would put bougainvillea outside the new building in Santa Monica, he promised himself, and he made a mental note to speak to Judy about carrying some over inside the lobby and restaurant. No one ever used it indoors the way they did in Positano. Then, with a tug at the tips of his bow tie, he entered the club.

Had he lingered on the bougainvillea a little longer, he might have noticed the vehicle parked directly in front of it, and perhaps, too, if he'd squinted, the man wearing sunglasses positioned behind the steering wheel. Had he been alert, he would have recognized the car as the same one he had passed when he turned from his street onto Sunset, the same man he glanced back at several times as he changed lanes on the freeway. He might have felt afraid of the man sitting there, watching him.

When Norman emerged from the party almost four hours later, a black-tie soiree celebrating the groundbreaking for a new animal clinic he had designed for the city of Marina del Rey, the same robust car-park jockey brought him the Jag. Immediately, Norman realized something was wrong. He could actually see, as the boy opened the door, the leather cushions of the front seats, something he'd not been able to do since he purchased the car fourteen months ago. "Took the liberty of sprucing it up, sir," the eager-for-a-tip young man sang through perfect white teeth. "Anything important, I put in the trunk."

"You little prick," Norman muttered.

"Pa—pardon me, sir?"

Norman slid into the car. "Ruined my goddamned day."

"Dude?" The boy couldn't comprehend. "I kept anything that looked like it was—"

But the car was gone. Norman had left the boy in the dust, standing with his mouth open, empty palm extended. The middle finger went up as the others curled into his palm.

Inside the car, Norman shouted, "In the trunk! In the goddamned trunk he puts things!"

The man hiding inside the trunk was feeling uneasy. He had left the marina immediately after seeing

Norman enter the restaurant. He'd returned three hours later, ready. When he'd put his own vehicle in the self-park lot, he'd seen the boy who had parked Norman's Jag working on it, detailing it, it seemed. All four doors and the trunk lid were open, and that gave him the idea. Norman would be driving to his boat, because he always did. It was only a distance of four or five piers, where he would park the Jag for the night. He would put it in a lot that was manned by twenty-four–hour security—and bring his killer with him.

That was, however, if Norman didn't open the trunk lid. When the boy had left the Jaguar to start retrieving cars for other party guests, the man had jumped into the trunk, pulling the lid down. He put the tip of his leather belt in the lock so it wouldn't latch from the vibration as they were driving. But now Norman was shouting about the trunk—what for? The concealed man was curled up in a sea of junk, papers and maps and trash. What would he want in there?

The car braked for a stop sign, then the passenger felt a hard left turn. As he rolled onto his sunglasses in his shirt pocket, he heard a crack. Thank God it wasn't the vial. The car was approaching the pier where the big sailing schooners docked, Norman's pier. Sure enough, he felt the Jaguar slowing significantly and then Norman was chatting with a woman who sounded either stupid or lethargic or both. "Mistah Lempke, it's good to see you! What you doin' down here all dolled up this time of night?" The man heard Norman explain his evening. Then the woman said, "Honey, you ain't be expectin' a pretty lady anytime later, would ya?" The passenger felt his heart race, anger filling his veins. Lady? Why didn't she just say "Judy?" Then they went through.

Norman's yacht, the biggest there, was at the very end of the dock. The minute the passenger felt the wheels stop moving, he readied himself. He waited a few seconds for Norman to kill the lights and then jumped out of the trunk and hid behind a blue van parked in the next space. When Norman emerged from the car, he noticed the open trunk, cursed the parking-lot attendant for not being sure it was securely locked, and walked toward his boat.

So did the other man.

At the dock security gate, Norman inputted his code on a keypad, eliciting a metallic click. He entered, leaving the gate to swing shut right behind him. His passenger hurried in, protected by the sound of the water slapping against hulls. Over the years Norman had done this hundreds of times. Another routine boater's Thursday night—a deserted dock, sleeping pelicans, only a few lights aglow in damp cabin windows, the moon shimmering on the glassy black water.

Norman's anger at the little prick who cleaned his car dissipated as he felt the calming effect that his boat always brought him. The martinis were kicking in as well. He looked up at the gleaming white mast and swelled with pride. He studied the words painted on the stern: *Hidden Agenda*. He'd wanted a grand sailing vessel for as long as he could remember, the hidden agenda behind his life's work of building structures on land. Water was nirvana, land was just dirt. But land had made him rich and famous and powerful, so he tolerated it. Water, however, nourished his soul, gave him life itself. With a burst of energy and enthusiasm, he bounded up the steps and onto his yacht.

The intruder stood up from behind the storage container near the gate. He looked around. He'd hoped the dock would be deserted, but it was still early and he could see people on two boats, lights on in a few others, and music coming from a power boat that was just docking. Grabbing a coil of rope that someone had left atop the storage container, he slung it over his shoulder to look more like he belonged if anyone should see him. Then he walked slowly toward the *Hidden Agenda*.

Norman lounged on an overstuffed down sofa in the yacht's elegant salon, amid priceless Asian antiques, a Steuben glass bowl on a marble coffee table standing on a custom wool rug, surrounded by refuse. He'd stripped off his tux, pulled on sweatpants and an Armani T-shirt—he'd designed Giorgio's new offices in Milan—and dirty big woolly sweat socks he'd picked up off the floor. He sipped the martini he'd shaken before even changing clothes, and opened a paperback he had found called *Ship of Gold in the Deep Blue Sea.* He loved books about boats, and this looked inviting. But he couldn't concentrate because the slight rocking motion of the water was putting him to sleep.

He rested, didn't let himself fall into darkness yet. He was content, at peace. The reason he'd bought this baby in the first place. Oh, yes, it made headlines that time he'd sailed it to Australia for the World's Cup, and it got him girls the way his late, great friend Malcolm Forbes had used his yacht to get boys. But more than that, he loved it.

He'd first set eyes on the sixty-five–foot Tayana Deck Saloon when Jennifer, his broker at Wagner Stevens Yachts, gave him a peek at the Annapolis Boat Show. She had sailed it from Taiwan and sang its praises. One look at the polished teak interior, the spars and rigging, the full equipment package, and he was halfway to heaven. An outing the next day on the Chesapeake put him in the clouds. He paid cash—a million two—and sailed it to California himself, with only the help of a small crew.

In the years since, he'd traveled the world's oceans with gusto, and his passenger log read like a Who's Who of the rich and famous. The parties were legendary, like the *Christina* in its heyday. The only thing was, being a confirmed bachelor, he more often than not was all alone on it.

But not tonight, though he did not yet know that.

* * *

The stalker removed his shoes when he set foot on the deck. He could well imagine modern forensic science tracking him down through the damn shoes. No, he'd have none of that. He pulled surgical gloves from his pocket and slipped them onto his hands. He felt invigorated.

He listened for signs of life below, but there was nothing. He looked down into one of the windows and saw a teak-paneled hallway. The wood was gorgeous, shining like a wall of polished dark, flat reddish diamonds. He went around to the bow and peeked through a lighted skylight, a kind of smoked-glass hatch that was lifted up an inch or two for ventilation. He saw a stateroom, all luxe and gleaming, yet strewn with underwear and socks and towels. But no one was there.

He peered down the stairs leading to the salon, poking his head in first, holding tight to the polished brass railing to keep his balance. Norman's back came into view. He was seated on a curved sofa, facing away from him, sitting so deeply that only his white hair, thick and lustrous for a man his age, was visible. He took a step down, placing one stockinged foot in front of the other in measured, thoughtful steps, until he was standing on a rug that seemed thicker than Korean grass. He waited a moment, his heart racing, adrenaline pumping through his veins. Then he walked up behind the famous architect and said softly, "Buenas noches, Norman."

He braced for the man turning his head around to

look at him, the surprise. But what he got in reply was a snore. Norman Lempke was fast asleep.

That was a laugh. He reached next to the man and picked up his martini glass and carried it to the galley. There he poured and shook another martini. From his pocket he withdrew a small vial with a dropper. He didn't even have to squeeze one drop of the greenish liquid into the drink. He simply touched the head of the dropper to the gin. He knew how powerful it was.

He replaced the elegant crystal martini glass where he'd found it, next to the sleeping man.

And waited.

Almost an hour had passed when the intruder, sitting on a stool at the stainless-steel counter in the ship's galley, looked up to see the captain of the ship was awake. Uncomprehending for a moment, Norman rubbed the sleep from his eyes, then stared at the younger man. "What. . . ?"

"Refill?" the uninvited guest asked, reaching for the open Bombay Sapphire bottle. "Had one myself. Good stuff. Didn't think you'd mind."

Norman couldn't believe his eyes. "I'm dreaming."

"Hallucinating a little, perhaps."

"What?" Norman shook his head. Reason set in. "What are *you* doing here?"

"Nice boat."

"I know. But—?" Norman stood in the galley doorway, trying to figure out why the man was there in his kitchen at—he glanced up at the clock on the microwave—almost one in the morning.

"God, but you're a pig. I mean, you'd never guess."

Norman's eyes took on the look of distrust that the intruder wanted. "How'd you get in here?"

"I opened the drawer here," the younger man said, nodding to a cabinet just under a block holding expensive knives. "Rubbers! Full of goddamned rubbers. You old fart!"

Slightly combative, the architect said, "I'm only sixty-two. I can still fuck as good as the rest of them, and better than some half my age."

The intruder held up a prescription bottle. "Bob Dole in particular?"

Norman shrugged. "I'm too exhausted for this game. Just tell me why you've come here. I'm tired and—" Norman stopped when he focused on the man's hands. "Why are you wearing gloves?"

"Cleanliness. Can't be too careful in this shit hole."

Norman looked perplexed, as if he were talking to a lunatic and needed to be nice, to humor him. "Listen, I'm a little drunk and I'd like to go to sleep."

"Like I said, buenas noches."

"You want me to go to bed?" Norman looked perplexed. "With you here?"

"I've already made sure you'll get the perfect night's rest," the intruder answered. "Just drink that martini there at your elbow."

Norman shook his head. "I shouldn't have any more."

"Should finish up your drink. It would be a less painful way for you to go."

Norman was wide-eyed. "Go where?"

"Straight to hell."

The intruder reached over to the knife block, removing a paring knife that glinted as he pulled it from the wood. "Good quality," he said with admiration.

"Everything I own is good quality," Norman responded. "Put that down."

"No. I'll show you a little trick."

In a split second, before Norman could move, the man tossed the knife up into the air, caught it by the blade, and then threw it across the room. It imbedded itself into the polished teak wall just inches from Norman's left eye.

Norman took a deep breath, but remained cool. He reached up, pulled the knife from the wood, and set it on the counter. "Very talented."

The intruder had already pulled another from the block, a long boning knife. Before Norman could say another word, the man threw it. Norman watched in horror as it plunged into his lower chest.

As the blood rushed out, the first sensation was heat, as if someone had poured boiling water down his stomach and into his undershorts. The second feeling was shock, that he was standing there with a knife protruding from his white Armani shirt. The third was white-hot pain. "What have you done?"

The intruder laughed. "I think it's pretty clear that I just put a knife into your . . . hmm, I'd guess your pancreas or spleen, judging from the height."

Norman grabbed the door frame with his left hand. Closing his eyes for a second, he pulled the blade out with his right. His whole body suddenly tremored with pain and shock. He staggered forward and took the dish towel the intruder was offering him, a cream-colored towel monogrammed with a big blue "HA," which turned crimson in seconds. "Help me," he begged the man who stood watching calmly.

"Help you?" the man responded. "That's what I'm doing. Helping you die."

"You're mad!" Norman gasped, resting his weight on the stainless-steel counter.

"Oh, I'm mad all right, but not loco," the intruder answered. "I'm mad angry." He reached for the knife block again. "So, let's see, which shall we try next?"

The intruder pulled one of the chef's knives from the block and ran his finger down the side of the blade. The sight of it filled the old man with utter terror, and he ran.

The knife stopped him in his tracks halfway down the teak-lined hallway leading to the master stateroom, where Norman thought he might be able to lock the door and call for help. The pain was incredible, paralyzing him for a moment, and when he gripped the wall to keep himself from collapsing, he realized he could barely breathe. The knife, which had entered his back high on the left side, had penetrated one of his lungs. It was still inside him. He began to cough blood.

By the time he was able to get a breath, a glance told him that he was alone in the hall. Continuing down the corridor to lock himself in his stateroom was no longer a good idea. The intruder would cut the phone line, and locked in the room, Norman would surely bleed to death. Instead he took a step back toward the salon, and saw that the man was not there. Hope surged through him. He walked as fast as he could, blood gushing from him, staining his expensive straw-colored carpeting with crimson splotches, until he reached the stairs leading to the deck. He gasped, choking, and spat up more blood. He was feeling faint, weakening by the second. But when he saw the man again, coming from the gallery doorway with yet another knife in his hand, he gathered the strength to force his feet up the stairs.

Outside, in the cockpit, he took what breath he could manage and yanked out the knife. With it gushed even more blood. He attempted to call for help across no more than thirty feet of water, to Captain Lyttle's yacht. The old salt and old friend had been commodore of the Annapolis Yacht Club for most of his life, and when he'd moved to California for his health, he'd refused to live anywhere but on a boat. Norman knew he would be awake. The man was a night owl just as he was. He could get Captain Lyttle's attention if he could only—

The call was feeble, impotent, wedged tight in the phlegm and blood gurgling in his throat. But even if he'd been able to shout, the hand suddenly clasping his lower face would have muted it. The intruder held him from behind, the gloved left hand securing his chin. In the right he saw another knife, a long knife that Norman didn't even know he owned. A wave of pain shuddered through him, and he let himself sink into the intruder's arms.

When he was down, the intruder knelt above him, leaning against the striped cockpit cushions, most of his weight on Norman, brandishing the blade in the moonlight. The loss of blood had weakened him to a point where he suddenly was blacking out, suddenly had no idea where he was and what he was doing. Then he felt his wrist explode with a searing pain. He looked to see his hand dangling, nearly severed, as he lifted the arm. The horror was too much for him. He broke loose and crawled on his knees. Blood painted every inch of shining white fiberglass and varnished teak. Then the intruder landed on his back and set him crashing to the deck.

Amid his pain, Norman heard these words: "You'll never have her again. The poisoner shaman has spoken."

Then, as Norman closed his eyes, ready to die—for it was inevitable now, there was no denying it—he thought of Cody and wondered how the dog knew early that evening that he would not be coming back. He wished he had lived long enough to see his building finished, just a few miles up the beach. And he thought of *her*. Oh, yes, he knew who the intruder meant when he had said, "You'll never have her again." The image of Judy was the last pleasure he would feel on earth.

Then it was suddenly cold. He felt frigid and weightless, the pain disappearing all at once, and the black water of the marina filled his lungs until they would fill no more.

Dear Diary:

For centuries the birdsongs have told the story of the land. Our land, our desert canyons, where our people have always lived. I would go there in the early mornings, at dawn sometimes, and I felt peace, a closeness. I wasn't frightened. I was home.

Palm Springs is home, the home of my people and myself. *Demron*, the old Indian said, which means respect your land.

That this man, the old architect of unpleasing structures, should die in the water is fitting, for he was not worthy to die on land. If you don't have land, you have nothing. We live in harmony on our land, and we are put here to protect it.

The harmony of our lives was interrupted by this intruder. I will grieve for him, for what I have done, for what I had to do. But as the poisoner shaman of the tribe, this is my responsibility.

Alvino Siva, a great leader of our tribe, said, "Like I tell the white people, it is hard to believe . . . the only way you can believe that is if you are an Indian."

I am a shaman. I am Indian. I understand.

Chapter One

When Judy Sussman stepped outside to get the morning paper, she suspected it was going to be one of those days when you could fry an egg on the sidewalk. It was way too early in the season for such hot weather, but for the past three days, high noon had registered in the nineties.

She loved it.

The Coachella Valley was in her blood. A transplanted New Yorker, she'd graduated from UCLA, where she majored in architecture, specifically in restaurant design, a field in which she had recently achieved great success. Still young at thirty-four, she was at the top of her craft. She chalked up her creative inspiration to the magic of the desert.

She glanced up at the blazing pink bougainvillea beginning to cover the broken, aged Spanish tiles of the roof. Amazing how fast it grew; it seemed Juan had severely trimmed it back just a week ago. Doves had nested in the lower branches, and five or six little hatchlings were squawking as the father flew in with food in his beak. Suddenly it occurred to Judy that bougainvillea was seldom used indoors—would it even grow indoors? She'd often cut them for centerpiece vases, but never tried to grow one. She'd have to find out, mention it to Norman. It could be interesting for the interior planters they were planning for the restaurant.

She spotted three calla lilies that had come into bloom overnight, and the Sterling roses were about to open as well, already revealing their delicate lavender hue to the morning sun. It was going to be one of those days she loved so much. In fact, she decided she wasn't going to drive to L.A. today. She went back inside the little Spanish bungalow that she had constantly been renovating, all the while attempting to retain the feeling of 1929, when Desi Arnaz had built it in the shadow of Mount San Jacinto. She picked up the phone and dialed a number in Beverly Hills.

She wasn't surprised to get the machine. Norman Lempke was a night person, and she seldom saw him around the construction site until well into the afternoon. But they had made a lunch date, and she wasn't going. She listened to his message, then said, "Norman, it's Judy. Too beautiful here today, I'm not driving around that mountain for anything. Call me later. Love to Cody and you too."

She walked into the den, where she'd left her coffee, which was now on the lukewarm side. She clicked the TV remote, already set on MSNBC. She heard the words ". . . Norman Lempke, the renowned architect" before the picture even appeared.

She couldn't quite make out what was going on. There was a shot of boats. A close-up of an ambulance, several police cars. Then a somber black-and-white photo of Norman standing on the stern of his boat. It froze there for a second, and then went back to the studio, where a woman said, "Norman Lempke, dead this morning at sixty-two." Then they went to a commercial.

The phone rang. Judy grabbed it without taking her eyes from the screen. "Hello?"

"Judy, have you heard?"

"He can't be dead. I just called him."

"He is."

"What happened?"

"Drowned," her mother said.

Judy felt her throat going dry. "What?" she gasped.

"That's what they said, fished him out of the water."

Judy was in shock. "I saw him. Day before yesterday. He was in perfect health. What was it? Heart attack? Stroke?"

"Nobody knows, but the police found blood all over the boat. Didn't you see the pictures?"

"Norman's dead?" Judy said softly, not accepting it. "My God."

"They said it looks like foul play," her mother added.

At that moment Skeeter rushed in, and Judy hung up. He immediately took her in his arms. "I wish I'd come back sooner," he apologized. He'd just spent two days doing his monthly perusal of Fancies Beverly Hills, his signature restaurant. "Just heard it on the car radio."

"Unbelievable," Judy said, "I saw him only day before yesterday."

She had been working with the "American architectural icon" (as *People* had one year named Lempke) for more than fifteen months, and though she'd been a little intimidated by him at the start, she quickly got over fearing his bark and had come to really enjoy him. Like her father, he was so damned smart. He was a Greek scholar, an accomplished musician, had a degree in history, and enough artistic talent for twenty men. He was bigger than life. This was a man who had climbed nearly to the top of Everest, a man who had flown a plane across the Outback, a man who had sailed every ocean on the globe.

She switched to CNN, and they watched the whole report. Judy felt empty, hollow. She could not fathom it. She hit the Mute button. "Who would want to kill him?"

"Someone who wanted his money," Skeet said.

"Nothing was missing on the boat."

He corrected her. "They *think* nothing is missing. Wait till they find the safe behind a picture that's minus a few million."

"I can't believe it. I liked being with him so much."

"I liked him too. I thought about asking him to design a Mexico City branch if we do it."

"No, you didn't," Judy replied. "You've got your hands full with Cabo right now. But thanks anyhow. You're just trying to make me feel good. He didn't do taco stands, even high-end ones, and you know it."

"A little cutting-edge contemporary might look nice down there."

Judy shook her head. "Why? That's what I don't get. Why would someone want to kill him?"

There was a loud knock on the back door, and a scruffy, handsome Latino poked his head in. "I'm late, sorry," he said to them both. Then he gave Skeet an apologetic look. "I was in Hemet visiting my sister."

"You have sisters everywhere," Skeet said and laughed.

"No, only in Hemet, and Elena in Todo Santos. All the rest are still in Caracas."

"Never left?"

Juan smiled. "All getting fat like our mama, making lots of babies."

"Juan," Skeet said, remembering why he'd asked the gardener to come over this morning, "check that sick cactus I told you about out by the street."

"Will do, señor. Cómo está, Judy?"

"Oh, Juan. *Has oido las noticia?*"

"News?" Juan asked in English.

"Come here. . . ."

* * *

Juan knelt on a ragged foam-rubber pad at the edge of the driveway. He had barely assessed the problem with the cactus when Judy's feet appeared in his line of sight. "Forgot, she went somewhere on a case," she said. Annie Chestnut was not only her next-door neighbor, she was Judy's best friend. And a private detective as well. "I want to know what she thinks about what happened."

Juan lifted the sombrero shielding his eyes and looked at her. "Met him that one time, Miss Judy, when you had that party. Real gentleman."

"He *was* a gentle man," Judy agreed. "Thought you were a fine landscape artist."

Juan's eyes widened. "Yes?"

"He did. When he saw the gardens at my parents' house."

Juan nodded. "I saw him study the yard, look closely at many things."

"He had an eye. He was gifted."

Juan stood up. "You will miss him."

"Yes, I shall. Very much." She fought back a tear, the first sign of breaking down since she had heard the news. She always found she cried at the wrong time, or at least the unexpected time. When she was seven, she started crying when she was supposed to blow out the candles on her birthday cake—because the week before, her cat had fallen from a window to its death fourteen stories below. She didn't cry when she got her diploma from UCLA, as so many of her fellow classmates did, but when a professor later told her he'd miss her "rambunctious" questions, the tears came. Norman was gone now, and she'd probably cry a month later, in the middle of a seemingly happy moment. "Sorry," she said, trying to hold back her tears.

"Kleenex on the front seat," Juan offered, with a nod to his truck.

She pulled open the driver's door and reached across the seat to a box of Kleenex that looked like it had been sat upon several times. When she tried to withdraw one, it came apart in her hand. She realized that they were damp. "Juan, your seat's wet."

"Oh, yes, sorry. Left the windows open last night. Sprinkler next door to my sister soaked it." He indicated his still-damp jeans, then reached into one of the front pockets. "This one is fresh from home."

It too was slightly soggy, but she said, "It's fine." She tried to put Norman out of her mind. "So, cactus rot?"

"No good," Juan said in a somber tone. "I'll replace it tomorrow. Got to get to your papa's house now."

"Mom wants some oranges." She looked at the Valencia tree standing against the garage, stately if somewhat scraggly. It was designed to seem that way, in keeping with the planned look of slightly overgrown natural plantings. "Why don't you pick what's left on it? It's already getting new flowers."

"Sí. But doesn't Skeet like them for breakfast?"

Judy smiled. "Let him eat grapefruit." Which they still had in abundance.

A few moments later, a car pulled up. Troy Skinner, Judy's favorite waiter from Fancies Palm Springs, a handsome fellow in his mid-twenties, jumped out and immediately hurried to Judy and took her hand. Juan watched and listened from the ladder, where he was picking the oranges.

Troy told Judy how upset he was about her friend and offered his condolences. She thanked him, but wondered aloud if he'd come all the way over for that. "No, no, for a delivery," Troy said, and walked back to his car to fetch a couple of foil-wrapped dishes from the backseat. "Skeeter wants you to try these, possible new menu items. I was supposed to bring them last night, but I forgot."

"Oh, he mentioned something the other day." She let him put them in her hands. "I just don't feel very hungry."

"I understand." Troy brought his hand to her shoulder and touched it compassionately. Juan peered down from the ladder, listening intently, aware of their closeness. "If there is anything I can do to help," Troy offered, "I will. I'd do anything for you."

Judy smiled and nodded. She knew the boy had a twenty-something crush on her, and it tickled her. But right now nothing could take away the pain of Norman's passing. "Thanks, Troy," she said, pulling away, "just say a prayer."

"I will," he told her, "to the Indian spirits, for forgiveness."

She looked uncertain, thinking that was a strange response.

"For the man who hurt him."

She nodded and went back inside.

Juan watched the boy drive away. Then he tossed an orange to the ground, spattering it to pieces.

Skeet was wrapped in a white towel, shaving, when Judy entered the master bath. The bungalow, one of the earliest structures in the area, had been added onto by subsequent owners after Arnaz. The new kitchen and master bathroom were Skeet and Judy's addition. They put in soapstone counters that complemented the reddish pink and yellow Mexican pavers on the floors. Judy slapped Skeet on the butt as she entered the room. "Juan says the cactus has to go."

"Figured," he said into the mirror. "What did Annie say?"

"She's in Texas, I think."

"Oh?"

"Case she's working on. Or a new book. Or both."

He dragged the razor over the cleft of his chin. "Didn't think Texas would let her back in."

"Maybe she smuggled herself across the state line in a nondescript van."

"Think she'll visit her ex-husband?"

"If she showed her face anywhere near that prison,

I swear he'd find a way to murder her, even through the bullet-proof glass."

Skeet put the razor away and splashed cold water onto his face. "Tap says 'cold,' but in Palm Springs it should be relabeled 'lukewarm.' "

Judy laughed. "Just part of the price we pay to live in paradise."

She honestly felt it was. Palm Springs was beautiful, yes, no one would deny that—but Judy had become a hard-core desert afficionado, where the perception of beauty went far deeper than the majesty of the mountains or the swaying palm trees or the incredible purple sunsets melting like giant scoops of raspberry sorbet over the sand. It was a powerful sensation that reached into the soul and sparked the very heart of her creativity.

She'd gone to the University of California in Los Angeles because of an article she had read while still in high school, the author of which was a young, brilliant professor who viewed buildings as near-human. They became friends, and Craig took on the role of mentor when he recognized her talent. On weekends they'd join her parents at their desert house, or use their place if they were in New York. When she graduated, the same professor, who by that time had become very close to her, helped her snare a job at a large architectural firm in San Francisco. She was not happy there, though. The prospect of spending years drawing bathrooms and closets for office buildings in Cleveland didn't have much appeal. She returned to L.A. and struck out on her own.

It was tough. She was unknown and a woman, two strikes against her in the male-dominated world of architecture. To make money as she struggled to find clients, she started decorating friends' houses and apartments. Born with her mother's eye for things tasteful but not too stiff, she could create a charming and inviting environment in a matter of days. Before she knew it, she was "designing" interior spaces as well.

Her reputation took off in her late twenties, when Doris Silverton, a woman whose house she'd redone, introduced her to her daughter, Nancy, at her daughter's restaurant, Campanile. Not till that moment had Judy realized Nancy was the baker behind LaBrea Bakery, whose breads she'd been buying and loving for years. They struck up an immediate friendship, and within six months Judy was designing a new restaurant for Nancy and her husband, former Spago chef Mark Peel. It took off, and Judy's career was established. She opened a design shop on Melrose Avenue, and moved into an apartment in a high-rise on Wilshire Boulevard in Westwood, where the salesperson couldn't understand why she didn't prefer an ocean view, as most of the apartments were built to provide. What ocean-view lovers didn't understand was that Judy wanted to face her own personal Mecca, far past the hills of Anaheim and over the smog of Riverside to the Coachella Valley: her beloved California desert.

Judy leaned against the bathroom counter and closed her eyes. "Who would want to kill him?" The thought was eating at her soul.

Skeet made an attempt to answer that. "You don't know his secrets, you don't know much about his life except what had to do with you. There could be a lot of reasons."

It was an answer she didn't want to hear. She said stridently, "He was a great man, a good man! Christ, all the wrong people die."

He knew she was thinking about Craig, her mentor, her professor, her lover, and his suicide so long ago. So he kept quiet. He reached out and splashed aftershave lotion on his face.

Then the phone rang.

"I'm going to the restaurant. Come for dinner?" Skeet said.

"Okay," Judy replied, and lifted the receiver. "Hello?"

"Annie here, babe."

"Here as in where?"

"Private jet," the woman said with a throaty laugh, as if she couldn't believe it. "Client was so pleased, she flew me back. We're gonna stop in Phoenix to drop off something and I'll sign some books in the airport, then on home."

"Where are you landing? Thermal?" Judy guessed that because the Random House plane she used to fly on with her parents usually landed at the smaller desert airfield.

"Palms Springs, baby. This is a 727."

"My God, just like Delta."

Annie howled. "Food's a hell of a lot better than Delta. Stewards too, flight attendants, whatever they call them now." She still had a touch of Texas in her accent. "Old gal's got a herd of Texas studs working this plane. You should see the pilot, hot little god named Peter. . . ."

"Annie, down girl."

"Yeah, well, an old battle-ax like me can dream, can't she?"

"Can I pick you up? I need you real badly right now."

"Figured," Annie said. "Honey, you must be devastated. I've already made some calls, I'll tell you what I know."

"When will you be in?"

"Pete says five o'clock."

"*Pete*, huh?"

"He let me play copilot for a while."

"No!"

"Now I know why they call it a cockpit."

"Annie!"

"Just trying to lighten things up. When it gets bad, honey, you gotta keep laughing, or the cowshit'll smother ya, ya know?"

Judy smiled. "Spoken like a true Texan. I'll be out front at five."

"Gene Autry Road side, we go to the Million Air Terminal."

"Yeah," Judy said, "you and Pete."

Jokes aside, Judy started counting the minutes. For she knew that of all the people in her life, Annie would be able to cheer her on this completely cheerless day. More important, she was the only person who might be able to learn who killed her dear friend, Norman Lempke.

Chapter Two

Judy watched Annie deplane. The woman was a character right out of one of her own novels. The wind that had kicked up was no match for her big, colored, lacquered-hard hair. She weathered the gusts with every strand in place. Fat and sassy, still sporting the bright red lipstick and tight pants she'd worn while miserably married to Texas oil millionaire Anthony Chestnut, she had become a private dick without wanting to. Her curious, snooping nature had compelled her to nose through her husband's private papers, which had made quite clear that he had bumped off his first two wives. Determined to put an end to that tradition, she'd led investigators to what she'd uncovered, and after seeing the good hubby safely in prison for life, she'd decided snooping wasn't at all a bad career choice. Moving across the Southwest from Austin to Albuquerque to Phoenix and finally to Palm Springs, she left behind a trail of successful cases and decided, for the hell of it, to write them down—each becoming a book in her successful "Desert Gumshoe" series. She'd met

Judy and Skeet when she bought the rotting adobe house next door to theirs, and hired her new neighbor to redesign, remodel, and refurnish it for her. She and Judy had been girlfriends ever since.

A man in uniform, looking no more than thirty, deeply tanned, with sun-bleached hair, a good build, and a very sexy smile, took Annie's hand and walked her over the tarmac to the fence. Behind them followed a line of stewards, looking like a contingent of male models, carrying Annie's luggage, a box of books, clothes in a hanging bag, and Scout, her hysterical soft-haired Wheaton terrier, whom she never traveled without. Annie saw Judy and gave a big wave. Judy hurried inside the fence to greet her. "I thought they abolished slavery."

"Not in Texas," Annie said, then gave her a big ol' Texas hug. "Judy, this here's our pilot."

"Pete," Judy said, "happy to meet you. Right on time too."

Pete lifted his cap. His eyes were a bright, brilliant blue. "Winds were a little tricky." He gave Scout a pat on the head. The steward carrying Scout set the dog down, and he immediately trotted off and peed against a post.

Judy smiled. "Driving here was just as difficult. Tumbleweed dodging."

"Now, sugar," Annie purred to Pete, "you call me, hear?"

"You promised me a book."

"Hell, yes, forgive my crusty manners." Annie

turned and snapped her fingers at the slave holding the box of books, whispering to Judy, "Just like Cleopatra, huh?" She bent down—Judy thought Annie's tight white pants were going to split—and fished out a copy of the newest novel, *Desert Dick's Dangerous Dilemma*. She quickly wrote what had to be a salacious dedication to Pete, because it immediately made his face go red. Then she gave him a little pat on the tush as he departed. Then Annie looked at Judy and got serious. "He was murdered."

"What?"

"Talked to a pal in L.A., cop working the case. Someone carved him up good," Annie said. "Had a wound clear through his pancreas, almost came out his back. Besides the severed hand."

Judy gasped. "Severed hand?"

"Someone hacked him up something fierce. Honey, let's get in the car. This wind's about to blow us back to Arizona." She turned to the waiting stewards, lined up like bowling pins. "Boys, in that thing over there." That *thing* was Judy's BMW X5. "If it doesn't all fit, you can deliver it personally to my place tonight." Annie put her arm around Judy as they and Scout followed the slaves toward the SUV. "When you're as old and fat as I am, you gotta do something."

Troy Skinner, the waiter who had brought Judy the tasting dishes earlier, brought Judy and Annie icy margaritas in chilled green Mexican glasses. They were nestled in a booth in Fancies Palm Springs, Skeet McCloy's famous eatery. Modeled after his first and overwhelmingly successful Fancies Beverly Hills restaurant, the place was a hit the minute it opened. In the past few years Skeet and Judy had become the new Wolfgang Puck and Barbara Lazar, the fabulous "in" chef and his beautiful designer wife who created the environments of all his restaurants

Only Judy was not Skeet's wife. Nor was she even his girlfriend anymore. They were soul mates more than anything. Skeet had always cooked, even when they were in college together, and had gone off to culinary school when he decided UCLA was not for him. He had been raised by his grandparents, who had taught him a love for food: his grandfather had run the last independent butcher shop near the ocean, on Rose Avenue in Venice, and his grandmother was constantly creating new dishes with whatever meats and poultry he brought home on a given day. Skeet had returned to California after studying cooking for a year in New York and another year working in a three-star restaurant in France, and Judy's father had backed him in opening the brash and delightful Fancies Beverly Hills.

Set in an old bank building, Judy designed the open space to feel much like the Pool Room at the Four Seasons in New York. The floors were rough green granite, with gradings of red and purple, and in the center of the space was a lovely rectangular pool, reflecting the lights from the ceiling, water gently spilling over the rock sides to a disguised drain. The furnishings were sparse and simple, cutting-edge design and muted, dark rich colors. Booths shaped from curved alder formed private spaces where the rich and famous could enjoy their privacy and yet still remain on public display. The former vault still stood in all its polished steel glory, now keeping cool hundreds of bottles of fine wine.

The Palm Springs restaurant opened in what had been a branch of Wells Fargo Bank, and Judy had the good sense to copy the same design she'd used in Beverly Hills. It was familiar, and it worked; why play with it? The only difference was that she used bright, vibrant Mexican colors on the walls and in the fabrics, a scheme that fit well with the desert. One lone cactus rose outside the front door, and only because it had been there forever. Norman Lempke had eaten there, and had admired it.

"No robbery at his house," Annie said, "nothing missing off the boat, car was in the lot. He was single so no one knew who was in his will, no insurance thing going on, nothing that makes any clear sense to me."

"What do you think, then?"

"Motive?" Annie licked the salt from the rim of her glass. "Somebody didn't like him."

"Enough to kill him? What could he have done?"

"We never know the secrets, honey."

Judy shrugged. "You sound like Skeet."

"How does she sound like me?" Skeet slid into the booth with them.

Annie answered. "I'm saying we never know a person completely. No matter how much you think someone's life is an open book, there's some horse-shit sticking some pages together."

"I don't have secrets," Judy said.

"I do," Skeet said.

"See?" Annie replied.

"What kind?" Judy asked him, curious.

"I hate cooking. What I really want to do is direct."

"Refills?" Troy asked with a smile to the girls. "Mr. McCloy, would you like something?"

"No, I'm fine," Skeet declined. "Annie? Judy?"

Annie nodded. "Sure, hell, yes."

Judy said, "Yes, but not a double this time, okay, Troy?"

Troy smiled. "Oh, I think you need one today. Again, I'm so sorry, I feel for you."

She smiled slightly and allowed him to take her hand briefly.

When he walked away, Annie said, "He's got eyes for you."

"Oh, please," Judy replied, the last thing on her mind.

"Secrets," Annie said as if she hadn't been interrupted, "you always find them. Look at my ex, that piece-of-shit Tony. Look at the secrets he had. Forget that he killed his first two wives. He had two more while he was married to me! Not affairs, not girlfriends, wives." She downed the last slug of her margarita. "In Nebraska and Puerto Rico, of all fucking places."

"Point well taken," Skeet replied. "We just don't know everything about people."

Annie said, "Which is great, 'cause it gives me more to write about."

"That may be," Judy agreed, "but I want whoever made Norman die such an awful, painful death to pay."

"I think the terror of it is what bothers me most," Skeet said, "that he died trying to fend off an attacker. It's really a horrible way to go."

Annie asked Judy, "Did he indicate he was frightened about anything lately? Scared, antsy, jumpy?"

Judy shook her head. "Not at all. He was happier than ever."

Troy brought the new drinks and gave Judy another warm smile. Annie raised her eyebrows. Skeet said, "Well, maybe you're right. Secrets." He took a sip of water as he watched Troy check on another table. "Makes no sense," Skeet said, "killing Norman just doesn't make sense."

"It will," Annie replied. "Just a little time, a little lifting of the rocks, and we'll see what comes crawling out."

Late that night, sitting on a huge rock on the desert floor, two men were sharing a bottle of tequila and talking. They'd driven in their separate cars after work, as they had done often of late. The younger of the two men was being instructed in the ways of Indian lore and culture by the older man, who called himself a shaman. He was explaining birdsongs to the other, a form of communication used by the desert tribes for centuries. There was a birdsong about a young man's emergence into manhood, and in the discussion the younger man asked when he could experience the ritual referred to in several of the stories, the ceremony of the sweat house.

"I know of one that still exists," the shaman said.

"Nearby?"

"Down closer to San Diego. In the mountains there."

The younger man's eyes lit up. "Can we do it?"

"There is going to be a group going soon."

"Man, cool." He took the tequila bottle from the shaman and knocked down a swig. "I want to do that."

"It has to be controlled. We must be careful. It can be dangerous."

"Who else is going?" the young man asked, psyched.

"People who have done this before, and one other acolyte, like yourself."

"Cool." The young man paused a second, then asked what he really wanted to know. "Will we do the plants?"

The older man looked hesitant. "I don't know."

"We have to, man. That's what it was all about for

the Indians. It's that trip, that out-of-body experience that I want."

"Your enthusiasm makes me think you should just go buy some crystal meth."

"Shit! Come on, you've been instructing me for months now. You know I'm no druggie. I want the hallucinations the Indian braves had, the knowledge, the visions, the wisdom."

The shaman smiled. He recapped the bottle. "It is getting late." He uncrossed his legs and rose.

"Shaman!" the young man shouted.

The shaman turned back.

"Yes? Will we?"

"I will talk to the others."

"But will we do the plants?"

The shaman nodded. "You trust me, my friend, I know that. And thus I trust you. We will do the plants." He got into his vehicle, started the engine, and the desert suddenly glowed in the beam of the bright headlamps.

From the window he said, "But remember, they are poison."

Dear Diary:

Dead, so his amigos can mourn. Dead, the man who desired her for his own.

Now there is another who desires her. People would say he is too young, too inexperienced to take seriously as a threat. Yet I am cautious, for in her grief her susceptibility is enhanced. The boy will not take advantage of her grief, her open heart.

He will go to the sweat house.

But he may never leave it.

Chapter Three

The funeral was huge. The service was delayed an hour because of the stream of cars and limousines lined all the way down Reseda Boulevard from the gates of Eden Memorial Park. Some of the most famous people from the worlds of architecture, art, politics, and show business gathered with grieving friends, family, and those who'd worked for Norman Lempke over the years, to say good-bye. Judy was overwhelmed by sadness. She leaned on Skeet's shoulder for support as she watched the casket being lowered into the earth. When she knelt to put a stone on the grave, she felt the full weight of her grief and finally tears came.

Annie watched from a short distance. Not having known the man, she was less mournful. She was looking around, hoping to spot the person who killed him. The authorities had come up with no motive and very few clues. Annie guessed that her friend had cared more for Lempke than she'd let on. She doubted they were sleeping together, but that might have been in the cards. Yes, the man was an old fart next to young, vivacious Judy, but he had a magic of the kind that Onassis and Kissinger and Niarchos had, the ugly brute who overcame that drawback by his personal style, his charm, his money, his power, and his mind. Judy had had "eyes for him," and she imagined the late architect, having had a reputation as a tireless ladies' man, had them for her as well.

So it would help if she could bring closure for Judy. After the funeral, instead of joining most of the other mourners at the Lempke house for food and remembrances, Annie drove down to Marina del Rey to look at the boat where Norman had met his maker. Detective Tom Sparks, an old friend and longtime member of the LAPD, happened to be standing on the dock when she pulled up. He blinked twice. "What the hell brings Annie Chestnut to the water?"

"Christ," Annie said to the man, "Rogaine was a crock, huh? You look more like Kojak every day."

"You sound like my wife," the balding man moaned. "Hey, I'm going to pot, what can I say? My belly's almost as big as yours."

She smiled. "Touché. So what you got here?"

"Why do you care?"

"A friend of mine knew him well. She's hurting. I'm nosy."

Sparks cast a glance around for any higher-ups. "Your lucky day. Come aboard."

They walked through the rusty security gate, down the pier to the slip. The *Hidden Agenda,* sparkling in the sunlight, rocked gently behind yellow plastic tape. Several uniformed cops stood guard. Tom Sparks reached out and helped Annie step aboard the yacht.

She groaned as she pulled her weight aboard. "My fat ass doesn't want to do this." She straightened up, got her balance, looked around. "Blood everywhere?"

"Everywhere."

She surveyed the area. Then she said, "Let's see down below."

"Nice joint," Sparks commented as they entered the salon. But for the bloodstains here and there, the boat was gorgeous. "Wouldn't mind having one of these myself."

"Not on your pay," she muttered. "Christ, this is classy. Got to set a book on one of these."

"Leave that to Patrick O'Brien," he warned.

"He's dead too." She laughed. "But I'm impressed, a cop who reads. Where'd it all happen down here?"

"Some here, some in the hall."

She nodded, studying every inch of the room and the adjoining galley. She noticed a gouge in the teak wall. "What's this?"

"Knife went into it."

She studied it. "Fresh. If it had been old, the wood would have darkened inside it."

Tom Sparks scratched his head. "Probably tried to stab him and missed."

Annie nodded, looking at all the dried blood. "They obviously tried again and succeeded." She turned to the counter on which sat the knife block. "Weapon?"

"Two of them. Diver found them yesterday, straight down."

"What kind?"

"Butcher knife. Chef's knife, I guess they really call it. And a long thin boning blade."

She looked at the indentation in the wall again. "Neither would have stood up," she muttered, then checked the floor. There wasn't a nick, much less a sign of a blade having dropped on it.

"What're you talking about?" Tom Sparks asked.

"A different knife from those went into that wall, and probably stuck there till it got pulled out. Chef's knives are too heavy for that small a tip stuck in the wood to hold. Boning knives are too long."

He rubbed his chin. "You're good."

She pointed at the three other knives in the block. "Check these for prints?"

He looked chagrined. "May be too late."

"Why?" But she knew the answer. " 'Cause someone already touched them."

"Yeah. One was lying on the counter, one of the forensic guys picked it up. The paring knife I used to cut up an apple."

She was dumbfounded. "An apple?"

He shrugged. "I was hungry."

"Leave it to you morons to dirty a crime scene."

He winked. "We have a long tradition in that line."

"And proud of it too," she said, half joking, "that's what's so irritating."

He pulled plastic gloves from his pocket and put them on, then scooped the knives into a Ziploc bag. "I'll test 'em anyhow."

"You do that."

She started to leave, but his voice stopped her.

"Just so you'll know, I did collect a couple of martini glasses in here. One of them looked funny. Might have had a drug in it."

"Hey, he wasn't poisoned, for Christ's sake. He was hacked to death."

He laughed. "Trying to reassure you that detectives really are doing their jobs."

"Captain Lyttle?" Annie asked the elderly man standing on the dock, smoking a pipe. He looked like a boater, from his worn deck shoes to the captain's cap on his thick white hair. She'd seen a picture just a minute ago, down in the boat, of Norman and him standing near an enormous fish one of them had caught.

"Howdy," he said softly.

"I'm Annie Chestnut. My best friend was close to Mr. Lempke. I'm a private investigator."

"He was a good man, good man," the old salt said, obviously very saddened. "Didn't attend the funeral. Mine's next, can't bear knowing that. Norm'll forgive me."

Annie smiled. "I'm sure."

He stared at the sailboat and shook his head slowly. "Who could have done a thing like that to Norman? And why?"

"That's what I want to find out." She leaned up against a piling. "Anything you can tell me that you haven't already told the police?"

He shrugged. "Afraid I'm no help."

"You were awake, Detective Sparks told me, and you heard the scuffle?"

He nodded. "Not real sure what it was, but I heard noises. But that's common here, people running up and down the pier. Sometimes a couple will get a little—how to say this?—a little too heated up and take their private stuff topside, seen that down here too. But never a murder."

"What did you do?"

"Went on deck. I'd been up. I'm a real insomniac."

"Did you see anything?"

"Heard the splash. Knew someone went overboard, that sound. Heard it before many times."

"What did you do?"

The man looked surprised that she didn't know. "Called out, of course. I knew it was Norman's boat, figured he'd had a few too many and fell in the drink."

"You didn't see anything?"

"That's my boat there." He pointed. "Motor yacht, not a sailboat like this. I was on the back deck. Sound came from *Hidden Agenda*'s starboard side."

Annie nodded. "What did you do after you called his name?"

"I went to see if he needed help. Hell, Norman could swim as well as the next man, but if you're pie-eyed. . . ."

"Been there a few times myself," Annie admitted. "But I've never had to swim."

"By the time I stepped onto the pier and rounded the slip, that's about when I heard the second splash, and when I got to the side of Norman's boat, there he was, floating facedown."

"Second splash?"

"Yes."

"You sure about that?"

"Eyes may be failing, but my ears'll be the last to go."

She looked fascinated. "Then he left by water. The police said they talked to everyone nearby, security guards and people who parked in the lot here, but I don't think anyone ever thought that he might not have left on land."

"Sure," Lyttle said, agreeing with her, "whoever killed Norman swam outta here."

When she left Captain Lyttle, Annie told Tom Sparks what she'd learned. Then she tried to put herself in the killer's shoes. Where did he swim to? Another boat was the most obvious answer, a boat he'd readied like a getaway car. Or perhaps another pier, where he avoided detection because there was no commotion and he ran off, or drove off. But how would she begin figuring out where? Start at the beginning. That meant retracing Norman's steps that night.

She started with the restaurant where he had spent that evening, but learned nothing of interest after talking to everyone she could find who'd worked that night. When she stepped outside, however, a perky parking-lot attendant offered to retrieve her car for her even though she'd parked it herself. She learned that he'd not only parked Norman's Jaguar that night, he'd cleaned it as well, an act of kindness to which the architect apparently hadn't responded in like manner. "Did you find anything in the car that you threw away?"

"McDonald's wrappers," the boy said. "Everything else I put in the trunk."

"Anything you remember about that night?"

He looked at her as if she was crazy. "Duh," he said, "like I remember all of it."

"Anything strange, I meant."

"Nope."

"Anything at all, did he talk to anyone, seem frightened, ornery—?"

"Ornery, yeah. Nasty dude, you know?"

"About the car?"

The boy nodded. "No tip even."

"He just drove off, then?"

He nodded again. "I was, like, dude! Pissed me

off, I shoulda got twenty bucks easy. He drove off and I gave him the finger."

"Did he see that?"

He shrugged. "Like I care."

"Didn't like him, did you?"

The boy blinked. "I didn't kill him, lady."

"Anything else?"

He shrugged. "Like?"

"Like a car follow him out of the lot, or was someone watching him, maybe someone tailed him from the restaurant?"

The boy looked like he didn't have a clue. He remained mute.

"Nothing unusual about that night? Before or after he got his car?"

"Dunno. Talk to the dudes inside."

"The *dudes* inside don't know diddly," Annie answered.

The boy smiled. "That's true."

She handed the boy her card—six inches long, bright yellow, one side reading *"POLICE LINE DO NOT CROSS,"* a clever spin on the usual business card that always drew comments, and served as a bookmark for her readers. She told him to call her if he remembered anything else. "My name's Annie."

"Jimmy."

She handed him a twenty, which prompted him to fetch her car, the huge, lumbering Cadillac DeVille convertible that she'd brought from Texas, still sporting its faux cowhide black-and-white-spotted seat covers. "Cool wheels, lady."

"You remember anything else, Jimmy, anything at all, you call me, hear?"

Juan had just finished Annie's yard. He brushed the sand and dirt from his shirt and pants, and took off his gloves. He preferred working there when she wasn't around, for all she seemed to do was yell at him not to cut this, don't trim that, stop before you clip another leaf! He never knew anyone so insistent that a yard look like it had no caretaker. He thought she should live in the jungle like his cousins in Venezuela, for that's what her place looked like. Judy kept the house next door overgrown but natural looking, and it took great care to achieve that look. Annie Chestnut, she wanted chaos. It almost made him laugh.

Driving down Highway 111 to Cathedral City, he cursed the fact that he was so stupid as to let the seat get wet. He was sitting on a towel now, but still he felt the dampness. It had penetrated. He turned on the radio. There was a report on the burial today of the famous architect who had been Judy's good friend. So that's where they all were. He was proud that Judy had told him Norman Lempke had admired his work. Then he remembered Judy's obvious infatuation with the older man and his mood got gloomy. He changed to a Spanish station and sang along, trying to lift his spirits.

Home was a tiny, dilapidated house nestled behind a strip mall on the wrong side of the highway. On the right side, a spanking new civic center and bell tower had been built, an Imax theater had opened, buildings had been razed, and businesses had been refurbished. But "Cath City," and Cathedral City Cove, which rose up the mountainside behind it, originally had been built to house the poor workers who serviced the rich houses and resorts and hotels, and the majority of the residents were still poor Mexicans who found this dusty, rundown place a step above the difficult life south of the border.

Put in Rancho Mirage terms, Juan's little frame adobe would be laughed off as a shack; in Palm Desert it would be considered a teardown. In Cathedral Cove, however, it was a desirable house. Consisting of a small living room and bedroom, a tiny kitchen and even smaller bathroom, it was filled with cast-off furniture from the Estate Sale consignment store. The walls were lined with bookshelves that he had built himself, filled with volumes on gardening. The postman had once asked him what he did with all the gardening magazines he received each month, and Juan showed him his bedroom. The bookshelves in there were stacked with every *House & Garden* from the past five years, and more. A laptop computer set on a rickety table was loaded with every landscaping program available in software.

He thought of himself as an artist. He had the temperament of the artist too, and had lost clients because of it. Given to extreme reactions, he often let his temper get the best of him, telling the very people who hired him that they were complete idiots and were interfering with his artistic imagination. But for all the people who had fired him for that reason, there were twice as many who put up with it, for the end result was his exquisite landscaping.

He took women's breath away as well. Handsome, tanned, and muscular from the outdoor work, he looked older than his thirty years, and had eyes that seemed to peer *through* you. He was always being watched out a window, or spied on from a pool, by both women and men, for several of his clients were gay, which was expected in a place with such a large homosexual population. But no one knew anyone who had ever slept with him. He was a loner who seemed to have no friends.

Tonight, he stripped down to his shorts and worked out with the free weights on his back patio, a slab of cracked concrete covered by a makeshift rippled green fiberglass canopy. Then he showered under cold water, and ate some tamales and a few ripe tomatoes Maria from next door had given him from her trip down to Mexicali. After he finished, he played with the computer for a few hours, designing the greenery for a house being built in the exclusive enclave called The Reserve, where Henry and Esther Sussman lived. The owner, younger than Juan, had admired the Sussmans's landscaping when looking at a lot nestled in the mountainside, just down the cul-de-sac from Bill Gates's new mansion. A little Gates himself, this brash smart aleck had just made an obscene amount of money in an internet IPO.

Tired of pondering over whether king or queen palms should flank the geeky punk's tennis court, he turned on the TV and watched a *Dateline* segment, where he saw Judy and Skeet at the funeral, taped earlier in the day. It was followed by a report on Lempke's half-finished building in Santa Monica, replaying an interview Judy and Lempke had done together some weeks before. Then he went to bed.

He slept naked, with the windows open. The nights were still cool enough to sleep comfortably, but tonight he tossed and turned. What was it? The tamales? He seldom ate Mexican food—not healthy enough, too much grease. No, that wasn't it. He knew what was making him so restless.

He reached up and ran his fingers over the one single beautiful accessory in the room, a picture frame made from silver, designed by an artisan in Guadalajara, exquisitely etched with a rope design. He could see it glint in the moonlight streaming in the windows. He gently caressed the photo of himself and Judy, clutched it to his chest, and finally slept like a baby.

Chapter Four

"Barnes & Noble Welcomes Annie Chestnut," the sign in the Palm Desert store proclaimed, and outside was the gaudy Cadillac parked in the middle of two of the handicapped spots. Annie was prone to a slipped disk now and then, but she wasn't exactly crippled. Inside the store, in an area roped off by yellow plastic tape reading CRIME SCENE DO NOT CROSS, she was autographing her latest book. Annie signed a copy to *Lisa Singer, from an old broad, Annie Chestnut.*

Next in line was a familiar face, Judy's mom. Esther Sussman was a tall, handsome woman, with a strong nose and chin like her daughter's, intelligent eyes, and a winning smile. She was well-groomed as always, wearing a lightweight suit even on this hot afternoon, not a hair out of place, with a bright Prada bag and matching sandals, dressed up yet dressed down. Two copies of Annie's new novel rested in her arm. "One for me, one for Henry, please."

"How the hell are you?" Annie asked warmly.

"Good, and you?"

Annie glanced at the line of people waiting for her signature. "Hand's gonna wear out."

"You should get a stamp."

"Not complaining. This is normal here, 'cause I'm local. When I get a crowd like this in Iowa, I'm thrilled." Annie started inscribing the first book to Henry.

"How's my daughter?" Esther asked about Judy, sounding concerned.

"Haven't seen her since the funeral a few days ago."

"I think she's taking this harder than anyone knows."

"Why's that?"

"A mother knows. I hear it in her voice. I've heard it before. It scares me some."

Annie looked up from writing a deliciously teasing note to Henry, with whom she played a game of "divorce your wife and marry me, you big old hunk!" Annie did think Henry was one of the best-looking men in the world, but the idea that Henry might leave Esther for Annie Chestnut was preposterous, and that was the fun of it. "When before?"

"When Craig Castle killed himself."

"Who?" It took Annie a moment. "Oh, UCLA."

Esther nodded. "Judy was in a deep, deep depression, though no one realized it for months."

Annie began inscribing the second book to Esther. "Skeet will help her through it."

"I suppose." It definitely wasn't supportive.

Annie looked up. "What's your problem with him?"

Esther glanced down at the cover illustration of the hungry, slightly unshaven, good-looking bare-chested man with a long-barreled phallic gun in his hand, and the words *Desert Dick's Dangerous Dilemma* beneath him. "I just think that Judy limits herself living with Skeet."

"How?" Annie said, recapping her marker.

"Every mom wants her girl to be happy. This non-relationship with Skeet, I think, prevents Judy from really meeting a man she could love."

"They're just best friends."

"She should be living alone," Esther said, "or with you."

"Christ, then *no* man would look at her."

Esther laughed. "I really doubt that."

"Listen, I got angry faces lined up behind you like we're in Albertson's and I'm the only checkout lane open."

"Sorry." Esther gathered up her books.

"Where are you going?"

"To Ross, but don't tell anyone. Don't want to lose my Prada image." She giggled. "But you never know what you will find. I cleaned out Loehmann's this morning."

"Can you have coffee with me in about forty minutes?"

"I'll just blast through the shoe racks," Esther joked.

"Meet you at Starbucks." Annie turned to the line and said, "Come on up, baby," to a young man looking a little trepidatious. "Annie Chestnut, private eye here, and I'm not gonna bite."

On the line at Starbucks, while the barista shot the expresso with a certain amount of flair, Esther showed Annie her loot. She was particularly proud of three pair of shoes at an average of ten dollars a pair, plus a cotton blouse, linen skirt, two throw pillows, and four pairs of socks for Henry. "I love a bargain."

"I love a book signing. We did one hundred and four today."

"Just like the temperature," Esther added wryly.

They bought two iced caramel Frappuccinos and sat outside in the shade. It was one of Annie's favorite meeting places in the desert. A couple of times, in the winter when the weather was cooler, she brought her laptop here, sipped coffee for hours, and wrote. "So," she asked Esther, "how's life in the exclusive enclave?" She was referring to The Reserve, the new project carved out of the rugged desert right next to another exclusive enclave, The Vintage Club, with million-dollar–plus homes dotting the hills, lakes, and golf course. The Sussmans had been one of the first families to move in.

Esther shrugged, that wry smile creasing her face again. "It's better than I anticipated. I really didn't want to move, you know."

"Judy said."

"We'd been in that house since Judy was born. It had such history for us. But Henry wanted something spanking new. I liked the Firestone house myself."

"Leonard Firestone? Isn't that the place next to the Fords on Thunderbird?"

Esther nodded. "And that's why Henry hated it. Besides disagreeing with his politics."

"Didn't know Jerry Ford ever had any politics. Thought he just golfed."

"Henry didn't want secret service nosing through our oleander. Grand house, though. Heard someone from Santa Barbara bought it."

Annie shook her straw. "Oh, by the way, where did Skeeter get his name? I never thought to ask, but it's intrigued me. Sounds like one of those soap opera names a wacky Texas housewife gives her kid."

"Almost. He was named for a country singer. His grandmother, who raised him, had a favorite song back then called 'The End of the World.' "

"Sure, Skeeter Davis!" Annie, being from the hill country, knew well. "Great voice, great song. One of the first crossover hits."

Esther, whose taste went to classical, Sarah Vaughn and Johnny Mathis, curled her nose. "If you say so."

"Why was he raised by his grandmother?"

"Parents were flower children. Remember the sixties? Sex, drugs, rock 'n' roll. He grew up with no boundaries at all, until his granny took over when Mom and Dad disappeared."

"Disappeared?" Annie sniffed another mystery.

"Nothing sinister. The father, who was a surfer like Skeet, did just that, in the ocean off Oahu. The mother joined a commune of hippies and died of a heroin overdose up in Redwood City. Terrible story."

"Judy said Skeet was a champion boarder."

"Won some medals, I think. Extreme sports. You ask me, it's just kid stuff like roller skating or riding a bike. He was raised by the grandmother in Venice, which means she must have been a flower child of sorts herself."

"Toking Granny," Annie mused. "I like her."

"White trash." Esther sipped her coffee and lifted a fingernail of whipped cream to her tongue. "I don't mean to sound so high and mighty, I just want my girl to be happy."

"They seem happy to me. She says she is." Annie was being very honest. "They are best friends. They care about one another. There's more to life than romance and sex and kids."

Esther sighed. "Perhaps. Just a mother's opinion. I want grandchildren while I'm still young enough to play with them."

"I loved him," Judy exclaimed.

Skeet boosted the flame on the front burner, then slid the heavy cast-iron pan onto it. Sweat was pouring down his forehead. "Of course you did."

"No, I mean he meant something to me. He was important to me. The opening means more to me because he's gone. I want you there."

Skeet poured a few drops of olive oil, shook the skillet, then tossed a handful of chopped garlic into the oil. They sizzled on impact and began smoking. He gave the pan another shake and then stabbed a ripe, thick rib-eye steak with a long fork and set it in the hot oil. "I'm due in Cabo and I can't change that."

"Why?"

He flipped the steak. The diner had ordered it rare. As the second side seared, he tossed a pinch of salt onto the meat, and then a grinding of pepper, and arranged the oversized plate, already set with a slow-roasted tomato, charred Yukon Gold potatoes, and some deep-green kale leaf for color. "I have meetings, local government, permits, all that shit you well know about."

She reached out and touched his hand. It was hot from the stove, but that is not what startled her. His fingers bore calluses, scars, and burns from molten fat. "Please, Skeet. I need you there with me."

He looked into her eyes. "I'm sorry, honey. If I could, I would."

"I thought you liked him too."

He groaned. "Oh, come on." He speared the steak through the smoke and sizzle and set it on the plate. "I was very fond of him."

"Then you should want to be there to celebrate the

opening. It's a great building. It's the best thing I've ever done."

Skeet handed the platter to Troy, who already held an oversized wooden bowl filled with fresh greens. Troy gave Judy one of his enamored smiles and left.

Skeet missed it as he wiped his hands. "Jane Wyman, dining with Ann Miller. Steak for one, salad for the other. Guess which?"

"Who cares?"

"You have a point."

"Skeet, come on," she attempted again. "I don't want to do this alone."

"I liked him, Judy, but I wasn't involved with him the way you were."

"What does that mean?"

"Involved? I don't know, you tell me."

"I wasn't sleeping with him if that's what you think."

"I wouldn't care if you were."

"I think you would."

He looked shocked. "Are you saying you want me to be jealous? I thought we were best friends. We made that decision long ago."

She looked exasperated and charged out the kitchen door, running smack into Troy. "You okay?" he asked, his hand on her shoulder.

"Fine, sorry about that," she said, and he took his hand away.

Skeet came through the same door. "Judy, come on outside."

She followed him out. He took off his apron and pulled out a pack of Winstons from his shirt pocket. "Calming down?"

She looked disgusted. "Christ, smoking again?"

"I only smoke when I get riled."

"I'm riling you?"

"You're doing a good job of trying."

She sat on the stone fence that separated the back parking lot from the garbage dumpster. It was late and she could feel the heat of the sun being swept away by the rising cold from the sand below. "Skeet, sometimes I think we should go our separate ways."

"We've talked about this, Judy." He lit up the smoke.

"But we don't resolve it."

He disagreed. "Sure, we have. When we had our affair, we were just kids. It was all about passion and heat. I thought this was now a mature, deep friendship." He blew out a puff of smoke.

"I'm not complaining. I love our friendship. It's just that . . ." Her voice trailed off as a car started in the parking lot.

"What?" he softly asked, taking a seat on the warm stone next to her. "Honesty is the foundation of this partnership. And we have someone to come home to, someone there for us, someone always down the hall." He flicked the ash and laughed. "At least the nights I don't sleep here at the restaurant."

She smiled slightly. She was warming to him again. He had a charm that melted everyone around him. "I don't know what it is. I don't feel complete is the best way to put it. I feel that I want more, but then I'm scared that there isn't more, can't be more, that I'm just fooling myself."

"I understand. But that has nothing to do with our friendship." He took another drag.

"Put that stinking thing out."

He did.

"Sometimes I feel that friendship is the best thing you can have in life, the most equal of relationships. But I don't know that for a fact. I feel I've always been cut off on the brink of feeling real happiness."

"You weren't happy when we were first together?"

She shrugged. "You said it, we were young."

"Or was it Craig that messed it up?"

She stiffened. It had been years, but it always still drove a nail through her heart. "I was completely honest with you about Craig. I was in love with him. He told me he'd been in love with me for years, in pain while he watched us have our affair. When we came together, it was perfect. And then he committed suicide."

"And you came back to me."

"You were there for me. You're the one person on earth who knows me best, you were the only comfort I had, you kept me from doing the same thing he did. And when it transformed into friendship, I knew it would be forever."

"Why are you so miserable, then?"

"I'm not miserable." She stood up. "Just missing

something. Restless. Unfulfilled. Getting old, you know?"

"I think it's the loss of Norman. You know he was attracted to you, and that made you feel good, it revived those dreams. But what we have now, hey, it beats the hell out of growing old alone."

His puppy-dog eyes melted her. "I'm sorry. God, I sound so needy."

"Yes, you do."

She sat next to him again and took both his hands in hers. "When I was little, I went to school with a Catholic girl named Rose. Rose Furloni, a looker. She used to tell me that all this stuff she learned from the nuns at catechism class. I remember her telling me there was a place called Limbo where all the little unbaptized babies went, and you also were sent there if you had racked up a few sins in your life that, I don't know, you didn't go to confession for or something. It intrigued me because she made it sound lovely, soft swirling clouds, a good place where you would be content for the rest of time. I feel like I'm in that place now."

"That's bad?"

"I said content. Not happy. It was a great place, but neither here nor there. Only those attaining heaven got to be happy, got to see God."

He bent forward and kissed her cheek. "I see God when I look at you."

"Oh, please."

But he wasn't kidding. "When I look into my

friend's eyes, it's the safest place in the world. If that's Limbo, I'm happy there."

That was just what she didn't want him to say. The frustration eating at her was that she truly wanted to take a stab at happiness with someone. He was content with the way their relationship was and had no interest in pursuing another.

But—and this was the deepest frustration—was that so awful?

The young man parked his car at the end of Sand Canyon Road, in north San Diego County, precisely at midnight. He waited a few minutes until he saw the lights of another vehicle approaching, and when it came near, he saw the shaman. When the man stepped from the car, the younger man asked, "Where are the others?"

"They are not joining us."

The young man blinked. "Why?"

"One of the men felt he was not ready. The other two want to wait for him. Shall we do the same?"

The young man looked as if he'd been told he couldn't have Christmas this year.

"All right, we will do it alone."

"Cool."

They climbed the rocky incline with the help of flashlights, but they did not have far to go. This place was well-known to those who were interested in Indian rituals, and had been used many tines. Most Indian villages throughout California had several of them. When the villages were small, they were constructed from hides and sticks, a pole frame covered with leather, where a fire would be burned on the earthen floor and a few men would gather to sweat and purify themselves.

But as the villages grew, the sweat houses grew larger, like this one. It was made of clay and brick, with a small chimney. The room inside, which was partially dug down into the ground, was large enough for many men.

The boy was attracted to the mystical side of the sweat houses. The ability to alter your mind and your spirit so that enlightenment and guidance reached your heart. When the sweat house shamans combined the experience of male bonding with drugs extracted from desert plants, the result was both incredible and alarming. The spirit world would be contacted, but the method of getting there risked death. Tonight, the shaman promised, it would be safe, and they would commune with the spirits.

They lit the fire, and while they waited for the room to heat up, the shaman told of birdsongs and tales of Indian tribes. The boy sang an Indian verse with him, and then they removed their clothing. They were, as the shaman had promised, not embarrassed in their nakedness, but felt closer because of it. There were no illusions.

They sat next to one another on leather patches placed on the rocky floor, chanting a low, almost melodic sound that the shaman had taught him, until sweat rolled from their bodies in the sweltering heat. Then the shaman withdrew a leather case from the backpack he had brought. He set it on the floor and withdrew a vial of liquid.

The young man nodded with anticipation. His chest heaved as he breathed deeply, his whole body shaking.

The shaman mixed the potion, a mix of cactus juice, oil, and Evian water. And then a drop from the vial. "This is called snakeweed," he said softly, "*Xanthocephalum sarothrae,* sometimes called 'broomweed' by the Indians."

"Why?"

"It grows rampant on overgrazed land, like a broom sweeping it, I was told."

"Livestock eat it?"

The shaman laughed. "None that live to tell about it."

The boy looked scared suddenly. "Really?"

The shaman touched his shoulder reassuringly. "What I have brought is very diluted, have no fear. It is called snakeweed because it hides snakes from sight. The Indians attributed great powers to it because of that. It is very bitter."

The boy knew. "I would like to be a snake. I would like to move like one."

"Perhaps you shall," the shaman said.

The boy watched his instructor put the cup to his mouth and close his eyes, tilting his head back slightly. The shaman's Adam's apple bobbed as he swallowed, and it seemed that he had swallowed a good mouthful. The truth was, the shaman had only let the liquid touch his pursed lips, and the moment he handed the cup to the boy, he wiped his mouth.

The young man was trembling so much that when he brought the cup to his lips, it nearly spilled. The shaman took it from him, calmed him by rubbing his shoulders, telling him to close his eyes and picture himself riding a great horse over the clouds, telling him to see himself as strong and courageous and magnificent.

The shaman handed him the cup. The boy brought it to his lips and sipped slightly. The shaman nodded and took the cup from him. The young man closed his eyes, feeling the euphoria, the release of his spirit, a feeling he had never before experienced as everything inside him seemed to rise into the air, soaring.

The shaman whispered to him to drink more.

But the boy suddenly felt a paranoia grip him that tightened his throat, choked his breath and prevented speech. He was overwhelmed all at once by feelings of fear and panic. The room started to spin. He bolted from the sweat house, bare-naked into the cool night.

The shaman found him kneeling in the rocky soil about twenty feet away, vomiting. He'd fallen, cut his knee, and blood had spread all down his shin. The shaman cleansed him with his T-shirt, onto which he poured some of the Evian water, and then helped clean the boy up. All the pupil could say was, "I'm sorry. I let down my spirit. I am a coward."

"No, my friend," the shaman said in a steady, comforting voice, "all men must admit they can be frightened." He helped him up to his feet, steadied him. "Next time you will be ready."

"I started to get sick. I fell—"

"Next time," the shaman assured him, "we will change the elixir so that you will tolerate it. There are many desert plants. We will find the one that will enhance your consciousness and bring you to the place you want to go." The shaman wasn't kidding; there was enough snakeweed in the dropper to kill twenty men. But next time he would use something that would not make the boy sick before he drank it all.

"Thank you," the boy said gratefully.

The poisoner shaman led the boy back to the car with his arm around his shoulder. "Till next time, may the spirits guide us, Troy."

Troy nodded and said good night.

Dear Diary:

We went to Joshua Tree one time, where we did some peyote and talked about girls and saw a scorpion kill a mouse. We came upon what looked like a little watermelon, and I was so stoned that I wanted to eat one. Thirsty as well. My friend cautioned me.

It was something called coyote melon, and even the coyotes shunned it, he said. He knew a great deal about drugs, everything you wanted to know about poppies and opium, mushrooms, grass, mostly organic stuff. He did not like manufactured drugs. Acid was forbidden. So he also knew a great deal about plants and their medicinal properties.

He showed me the power of the coyote melon. The same scorpion who was feasting on the mouse was to be our lab animal. Adios, I should have said, and vamoosed. But I stayed and watched it as he put bits of the melon onto the bloody corpse of the mouse.

That scorpion just curled up and died in seconds. It was powerful. I understood the stories of the ancestors after that.

Men can become bears. Women can become rattlesnakes. There is power in nature and power in the human mind. Together, they accomplish great things.

Snakeweed is not lethal enough. Coyote melon is. I wonder, had the architect drank the melon extract, would he have curled up and died as quickly as the scorpion?

I will have to bring coyote melon for the boy next time.

Chapter Five

Judy went alone to the dedication of the building. She spoke for a short time about how the building would forever be a monument to Norman Lempke's skill, talent, and taste. She told the gathered throng that she was especially proud of the bougainvillea in the lobby and the restaurant, and knew that it would have tickled Norman as well. She didn't mention that to keep it growing in there, it had to be changed every three weeks.

Skeet went to Mexico to put the finishing touches on the plans for Fancies Los Cabos, in Cabo San Lucas. He'd first gone there on a fishing trip when he was only eighteen, when the place was nothing more than a sleepy fishing village catering to macho Americans wanting to play Hemingway. But then a Hard Rock Café had arrived, followed by a hundred T-shirt shops. It was still an enchanted piece of the Baja Peninsula, though, and now he was planning to open a restaurant and perhaps retire there one day.

He stayed nights on his boat, a thirty-seven–foot classic Egg Harbor Sports Fisherman, which he kept docked at the marina there. It had a spacious master stateroom, a comfy main salon where four could relax in comfort, and he'd remodeled the forward cabin to become part of a galley set up for a master chef. He'd serve friends a fabulous dinner made from the marlin he'd caught just hours earlier.

The plan was to open the restaurant in a building off the beaten tourist path, not far from another eatery that had flourished in the last few years, that of his friend J.W. Stowaser, Macaws. Located on a dirt road near the popular Melia San Lucas Hotel, Skeet first thought J.W.'s location too iffy for a fine dining establishment. The road was dirt, after all. J.W. told him he had decided he didn't want to compete with the tourist places out on Avenida Lazaro Cardenas, the main drag. And J.W. had been right. Word of mouth was good, and people had come. It helped a lot that his executive chef, Doug Miller, was brilliant in his reinterpretation of classic Mexican cuisine.

Trouble was, Skeet couldn't be in Cabo all the time, and he needed an executive chef whom he could trust, just as he'd found for the Beverly Hills branch. So Doug was helping Skeet look for a cook, putting his nose into the subculture of chefs. They all knew one another, it seemed.

Today, Doug told Skeet he had a prospect, a chef who had been cooking at one of Vermont's finest inns for two years now after spending a year in Paris at a three-star establishment. Trouble was, he hated cold weather, didn't ski, and ran down to Florida whenever he could. Skeet called him the minute Doug handed over the number, and the guy agreed to come down again the following week, at Skeet's expense, to "really talk about this."

Skeet called Judy. "I'm not coming home for a while."

"Why?"

"Found a chef, but he can't fly down to meet me till next Tuesday. I'll do some fishing, and God knows, there's enough going on here to keep me busy."

"Bring lots of cash?" she quipped. She knew that almost everything accomplished in Mexico required greasing palms under the table.

"Bribe suitcase is brimming. How are you?"

"Okay." Her voice was flat.

"Working?"

"No. I'm just not feeling particularly creative right now. Decided I can afford to take a few weeks off and just do nothing."

"Plunging into work would help you get over Norman."

"I'm fine. I'm just fine."

But she wasn't, of course. She had been sitting home doing nothing, not even venturing out to the gym, which was something she seldom missed. Her mother thought she was depressed, and her father worried that she would lose future commissions if she moped around any longer. Annie tried her best to rouse her with plans to do things together, but nothing worked. Chad and Malinda, the owners of Cabana Boy Pool Company, who'd been servicing her pool since she moved there, even invited her to a party, but Judy declined. Everyone she knew tried to cheer her up, but only Juan, with his gentle, quiet nature, seemed to penetrate. When he was tending to the yard, she brought him iced tea, and they sat and talked a bit. Shy and almost painfully private, he could converse about trees and soil, but had a difficult time relating to anyone on a personal level.

Judy didn't know why, but she felt she could talk to him more easily than others could, and while he loved this confidence, it made him very nervous. Their conversations, though they started off just fine, went nowhere. But he touched her on some level. Judy always suspected that Juan had a bit of a crush on her, and that that made it difficult for him to talk to her one-on-one. It was harmless. Truth was, she rather liked it. It gave her a secret thrill to be desired by this intensely handsome young man—provided she knew it would go nowhere. She had no attraction to him at all.

One morning, after Skeet had been gone a week, Judy's father drove over, handed her a sack of coffee beans and said, "Brew some. It's Arbuckles'."

Judy saw the colorful label on the brown paper bag. "What's Arbuckles'?"

"Cowboy coffee. This was the joe on the range, the stuff that real cowpokes drank."

That didn't sound promising. "The sludge that sat over a fire all day?"

"Most famous coffee in America a hundred years ago. John Arbuckle of Pittsburgh was the Starbucks of his day. You could tell a ranch hand he was worth his weight in Arbuckles', and that was a compliment as good as gold."

"How do you know all this?"

"*Gourmet*. Read an article, sent in for some, and saved it for a special occasion."

Judy opened the sealed bag. The smell of peppermint hit her. "My God!" There was a peppermint stick in with the dark, almost black beans. It was like finding the Cracker Jack surprise.

"That's the Arbuckles' signature," her dad said with a smile.

"And how do you know that? Oh, don't tell me, *Gourmet*." She laughed and poured some beans into the grinder.

The coffee was pretty good, dark, hearty, and rich—with, thankfully, just a hint of mint. What touched Judy was that her father had taken the time to come see how she was. "Aw," the big man said, "I'm not real good at sitting here and helping you psychoanalyze your problems. That's more your mother's style. I just want to do something with my daughter."

"Huh?"

"You know," he said, looking out the window to

the mountain baking in the sun, "all the years I've been in Palm Springs, I've never been up the tram."

She couldn't believe it. "Never? You took me when I was a kid. I remember."

"Your mom did."

"You didn't go?"

"So many times I've thought about it, planned it, but we never seem to get around to it."

"You want to today? I read that they have rotating cars now."

He didn't even blink. "Love to."

"Me too, Dad."

Judy had been born very much a New Yorker in the Beresford, one of the great pre-war apartment buildings on the Upper West Side. She began her yearly California trek at age three, when her parents started spending December fifteenth through January fifteenth of each year in Palm Springs. The tall, distinguished Henry Sussman was at the time the publisher of Random House, one of the great movers and shakers in the publishing industry, and he often invited colleagues to the desert for a good game of golf, food, and book talk.

When Oscar Dystel, another powerhouse who guided Bantam Books to prominence, visited with his family one year, he brought along his finest editor, Esther Stein, and Henry was smitten. After trying unsuccessfully to hire her away from Bantam, Henry married her instead. After a year they gave birth to what would be their only child.

"The tram, are you sure?"

She was a little taken aback. It was a tourist attraction, something she would never have thought of doing on her own. But she hadn't done anything alone with her father in a long time. They used to go sailing off Nantucket together when she was young. They rode bikes together up and down the coast of Maine while vacationing in Kennebunkport. They even went mushroom hunting in the fall just a few miles outside New York City, where Henry knew a farmer who had a lot of wet, wooded acreage that now held a Costco warehouse store. This would be, Judy knew, a special day.

The desert floor looked just the way it did from an airplane. Only up here she could take her time and pick out the buildings and landmarks. The golf courses looked like acres of green carpeting. They could not see his house in The Reserve because it was blocked by the mountains, but they could pick out Judy and Skeet's and Annie's. Judy dug a quarter out of her jeans and put it into one of the high-powered binoculars standing there, and looked almost straight down, toward her street.

After a couple of misses—wrong pool, wrong roof—she found her house and squealed with delight. She focused and saw Juan, working with his shirt off, something she'd never seen him do when she was home. But then again, he was shy. A second later, she spied Annie in a bikini carrying her laptop to a chaise out near her pool. Then she saw Juan start to stare across the fence and—

The machine went dark.

"Damn! Just when it was getting good," she said, without looking up. "Dad, got another quarter?"

There was no answer. Judy tried to hold the machine steady so she wouldn't lose the spot when the picture came back. This time she *demanded* another quarter from her father, whom she could sense out of the corner of her eye. "I need another quarter, Juan's spying on Annie!"

Click. The picture returned as she heard the quarter drop into the machine. She lost the street, however, and found herself looking into a parking lot. "Shit," she said. She expected her father to comment on her language, but he didn't. Then she found it again. "Oh, my God." Annie, who had not seen Juan (or maybe she had), was ignoring her laptop and stretching out in the sun, removing her bikini top. Judy saw Juan still watching from the protection of the fence and bougainvillea. Annie ran her fingertips over her nipples. "Dad, you're not going to believe what I'm watching." Then, just as she said it, the picture went dark again. She kicked the machine. "This is a rip-off, a quarter for less than a—"

Click. The picture returned again as she heard another quarter fall into the metal box inside the machine. "Thanks, Dad."

"Don't mention it."

It wasn't Henry's voice. She lifted her head. A guy

stood there, dark, thin, pleasant-looking, with a wry smile that said he was amused that she'd finally figured out that it was he who was funding her view, not her father, who had walked into the building behind them long ago.

"Hi," he said, in a pleasant, secure voice, "I'm Ben."

Dear Diary:

Mount San Jacinto has arms so big and strong, it can protect an entire nation. Our nation has been held in its great bear hug for centuries. I am reading *The Heart Is Fire,* which is all about my people and their lives and traditions. I have heard before that we are related to bears. But here it is again.

The bear used to carry the boy up the mountain, into the canyon. That was his father, the bear. We are so closely related to the bear. We cannot eat bear meat because we are eating our kin. *They would say that when you looked at him and he was still dancing, all of a sudden you would see a bear.* Then he would disappear, and become himself again. You cannot believe this unless you are Indian.

The shamans would go to the top of Tahquitz Canyon, which is very close to the top peak of Mount San

Jacinto, where the tram stops. There they would be closer to the spirits. They could look down on the world, on our land, and roar like the bear.

To frighten off the intruders.

Chapter Six

"What were you watching?" the guy asked. "Car accident?"

Judy laughed. "My gardener sneaking a peek at my neighbor's big bazoongas."

He looked a bit startled. "Okay."

"I'm Judy. I thought you were my dad."

"Gimme a break. I know my hair is thinning, but I don't think I could pass for your father."

She smiled. "He was standing next to me when I started looking into that thing. I just thought—"

"He went back inside. I was waiting my turn."

"Oh, go ahead." She stepped back from the binoculars. He stepped up. "If I keep it where you had it, do I get to see your neighbor's big bazoongas?"

"Annie's got enough for the whole bank of binoculars," she said, "and if she knew we were watching, she'd probably put on a real show."

"I'll pass." He dropped a quarter in. "But I'd like to see the town."

"Where are you from?"

"Originally, New Jersey."

"First time here?"

He hesitated, then said, "Yup. A desert virgin. What am I looking at?"

"Palm Springs proper. The Movie Colony, I think."

"Movie Colony?"

"Where the stars built their houses in the early days."

"Cool."

She saw him move the scope around. "Big houses, lots of walls?"

"Yeah."

"That's the Movie Colony, then." She guided the scope gently to the right, slowly so she wouldn't break his nose. "That should be where we live, straight down the mountainside from here. Tennis Club they call it, because the first big tennis complex was built there. It's lovely, but funky."

"The whole place is like a checkerboard. Why all the barren spots?"

"The barren spots, for the most part, belong to the Indians. You have to lease the land from them."

"Ah. What's this big street?"

She took a peek. "Tahquitz-McCallum Way, though everyone just calls it Tahquitz these days. Ends at the airport. Now," she said, directing the telescope, "continue down the street, you're moving toward Cathedral City, then there's Rancho Mirage—"

"Very green."

"Yeah, lots of golf courses."

"Lots of water." And he was rather attractive too, she realized, in an odd way.

"Plane landing," he said, focusing up an inch. "Bouncing in the wind."

"The Coachella Pass is the second windiest place in America. Chilly winter nights, rain from Baja, a convection oven in August and September, wind. The price of living in paradise."

"What's the first windiest place?"

"Altamont Pass outside San Francisco," she answered, adding, "I think."

"Streets of Chicago, maybe," he joked. Click.

"Where do you live in New Jersey?"

"I don't. I live in San Diego now."

She was stunned. "Then you've been here!"

"Nope."

"You live in San Diego and have never been to Palm Springs? How can that be?"

He shrugged, looking slightly embarrassed. "Just never did it. Went to UCSD, then back East, worked in Virginia for a long time, then came back West a few years ago. Always wanted to see Palm Springs. Now I'm really glad I came. 'Cause I met you."

They stared at each other. And in that moment, in her smile and his gaze, something happened. He was a nice man and she found him attractive. Not that there was anything remarkable about him. He was good looking, no one would deny that, but at the same time, his hair was indeed beginning to thin, his arm muscles had lost their ripple, and a few extra pounds were beginning to settle around his middle. He was the antithesis of blond, tanned, handsome Skeeter—or even a Norman Lempke. Yet his eyes seemed to exude intelligence. There was a gentleness about him that Judy found soothing.

"I should go find my father. Thanks for the quarters."

"Sure enough. Judy, was it?"

"Judy Sussman."

He held out his hand. "Benjamin Spiegel."

She took his hand—a strong, secure grip—and shook it. "Did you drive up?"

"Hopped on a commuter plane yesterday. I'm actually on my way back East to see my mom after Passover."

"Not spending it with her?"

He rolled his eyes. "She's with her cronies in Florida, a place I detest."

She nodded. "I understand."

"I'm here because school is out for Easter. I teach."

"What?"

"High school."

"That's great."

"Only when the metal detectors pick up the knives and guns."

She shook her head. "It's a different world."

"Judy?" The voice came from behind her.

She saw her father. "Gotta go . . . oh, wait, meet

my dad." She took Ben's hand and pulled him over toward her father. "Dad, this is Ben Spiegel. Ben, Henry Sussman."

They shook hands. "Henry Sussman?" Ben asked.

"That's right," Henry said.

An awed look came over Ben's face. Then he dropped it, as if telling himself no, it couldn't be. Then he had to ask anyway. "*The* Henry Sussman?"

Henry laughed. "What, I owe you money?"

"From Random House?"

Henry nodded. "Retired."

"You published my father."

Henry lit up. "I did?"

"In 1967. He wrote a book on the aftermath of the Second World War."

Henry sifted through his brain. "Spiegel, Spiegel . . ." Then it hit him. "History professor at Princeton?"

"Yes."

"I remember that. What was it called? *The Hollow. . . ?*"

"*The Hollow Soul,*" Ben said proudly.

"First book, I recall, that dared suggest collusion between Pius XII and Hitler."

"Dad was ahead of his time."

Henry was impressed. "Quite the mind, a good man."

"He died last year."

"I'm sorry. Didn't read everything we published, of course, but that book was a stand-out. He should have done more."

"He was working on one when he passed away."

Judy said, "Ben's here for Passover."

"Please," a delighted Henry said, "join us. Do you have your family with you?"

"I'm not married, sir. Just your basic bachelor schoolteacher. Thanks, but I couldn't impose."

Judy was glad to hear he wasn't married, but she hoped he'd accept. She dug her card from her bag. "Here, in case you change your mind."

Ben pocketed the card and smiled. "I'm gonna go back to the telescope."

"They're a rip-off," Judy said.

"Hey," Ben joked, "they're my quarters."

"Ready, honey?" Henry asked.

"I need something to eat," Judy added. "Bye, Ben. It was nice meeting you."

Ben nodded to her, and again to Henry, and turned to put another quarter in the machine as she walked away. Had she turned when she entered the door of the building, she would have seen him looking at her once again.

"Why are you so perky?" Annie asked from her raft as Judy joined her by her pool.

"What do you mean?" She started slathering herself with suntan lotion.

"You've been in the dumps since Norman died. Today you're glowing."

"You're nuts."

"Girlfriend, something happened."

"Nothing *happened*."

Annie paddled closer toward her. "Get laid?"

"Annie!"

"Well, whatever it was, I'm glad." She grabbed her Greta Garbo–sized sunglasses, covered with rhinestones, from the pool rim and slid them on. "Wish it had been me, goddamn it."

"What happened to Pete?"

"Pete the pilot? Lotsa talk, no action, typical man."

Judy looked down at her. "Tell me something, girlfriend to girlfriend. Did you really play around with him in the cockpit?"

Annie looked around, as if to be sure no one was listening. "He took a little bite of Trixie." She had long ago named her boobs Trixie and Bubbles.

"While flying the plane?"

"Sure. It's easier than driving a car. I mean, there's no curves, no trucks, no blind Chinese women in old Toyotas to look out for. Tell me, why can't Asians drive?"

"What did you do to *him*?"

Annie giggled. "Took a little bite of Tommy."

Judy sat straight up. "Tommy."

"Named his balls Tommy and Bobby."

Judy knew she was putting her on. "You're disgusting."

"You asked."

"I wanted the truth." She nestled down in the soft lounge chair and felt the sun drench her.

They said nothing for about ten minutes, lapping

up the sun. Then Judy's voice cut the silence. "Saw you from the tram."

"Tram?"

"Dad and I went up San Jacinto. Did you know Juan was watching you?"

"Suspected. Thought I heard the bushes rustling. Wouldn't be the first time some boy plays with himself peeking at a woman."

"Strange bird, isn't he?"

"I'll say. He has a crush on you, you know."

"I suspected."

"Bother you?"

"He's harmless."

"It's a plus. You get the best-tended yard in the desert."

A few moments passed. Annie got out of the water and wrapped herself in a towel the size of a bed sheet. "Gotta dry my hair. Driving into L.A. for a book signing later." She sank into one of the chairs under the umbrella where her laptop was waiting. She stared at the screen, but could barely see it in the glare. "Desert Dick is about to shtump the blonde."

"*Shtupp*. You need Yiddish lessons."

"Desert Dick is about to *screw* the blonde."

"So crass."

"My best feature." But Annie wasn't up for it. "Don't feel like writing sex right now." She clicked to another file. "Need a name for blondie's boyfriend."

"Joel Stedman."

"Too WASPy."

"Joe Van Zandt."

"Sounds like a Nazi hairdresser."

"I think it's Dutch, actually."

"What's with the Joes?"

"What's the character like?"

Annie groaned. "Sweet, trusting dull guy."

"Ben. Call him Ben Spiegel."

"A Jewish desert rat?"

"Why not?"

Then it hit Annie. She looked up. "Who's Ben Spiegel?"

"A guy Dad and I met today."

Annie removed her hands from the keys. "Aha! That's why you're so perky."

"Oh, please."

Annie Chestnut finished at the Bookstar store in West Hollywood—the gay boys from that neighborhood had treated her like Judy Garland back from the grave—and drove not east toward Palm Springs but west some more, until she came to the ocean. Navigating her way down the coast to Marina del Rey, she piloted the big pink Caddy up to the restaurant where Norman Lempke had eaten his last meal. Jimmy remembered her right away. "Hey, cool wheels."

"You already told me," Annie reminded him. "So, what's up?"

"Just hangin'."

She hadn't come all this way for that answer. "You

left me a message this afternoon. Figured since I was in L.A. I'd stop and see what you wanted."

"Oh, right," Jimmy remembered. "Gotta park it first."

"I'm not eating."

"I'll get in deep shit."

"Keys are in it."

He moved the car to a space way too small for it, somehow wedging it between a couple of Mercedes. When he returned, two diners came from the restaurant doors, and he had to retrieve their behemoth Lincoln Navigator while Annie waited some more. She hoped it was worth it. After he saw them off, he turned to Annie and said, "I remembered what you told me. About calling you if I thought of something."

"I'm listening."

"That night. There was something strange. Sorta."

"How?"

"When I left work. I mean, I was done and I just sort of hung out for a while with this girl Claudia who waits tables here."

"I know who. I spoke with her the first time I was here."

"We heard all the sirens and stuff."

"Someone discovered the victim at one o'clock."

"That's about right," he said.

"Yes. And?"

"Just before the sirens and all, there was a guy by my car."

"Where was that?"

"In the self-park lot, where you put yours last time." He nodded over that way.

"What about him?"

"I didn't think of this till today," Jimmy said, "but it was weird. He was between my car and his own. Standing there. Taking off his clothes."

"What?"

"Yeah, as I walked toward my car, this dude was like stripping. But he left his pants on."

"Then what?"

"He got into his car, started it, and drove out as I was getting into mine."

"Hmm. That is weird."

"There's more weird. Where he had stood was all wet."

Annie's ears perked. "Wet?"

"I thought at first—" Jimmy laughed out loud. "I thought at first the dude had taken a leak there. Man, I was pissed, 'cause I stepped in it—"

"Nice pun."

"—but it was water."

"Salt water?"

Jimmy blinked. "Salt water? How would I know? Like, I didn't taste it, you know? Just the dude was wet, real wet, 'cause there was like this little lake down on the ground there."

"He was all dressed at first? Then he took everything off but his pants?"

"Yeah. Then he sat there for a while. And finally left."

"Why didn't you tell me this sooner?"

"Like, I didn't even remember it was the same night. I never connected it till I read this thing in a *Newsweek* my dad showed me today. It said the cops think the killer might have swam from the boat to escape."

"Back to his car in the lot where yours was." Annie sounded enthused now. "Okay, Jim, my boy, did you see what he looked like?"

"Nah. Too dark. I wasn't paying attention."

"Tall, short, fat, skinny?"

"Tall. Slim."

"Wearing?"

He groaned. "Hell, I don't know. Shirt and pants. You sound just like the cops."

"You tell them this yet?"

"Nope."

"You should. Call Detective Sparks, friend of mine. He's a cool . . . dude."

"Cool."

Annie smiled. His was a language she would never quite master. "Hey, Jim, think hard. What kind of car was he driving?"

"He wasn't."

"I thought you said—"

"It was a truck."

"What kind of truck?"

"Dark, old, kind of a beater, I'd say."

"License number?"

He spun around, a little on the dramatic side. "Come on, lady."

"Just thought I'd try. Anything else about it?"

"Hmmm."

"Come on, Jimmy, this is very good, but I need more to go on. Give me something to distinguish that truck—black, white, striped? Van or open bed? Advertising on the side?"

"Rakes and shit."

"Pardon me?"

"Rakes sticking up in back, man."

"Rakes?" She didn't know if he was speaking his post-teen tongue again. "Like raking leaves?"

"Yeah. A pickup like gardeners drive."

Juan Torres sat at his computer. He had tried to go to sleep, but tossed and turned for nearly an hour. He knew what the problem was. Same thing it was earlier, when he peered over the fence from Judy's yard and saw the nearly naked woman. The sight of her enormous breasts amazed him. Didn't turn him on exactly, but stirred him nonetheless. The nipples, he'd never seen any so huge, not even in magazines devoted to such things. He was erect when he got up from the bed, and even writing in his journal didn't make it stop.

He knew what he could do. He could be a bad boy. He could simply slip on a pair of shorts and sandals and walk down the street. Well, no, the nights were still a little too crisp for that. Perhaps jeans and a sweatshirt. But no underwear. Underwear would only get in the way. It would only take a few moments, and nothing needed to be said. He'd be serviced by someone very willing to help out, and then he'd walk home and sleep like a baby. Why should tonight be any different from all those other nights?

Because he heard his mother's voice resounding in his head. The time she had caught him with Jose. Jose had been three years older than Juan's thirteen, and he was determined to pass onto little Juan all that he'd learned about sinful pleasure. All of Caracas had heard Mrs. Torres shouting that day, screaming. She dragged in a priest to "save" him. The good father was in his thirties, a pious, affable but also athletic man who worked with teenagers to get them to channel their urges into sports, civic service, crafts. Father Hernandez was so liked by Juan's mother that he became a regular fixture for arroz con camerones every Friday night. What Juan's mother didn't know, of course, was that the good father had begun teaching Juan pleasures that the punk Jose hadn't even imagined.

As soon as he was old enough to really figure it out, the hypocrisy made Juan laugh. Yet the shame his mother had instilled continued to dog him. That's why he only did it in the cover of night.

Tonight, the climax relieved him. Right there, sitting in the chair, without even putting a hand on himself. Was it the powerful thought of what could happen in the bushes or in some automobile parked down the street?

Or was it the fact that he was writing about Judy?

Chapter Seven

Gold's Gym was adjacent to the runway of Palm Springs International Airport. From the upstairs level, Judy could walk/run/climb/step her way to cardio heaven while watching planes taking off and landing against the mountain backdrop. She had worked out in a lot of gyms, but this sunny, bright, open space remained her favorite.

She put her gear into a locker next to Babe's, which was her name for a woman who was about eighty years old, wore pink mittens and gold jewelry to work out, and put everyone in the place to shame. She had been a dancer her whole life, Judy had heard, starting as a Ziegfeld Girl, and was still hoofing it in the Palm Springs Follies, a sell-out production of old-timers strutting their stuff.

Judy grabbed her towel and water bottle, and high-tailed it up to the second floor, where she saw all the elliptical cross-trainers were taken. So she hopped onto a treadmill, chose her program, took a deep breath, and pushed the start button. When she got up to speed after two minutes of limbering up, she had the feeling she was being watched. Sure enough, the guy next to her, while keeping a good pace on his belt, was looking at her. "Ben!" Judy said, surprised. "Hi!"

"Howdy." He wiped sweat from his neck.

"Been here long?" She glanced at his control panel and saw that he'd been on the treadmill for forty minutes.

He slowed down. "How are you?"

"Fine, you?"

"After the heart attack, I'll be just great." His tank top was soaked, but that helped Judy see that he had more muscles in his arms and a stronger chest than she had guessed. "Trying to keep the flab off the middle."

"It's impossible!" shouted a guy who was approaching the step machine just in front of Ben. "I burn like seven thousand calories a day and still can't eat a good ravioli dinner."

"That's Dennis," Judy explained. "He's a great guy and very outspoken."

Ben looked out the window at a plane taking off.

"Hey, hi!" Dennis said to Ben.

Ben looked a little startled. It seemed that Dennis recognized him.

"Remember me?"

Ben shrugged.

Judy said, "You know each other?"

Ben shook his head.

"Wasn't that you about a month ago?" Dennis

asked. "I grabbed your tennis shoes after my shower?" He laughed out loud. "And they fit!"

Ben shook his head. "Must have been someone else. First time here."

Dennis looked perplexed. "I could swear," he muttered, and went back to concentrating on his machine.

"You work out regularly?" Judy asked Ben.

"I'd look better if I did. I get some exercise at school. I'm a swim coach as well as history teacher. Geography too. Hotel I'm at gave me a pass here."

"Well, if you want to come back, just tell the manager that you're my friend. Aaron is one of the good guys."

She tried to concentrate on running, but it was somewhat silly trying to do it next to him. The legs, in gym shorts now, were every bit as sexy as she'd remembered. But she was curious about more than his physique. "So your father taught at Princeton. You go to school there?"

"Yup." He nodded. "Mom still lives in Lawrenceville. Just down the road from Princeton."

"Only child?"

"No. Two older sisters. You?"

"One and only."

"Like that?"

"No. Always wanted a brother."

"Me too. Though one of my sisters is as close to a brother as a girl can get."

She decreased her speed, but upped her ramp resistance. "If I had kids, I'd have three."

"Sounds good. If at least one is a boy."

"Like kids?"

He laughed. "I'm a teacher. I'd better."

"None of your own, though?"

"None that I know of."

She laughed at that. "I guess being with kids all the time fulfills the needs of being a father, huh? I seldom have contact with children. I hate that."

"Not too late." He hit the stop button on his machine. "I'm whipped."

"I'd have to find a man to help."

"Can't believe you haven't," he said, meaning it as a compliment, his mischievous eyes flirting as well.

"The why not is a complicated story." She upped her speed. "I'm on a roll!"

"Catch you later." He started walking away.

"Leaving?" she called out.

"Free weights."

"See you down there."

He walked to the water fountain in the corner, and she snuck a look as he bent over to drink, got the affirmation that her assessment of his ass yesterday was right on. Then she turned away when he stood up straight, not wanting him to think she was too interested. But his eyes caught hers again as he started down the stairs, and they both sent each other a warm smile. She upped her speed again. She was energized now.

* * *

Ben finished his last set of curls. "God, does that hurt."

Judy stood watching, lifting light weights to strengthen her shoulders. "Where else do you like to vacation?" she asked.

"Oh, used to go to the dreaded Florida with my folks. When we were little, they'd get all excited and say hey, kids, guess where we're going again this summer? And we'd cover our ears and scream no, no, please God, make it not be Florida."

She laughed. "Why?"

"Bugs, snakes, humidity for starters. We went to my father's uncle and aunt's house in a place called Titusville where nobody was under eighty. The big event of the day was squirting my sisters with a hose. Horrible."

"Was it clear that you were miserable?"

"Tante Blanche finally died, thank goodness. They put Frank in a home. We never went back."

"That was the sum of your travels?"

He said, "Chicago to visit old school friends. I don't do it much."

She thought that meant he was probably boring and unadventurous. "I just live for the next flight to Rome or Hong Kong," she told him.

"Do it often?"

"Not since I've become successful."

"You design restaurants," he said. "It came to me

when I was driving back to the hotel yesterday after meeting you. Your name sparked something."

"That's what I do."

"But aren't you married to Skeet McCloy?"

"Join the list of the thousands who think so."

"Sorry."

"It's okay, a compliment really. Skeet's a great guy."

"I don't travel much now because I joined the Peace Corps after college."

"Oh?" He was beginning to sound more interesting.

"Went everywhere. Honduras, Colombia, then Bulgaria, and finally Malaysia. Backpacked through Burma—that was a trip—and ended up in Paris, starving, aimless, worked for a bookstore over there for a while."

She was bowled over. But she didn't let on. "Which one?"

"Shakespeare and Company, where else? My French wasn't very good."

"My God." Her notion of a boring man never having had any life experience was shattering right before her eyes. Backpacking across Burma! And she thought she had problems dodging cars on the Via Condotti!

He started doing deep squats, looking in the mirror. "That's what shaped my future, though, because I'd always been aimless and suddenly I liked encouraging young people to read. As a kid, I experienced adventure through books. I had been lucky that I'd gotten to travel all over the globe, but I realized that was rare. Most people would only feel that sense of emancipation and thrill through books. So, teaching travel sounded good to me."

"History," she said, nodding, "geography." She added, "Wow." Because she meant it.

"Well, reading too. I do that on the side, tutor special kids who can't grasp reading. It's very rewarding."

I design light fixtures and tables, she thought, feeling wholly inadequate.

"I've got a friend named Connie, an actress in New York, who has written the most amazing series of children's stories. They teach values in the most unique and accommodating way. I've been reading them to the kids—I tutor real young ones—for years. They're crazy for them."

"I love children's books. My dad published thousands of them, and I was the kid he tried the manuscripts on."

"You'd love Connie's."

"I'd like to read them."

The smile that crossed between them lasted longer than the connection up at the tram. It said that they were getting closer, and that they liked each other. "Grab a hi-pro drink with me after?" Ben asked.

"Love to," Judy answered.

They sat on the outside patio across from the gym, at Extreme Blends. Ben ate an oatmeal bar and drank a fruit juice concoction, while Judy stirred and sipped a smoothie. A warm wind had kicked up. Tumbleweed rolled over the airport runway. The breeze rustled the palm fronds overhead. "Where are you staying?" it suddenly occurred to her to ask.

"Hyatt. Right downtown. Package deal, rental car and all."

"Next time you come, book one of the little inns, like El Sueño or Estrello. But where you should really stay is Korakia Penisone. It's very special, a reminder of what Palm Springs used to be."

"I know some of the history of the area," he admitted, "and I guess I should, teaching it. Love the Southwest. Always wanted to live here. Aim to hike the Indian Canyons tomorrow."

"I know the perfect place to have lunch."

"That an offer?"

She blinked, straw in her mouth. "Offer?"

"You bringing lunch for our hike?"

She sat back and tried to hide her delight. But she didn't do a very good job. "Sure!"

"You're positive?" he asked, sensing her hesitation. "I don't want to overstep—"

"Bring water, sunscreen, a pair of sensible hiking shoes, and I'll do the food."

"You cook?" he inquired.

"I live with a chef, are you crazy?"

Her straw made sucking sounds on the bottom of her glass. "What are your plans for dinner?"

He shrugged. "I'm here alone. Know absolutely nobody but you. And your dad."

"Warning: it's a little stuffy going to dinner at their house."

"I didn't mean—"

She just continued. "Besides, I'm going there for Passover, that's enough. Maids and all, you know?"

He didn't, but he nodded politely.

"How about joining me at Fancies tonight?"

"Well, sure. I'd love to." His delight was apparent.

"I'll pick you up. Eight okay?"

"Great. But I'm buying, all right?"

She nodded. Then she stood up, slung her gym bag over her shoulder and shoved her sunglasses back onto her face. "This has been fun."

He rose as well. "I'm sure glad I went to the tram."

As they were leaving, one of the waitresses saw Ben. She glowed and said, "Buenas tardes, amigo!"

Ben just stared at her blankly. "Good afternoon."

"Ah, will we see you tomorrow?" the plump woman inquired.

"No," he said, "we have other plans."

"It is good to see you again, amigo," the woman called out to them.

Judy looked at Ben. "Do you know her?"

Ben shook his head. "That's really weird. I never met her in my life."

"Sparks?"

"Yes?"

"Annie Chestnut here."

"Annie, how's your chest nuts?"

"Funny. I've got a tip that's going nowhere for me, but might help you guys out in the Lempke investigation."

"We could use it," the detective said.

"Check out Lempke's gardener. And gardeners around the marina where he kept the boat. Kid who parked his car that night thinks the perp might have left the area in a gardening truck."

"Who's the car parker? I'll talk to him myself."

She gave him Jimmy's name and the restaurant number. "So what do you know that I don't?"

"Well, the test we ran on the martini glasses turned out to be an interesting one."

"How so?"

"Ever hear of something called coyote melon?"

"Huh?"

"Bitter fruit, grows in the desert, poisonous to man and beast."

"It was in his drink?"

"Yup."

"Enough to kill?"

"Had he drank the whole glass, yes."

"Coyote melon?"

"That's what I said. Listen, it's all zilch so far, despite that. No motive in the world. No one disliked this guy. Except maybe his gardener."

Annie wished him well and hung up. She finished her coffee and went outside to get the mail. Just as she emptied the box, Juan drove up. "Howdy," she said.

"Buenos días, Annie." He flashed a nervous smile, then bent down to study the sick cactus near the road.

Annie sorted through the bills as she started back toward the house. Then she stopped, dead in her tracks. She turned back, not saying a thing, looking over Juan's head to what was parked just behind him. His truck. An old, beat-up, repainted, greenish Chevy pickup. It was no different from the fleet of thousands of gardening trucks keeping Southern California green and clean. What got her was looking at it from the back, all she saw was the tailgate and a single, solitary rake sticking up almost defiantly from the bed.

Dear Diary:

His death was the most excruciatingly painful I have ever seen.

I fed him a drop of Thorn-Apple to start, which I knew would not kill him, but get him high. He was a drug addict to begin with, and I had teased him with cocaine and grass earlier that night, preparing him. His addiction was great. I told him we would go to a sweat house in the hills there in Scottsdale, and he was surprised such a place existed. It did not. I made it up.

It got him hallucinating, and he went through a long, drawn-out fantasy about a bird or something about wings, I could not clearly tell what he was babbling. Then I fed him more of the liquid, and he started to feel pain. I think clarity returned for a moment when I told him to crawl in the sand, crawl to the weed growing there, it will cleanse you, I told him, it will make you well, it will bring Judy back.

He put his face into the vine of Thorn-Apple and drank in the scent, which is terrible. I had seen it growing out behind the wall of the compound the day previous, and it was a godsend. What would it be like to make someone eat it?

The poisoner shaman this time would not kill by the elixir; death this time would come from ingesting the actual plant.

I picked some in my hand and stuffed it into his mouth. He fought me, coughed, groaned as his stomach retched. But I told him it was lettuce, it was delicious, it was a salad from the gods that would bring Judy back into his life. Oh, he had run from her lack of commitment, I do know that. But he longed for her. All the drugs he was doing then were to put the pain of Judy from his mind.

His mind must have exploded in the sand there that night. Eating the vine, the flowers, the green leaves, eating sand, crying out in pain and vomiting, then choking on that vomit. He screamed and doubled over, and then spit up blood. His eyeballs turned yellow, and his face—and he was a handsome young man—seemed to sink into itself, as if the dream plant were digesting him from the inside out.

He carried on like that for almost an hour. He was young, virile, in good health despite all the drugs he had put in his body over the years; he put up a fight. But, in the end, no one is strong enough to counteract the spirit plants.

I wept for him as I wept for the others.

Chapter Eight

Troy fought another waiter for the chance to serve Judy and Ben. From the moment Judy met Ben in the Hyatt lobby—attractive in faded chinos, loafers, shirt and tie with the sleeves rolled up—he seemed to be having a ball. He loved being in the famous restaurant he'd heard so much about, and though he wondered about the wine list, Judy assured him it wasn't necessary, that Troy would be bringing them "something special." But Troy seemed oddly nervous about Ben.

"He thinks *you* are something special," Ben said, observing the way Troy fawned over her.

As they talked, Ben kept looking past her. Judy turned once, trying to see what was getting his attention, but had no idea. "What are you looking at?"

"Is that Mary Bono?"

She grinned. And glanced. "Yup. You impressed?"

"Yeah."

"Well, don't look now, but over *your* shoulder sits Madonna."

He turned quickly, not at all subtly. He didn't see her. "Where?"

"Fooled you. But Dolores Hope and Barbara Sinatra are over in the corner."

Ben said it was the best lobster of his life—grilled with cilantro, lime juice, butter, and a sprinkling of chili pepper, with roasted cactus on the side—savoring every bite, for neither of them wanted the evening to end. "There were a lot of pluses growing up as an only kid," Judy continued as they discussed their histories, "but I think I'd have traded all that for a brother or even a sister."

"My sisters and I are close. One is gay."

"Was that a problem?" she asked.

"No, never. I think, because my parents were educated people, there was less resistance because there was less guilt that they'd done something wrong."

"Is that the root of it usually?"

He finished the last of his wine. "I believe so. We always fear what we don't know, and we think, in the case of parents, that our kids won't ever be happy—thus we want them to fit the mold. When they don't, we take it as some kind of flaw in ourselves."

"You're sounding like a father."

"Or a schoolteacher."

"You had a good father, I think, like I have."

He nodded. "We were all with him last year when he died. In Minnesota."

"Mayo Clinic?"

"Yes. Cancer. He was so young at heart, his mind was sharp as a pistol, but the body just gave out. He loved the musical *Evita*, and just before he died, when we were telling him to fight, to hang in there, he quoted a lyric from a song in it: 'What's the good of the strongest heart, in a body that's falling apart?' "

Troy, returning with a melon–and–cactus-flower concoction that he said was "on him," had the misfortune of dropping their empty wineglasses when he tried to balance them on the plates he was removing. "What's up with you tonight?" Judy asked, thinking he'd seemed nervous. She wondered if it was just being in her presence.

"I'm doing something tomorrow," Troy admitted. "Something exciting."

"Date?" Ben inquired with a grin.

"An experience. Instruction. It's an Indian culture thing, hard to explain."

Ben said, "I teach it sometimes, do field trips. Fascinating, huh?"

"I'll say," Troy admitted. "It's gotten me in touch with my spiritual side."

"What exactly are you gonna do tomorrow, if I can ask?" Ben inquired.

"Sweat house experience."

Ben nodded. "I've done a few of those."

Judy regarded Ben curiously. Here was another interesting thing about him. "I hope it turns out to be the experience you want it to be." She looked at Troy warmly.

Troy seemed energized by her words. "I know it will. I'm ready."

When he walked away, Ben said, "It can be a powerful experience."

Judy watched Troy disappear into the kitchen with a final glance back at her. "I don't know, but I have to say he really is adorable."

"So are you," Ben admitted, "so are you."

J.W. poured tequila shooters for himself, Skeet, and Doug, now that the crowd at Macaws had thinned. "Here's to the new chef."

Skeet lifted his glass. "Here's to Doug, who found him for me."

Doug said, "Here's to the new competition."

Skeeter laughed. "We're a fancy taco joint. No competition at all."

They licked the salt on their hands and drank fast. The tequila was a bottle of vintage Patron that J.W. had been saving for a special occasion. This was reason enough to drink it.

The interview had gone well; Skeeter had liked David Storey, the chef who'd flown down from Vermont, and the guy had liked him and Cabo and the kind of lifestyle he could have there. Fancies Los Cabos would be *his* kitchen, Skeet had promised him, and, in time, his menu. J.W. and Doug both doubted that because, first of all, Skeet McCloy was a control freak, as most executive chefs are, and second, he was building himself a house down in Cabo. That meant he was planning to spend a lot of time there. But for now, the plans were set. Fancies Los Cabos would open in a few months, as soon as David could break his contract with the inn and the Mexican paperwork could get done. Skeet felt he had jumped a hurdle.

Doug was called back to the kitchen. The straggling diners over in the corner had requested dessert after all, and he had to go whip up a chocolate flan. J.W. asked Skeet when Judy was coming down.

"Soon as we get to the interior, get all the pieces there."

"I got a guy for tables, if you need. Woodwork, the best. Built me a great armoire for the house."

Skeet nodded. "Can he work from Judy's sketches?"

"Showed him a pic from a magazine ad, a Kreiss Collection piece, he copied it perfectly, for less than half the cost. He's up in Tijuana."

"I'll go see him tomorrow."

J.W. handed Skeet the man's card. "So, what else is wrong?"

"Huh? Oh, Judy's in a rut. But I've seen it happen before."

"How so?" J.W. poured each of them another shooter.

"She's going through her dance again about independence and motherhood. Every so often those hormones kick in, and she starts feeling unfulfilled."

"Those things mean a lot to women."

Skeet nodded. "I'm supportive, I want her to find someone, but every so often she blames me for holding her back."

"Maybe it's constricting her," J.W. suggested. "Maybe you shouldn't be roommates anymore."

"Listen," Skeet made clear, "I've seen it again and again. She falls for some dope and then she loses him and ends up blaming the security we have."

"Better than marriage," J.W. said confidently. "Take it from one who's been there. But how about you? I don't think I've seen you date anyone else in all these years I've been fishing with you."

"I'm married to my job." Skeet leaned over the table. "Judy gives me the companionship. I want sex, I find a girl for the night. It's a good life," he said, winking.

When Skeet returned to the boat, the phone was ringing. He grabbed it just in time. "Oh, Meester Skeeter, I about hanging up!"

"Buenas noches, Anna. Just got aboard. How's everything?"

Anna Bocwinski Sepanski, the classy Argentinian who was the hostess at Fancies Palm Springs, called every night, no matter where Skeet was in the world, to give him a report. "Dizzy blonde lady again early coming in."

"Who?"

"The famous one."

"There are lots of famous dizzy blondes. Oh, you mean Suzanne."

"Yes, that one, rerun queen with her cooking books. 'We Somersizing!' she screaming to everyone in the place. 'Order beef, order fat, lotsa fat!' she yelling. She wipe us out of beef."

"Beef?"

"Prime rib. She eat it all. Need greens and scallions too. Lobster go fast. Judy and friend have."

"Judy was in? I'm surprised."

"Nice tip man leave, Troy very happy. He glowing about day off tomorrow."

"Man? Who?"

"Nice man, say he friend, never see him before."

"Interesting." He waited a beat. "Call Desert Produce and get them to bring you out whatever greens you need in the morning. Go ahead and order more beef and call Fish Louie and see if you can't get some lobster from him, our shipment won't arrive till Tuesday morning."

"Okay, I doing, Meester Skeeter."

"Bye, Anna."

"When you coming home, Meester Skeeter?"

"Perhaps sooner than I'd planned." He hung up. And immediately lit a cigarette.

Juan lifted weights out back of his house in the dark, till the sweat ran into his eyes. He was fighting the urge again, he knew it, and he was going to lose, he was also quite sure of that. He rinsed off outside, spraying himself with the garden hose, but it only froze his pecs, gave him goose pimples. It didn't have the desired effect on another part of his body. When he got caught up in a horny frenzy like this, he could not live with himself until he had found relief. Only one woman could give him that relief. Judy was the one person in the world he knew he could make love to. But she was not his. So he'd have to go to confession again.

That's what he'd always called it. He'd sometimes tell people, "I'm going to confession tonight." They'd respond how nice that was, good for him. What a fine religious boy. No one had any idea of what it really meant, though it did entail getting down on one's knees.

He slipped on gym shorts and a tank top. He knew he'd score faster with more skin showing. He left the house and walked the two dusty blocks over to the parking lot between Palo Verde and Melrose, where, behind high walls and lots of foliage, was a men's resort called the Cathedral City Boys Club, or CCBC. It was a popular place, and, he understood, not only for the pool.

All he had to do, he'd learned long ago, was stand in the parking lot. Someone, sooner or later, saw him. Approached him. Touched him. Took him into the oleanders. Or between two SUVs. Did what the priest used to do. And tonight was no different. A fairly handsome, masculine guy who sported a wedding ring stopped his Jeep, gave Juan a glance, then parked at the end of the long line of spaces. The desert sky was so dark that no one could see what the two guys were doing. They didn't speak. Juan walked up to the truck as the guy opened the driver's door. Then Juan simply yanked his shorts down over his butt. The guy moaned a little in anticipation, and in a moment he was on his knees in front of Juan. It was over in about four minutes.

But it had an effect Juan could have predicted, yet never thought about beforehand. He invariably felt that he'd been a bad boy, that he would go to hell, that he had sinned. The need for confession raged through him, as hypocritical as it was. Where was the priest now?

In the photo that Skeet had taken of them one afternoon quite on the spur of the moment, Judy gazed at him. His only memento of his secret love for her. Guilt riddled him. He'd cheated on her. No, he hadn't, it wasn't with another woman, so it didn't count. Just the kind of reasoning the guy in the Jeep probably used on himself when driving into his suburban driveway, ready to greet the wife and kids. Boy, how we fool ourselves, Juan thought.

Annie was on hold for what seemed like years. She finished a whole bottle of beer in the time it took for the person who answered to locate Jimmy. He was probably retrieving a car. "Hey," he said finally, instead of "hello."

"Hey, dude," Annie joked. She figured she'd talk

to him in a language he'd understand. "You called me?"

"Right. Listen, I thought of something else."

"You remember something more about the truck?"

"The name was painted over."

"What name?"

"I dunno. Toyota. Or Ford."

"You mean on the tailgate?"

"No," Jimmy said sarcastically, "on the windshield."

"Cute."

"You know how they have M-A-D-Z-A in white on the back or something?"

"I think it's M-A-Z-D-A."

"Well, on this one it was the color of the truck."

"You sure?"

"Yeah, otherwise I'd be able to tell you the make. I looked right at it from behind."

Annie was trying to remember if Juan's truck had a painted tailgate or not. But that was absurd. Juan didn't have anything to do with this. He just happened to be the only gardener she knew.

"Lady, you there?"

"Jim, my boy, thanks, that might really help."

When she hung up she knew how silly it was to even consider that Juan had something to do with this. He had a connection to Judy, not to Norman. He had no motive. He was no murderer.

But she'd said the very same thing before. So she

grabbed her car keys, Scout, and set out into the night.

Juan didn't know it, but while he was writing in his journal, a big pink Cadillac convertible with a woman and dog in it was passing slowly by his house. His truck was parked in the dirt out front. She had thought she might need a flashlight, and had one resting between her thighs, but it wasn't going to be necessary. She could see, by the light of the neighbor's garage light, that the name on the tailgate had been painted over.

She continued on by without even applying her brakes, memorizing the plate in a single glance.

Dear Diary:

As the Indian once probably said, This shit ain't easy to find!

Sacred datura blooms at night, and it spreads to fifty feet, which makes you think it might be easy to locate. I walked for miles in the desert sand, up hillsides, down arroyos, searching for a sign of the flowers. Coyotes ran from my flashlight beam, snakes slithered over my boots, and rodents ran from my path. I saw every imaginable plant but the one I was searching for.

I sat down near the water. Whitewater was nearby, where I'd left the car, and if I followed the stream it would take me right back. I had been frightened that in my meandering I'd gotten lost. I decided that without the datura, I would have to put off the sweat house rendezvous with Troy. I have coyote melon, yes, stored in the refrigerator, but it is too close to

Norman, it has been in the news recently, people are very aware. It would be a mistake. This should look like a boy playing with fire. And the fire burned him.

I stretched, splashed some of the cooling water on my face, and decided to give up. But lo and behold, the Indian spirits were looking down on me this moonless night. For there, at my very feet, spread over at least twenty feet of land, were the gorgeous pale white blooms. I fell to my knees and gathered up a large quantity, cut the plant stems as well as the flowers, and the sticky seeds, and gathered them into my bag. It was a windfall.

I have extracted the syrup now, the golden green elixir, ground the seeds into it and blended the entire mix. It is done.

Sacred datura.

I have done this before.

Chapter Nine

"Good morning," Ben said energetically when Judy opened the door.

"I'm almost ready." Judy didn't see a car out front. "You walked?"

"Figured it would warm me up for the hike." Ben entered as she pulled the door open, then set his backpack down on the vestibule floor. "Wow," Ben said, charmed by the decor. "This is great."

"It had better be," Judy said, "or I should be doing something else in life."

Ben's eyes swept the living room, a comfortable mix of old Mexican—white fabrics on dark woods, gold-leaf accents on carved picture frames, all set on saltillo pavers laden with rich, faded old carpets. He found his own focal point, a brown leather sofa that looked ancient and as comfortable as his favorite pair of jeans. "Where'd you get this?"

"The Snow Creek Hotel, middle-of-the-desert ghost town, used to be in their lobby. They claim Wyatt Earp and Billy the Kid rested their butts on that hide."

"So will Ben the Schoolteacher." He sat down. "Oh, never ask me to get up."

"Can I get you anything to drink?" Judy asked as she turned toward the kitchen.

"No, I'm fine. Thanks."

He studied the place, the beautiful French windows framing the pool area, all rock and natural desert plantings, bougainvillea leaves floating on the water. The walls behind the old, battered antique table were covered with restaurant photos—Skeet with Judy with presidents, politicians, actors, writers. He picked out Madonna, Mick Jagger, Pete Sampras, Nicole Kidman, Bill and Hillary Clinton, Steve Forbes.

He saw several photos of Skeet and Judy alone through the years—hugging photos, close photos, photos that told him there was more to their relationship than she was saying. He almost felt guilty for being in the man's house.

"So, you sure it's okay . . . this hiking thing," he asked as she came back in.

"Okay how?"

"With Skeet?"

She smiled, understanding. It happened all the time. "Trust me, Ben. We really are just roommates."

He felt just slightly uncomfortable with so many pictures of her with her "roommate" staring at him.

He followed her this time when she went back into the kitchen. She put sandwiches and some other foods wrapped in foil and Ziploc bags into a backpack. Then she tugged on the big Sub-Zero freezer door and withdrew a frozen plastic ice pack and slid it in between the food. "Rosemary chicken on foccacia," she said.

"In that case, skip the hike and let's just eat."

She giggled. He zipped up the backpack and grabbed it with one hand while she picked up another and a Gap baseball cap. As they walked out of the kitchen, Judy didn't realize that someone was watching through the French doors, hidden from sight behind a large sego palm. Curious, the man immediately moved around to the front of the house, and waited for them to emerge.

Outside, Judy immediately saw Juan's truck. What was he doing there? It seemed that he'd been stopping by every day, not his normal twice a week. "You here again?" she asked him when she saw him rounding the corner of the house.

"I think I'm obsessed with this yard," Juan admitted.

"Great job," Ben said, looking at the neat splendor of it.

"I won't charge you any more, Miss Judy," Juan said emphatically. "I just can't stay away."

"We like that," she assured him.

The gardener smiled at Ben as he passed him, and he smiled back. "Ben Spiegel," he said, offering his hand.

"Juan Torres," Juan said softly, "muchacho."

Judy said, "Juan's like part of the family."

Juan blushed and went back to work.

They climbed into the SUV, and Juan gave her a wave as she put the vehicle in gear. "Bye," she said, with a little wave of her hand as well. Ben just smiled.

"Juan looks like that singer, Julio's son . . ."

"Enrique Eglesias? Yeah, he does. Very sexy."

Ben looked back at Juan, who was still watching them as they drove down the street. "I'll bet he's a lady killer. Yup, for sure."

Juan felt anger brimming inside him as he watched them drive away. He tried to concentrate on what he was doing. But even on his hands and knees in the sand, he could only think about one thing: Who was that guy? He had never seen Judy glowing so. She'd been all aflutter when she was working with the dead architect on that building, but it was different from this. This was apparent, palpable. God, Juan wondered, was she dating this guy?

He never could figure out the arrangement that she and Skeet had. It just wasn't normal. She had been crazy about that hotel pool boy, she even spent nights with him, and Skeet seemed not to mind. Had she been Juan's woman, *his* "roommate," he would have paddled her good. Flaunted it, she did. It was this reverse image of her that troubled him, but also made her so irresistible. The fact that she had a slutty side intrigued him, made him sweat, got him hard.

Where had she gone with this new lover? Off to

have sex somewhere? They had packed food, taken backpacks. They were going out in the desert, perhaps up to Whitewater to lie by the rushing water. He'd been there, seen people screwing on blankets between the rocks and scraggly plants. The idea of her lying there, naked, under this man he'd just met sent shivers of anger and hatred through him. But at the same time, he found the image of it very powerful, so strong that when he closed his eyes he could actually see it, envision every thrust and passionate moan.

He suddenly realized where he was and what was happening. His hands went down to his crotch to cover the outline of his erection, in case anyone was looking—especially that fat broad next door—and he tried to switch channels in his mind to get rid of the image. But he shuddered. He had been close to orgasm.

Ben, he thought as he walked to the truck to get fertilizer. Ben Spiegel. Fuck him.

Judy took the road with the sign to Andreas and Palm Canyons, the Palm Springs Indian Canyons. Ben wasn't much impressed at first, because the terrain seemed like everything else in the sun-parched desert: dry and rocky. But as they started to climb, the land changed. The dry chaparral and cacti turned to green foliage. He heard a babbling brook, and when they finally made their first crossing of the stream, he was impressed at the icy coldness of the water. "Snow melting above," Judy explained.

"Just like in Vermont—in June, however."

"I am awed by this place," she said to him, "because of the Indians. They have kept it what it is, and it is very meaningful to them. There is a purity here that speaks of their lives and culture."

Up the trail, they came upon the palm trees that grew wild in the canyon, first just a smattering of them, then huge clusters that looked like they'd been there hundreds of years. Some were so wide, Ben thought them to be the Redwoods of palms. Judy told him there were eight miles of them.

"Washington Fillifera."

"How'd you know that name?" she asked, reasonably impressed.

"Told you I'm nuts about the Southwest."

Ben took several pictures. A bit higher they found the springs that also fed the stream, which, Judy explained, was the reason people first started flocking to Palm Springs. The waters, so said the Indians, were healing. In fact, the local band of the Cahuilla Indian tribe, who lived close to the hot mineral spring bubbling forth from the desert floor, named themselves after it: Agua Caliente, or hot water. Even back in the 1920s, the Hollywood set loved a good spa.

They found a spot for lunch that Judy had been to many times before. She had once made love up there, under the stars with Craig, shortly before he died.

They'd hiked up in the late afternoon, and when he surprised her with a bottle of wine and two plastic glasses, they'd drank every drop, and found themselves unable to walk. It was a hot night in summer, so they decided to just stay. And then some.

But she didn't mention that today. She felt slightly on edge because she knew she liked this gentle man, and she didn't want to scare him away. It was that time when she would be on her best behavior with someone new in her life, when she gauged what he liked. It wasn't dishonest, exactly, more like sliding over the sharp edges.

As they sat across from one another on two large rocks by the cold, flowing water, she was ready to get to know him better.

Annie sat writing. Desert Dick was anything but inspired today, for she was turning out page after page that went right into her computer's recycle bin. She got up and ate two brownies, and even that didn't help. Trouble was, she wasn't concentrating. Her mind was on what Jimmy had told her. A truck that matched his description belonged to her own gardener. It was preposterous that the perpetrator would turn out to be Juan, and she tried to put it out of her head. But it wouldn't go.

Her friend at the LAPD, Tom Sparks, called. "Annie, honey, Lempke's gardener turns out to be a ninety-year-old Chinaman who had his driver's license taken away six years ago. Lives in a guest house on the property. The restaurant doesn't have a gardener—nothing to garden—and nobody down on that pier, or anywhere around, uses one. Dead end."

"Any trail of water from the dock to the self-park lot that night?" she wondered.

"Checked on it, but it would have dried by morning. And no one thought to look that night."

"Anything more?"

"Nothing. You got something for us?" Sparks asked, hopeful.

"Gardening truck bothers me. Don't know why."

"'Cause maybe it don't mean a thing," Sparks said.

"Yeah. And Desert Dick ain't doing so well today, writer's block."

"Use this stuff," the man suggested.

"How so?"

"Fictionalize this story and see where it takes you."

Annie brightened. "Not a bad idea."

"And if Dick solves this one, let me be the first to know."

Annie laughed. "You can damn well buy a copy and read about it like everybody else."

"Annie, baby," Sparks said in the most sexy voice he could muster, "I'm not like everybody else."

"No, you're probably smaller." Touché.

"See ya, babe."

"Bye." She hung up the phone and stared at the screen. Crap. Just crap.

The dog was scratching at the door. When she opened the door, Scout scampered between her legs toward his food bowl. In turning to watch him, she glanced at Judy and Skeeter's yard, and saw Juan sitting on the wall, under the lemon tree, writing on a yellow pad on a clipboard.

He seemed to be in another world, lost, like she was when she was writing a book. There was a look on his face of rapture, then despair, then it would fade to anger and finally complacence. It fascinated her.

But what was he writing? What was causing these emotions to spring forth in him? And why there, in Judy's yard, when he was supposed to be working? If she could only take a peek at what he was scribbling.

He finally put his pen away and started to gather his gear. He went around the front of the house to his truck, and she ran through the living room to watch him set the clipboard on the front seat. Then he put his tools away and took off the wide-brimmed straw hat he wore to work in the sun. Instead of leaving, however, he turned and went back around Judy's house.

Annie crept out her back door, feeling ridiculous, but she wanted to see what he was doing. She made her way under the extended back eaves, and peered up over the wall between the yards to see Juan standing at the side of the pool, just staring at the diving board. She couldn't imagine why. She watched him walk around the side of the pool, and then, just before the diving board, he stopped and gave a fast look around to make sure no one was watching him. Then he picked up a piece of clothing that she would swear was a bikini top from the way it dangled as he balled it up and shoved it into the front of his pants. He was stealing Judy's bikini.

Sunlight filtered through the swaying palm fronds, bathing Judy and Ben in cool light. "We hiked up a mountain in Burma," Ben was saying as they ate, "that we shouldn't have attempted."

"Too difficult?"

"Too risky. I was with two guys who collected artifacts, Asian pieces that they'd resell in England for outrageous sums. They wanted to find an old monastery and temple they'd heard about, and sure enough, it was up there. Abandoned, filled with ruined pieces, broken crockery and stuff. A mess, but they sifted through it and found all sorts of intact things, which was highly illegal because nothing could be taken out of the country without government approval."

"They call it Myanmar now, and I understand it's worse." Judy finished her sandwich and took a sip of water. "Chop your hands off if they catch you stealing."

"The government didn't get us, bandits did. Here we were, loaded down with this stuff and bullets flying all around us. I've never been so scared in my life."

She swallowed a delicious piece of melon. "What did you do?"

"Dropped the backpack. Ran like hell. The one guy started yelling at me, how could I do that? Hell, I wasn't ready to give up my life for some ancient Burmese parchment rendering."

"I did that once in Thailand," she remembered. "Set my bag down, got lost in a crowd of people, never saw it again."

He was eating his sandwich with obvious pleasure. "Someone stole it?"

"I didn't want it."

"Why?"

"Grass. Craig and I, well, we were smoking then—this is back in my last year of college."

"Craig?"

She nodded. "My teacher. My lover."

"You were having an affair with him by then?"

She nodded. "He was a pretty heavy user, grass, magic mushrooms, some desert plants that had hallucinogenic properties."

His expression suddenly changed. "Heavy."

"They killed him. He taught Indian Studies at UCLA."

Ben blinked. "Craig *Castle*?"

She gasped. "You know who he was?"

"I took a course with him one summer. Went to a sweat house with him. Did the Hopi ruins in New Mexico on a field trip."

"My God." Judy was in shock. "Small, small world."

"I'll say. It was over ten years ago, but I remember him telling us about his girl. That was you."

She was still disbelieving. "Where was I? I mean, if you did a whole summer's course with him, why didn't we ever meet?"

He tried to recall. "Hmmm. Were you were traveling with your family part of the time? I think he showed us a postcard from you—"

"Bangkok! That's the story I was starting to tell you. It was that summer. I was in Thailand with my family and Craig said bring back some good dope. I bought some off this guy on a boat, a little sampan at the floating market while my mother was haggling over fake Rolexes and bok choy. But I was so scared that afternoon when we were shopping, so paranoid that everyone knew what was in my bag, that when I saw a cop look at me in the Orchid Mall, I just froze, went to the ladies room and left it there."

"Yikes."

"Skeet was a lot more vocal than that."

Ben took the opportunity to decipher their relationship better. "He makes you happy?"

"He's always there for me."

"That means a great deal. I've never had that."

She was surprised. "No friend like that?"

"Good friends," he said, finishing his food, obviously pleased, "but no one ever that special."

"Confirmed bachelor, then?"

"Not if I can help it. I love kids too much."

"You want your own?"

He lit up. "Oh, yes. At least two, maybe four. You?"

"Don't think I'll ever get the chance."

"Never say never."

"If I ever get married," she added, "Skeet will do the reception food. At least people will remember the cake!"

He stretched and stood up. "It's gorgeous here. Thanks for bringing me." Then he looked around, seeming slightly anxious. "We in a hurry?"

"No, why?"

"We have an hour at least?"

"Sure. What do you want to do? Climb more?"

"No," he said, "not at all." He grabbed his backpack and started opening it, adding, "I want to paint you."

"Palm Springs Police, Sergeant Steve Sanders speaking," a pleasant voice said.

"Sergeant, is Selma Sherman there?"

"May I ask who's calling?"

"Tell her her old friend Annie."

In a flash, an excited voice burst over the line. "Annie Chestnut, how in the heck are you?"

"Great, Selma, you?"

"Never been better," Selma assured her. "Haven't seen you at Gold's lately."

"Gyms make me break out in a rash lately."

"Come on, ride the bike next to me at least, we'll gossip."

"Writing a new book. No time."

"I'll bet you're getting fat again." Selma never minced words.

"Me? Fat?" Annie sounded horrified in her most self-deprecating tone. "Just pleasantly plump. Honey, wanna run a name for me? Got to know if this guy's got a record."

"Got a social on him?"

"I could get it. Have a plate number on him."

"Annie," Selma said emphatically, "you could get anything. So, you want this fast?"

"Fast as you can manage."

"Tomorrow morning."

"Now that's service."

But Selma had a condition: "At Gold's."

Annie groaned. "Selma, don't make me do this."

"You want info, you meet me on the machines. Be good for you."

Annie protested. "It's Passover, isn't it? Aren't you supposed to refrain from physical exertion?"

Selma laughed. "I love when goyem suddenly become Jewish for the holidays."

"I rest for Easter too."

Selma laughed. "Honey, we need to exercise

harder to get ready for all that food we're going to eat. See you in the morning."

Annie hung up and looked down at Scout at her feet. "What a girl won't do for a good lead."

Dear Diary:

It was in the sweat house that I knew Craig must die.

He revealed everything to me about his relationship with Judy—way too much. He did not know that I was in love with her as well, so he did not realize that losing him might convince Judy to accept me in her heart. He described his feelings for her, described their erotic couplings as if writing pornography, and went on about their "spiritual quest" together like a loon. Of course, he was high on smoke and some kind of elixir he'd cooked up. Truth serum.

The way he described Judy, however, made her seem a goddess, almost untouchable, an angel or madonna or fairy princess. She took on a magic that was completely of the spirits, not bound to earth at all. She soared in our minds and in our consciousness! Craig thought she only existed there in his. He was so wrong.

It was from Craig that I first learned about poisoner shamans, and when I told him I felt it was my destiny to become one, he instructed me. He taught me everything I know about the plants, about the traditions. That summer was the most education I had ever packed into three months in my life.

I became the poisoner shaman because of Craig.

I became the poisoner shaman with Craig.

For it was Craig whom I first poisoned.

Chapter Ten

Ben sat on the rock on which he'd eaten lunch, painting with the watercolors he'd brought in his backpack. He had explained to Judy that this was his favorite hobby. He wasn't very good at it, but it didn't matter. He felt he could express himself better through painting than he could through writing or speaking. And he was feeling inspired to paint her. "I don't often do people," he warned, "so forgive me now if you turn out looking like a bowl of fruit or a coyote."

He dipped his brush in the flowing spring water and dabbed it lightly in red, then yellow, creating an ochre that echoed the desert sunrise. "Lift your chin just a little." She did, and he was pleased, wiping the brush onto the paper over her image, and then sweeping it quickly all the way to the other side, and off the page. He worked for a while, then announced, "I think that's it."

"Do I get to see?" she asked as she relaxed and stretched her arms.

"Sure." He handed her the painting.

She took it and said nothing for the longest time, just staring at it. He watched closely, seeking her approval. "This is really wonderful," she finally said.

"It's just you." He meant it as a compliment.

She took it as one. "It's just so . . . sensitive. Delicate. And I'm not, so that must be the artist."

"Painter," he corrected her.

"Artist," she insisted. "Ben, you're good!" She was getting charged now. "It's really quite amazing, I mean, you caught what I look like, but you added so much more. . . ."

"It's how I see you. I try to paint the inside as well as the external, the spirit, the feeling, the subject's inner beauty. I'm getting too poetic. There is a dazzle behind your eyes that I tried to put in there."

"Oh." So many times in her life, with so many men, she'd been told she was attractive, or that she was smart, or elegant, and that would lead into more compliments, and then the guy would make a pass at her. This time the compliment had been put into a picture.

Ben walked toward her, sure of himself. Her arms opened, and her lips met his hungrily.

They kissed only once, but it seemed to go on forever.

When Ben finally pulled away, he looked into her eyes. "I didn't quite capture them. Not exactly right. So, can I try again before I go back home?"

She smiled from ear to ear. "I'd hate it if you

didn't. Plus, I still want to give you the hip architectural tour."

He shrugged off the sexual excitement. He had to or he would either burst or end up attacking her right here on Indian land. "So, shall we head back?"

"I guess so," she said, almost not wanting to go. "The days are getting longer so we have time."

He packed up his paints and whatever was left from their lunch and rolled the painting around the small cylinder the paper had been wound around. "Would you like it?"

"Oh, can I?" she said, thrilled. "I've never had anyone paint me before."

"My pleasure."

"You'll sign it, won't you?"

"Sure." He pulled the straps of his backpack over his shoulders. "Ready?"

She did the same, made sure they'd picked up everything. "Ready."

They began their descent, crossing the cold water several times, meeting other hikers they'd seen climbing earlier in the day, finding a group of people singing around a guy with a guitar under a clump of trees, looking like the last descendants of a band of hippies. "Speaking of magic mushrooms," Ben remarked.

She giggled. "They're probably stoned on the plants that grow here. Indians did that. Powerful stuff."

"Yes, I know. I knew Craig, remember?"

She nodded. "God, how could you do a summer session with him and never have come to Palm Springs?"

He stepped over a fallen branch. "I took a week off to visit my parents. Missed this experience. We did Joshua Tree, and other places, though."

"What are you doing tonight?" Judy asked Ben when they got a little farther down the trail.

"Going to the Follies."

"Oh, you'll love it! I know a gal in it, see her at the gym all the time."

"I hear it's great fun."

"What about tomorrow?"

He shook his head. "No plans."

"My father invited you to join us for seder."

"I couldn't."

"Why?"

He had no good answer for that question. He certainly looked as if he wanted to. "You sure?"

She stopped walking, turning back to him. She bent forward and kissed him on the lips gently. "I'm sure."

That was all he needed.

Troy had waited for hours, sitting near his car at the end of Sand Canyon Road, watching the sun—and his hopes—die over the mountain above the sweat house. He was dressed in shorts and a tank top, sandals, and a bandana wrapped around his forehead, which would keep the sweat from stinging his eyes. He was getting antsy, but he told himself it was because of his anticipation, never doubting for a moment that the shaman would show up.

A vehicle came up the road, one he did not recognize. He felt fearful for a moment, but when the door of the car opened, his trust was restored. The shaman got out, looking exhausted and exasperated. "I'm sorry I'm so late."

The boy said, "I knew you would come, my teacher. Whose car is that?"

"I had to rent one because mine broke down. Hell of a day. I need this experience more than you do tonight."

"I am happy to hear that."

The shaman looked up at the sky. "This is a good time, as darkness envelops us, chasing away conscious thoughts and spirits."

"Yes, my teacher," Troy obediently said, and followed the man to the same sweat house where he had lost his courage the previous time. Tonight, he was sure, his faith in himself would be realized fully and completely.

In less than an hour, the wood had burned down to glowing hot coals. The shaman said, "In the original sweat houses, the men and boys of the tribe would collect sticks and brush, tie them in a bundle, which they carried on their backs, and sang songs for what they wished for in life—prosperity, good health, many children. When they made the fire in the sweat house, it looked like it was on fire itself, because the smoke would come out of the crevices where the wood and hides were joined."

"Those were the real kind?" the boy asked.

"This one," the shaman said, standing at the entrance to the sweat house, beginning to remove his clothing, "is more modern, well built. It has been here for many moons, as Tonto might say."

The young man laughed and eagerly took off his tank top. "How long would they stay in it?"

"Thirty, forty minutes, when the sticks had formed the hot coals. Then they would come out the small door, steaming, weak, and limp, and lay flat on the stone platform and sing the same songs, but in a more doleful way."

The boy removed his shorts and stood naked in the early night.

The shaman did the same. "They would dine with the women, then go back to the sweat house for the big smoke, which is when they laughed and talked of different topics, told amusing tales." He entered, and the boy followed. "And they would also become very spiritual and raise their consciousness."

The shaman set his leather bag down, then sat cross-legged. The boy sat facing him. They said nothing for a while, drinking in the heat, feeling the sweat beginning to appear on their flesh. "Sometimes they slept in the sweat houses."

"Really?"

"They would be drunk, I suspect, and find it difficult to walk. They would put the wooden pillows under their heads and just sleep like that. The place would stay warm for a good twelve hours, even in winter."

"It's hot now."

"Yes, Troy, it is." The shaman took a sip of water from a bottle. He offered it to the boy, who drank as well. "But we know for a fact they didn't have Evian."

Troy laughed. "I want to experience what I failed at last time."

"You did not fail, my boy. It was the wrong plant. This time I have brought sacred datura."

Troy's eyes widened. "I know that's dangerous."

"Very dangerous. In the wrong hands."

"You have done it before?"

The shaman smiled. "Many times." Then he got to his knees and started to massage the boy's shoulders, firmly rubbing them, moving his hands up the sides of his head, to his temples, where he gently massaged him, telling him to relax, to go to a spiritual place, feel the stress and the pain flow from him, allowing his vessel to open to a new experience, a new enlightenment.

"Yes," the boy whispered softly, excited now, but very calm at the same time. "I am a warrior, and I see weather."

"Weather?"

"I can feel the change coming in my bones, I can sense the rain a hundred miles away, I can tell the tribe a storm awaits, or drought is imminent."

The shaman smiled. He knew the kid was a weather freak, actually one of the few people he'd ever met who actually *watched* the Weather Channel. He played along. "You shall predict the storms based on the pull of the sun and the moon, and you will help save your people."

Then he mixed the elixir.

The boy shuddered in anticipation. "It's so dark and cloudy."

"Not pure like snakeweed," the shaman agreed. "I have ground the seeds into it."

"It won't make me sick?"

"We will drink the dark fluid of the gods, let our minds soar, and our spirits free." He held the cup up in front of him, like an offering to the gods. But he was offering it to the boy.

Troy took the cup in his hands. They did not shake this time as they did the first; he was finding confidence. "Oh, master," he said, "I want to reach the other world, the world beyond this one."

"You shall, my boy." He gently touched Troy's wet, hot shoulder. "Drink."

Troy sipped. Closed his eyes. "Oh. . . ." It was almost a gasp of pleasure. He could feel his body changing, transforming.

"More," the shaman urged.

Troy drank it all. His eyes widened in a flash, as if startled, as if he'd been stuck with a red-hot poker. The cup tumbled from his hands, hitting his stomach, rolling off his penis to the dirt floor. Then the boy froze, his whole body suddenly as rigid as a steel girder as his face filled with an emotion that looked like heaven and hell at the same time.

And then his heart stopped.

It happened so fast. No real pain, no anguish, no fighting for his life. No drama. The shaman was almost disappointed. It should have been more amusing than this.

The shaman packed his things into the leather bag, making sure he left nothing in the house that could be a clue. He dusted the floor with an old rake that had been left there to smooth out the dirt, and then, outside, he dressed quickly, and felt his clothes getting soaked with perspiration. He knew his shoes would never be traced because there were hundreds of other footprints all around the place. He made his way back down to the rented car and tossed his bag inside.

It was done.

Chapter Eleven

"Glad you liked our Follies," Henry Sussman said as he carved the roast beef. "So, Ben, tell us about your family. I know about your father, but do you have brothers? Sisters?"

"Two sisters, older. One's a performance artist in New York. And the other"—he said this with a straight face—"is a tugboat captain on Lake Michigan."

"My God," Esther gasped, "that's diverse."

"I'm the dull one, obviously," he said with a laugh, "with the unrisky genes."

"Tugboat captain? Don't tell me her name is Annie."

"We've got our own Tugboat Annie in this family," Judy interjected, and both her mom and dad smiled.

"Her name's Cricket," Ben answered.

"Cricket?" Henry said. "What kind of name is that?"

"She was born Carol, but she had it legally

changed because she was madly in love with Connie Stevens when she was a teenager."

"Cricket!" Esther exclaimed. "I remember, *Surfside Six* the show was called. I thought Troy Donahue was so cute."

"She never had any trouble telling us she was gay because we lived for years with a room filled with posters of Connie 'Cricket' Stevens, and we knew her passion sorta crossed over the boundary of fandom."

"I'm sorry for laughing," Esther apologized, "but it seems so stereotypical."

"Down to the marine haircut, sweatshirts, and the boots," Ben added, "but you'd love her. She really is unique."

"The performance artist sounds unique," Judy said, fascinated to hear more about him and his life, and again finding herself feeling guilty for having judged him to be so uninteresting when they first met.

Ben shrugged slightly. "She's . . . unusual. She does these things—like shaving a bald spot on her head to experience prejudice against male pattern baldness."

Esther stopped chewing. "No."

"For real?" Judy asked.

Ben nodded. "That was nothing. Went to Moscow for three whole months to study tattoos in prison."

Henry froze with a forkful of food in front of his mouth. "Tattoos?"

Ben said, "The guys in jail there don't have much

to do, so they brand themselves, apparently everywhere. She did a whole tattoo performance where she got 'scored' in front of an audience."

"Don't tell me where!" Esther shouted jokingly.

Ben just grinned. "She's a handful. I remember my father sitting with me and my mom at the first show she ever did, in some grungy theater down in the East Village, just shaking his head as she stood there, butt-naked, breaking eggs on her breasts."

Esther reached out and took Judy's hand. "I'm so glad you do what you do. As a mother."

They all laughed. Ben added, "She's been very successful, as performance artists go, I guess. She's really quite gifted. She painted and acted when she was younger, she was brilliant. She just went down a different path. She's the talented one in the family."

"And so are you," Judy said. "Ben paints beautifully."

Esther looked dreamy. "I took classes for years, always wanted to master watercolors, never did. But I enjoyed it."

"I use only watercolor," Ben said.

"Just thought of something," Judy suddenly said. "Your friend who writes the children's stories—"

"Connie."

"Why don't *you* illustrate them?"

Ben looked interested. "Never thought about it."

"It might help get them sold."

"I thought publishers assign people to do that," Ben answered.

Henry piped in. "In the old days, when we had real editors. Now agents are editors. Editors buy and sell and lunch. Today you have to come in with a completed book or you don't even get looked at. Hell, pretty soon authors are going to have to submit cover art with the manuscript."

"Didn't know that," Ben said. "I'll tell Connie. Great food, Mrs. Sussman."

"Esther."

He smiled warmly. "Esther."

"Okay, son," Henry said, balling up his linen napkin, pushing his chair two feet from the table, crossing his legs. "Tell me about these children's stories."

Later, they strolled hand in hand on the dark golf course that wound under the shadow of the mountains behind the lush houses of The Reserve. "I liked being a part of your family tonight," Ben said.

"They adore you. Mom whispered to me as we were filling the dishwasher, 'This is a good guy. And cute too!' Dad liked you as well."

"He seemed genuinely interested in Connie's stories."

"He wouldn't bullshit you. Please send them to him."

"First thing when I get back from my mom's."

She felt a lump in her throat and squeezed his hand. "Which is when?"

"Next Friday."

"I could come down to San Diego to see you."

"I'd love that. Or I could come back here." He looked into her eyes, moonlight illuminating the whites. "Hell, I'd go just about anywhere for you."

"I like you so much," she said emphatically. Her heart was bursting, she was wanting to say more, but she wouldn't let those words come because she knew that, this soon, love could not be part of the picture. Perhaps at sixteen, or even twenty-six. But not now. Not this fast.

"I've never liked anyone so much so quickly," Ben admitted, echoing her very thoughts.

It was the perfect opening. "Has there ever been anyone?"

"Yes. For four years, just after I started teaching, when my wandering days were over."

"Were you in love?"

"Very much so."

"What happened?"

"We planned a wedding. It's quite a story. She left me standing at the altar."

Judy gasped. "You don't mean it."

"Right there, rabbi waiting under the canopy all covered with flowers, our parents beaming in the front row, Aunt Sadie and Cricket and Julie and everybody all thrilled for me. The music plays, the bridesmaids start walking, but her dad is standing there alone. She's gone."

Judy put her hand to her mouth. "My Lord."

"She had fled, at the last second. Got into a cab, in her wedding gown."

"*Rhoda* did that," Judy recalled.

"She told me later that she 'just couldn't do it.' It was pretty funny, actually, in the end."

"Yeah, it sounds like a riot," she said.

"No, really, we had a party. My parents had paid for everything because her family had no money, and my dad figured why waste all that food and a good orchestra? And as people got drunker, they all started to tell me things."

"Things?"

"Like Aunt Sadie, whom I thought adored Kathy, starts whispering in my ear things like, 'Oy vey, the pain she would have brought you!' "

"No!"

"The rabbi himself says to me, 'She was a goy through and through.' "

"My God. Why'd he call her a goy?"

"She'd converted for me."

"So people started trashing her?"

"Honest, it was nuts, everyone was telling me stuff that they would never have said in a million years had we married. 'We never liked her.' 'We knew better, little Benji, but we bit our lip for your happiness.' Stuff like that?'

"How did you cope?"

"Drank a lot and danced with everyone there, twice. I was in a state of suspended animation, going through the motions but feeling empty, embarrassed, wondering what I had done to cause this."

"Had you?"

He shook his head. "I've never been able to figure out what exactly happened." His voice sounded sad.

"I'm so sorry."

He nodded, took her hand and started walking back toward the house. "She married some guy in Seattle a year later, my mother heard."

"That hurts."

"No, turns out it was for the better. For me. She's already divorced the poor jerk. Aunt Sadie was right, she's a little nuts, if you want to know the truth. She's still finding her way, maybe. Hey, everyone deserves to be happy."

"You and I included?"

Near a magnificent jacaranda tree just beyond the long, shimmering Sussman lap pool, Ben stopped and took her in his arms. "You and I especially," he said, and then kissed her passionately. He ran his fingers through her hair, and felt her body press closer to his, as if wanting to join together to prevent him from getting on that plane tomorrow. "I'm going to miss you like I can't say," Ben whispered in her ear.

"Oh, Ben," she said back, "if you only knew . . ."

"Judy?" Another voice joined theirs. "Judy, hey!" A man's voice that was not her father's.

Judy pulled away from Ben instinctively, shocked. She turned toward the house and saw the figure standing just past the pool, on the floodlit stone patio, glass of wine in one hand. "Skeet?" Judy called out.

"Hey, honey, I can't see, the lights are blinding me."

She was a little glad of that. She stepped from the shadow of the jacaranda tree. Ben followed her, feeling sheepish, as if caught sneaking a kiss with the farmer's daughter behind the barn. "What are you doing back?"

"I was done down there, that's all," Skeet said. "Remembered you'd be here for Passover."

Ben realized he was meeting the famous Skeeter McCloy. "Hello," he said, trying to gauge the man's reaction to his sneaking through the bushes with the girl he lived with. "I'm Ben Spiegel."

"Friend of the family?" Skeet asked, shaking hands.

"Yes," Ben said firmly, for as of today it was true.

"Ben," Judy added, "this is Skeet, whom I've told you about."

"Pleasure," Skeet said affably.

"Ate at Fancies the other night," Ben said, "it was great."

"Thanks. Listen, I'm starving. Esther is heating some latkes and brisket for me, has dessert ready for you."

"Let's go in, then, shall we?" Judy said, feeling just the slightest bit uncomfortable.

"After you guys," Skeet said, "please."

* * *

Judy's fears diminished as Skeet took to Ben almost as quickly as she had. They talked for hours, with Henry, Esther, and Judy as well, about everything from food to politics, from the maddening difficulties associated with opening a restaurant in Mexico to how to keep guns out of schools. Ben and Skeet shared some common interests. Both loved fishing, and Ben reveled in Skeet's deep-sea stories, admitting that his own were more of the "stand on the bank with a worm on a hook and wait" variety. Another interest they shared was Indian culture. When that came up, Judy said, "Ben knew Craig."

Skeet blinked. "Craig Castle?"

"Did a sweat house with him even."

"Oh, God," Esther Sussman said, rolling her eyes.

"No kidding?" Skeet responded.

"It was great."

"Where?"

Ben said, "Down near San Diego. I've been there since, a couple of times."

"I only heard about that one," Skeet said. "They say there's a better one up near Yucca Valley."

Ben told Skeet, "I did Craig's summer workshop, and really got into that stuff. I teach a course to high school kids on Indian legends and customs."

"I try to use a little Indian inspiration in my menus."

"Hey," Ben said, offering Skeet his hand, "we should do a sweat house sometime."

"You're on, buddy," Skeet said.

Judy was thrilled that they were getting along so well. She feared Skeet would feel too protective, especially when he had found them embracing under the jacaranda tree, but she had been wrong. The evening was simply wonderful, and she left her parents' house that night thinking how pleased she was to be with the two men who meant so much to her, her soul mate and her new . . . boyfriend?

Only after she'd driven Ben back to the hotel did Skeet make a comment about him. He was already in his room lying on the bed, reading a big novel as he usually did to put himself to sleep. She knocked, pushed the door open, and saw him lying there on top of the big fluffy comforter. "Buenas noches," she whispered.

"Hey, you too," he responded, looking up from the book. "I think it's time for me to turn out the lights."

"See you mañana," she said, and started to go.

But his voice stopped her. "Were you two kissing when I walked out on the patio tonight?"

She froze for a second, turned back, but then reassured herself that it was an honest question, one she would ask if the situation had been reversed. "Yes. I like him."

He clicked off the light. But he mumbled, "Yeah . . . I do too."

And that was that.

* * *

Juan peeled off his T-shirt the minute he got out of his truck and realized he'd been sweating. He flung it into the branches of the old citrus tree out back of his house to dry, and went inside. He called his sister down in Todo Santos, and talked for a lot longer than he would have liked. Of all his seven siblings, Elena was the one who drove him to the edge with her complaining and her fears and her Catholic dictums inherited from their mother. She should have been a nun, he always thought, cloistered so they could only speak through a little hole in a door.

Tonight, Elena had railed on about their sister, Marguerita, the one in Hemet, complaining that she never called, how she didn't care about the family anymore because she was in America. Finally he had promised to drive down in the next few months. Truth was, he did enjoy visiting her, for she lived in a wonderful hacienda on a hillside not far from the ocean, in one of the most charming towns on the Baja Peninsula, just nineteen miles north of Cabo San Lucas.

Because the classically charming town with its nineteenth-century brick and stucco buildings had always been a haven for artists, Hector, Elena's good-for-nothing husband, who was a licensed medical doctor when sober, but considered himself an artist of some sort when drunk, moved them there right after they married. After finding Hector doing less medicine and more painting on Playa Migrio and Punta Gaspareo, Elena seized upon an idea to rent rooms to tourists. With Elena doing most of the bed-and-breakfasting work, they had a lot of repeat customers. This was dusty, untouched Mexico, despite the housing developments on the perimeter and newly installed traffic lights, with chickens in the streets and wash on the lines, where people were not overwhelmed by towering hotels and cruise-ship and time-share barkers.

When Juan hung up, he had an itch. Not for sex, but for a drink. His refrigerator held nothing but milk and juice. So he did something he hadn't done in years. He showered quickly and dressed in a zoot-suit jacket and skintight black pants, boots with buckles. *Es buena onda.* He'd knock 'em dead.

Juan drove downtown, parked, and walked Palm Canyon, along with the usual tourists, the shaved-head boys from the military base, the Valley girls in from L.A. for Easter weekend, the neighborhood locals out for a stroll. He ended up doing tequila shooters with a total stranger he got to talking with at an open-air bar across from the Hyatt Hotel. He was in mid-shot when he froze, his eyes focused on Judy dropping Ben off in the circular drive.

He watched as they talked for a moment, bellhop holding the SUV door. Then the bellhop was sent away. They kissed, a long and passionate kiss. It made Juan's hand tremble so fiercely that he had to set the shot glass down.

"Man, you okay?" his drinking partner, a young marine, asked.

Juan said nothing. He glared at the embrace going on in the car, then saw the look on Ben's face when he stepped from it, a mask of excitement, tenderness, and reluctance. So Juan had been right about this guy. Then he got a good look at Judy as she turned her head, and he swore that she wiped a tear from her eye. Then she drove away, with Ben just standing there as if lost without her.

When Ben entered the hotel finally, Juan downed the shot. And immediately did another.

"Man, you're gonna get wasted," the marine said, delighted.

"Fuck," Juan muttered. "Gonna get drunk."

"Hell, buddy, let's go there." The marine did another as well. "Was gonna find me a girl tonight. Gonna find some pussy, I said. But shit, all that bull-crap you gotta do first, all the talk and nonsense. Let's just get wasted."

"She kissed him," Juan said, not hearing a word the kid had said.

"Sure did, man." The marine had seen what Juan was watching. "Serious kiss."

"Fuck."

"They probably did that too," the marine said, laughing at his wit. "Lucky dude."

Juan glared at him suddenly. "Fuck you."

"Huh?" The marine saw the intensity on Juan's face. "Chill, man."

"Get outta here."

"What?"

"Get lost."

The marine smiled. "You're kidding, right? Yeah, this is getting tired. Let's go find some babes."

Juan was silent, his tight body language making it clear he wasn't going to say another word. The marine finally caught on, got up, dropped some money on the table, and said, "Hey, catch ya later, man." And as he walked away, the word "weirdo" could be heard under his breath.

Juan sat there, finishing what was left of the bottle of tequila on the table. When he got up, the bar spun around him, and he dropped backward, onto the table, knocking it to the floor, smashing the bottle and the glasses, landing in a woman's lap some three feet away. He was so drunk that he could not stand up. Then he passed out cold.

No one knew what to do with him. The bartender reached into his jacket and found his wallet, paid himself for the booze first, and then looked for a phone number to call, but there was nothing in there but cards for Juan's business. He was about to dial the police when he saw Juan's drinking buddy, the marine, strolling past the outdoor tables. He called to him, explained the situation, and the marine ended up taking Juan's somewhat lifeless body off his hands.

When Juan woke in a bed in a tacky motel in Desert Hot Springs at four in the morning, he had no idea where he was or how he'd gotten there. But he felt the warmth of a body lying next to him. In his fried brain, he thought at first that it was Judy, that somehow he'd driven off with her after she kissed Ben good night. But when his hand reached out and felt hairy legs and boxer shorts he knew he was fantasizing.

"Hey, man," the faintly familiar voice said, "I'm not into that. But we could check out some porn if you want."

Juan realized who it was. And what probably had happened. And then the room started to spin and he let go, figuring that was a whole lot better than the dismal reality of where he was.

Annie had had one of her inklings. She got into her Cadillac and drove down Highway 111 to Cathedral City. Juan's truck was parked outside his house, which looked more like a shack to her, but she had long ago learned not to judge the value of a steer by the pile of crap he left behind. Magnificent homes hid behind the ugliest, plainest exteriors.

She parked around the corner and walked back to the little house. She put an ear to the wall and heard the shower running. Good, it gave her a little time. This was all ridiculous, of course. She could easily have checked out his truck when it was parked out front of her house, or Judy and Skeet's. She'd have a reasonable excuse then if caught nosing around. Here, what would she say? *Just in the neighborhood and wondered if this was yours? Did you take my garden shears by mistake?*

Nevertheless, she gave the truck the once-over. What she was looking for, she had no idea. In any case, she found absolutely nothing.

She saw him through the window suddenly. He was preening, dolling up in what looked to her like one of those slick designer ads in *Wallpaper*. He was obviously going out. She'd wait.

She sat in her car for the longest time, wondering what in the world she was doing here. An old queen parked next to her and gave her an odd glance, then a smile, obviously thinking her pink Cadillac the epitome of camp. From the corner of her eye, she could see the bumper of Juan's truck. When it finally pulled out, she moved in.

Getting into his house was easy. The doors were not locked. But there was little inside of interest. A dump, of course, as she'd expected. The walls of gardening books she didn't expect—a nice touch. Lots of books on cacti, native desert plants, Indian lore, even one about plant extracts with case histories of those who'd ingested them and lived to tell about it. One plant called sacred datura was circled.

His computer was on, but it needed a password to enter. Shit. She liked peering into people's hard drives better than peeping into bedrooms. Everything was there these days, all the stuff you wanted to hide, thought you were keeping secret. And it was secret, unless you had the password.

She didn't find anything that had to do with Norman Lempke. No note or picture or calendar notation. No book on the man, no newspaper articles circled and cut out by madman's scissors, nothing. But there was quite a collection of things about Judy.

In fact, Annie thought, there was too much for comfort. There were clippings and magazine articles, photos of her and Skeet from various restaurant functions, even pictures he must have taken with his own camera, of Judy lying in her bikini at the pool. And then, sure enough, in his underwear drawer—why did they always keep the important stuff in their underwear drawers?—was the bikini top that she'd watched him filch. She sensed an obsession.

On the bathroom sink was a toothbrush set on a silver plate. It would have meant nothing had Annie not given Judy that toothbrush when she returned from an American Booksellers Convention in Atlanta. It had been a promotional gift to publicize some dentist's tome on how to make cavities disappear through meditation or some such thing. The gold-plated brush had been so campy that she thought Judy would appreciate it. She remembered Judy telling her a few months ago that she didn't know how she'd lost it. Now Annie did.

Next to the bed was a framed photo of Judy. And, on the bed, almost lost in the tousled sheets and comforter, was the clipboard she'd seen him writing on earlier in the day. She pulled it from the folds of the bed linens and was amazed at what was written there: Judy's name, about three hundred times. Just JudyJudyJudyJudy, over and over again, till it ran off the bottom of the page. "My, oh, my, Desert Dick," she said, as if talking to her best creation, "we do have a sick one here."

But did that make him a murderer?

Chapter Twelve

"If I have a coronary, it's on your conscience, Selma Sherman!" Annie called out, gasping for breath.

"Come on, girl, go for the gold!" Selma urged.

"Jesus!" Annie was dripping wet. "These things are killers." She was on an EFX Elliptical Crosstrainer for the first—and last, she swore—time in her life. "You're a sadist, Selma."

"Your arteries will thank me," Selma assured her, pumping even harder next to her. "Keeps ya young!"

Annie shut the machine off. "I'll go gladly into old age, with all its aches and pains, rather than croak, thank you, in a goddamned gym."

"No, no, no," Selma admonished, "you gotta cool down slowly. . . ."

"I'd like to jump into ice water." Annie took the wet towel from the back of her neck and wiped it over her face. It didn't help much. She was a mess.

Selma fared better, but she was a pro. She did this every morning at six. She'd called and gotten Annie up at five, which was only three hours after she'd gone to bed. Annie knew she was going to be a goner for the day, and of all days she was speaking at a book luncheon. Selma cut the pace on her machine and started to wind up her workout. "So, I'll bet you wanna know about your friend Torres."

"No, I came here for fun," Annie snapped.

When Selma had wiped down her machine, she sat down with Annie on one of the upstairs benches, far from other ears. "Okay, here's what I got." Stuck inside a copy of *Vogue* was the police report. Annie read it with interest.

Juan Torres had a record. He had been arrested for possession of marijuana, stealing a car, two petty thefts, an apartment robbery for which he served three months in the Riverside jail, and assault, beating up a guy in a bar last year. "Eugene, officer I know, made the collar," Selma told her. "Mashed up a marine he said made a pass at him."

"Well, well, well," Annie said, still wiping her forehead with the towel, "my gentle little gardener has quite a history."

"Your gardener?"

"He's very good," she told Selma. "I recommend him."

"Thanks, but I've got an association."

Annie folded the sheet, but didn't know where to put it to keep it dry. "Maybe I'll just get going."

"No, you won't, you gotta do some butt work."

Annie'd had enough. "You go do some butt work. I've got a busy day."

"Excuses, excuses," Selma admonished.

"Selma, I got what I came for." Annie gave her a wave and started down the stairs. She felt miserable. "And I paid for it too," she shouted back upstairs.

Annie showered the minute she walked in the door, then looked at her computer and saw the headline about a young man, now identified as Troy Skinner, a Palm Springs resident and waiter at Fancies Restaurant there, found dead from poisoning from a toxic desert plant called sacred datura. She called next door, but there was no answer, so she tried both Skeet's and Judy's cell phones, but neither answered, so she left messages. The news shocked her, not so much because she knew Troy well, but because of the way he died. She called Tom Sparks in Los Angeles and told him to check it out. Troy Skinner and Norman Lempke had tasted the same drink, and it wasn't a Cosmopolitan.

Checking on Juan on the Net provided her with little more than Selma had given her. Juan had been in the kind of trouble—marijuana, "borrowing" a car for a joyride, lifting a few CDs, trying to rob an apartment of the usual stereo equipment—that was fairly commonplace. The one she laughed at was his arrest for stealing three books on gardening from a bookstore. She probably saw them on his shelf.

Beating up a marine bothered her. It told her he had a violent streak, and that he was probably homophobic as well. Yet the rest of his record was well in the past, when he was young. He'd cleaned up his act when he moved to Palm Springs, putting his trouble behind him, starting a business for himself—tough for an uneducated guy to do, especially one who didn't speak the language at all at first—and seemed to be doing well. Murdering Norman Lempke just didn't ring true to her. She was barking up the wrong tree.

Barking. Yes, Scout was barking, howling for the breakfast she had never fed him. She let him in with apologies. As she dished out his Mighty Dog, she looked at the clock. Christ in heaven. It wasn't even nine yet.

Judy parked haphazardly in the Palm Springs Airport parking lot and literally ran to the terminal. She was in such a hurry, she'd even forgotten to turn her Nokia on. It was ten minutes after nine. Ben's flight left in half an hour, so they were probably already boarding. She hurried through security—she'd left her bag in the car, and had shoved the keys on top of the front wheel so as not to have to take time inside with them—and made her way to the American Airlines gate. There was a line of people at the podium, and the door to the jetway was still closed. She looked around, studying faces, searching for Ben. There he was.

"Judy!" He started to move toward her.

"Ben, I came to see you off."

She went right into Ben's waiting arms. "I was

hoping I'd see you one more time," he said, his heart pounding.

"I didn't sleep all night."

"Come on, walk with me to the gate," he said, kissing her on the cheek. "I had a tough time as well."

"I want to see you again. Soon."

"Me too. I was already looking at the calendar to see when I can come back."

She brightened. "Yes?"

He shrugged. "Not for a few weeks."

"I'll come to San Diego then." She was emphatic. "I don't have anything pressing, it's not like I have classes I have to be at—I'm just your general irresponsible designer."

He laughed. "You probably have to work only one job a year to get what I get busting my butt for nine months."

Just then a young woman going past recognized Judy. "Hey, gal, what are you doing here?"

"Joan Jordano! You're still in the desert?" Judy asked.

"For another few weeks. Done slinging hash, gonna get married, move to La Jolla," Joan said brightly as other passengers made their way around her.

"Congratulations," Judy said warmly. "Oh, I want you to meet my friend Ben Spiegel."

Joan looked at Ben. "My God. I know *you*!"

Ben seemed surprised. "You do?"

"Plasta Italia, Palm Desert," Joan reminded him. "Ice in your red wine."

Ben laughed. "There's a twin somewhere, I swear."

Joan looked perplexed, then with a smile to them both, continued toward the check-in counter.

"That's so weird," Ben said.

"I'd like to meet this double," Judy said and laughed. "What a fantasy: two of you."

"One is plenty, I fear."

Soon they called for boarding, and after a passionate embrace, Ben was off. Getting on the plane, he saw the woman seated in an aisle seat. "Please," he said urgently to Joan, crouching down with a glance back at the entrance, "if we ever meet again in Palm Springs, please play along with me. I'm the wrong guy."

"But you're not." The woman was clearly upset.

"Please."

"Honey," she reminded him, "you kissed me one night!"

"I'll kiss you again if you promise me," he begged seriously. "It would really make things difficult if you don't, okay?"

"Did you hear?" Skeet asked when she walked into the kitchen.

"What's wrong?" She could tell from the look on his face.

"Troy. He's dead."

It didn't register at first. "Troy? Oh, my God, Troy Skinner!"

"Annie called and left a message. She said your favorite waiter had died."

Judy was beside herself. "How? Where?"

"In a sweat house accident."

It shocked her. "He told us he was going to do that, he was all excited about it! How did he die?"

Skeet explained he had not been able to get more details than that the young man was found dead in San Diego County—he figured it was the same sweat house Ben had talked about—and that they were going to do an autopsy, but that it looked like it was some kind of poison.

"He told Ben and me that he was excited about an upcoming Indian experience," she recalled, "when you were down in Mexico."

"Jesus, why would anyone be so crazy as to play around with dangerous plants all by themselves?"

"Craig did," she reminded him.

Skeet poured himself another cup of coffee. "Craig was, as we both know, nuts. Want some?"

"Oh, no. Thanks."

"Where'd you get the mint stuff? I made a pot thinking it was Starbucks and nearly gagged."

"My dad brought it. Jesus, Skeet, he wasn't there alone."

"Troy?"

It had dawned on Judy. She froze. "He said he had an 'instructor.' "

Skeet blinked. "You mean he might have been murdered?"

Judy shook her head. "I don't know. Accident, probably, but someone else was there, that person knows the truth."

"I never took Troy to be a druggie. Kyle yes, Troy no."

"Kyle didn't do plants."

"Kyle did *everything*," he reminded her. Her face darkened at the memory, and he hurriedly dropped the subject. "The restaurant is going to miss Troy. I'm going to miss him. I was fond of him. He was the best." Skeet looked forlorn. "Which reminds me, when are you coming down to Mexico?"

"Is it time?"

He nodded. "I think so. I've got a chef. Ready to start on the interior soon and that's your department."

"When do you need me?"

"How about next weekend?"

"Oh, can't."

"Why not?"

"Going to Los Angeles on Friday."

He blinked. "When did you decide this?"

"Meeting with Restaurant Associates from New York." It was true, but then she added the real reason she couldn't go to Mexico the next weekend. "Then I thought I'd drive down to San Diego and see Ben again."

"One delay after another. If it's not the Mexicans, it's you."

She didn't like his tone. "Listen, I have a life too. It's a lot to spring on me overnight, you know?"

He blinked. "Don't be so defensive."

"I'm not defensive."

"You are. You're embarrassed at your infatuation with the schoolteacher."

"Sometimes you sound like I'm your slave. I'm supposed to be wherever you want me to be, answer to the snap of your fingers."

"I just said you were delaying me."

"Too bad. You've been delayed before."

"Hey, lady, I'm the one who should be upset here. My friend and best employee is dead."

"Well, don't take it out on me!" Judy shouted.

"Judy, what's bothering you?"

She crumpled up the paper grocery bag that she'd been trying to fold and stormed from the room, shouting, "Everything."

Judy told Annie she wanted to drive because her hair would never survive the Cadillac, but Annie prevailed, saying that pulling into the Rancho La Quinta Resort in the pink Cadillac would cause a sensation, and she needed to sell as many books as she could. It was always one of the best gatherings in Southern California at which to do that, and authors killed to be invited to speak. A great lunch, in a great setting—Rancho La Quinta was an elegant, old Spanish-style hacienda hotel nestled into the Santa Rosa mountains. What was not to like? And Annie always lapped up the fuss the cute bellhops made when she pulled into the place with her land barge. No, she'd drive. To hell with Judy's hair.

Wrapped with a turban, Judy's coif stayed pretty much close to her head. They stopped in Palm Desert to pick up Esther Sussman, who ran back into the house to get a sunhat when she saw what they were riding in.

Rancho La Quinta sparkled in the noon sun, with perfect plants blooming as if in a florist's window. Almost on cue, the bellhops in khaki shorts and white polo shirts flocked around Annie's big boat and gushed a welcome. She picked the cutest one to hand the keys to, and told him, "Be very careful with it. It's an antique, you know. Like me."

"Yes, ma'am!" the bright-eyed lummox said.

Esther hugged Tori St. Johns, an attractive woman whose grandmother had founded Round Table West, and was happy to see they were sitting with Margaret Burk and Marilyn Hudson, the two women who *were* Round Table West and who had done so much for literacy in Southern California. Esther and Tori compared notes on the volunteer work they did, while Annie greeted people she'd seen before at these gatherings.

Then the program got started. Annie was the last of four authors, and it was a wise decision, for she followed three rather uninspiring men, one of whom talked drolly of golf. Thus, the audience took delight in Annie's crusty, off-color stories, her few truly awful jokes, and her genuine love for the work she did, both investigating and writing. She inspired everyone to read her latest book, if not all of them. "And if you don't," she warned with beady eyes, "I've got a gun in this bag." She patted her purse. The audience ate it up. When the program finished, Annie's books, which had been piled high on a table to the side of the big meeting room, walked out of the place.

Annie, Esther, and Judy stayed till the very end, sipping iced tea and talking with various women and men who hated to see the afternoon end. Judy, who had never been to one of the gatherings before, was surprised that so many young people were there. "I was expecting bored old yentas with nothing to do."

"I resent that," her mother joked.

"Lots of interesting people," Annie said. "They got stories. Better than I can create, some of them."

"How's the new one going?" Esther asked.

"I think the gardener did it," Annie answered.

"The gardener?" Esther asked. "Like in the butler did it?"

"Yeah."

"Patterning it after Juan?" Judy asked.

"You read my mind."

"He'll love it," Esther exclaimed.

"Not so sure," Annie admitted. "I'm making him handsome, of course, but really pretty psycho.

Annie was dying to go further. She wanted to ask Judy and Esther both if they knew where Juan was the night of Norman's murder. But she didn't dare tip them off that her new Desert Dick story about a killer gardener was based on reality. So she tried another approach. "You know, Judy, ever since you told me Juan was getting his jollies looking at Trixie and Bubbles—"

"No!" Esther exclaimed. "When?"

"No, Mom," Judy warned, "it's not like it sounds. He was just watching Annie sunbathe."

"He watches you too, babe," Annie added.

"So he likes women," Judy said, "like most guys."

"Hell," Annie relented, "if I were a man, I'd probably look every chance I got too." She sipped the last of her tea, and suddenly got an idea. "Judy, gotta ask you something. You don't think Juan might have been using my pool while I was in Texas, do you?"

Judy was taken aback. "Why do you ask?"

"Swear someone was skinny-dipping back there."

Esther looked perplexed as well as Judy. "You were gone. How would you know?"

"You know the old bat who lives over the back wall?"

"Mrs. Hennessy?" Judy asked.

"The one with the big black hair."

"Carole Hennessy," Judy confirmed, "former actress, completely mad."

"She said she saw some man naked in the pool." Annie was doing her best to make all this sound believable.

Judy groaned. "Oh, please, she's crazy. And a gossip."

"She sounds like fun," Esther interjected, smiling at this exchange.

"She is mostly lucid." Annie knew Carole Hennessy wasn't crazy at all, that this was going to be a hard sell. If only she could just get to that night. "She said the day before I got back, some young man showed up in the middle of the night, his swimming woke her up. Naked as the day God made him, she claimed. Full moon."

"That's the night Norman was murdered," Esther remembered. "Full moon."

And Judy remembered something as well. "Then it's impossible. At least it wasn't Juan."

"Why are you so sure?" Annie asked. "He's the only guy besides Skeet who has a key to the backyard gate."

"Because Juan was in Hemet that night visiting his sister."

Annie felt a surge. She'd finally gotten to it, and it was the answer she wanted. Now she could give up on this silly lead. To make the conversation sound natural, however, she asked, "How do you know that?"

"Because he told me."

Esther played devil's advocate. "Just because someone says so doesn't mean it's true."

"Ma," Judy said, "whose side are you on?"

"I think," Esther laughed, "this nutty Mrs. Hennessy's."

"That's right," Annie replied, ending the discussion. She stood up, eyed the table where they were still selling books. "Okay, gals, let's see how much this afternoon has added to my next royalty check."

"Listen, Mom," Judy said, unable to end the conversation, "I don't believe everything anyone says to me, but I know that Juan wasn't lying."

Esther stood too, fluffed the wrinkles in her skirt, picked up her bag from the back of the chair. "How?"

"His answer was so spontaneous."

Annie got curious again. "Answer to what?"

"I went to get a Kleenex from his truck the next morning," Judy said. "I'd been crying about Norman. When I reached in, the seat was all wet."

Annie almost fell to the floor. "What?"

"The seat of his truck was wet. I asked him why. He said he'd spent the night at his sister's in Hemet. And the neighbor's sprinkler came in through his open window."

"Hmmm," Esther said. "The sprinkler story sounds pretty convenient. If you took a naked swim and didn't have a towel to dry yourself, you would soak the seat, right?"

Annie thought, Or if you crawled out of the ocean in your clothes.

Esther headed off toward the book table. "I want a copy of that biography before we go."

"Mothers," Judy muttered to Annie.

But Annie wasn't listening any longer. The word *wet* was searing her brain like a blast of steam. And yet another word: *guilty.*

Annie didn't mention Juan again as she drove them home, but once inside her house, she located seventeen people with the surname of Torres in Hemet, California. Opening a beer to get her through, she started calling all of them. On the thirteenth try, she found Juan's sister. She was a young, unmarried working mother with two small kids who cut hair at Supercuts. Annie pretended she'd talked to Juan when he was there at her house a week or so ago and wanted to find out his number to hire him for some landscaping. Marguerita Torres said, "Juan is gardener, sí, but Juan no come see us for many week."

Annie felt her stomach turn. "You sure, honey?"

"Sí. Not since my baby had his birthday, first week in March."

"Oh, hell," Annie said, doing her best to sound unsure, "maybe it was way back then." She let the woman give her Juan's number, which she didn't need, and thanked her and hung up. And then she wondered, why had he lied to Judy? Where had he really been that night? What was the real reason the seat was wet? He might have indeed taken a dip, but not in her pool. In the Pacific Ocean.

Then she started to wonder: Where had he been the night Troy Skinner died in the sweat house?

Chapter Thirteen

Judy hurried into the house, balancing a heap of mail in her hands. She kicked the front door shut behind her, read the postcard from her friend Kervin from London, then set the pile of envelopes, magazines, and bills on the hall table—or where the hall table had been. For years, ever since Skeet and Judy bought the house, the foyer had held a lovely Baker reproduction of a rural French farm table. Now, in its place, was a piece that she'd discovered in a design shop on Melrose Avenue, but which wasn't for sale. For three years she'd begged the owner to sell it to her. It was a handsome, finely detailed altar table that had come from one of the convents in Portugal that had been converted by the government to pricey tourist posadas. Today, it stood regally in her hallway. The two brass lamps, the big Mexican pot, the carved wooden cherub statue encased in glass that had sat on the previous table for ages now rested on the altar table as if it had always held them. She couldn't contain her excitement.

She ran to the phone to call Skeet, overflowing

with curiosity. How did he get it? But as she lifted the receiver, she saw the message light blinking. She punched the button. At the same time, she pressed the auto dial button for Fancies Palm Springs. The message started first: "Judy, this is Ben. Hi there."

"Fancies Palm Springs," sang Anna in her strongly accented Spanish warble.

Judy was about to express her condolences on Troy's death, but she was so mesmerized by Ben's voice on the machine that she just hung up. "Judy, I'm in Dallas. I, um, guess you're not there. I hope you don't mind that I called. I was just, um, thinking of you. Gotta get my other flight now. I'll try you tonight when I get to my mom's. Okay? Well, bye."

Her heart was in her throat, and her stomach went tight. He called! She looked at the time, quickly computing the difference to East Coast time. It was almost nine there. He'd probably land at ten or so, maybe call by eleven? She couldn't wait.

She was so thrilled with the anticipation of Ben's call that she forget that the Portuguese table was even in the house.

Annie woke up when Scout had finally reached the end of his patience and jumped on her. He'd been nudging her ever since it got dark, yapping, barking, but she snored through all of his best efforts. She'd sat on the sofa right after the call to Juan's sister, put her head back with the enormity of what she'd just learned, and passed right out. Day turned to night, and the poor animal had been trying to revive her. "Baby, Mommy's sorry," she cooed.

She let him out, looking at the time. Almost nine. She was starving, and didn't feel like fixing anything. Then she got a brainstorm. Many a day when she felt like this, Skeet came to the rescue. All she had to do was show up at the restaurant and he'd find her a cozy booth, a great martini, and a steak the size of Texas.

She jumped in the shower and emerged a new woman.

Dolled up, she reached the restaurant just before ten, but she never made it inside. Something caught her eye—a gardener's truck in the corner of the lot behind the building. It was like a magnet pulling her. She parked right next to it. And realized that it was indeed Juan's.

She figured he must be inside the restaurant, though it surprised her because she didn't think he could afford places like this. Well, hell, Skeet employed him, how dumb was she? Hopefully he was having a nice dinner with friends. At least long enough for her to accomplish what she suddenly felt she needed to do.

Could you tell, after something had dried, if it had been wet with salt or fresh water? She was sure salt residue would remain, and thus it could be identified. If the cushion of Juan's truck turned out to only have fresh water soaked on it, he was clear. But she had to have it tested. What better time to find out than right now? The driver's door was locked, but the passenger door wasn't. She opened it.

It smelled like freshly mowed lawn, a smell she always liked. There was a water bottle on the seat, a battered box of Kleenex, probably the ones Judy had found were damp, and the clipboard with a bunch of addresses on it. On the floor were various wrappers from all the fast-food places in town. "Pig," she muttered. She could see the seat bottom was in bad shape, and there was a towel under where the driver sat. She lifted it. The cushion was almost coming apart.

She reached over and unlocked the driver's door, then got out on the passenger's side and walked around the back of the vehicle, glancing at the restaurant. The coast was still clear.

She opened the driver's door, folded the towel back, and dug her fingernails into the seat cushion. She lost two perfectly good press-on nails, but a good wad of stuffing came out with her fingers. She smelled it, trying to see if she smelled the sea. It only smelled stale, like the locker room at Gold's. God, sniffing the sweat from his butt, that turned her off. She rolled the towel back over the hole with her free hand, and turned to close the door. And found herself staring into Juan's eyes.

She shouted in surprise, "Shit."

"What are you doing?" he asked flatly.

"Jesus, you scared me."

"What are you doing in my truck?"

"I'm a pushover for that just-mowed-lawn scent." Annie wondered how she was going to explain this. She was a bullshitter from word one, but how would she fib away the handful of seat padding she was so clearly grasping?

"You broke in," Juan said.

"It wasn't locked."

"What is that?" he asked, looking at the white foam.

She gave him a silly grin. "Probably wouldn't believe me if I told you I was trying to stuff my brassiere, huh?"

It didn't play. He looked violated and suspicious.

"Okay," she said, figuring the truth was best. But better to start out on the offensive. "Why did you lie to Judy about being at your sister's in Hemet the night Norman Lempke was killed?"

He was so startled by the question that his mouth fell open. "What?"

"You heard me."

"What is this about?" he demanded.

"This is about saving your cute butt."

He shook his head. "This is loco!"

"What do you know about sacred datura?"

"Nothing."

"You had it circled."

"What?" He looked dumbfounded.

"I just learned Troy Skinner's autopsy showed he died from swallowing sacred datura."

Suddenly a third person joined them. Skeet, cigarette in one hand, walked up. "What's going on? Hi, Annie."

"I caught her in my truck," Juan said, fuming.

"Caught her?" Skeet said, surprised at his choice of words.

"For good reason," Annie shot back. "Now tell me why you lied to Judy."

Skeet piped in again. "Lied about what?"

"This is between Juan and me," Annie said tersely.

"What are you accusing me of?" Juan demanded.

"I'm only asking a question. Why did you lie? Why was your seat wet?"

Skeet looked at her as if she had lost her mind. "Seat wet?"

"This!" Annie said, clutching the foam in front of Juan's face.

"What the hell is that?" Skeet asked.

"You ruined my truck!" Juan shouted, trying to grab the foam in her fist, but she pulled it away too quickly.

"Not hard to do," Annie quipped.

"Bitch," Juan swore.

"He lied," Annie said, "about being at his sister's in Hemet the night Lempke died."

Both men froze. Skeet looked at Juan. Juan looked at Skeet. Then Skeet burst out laughing. "Sure, he lied. I told him to."

Annie thought she hadn't heard correctly. "*You* did?"

"Yeah, so Judy wouldn't find out."

Annie sucked in her breath. "Find out what?"

"The table," Juan said, now looking in his front seat to see what kind of damage she'd done. He lifted the towel and swore in Spanish at the gouge.

"Table?" Annie was lost.

Skeet explained. "Juan was with me in Los Angeles that night."

Annie's eyes popped open. "With *you*?"

"Yes," Skeet replied, laughing out loud. "He drove in because I needed someone to truck back an antique table that Judy has had her heart set on forever. We just moved it into the house today, as a matter of fact." He suddenly looked disappointed. "Surprised I haven't heard from Judy."

"You two were together in L.A. the night of Lempke's murder?" Annie was truly surprised to hear this piece of news.

"Drove back the next morning," Skeet said. "Put the table in the shed here until today."

Annie glared at Juan. She wanted to get this right. "You told Judy you spent the night at your sister's because you didn't want to tell her you were in L.A. with Skeet because this table was a surprise for her?"

"Sí." Juan sounded completely believable.

"Oh, boy," Annie said.

"Listen, God's truth," Skeet assured her. But he was more than curious now. "What the hell is this all about? What are you doing?"

"Wrecking my truck," Juan said.

"I had good reason to believe I might be on to something," she replied in her defense.

"Annie apologizes, kid," Skeet said, stepping on what was left of his cigarette. "Annie, say you're sorry."

"I'm not sorry. I had to investigate."

"Investigate what?" Skeet asked again.

Juan didn't let her answer. "Hey, fat lady," he yelled into her face, "I quit. No more pulling your fucking weeds."

"Juan, hey, man," Skeet said, trying to play peacekeeper, but Juan jumped into his truck, started it, and pulled out without another word. Skeet shook his head. "Jesus, if I'd have known this was going to happen, I'd have just taken a U-Haul to L.A."

Annie shook her head. "I knew I was sniffing the wrong dog's ass."

"Sniffing for what?"

"Lempke's killer."

Skeet almost fell over. "What?"

"You heard me."

"Come on, babe, I'll make you dinner." He took her arm and started leading her toward the building. "Got a nice Maryland rockfish tonight. I want to hear this whole story."

The fish was delicious, if unexciting. The conversation, on the other hand, was anything but. She told him that she'd gotten to the point that she thought

Juan had something to do with the brutal killing of Norman Lempke.

"You considered our gardener a suspect?" Skeet asked incredulously.

She nodded.

"Why?"

She told him about Jimmy having seen a man who could have been Juan who left a big puddle behind, so on and so forth, to Judy having mentioned today at lunch that Juan's front seat had been soaked that next morning. Skeet was fascinated, but laughed it off. "Juan did leave his truck window open that night, and the sprinklers outside my building in Beverly Hills soaked the inside. He told me so that the next morning, when we loaded the table. He lied to Judy for me. You're barking up the wrong tree, Annie," Skeet said, "and you know it. The kid's no killer."

"That's what everyone said about Cary Stayner up at Yosemite. And Ted Bundy. They probably said it about goddamned Lizzie Borden too." Annie softened. "To be honest, it's been hard for me to believe Juan had anything to do with it. But it was a gardening truck like his, a wet seat, he's got a record, lied to Judy, put that all together—"

"Annie!" he said, like she was crazy and he was reining her in. "What would be the reason? I mean, why would he do it?"

"I thought in some way it had to do with Judy. He's got eyes for her, as my mom used to say."

Skeet nodded. "We all know that. It's harmless."

"Troy did too."

Skeet looked astonished. "You don't think someone killed Troy because he had a crush on Judy, do you?"

"Could be."

Skeet leaned back in the booth and really started laughing.

"What's so funny?"

"It's all so preposterous. And you, standing there with a handful of his seat cushion!"

Annie realized how silly it must have looked. But she assured him, "I've been caught with stranger things in my hands."

He gave her a sly look. "I bet."

She got off the subject, since it was making her seem so foolish. "So, what's this precious table like?"

"You'll see. And it is precious, cost me fourteen thousand bucks."

Annie choked on her sugar snap peas. "Fourteen thousand smackers for a goddamned table?"

Skeet had a revelation. "Hey, when did Judy leave that luncheon thing you guys went to?"

"Four-thirty," Annie said.

"She go right home?"

"Watched her get the mail and walk in the front door."

"The table is in the front hall."

"Oh," Annie said.

He looked very disappointed. "You think she could have missed it?"

"Even I wouldn't miss a fourteen-thousand–dollar table," Annie said, "and I'm menopausal, unfocused, and half blind."

Skeet reached under his apron for his cell phone. In a moment, he said, "Honey?"

"Skeet, I'm on my cell phone," she said flatly, almost testy that she had been interrupted, "I'll talk to you when you get home, okay?" She hung up without even giving him a chance to respond.

He looked even more disappointed. He looked hurt. He turned off his phone.

Annie asked, "What? She doesn't like it?"

"She didn't say."

"I miss you," Ben said.

"I miss you," Judy said with equal passion, for the tenth time in the past hour.

He called her the minute he got to his mother's house, near one in the morning his time, and they spoke as if they hadn't conversed in years. When Ben admitted he had to go to the bathroom—he'd been drinking a lot of water on the plane to keep from getting dehydrated—Judy said she'd do the same, and called him back on her cell phone. When Skeet interrupted her, she barely gave it a thought.

She told Ben about the boy who had waited on them, what had happened to him in the sweat house. Then she went on to happier subjects, reminding him that her father really wanted to see his friend's children's stories. He in turn told her how uneventful the flights were, but crowded due to Easter, how he tried to plan a lesson for the following week but his mind kept wandering to her. He even admitted that he was half-sleeping on the second flight, dreaming of her, when the woman in the window seat asked him to allow her to get out. He stood up and realized he was excited by thinking about Judy, and had to cover himself with his hands.

Just then she heard a car drive into the garage. "Skeet's home," she said.

"Do you have to go?"

"No, but I should anyway."

"Don't."

She heard the garage door shutting, heard Skeet enter the house, heard the door lock. She lowered her voice. "I have to let you get some sleep. Ciao." She clicked off the phone and walked into the living room, where Skeet was taking off his shoes. "Hi."

"Hello," he said flatly. "Who were you talking to at this hour?"

"Ben."

"Oh. Thought he left today."

"He's at his mom's. Just wanted to tell me he arrived safely. How was your day?"

"Broke up a catfight between Annie and Juan, but other than that, it was uneventful."

"Annie and Juan?"

"I'll tell you about it tomorrow. Too stupid to waste time on."

"Something's wrong," Judy said.

"Well, what do you think?"

She thought about it. There was only one possible answer. "Ben?"

"Oh, God," Skeet muttered and closed his eyes.

Judy tried to put things into perspective. "Listen, I've been hurting ever since Norman died, and Ben just makes me feel good. I don't know what it's about, whether or not it will go anywhere, but I like him and he likes me, and there is an attraction, and I'm not going to cut myself off from experience—"

"Judy," he said, trying to stop her dissertation, but she rattled on.

"—and I think this is really healthy for me right now because I've been feeling bad about myself lately, with all that's happened. It's like I felt when I was going out with Kyle. Please don't judge me. I know it could be just silly infatuation. And sometimes you still get jealous, even though we are just friends. I wasn't jealous when you dated that Chinese girl for almost nine months."

"Eight. And she wasn't Chinese."

"Wendy Wong?"

"She was Caucasian."

"What?"

"She was married to a Wong."

Judy gasped. "Married? She was *married*? You never told me that!"

"Give me a break."

"We always get into these little battles, Skeet, when it comes to others in my life, and it just isn't fair, it's not part of our agreement."

"Judy, it's not about—"

She cut him off again. "You said something was wrong."

"Yes," he said. "Something is wrong, but you're the one who said it, not I."

"Blame me."

"What's wrong," he said pointedly, "is not Ben or anything to do with Ben."

She was startled. "What then?"

He started walking toward the door, hurt and angry.

"Skeet! Stop. What?"

He turned back to face her. "Try a certain table."

"Oh!" It suddenly came back her. She felt like a complete, ungrateful, selfish heel. "Oh, Skeet, I totally forgot."

"Nice to feel appreciated," he muttered, storming out.

"I love it," she called out. "It's gorgeous . . . I . . ." Her voice trailed off with no one to hear it. "Boy," she whispered to herself, "did you blow this one."

And she knew why.

Because she had suddenly become obsessed with Benjamin Spiegel.

Chapter Fourteen

It was not the best week of Judy's life. She had hurt Skeet deeply. She had coveted that piece of furniture more than any object she could remember. Though he barely spoke to her the next day, she wrote him a note telling him how sorry she was, how much she loved the piece, but also how much she loved him for going through so much to give her this joy—and for what it cost him. She had flowers sent to him at the restaurant with a card that said, "Forgive me?" He stayed at the restaurant that night, upstairs in the little apartment he kept for days when he worked too long.

But the next morning, when he came home for a change of clothes, she confronted him. "Aren't you ever going to speak to me again?"

He smiled. "Sorry. Of course."

"I'm really ashamed of myself."

He nodded, with a look that said she should be. "Your declaration about Ben was pretty telling."

"That's why the table didn't imprint on my mind. His call sorta hijacked my thoughts from what was going on here."

"Ah." He gave her a cautious look. "It's happening pretty fast with this guy."

She sat down at the table with him. "Skeet, I really like him. I know it's probably just infatuation, but I feel good when I think of him."

"I like him too. But he didn't strike me as being all that seductive."

She smiled. "I think you see him through different eyes."

He laughed out loud. "I hope so."

"You're not upset?"

"Nope. I just don't want you to get hurt."

She reached out and took his hand. "If I do, I have no one to blame but me."

"You going to be gone long?"

She shrugged. "The weekend, back for sure on Monday."

"Fly to Cabo from San Diego."

She smiled. "You got it. I need to get back to work."

"I have a surprise for you down there as well." His eyes were teasing.

At that moment she noticed Juan out back, feeding the blooming fruit trees. She took him a cup of coffee.

"Buenos días, Miss Judy."

"Hear you and Annie have parted ways."

His face showed the strain. He wanted to tell her what he'd caught the fat bitch doing, but Annie was her friend. "She fired me."

"She said you quit."

"Mutual agreement."

Judy was curious. "What happened? She wouldn't tell me."

"She was very bad to me," Juan answered, and that was all he would say. He turned back to his work.

When she pressed Annie on it that afternoon, all Annie would tell her was that they had had a "misunderstanding." And that was that.

"Damn," Annie said to Esther Sussman as they put their clubs away and hopped back into the golf cart, "I'm worn out." They were only on the seventh hole on The Reserve course, and Annie already was exhausted.

"We haven't even started."

"What?"

"We're doing eighteen."

"It must be a Jewish thing, athletic genes. Selma, the same way."

"Your heart needs it."

"Talk like her too." Esther drove to the next tee. Annie fanned herself. "But this is so boring! Swat a ball, drive a mile, swat again, drive a mile, push it into a hole, and do it all over again. Eighteen goddamn times."

"You're ornery today."

"Book problems."

"How so?" Esther inquired, pulling up to wait for the golfers before them.

"I made the mistake of basing this new opus on Norman Lempke's death."

"Yes," Esther remembered, "the gardener did it."

"Yeah, I was going to make him the perp."

Esther looked confused. "What would his motivation be?"

"An obsession with the girl who was working with Norman. He perceived them to have been falling in love."

"Judy?" she gasped.

"It's fiction," Annie cautioned, "don't go jumping to motherly conclusions."

"It sounds stupid."

"Oh, it's gonna be good. Until Dick starts to learn that other guys who were close to the girl got bumped off as well. A whole pattern emerges, but he's gotta prove one guy did it."

"Craig! You're using Craig Castle and that Kyle guy, aren't you?"

"Loosely. And Troy, the waiter who died in that sweat house. And some made-up characters as well."

"Glad to hear there's still *some* fiction in it. Where did this come from?"

Annie looked a little blank. "Who knows? Started out with the gardener thing and then I had to find myself a motivation, so that seemed like the perfect invention." She saw something, suddenly, on Esther's face that she hadn't seen before, a kind of knowing worry in her eyes that surprised her. "What?"

Esther averted her eyes. "What?"

"What are you thinking? You have a look in your eyes."

Esther closed her eyes for a moment and leaned on her club. "Okay. I've never told anyone but Henry this, and he stopped me right off by saying I was nuts."

"Spill."

Esther moved closer to Annie, as if someone might hear them in the middle of the expanse of golf course. She even lowered her voice. "I have never believed that Craig committed suicide."

Annie drank it in. "What do you think happened?"

"He didn't overdose. I think someone killed him."

"What makes you think so?"

"He had everything to live for. He wasn't depressed. He wasn't at all the kind who would kill himself."

"Mmmm," Annie said, "suddenly talking like Desert Dick."

"Read too much of him, it's rubbing off. No, honestly, Craig seemed to be the most grounded fellow that Judy had ever dated. I was shocked to find he did drugs. I know Judy experimented then too, everyone did. But I think someone killed him and made it look like he OD'd."

"Okay, Desert Dick, what's the motive?"

Esther shrugged in the hot sun. "Drug deal gone bad."

"Too easy."

"Something happened about three weeks before he died, something that we all knew was troubling to him. He wasn't himself, he was nervous, upset, scared."

"What was it?"

"Don't know. I suspect he was in over his head owing drug money. You could ask Judy, though she has always told me she didn't know either. But something happened to that man."

"Some kind of trouble," Annie said, "which led to suicide."

"Or murder."

"Well," Annie said, amused, "could be good for my book."

"Your gardener would have to have known the girl way back then for his motive to work."

"So," Annie said, realizing this, "Juan is old enough. He could have killed the guy when he was in his late teens or early twenties."

"Make him older in the book. Then I'll believe it."

"I already have."

Judy was tingling. She'd driven to her meeting with Restaurant Associates at the Four Seasons Beverly Hills, and then beat the rush hour down the 405 Freeway to the 5 all the way to San Diego, just in time to meet Ben at the airport gate. He swept her off her feet in a wild, exuberant hug. They kissed and delighted in the fact that they were together again. Only five days had passed, but it had seemed like weeks. In the car, in the parking lot, they kissed so passionately that the windows steamed up. Driving the short distance to his apartment in the old, hip, funky Hillcrest section, they held hands.

They made love for the first time the minute they entered his home. They had planned to talk, to unpack, to have a drink, get to know each other better, but the minute he closed the door, all the fantasies they'd both had all week long became real. He held her head in his hands as he kissed her lips, then licked her chin, then moved his moist lips down to her breasts, and kissed them with as much tenderness and passion as he had her mouth.

She opened his pants and pulled him out through his boxer shorts. He pulled his pants off while she still had her fingers clasped around him, and he lifted her skirt and pulled down her panties with one hand, one strong gesture. Then they joined together there on the floor of his vestibule, with the wheels of his bike to one side and the antique umbrella stand to the other.

They reached orgasm too soon, but their passion was so overwhelming that there was no way to stop. Ben leaned back, head on the floor, his left hand caught in his bike spokes, his right on Judy's thigh, and he groaned, then laughed, shuddering with pleasure that was still rippling through his body, and said, "So, welcome to San Diego."

Judy gasped for breath and started laughing. She

was a lovely mess, her hair mussed, her panties ripped where her knees had pulled them farther and farther apart. "If this is the welcome wagon, I want more."

He gave her what she wanted. He sat up, kissed her breasts, softly, slowly, then her lips again, and said, "May I help you up?"

He stood, put himself back into his shorts, and lifted her till she was standing. She pulled up her ripped panties, let her skirt fall back into position, and hastily put her blouse back on. "Before I turn the lights on," he said, "I want to show you something." He led her to a picture window from which, being on the ninth floor on a hill, a city of twinkling lights glowed at their feet. Beyond, the darkness of the water swept out to the ends of the earth.

"It's lovely here." And it was, the perfect bachelor pad. She wasn't wild about the matching sofa, chair, and ottoman, but she figured they'd been a package deal. There was a wall of books, and some old pieces that he'd told her he'd gotten from his grandparents' farmhouse, and various clutter that you'd expect a bachelor to have. School papers were piled up everywhere. The best thing about the apartment, however, was the art on the walls. All the paintings were watercolors, his.

She showered, and when she was done, he had a snack ready—he'd popped popcorn with lots of butter. She had a glass of white wine. He drank a beer.

He told her he had an incredible plan for the weekend.

"What are we doing?" she said, excited.

"Nothing."

She liked that. "Actually, I had hoped to catch up on my sleep."

He loved her sexy tone. "Just what I meant. But not alone."

When Judy Sussman looked into the bathroom mirror the next morning, she admitted she was falling in love.

They spent the morning in bed, reading the paper, watching cartoons while he corrected some test papers, eating breakfast off trays, making love again. In the afternoon, while Ben was preparing Monday's class projects, she studied his bookshelves and was surprised to find several on Palm Springs, and two on the Agua Caliente Indians. She asked him about them, and he told her since their hike up the Indian canyon, he had gained an interest in the Palm Springs desert tribes. He had what seemed like hundreds of books on Southwest Indians, from New Mexican tribes to those in Arizona and California. Sticking out of an old textbook was a faded photograph of Ben with a big cowboy hat on, obviously taken some years before, standing incongruously against a palm tree in front of a hot dog place. She knew he'd probably long ago lost track of it, and his bright, smiling face so touched her that she stole the photo and put the book back on the shelf.

They went to dinner at one of his favorite dives, Corvette Diner, where they had great burgers, malts, and onion rings. They walked hand in hand afterward, for blocks and blocks, window shopping, talking, enjoying the pleasure of one another's company. Two boys who were in Ben's classes passed them on rollerblades, saying hello and giggling to themselves that they'd caught their teacher holding hands with a beautiful woman. Cool.

Sunday morning came too quickly. She was due to fly to Cabo tomorrow, which suited her fine, because she'd leave her car in San Diego, which meant she would have to return to get it, which meant she would see Ben again. After a light breakfast, they went to his gym, worked out, then had a great brunch in Old Town. Ben told Judy that he'd get Connie's Missy Potato stories off to her father the next day.

Talk about the East Coast led at some point to his mother, still living in Princeton. "Ever been there?" he asked.

"Yes, once. I went there for two days with Craig. He'd gone to school there and was returning for a reunion, so I tagged along. Charming town, great campus."

"Didn't know he was a Princeton man. You know, I never had contact with him again after that summer I knew him. It was a shock to me to learn he died. Tell me about it."

"He killed himself."

"Yes, but why?

She shrugged. "If I knew the answer to that, I'd feel a great deal more peace inside."

Chapter Fifteen

Annie called a detective who'd worked on the investigation into Craig Castle's death, but she didn't learn much except the fact Craig had died of an overdose from sacred datura. The death had been a long time ago, and he didn't remember the details.

Once Annie hung up the phone, she suddenly had a brainstorm. She dialed Esther.

"Hello?"

"What was that other guy's name?"

"Annie?"

"The guy who Judy was involved with."

"There were a few," Judy's mother said, a bit unapproving.

"Two years ago, the one who disappeared. You mentioned him the other day on the golf course."

"Kyle? Hold on." She asked Henry what Kyle's last name was. Then she told Annie, "Hulsebus. That was it."

"What do you know about him?"

"Hmm," Esther pondered, "let's see. He was from Rochester, I think—" Annie heard Henry say something in the background. "No, Rockford, Henry says."

"Rockford, Illinois?"

"Yes."

"I did a signing there at Borders last year, they loved me."

"Who doesn't? Kyle was a lifeguard at the Hyatt Grand Champions down here in Palm Desert."

"What happened to him? You said he drifted away?"

"He did. Poof, gone. We just figured he went as easily as he came."

"Most of my men do that," Annie joked with a sexy voice.

"You're incorrigible. We didn't get it, though, because he seemed to really love his job, loved the desert, and I think he loved Judy. He was a few years younger than she was, but I wouldn't have thought he would just pack up and leave without saying good-bye."

"He take his stuff?"

"I think so. I think Judy found everything gone. She was devastated."

"Did anyone report him missing?"

"I don't know. Probably not. He was an adult. We all were very angry with him, that he could do such a childish thing. Judy said something about his leaving because she wouldn't make a commitment to him." She took a breath. "Why do you want to know all this?"

"The book," Annie said, "the book."

"Right," Esther answered, realizing she should have known.

"Thanks, babe," Annie said, hanging up. She reached under her desk, for the desert phone directory, then thought better of it. "Faster on the Net," she said to herself, and sure enough, within seconds she had looked up Rockford, Illinois, and saw a list of people with the last name of Hulsebus. She hit the print button, and started calling from the top.

Pretty soon she hit pay dirt. "Mrs. Hulsebus, I'm sure this is causing you pain, but I assure you, I'm not trying to—"

"No one's going to bring my son back!" the woman said.

"Back from where?" Annie didn't get it. Kyle's mother at first seemed receptive to Annie's telling her she was a writer and all, but when she got to the part about wondering what happened to her son, the woman dissolved. Annie heard enormous pain in her voice, and was trying to figure out what she had triggered. "I don't understand, Mrs. Hulsebus. We don't know what happened to Kyle since he left Palm Springs."

"Questions, questions, questions," the woman said wearily. "They all ask the same thing and I tell them the same thing and then I get more questions, and nothing brings Kyle back to me."

"So he did disappear, then?" Annie asked.

"Disappear?"

"That's all we know."

"Like martians took him up in a spaceship?"

Annie took a deep breath. "No, like never heard from again."

"You don't know what happened to my boy, do you?"

Annie realized she was missing something grave. She said, "No, I do not. That is why I'm calling. That's what I'm telling you."

"This some kind of joke?" The woman seemed to come apart. Through her sobs, she angrily said, "Just leave me alone, leave me be, please. . . ." And the line went dead.

Annie thought for a moment. What the hell was the name of the booking person at that Borders store in Rockford? Maybe she could arrange a book signing, make the trip worth it, write it off. Hell, it was a long shot, but the woman's edgy response had stimulated her prying mind. Whatever had happened to Kyle Hulsebus, his mother seemed to know.

And Annie had to find out.

Dear Diary:

I heard, from someone who knew him, that he was just having fun. Getting laid. A beautiful, older famous woman, who would not love it? Then I heard that he was emotionally involved. I saw that she was not. Or was she? It was never quite clear. She seemed she wanted to break away from her routine, her relationship she had been in for so long. She wanted freedom, and then again she did not.

Lifeguard. A pool boy. That says it all. What had she been thinking? It had to be sex and nothing more. Yet sex is a very powerful drug itself. Could she become the addict that he was? It went on, up and down, for almost two years. I watched, and said nothing. Then I had to do something, for she was losing clarity, losing sight of herself. In the old days, sex was not discussed, it was not flaunted. It was private, between husband and wife. Braves grew excited in the sweat house for the possibility of a woman one day, but not all women, *one* woman who would be theirs forever. This pool boy was stealing the heart of the woman meant for me.

He loved the desert. We had that in common. And he died in the desert, I saw to that.

Chapter Sixteen

Skeet met with the Cabo "officials" who had said three months ago they were ready to cobblestone the dirt road that led to Macaw's and Francies. But nothing had happened, despite the assurance that the road makers were ready, crews gathered, all set to start. So, what was the problem? The material, it is not good enough, one man said, need to get better stuff from another supplier. That translated to pesos. Always more pesos. Skeet got so pissed off at the constant blackmail that he overturned a table and kicked his way out of the room.

"Man," J.W. said to him, "that's not going to solve anything."

"Fucking wetbacks think all gringos are made of money."

"We are. To them."

"I'm not gonna take it anymore. Not gonna be held ransom for everything."

"Baja is still the frontier," J.W. reminded him. "They barter, they cheat at cards, they settle a score by driving someone out in the desert and shooting them."

"I'm not afraid."

"Just be careful."

"Fuck you, telling me what to do."

J.W. saw through his rage. "Hey, Skeet, what's up, man? What's this really about?"

Skeet kicked at a mangy dog that was wandering by. "I think, to be honest, that I don't want to live alone."

"This thing with Judy and her new man getting heavy?"

"Yes."

"She really love this guy?"

"I think so," Skeet said. "At least she thinks she does."

"It could fade."

"Getting stronger, you ask me."

"Give it time. They say men think with their dicks, but women become infatuated all the time. Head over heels, off the deep end. But they come back to the surface."

Skeet was gazing off into the distance, thinking of something. "Hey, you ever go into a sweat house?"

"Huh?" J.W. looked at him as if he were suddenly speaking Chinese.

"Haven't done it in years, but been thinking about it since Judy's guy mentioned it. We might do it together. Thing is, a waiter of mine just OD'd in one. That's pretty heavy."

"Drugs in a sweat house? That's like zoning out before you go into a steam room. Fool."

"Annie, my neighbor, thinks he could have been murdered."

"Why?"

Skeet shrugged, but then said, "Something just occurred to me, something outrageous, something I don't even want to say."

"But you will."

"This is nuts. But this guy, Ben, shows up out of nowhere right after Norman Lempke gets killed, and then Troy, my waiter, dies, and Ben knew Judy's first lover, Craig, who was into all this Indian shit, used to call himself a shaman actually, it just makes me wonder."

"Wonder what?"

"Well, Troy had a crush on Judy. So did Lempke. Craig loved her. They all died, and all the deaths had to do with poisonous desert plants."

J.W. looked aghast. "You suspect Ben?"

Skeet shook his head. "I said it was nuts."

When Judy arrived, Skeet was careful not to let the slightest suspicion of Ben pass from his lips. He encouraged her to talk about Ben, share her thoughts about him, and her hopes for a future with him. But she was here to work, and that's what they did.

The restaurant had a lot of problems, from the sign out front to the tile on the floor. The lighting had to be changed from what she'd proposed because they realized the lanterns she'd had made in Tijuana didn't cast enough light on the dining tables. The tables themselves were not sturdy. The last thing Skeet wanted was someone to try to cut through their leg of lamb and end up on the floor. The stemware, in a gorgeous cobalt blue, looked great, but the color flaked off in a test in the dishwater. It was hell.

While Skeet worked on the menu by e-mail with the new chef in Vermont, Judy took charge of the physical plant. She spent five days at the place, driving the lackadaisical workers hard, and finally getting results. On the sixth day, she had hopes that things would turn around.

She stayed on the boat the five nights she was in Cabo, and that was more difficult. Judy knew Skeet was worried that their affair with Ben had come on so fast. He reminded her of her wild passion with Kyle Hulsebus, which was not all that long ago. "You were addicted," he recalled. She nodded, for she believed him; apparently it had scared even Kyle into running from her. No one knew why he'd vanished. She did. He'd run from the intensity of her feelings.

"It's all about trust," Skeet reminded her, "trust is everything."

She nodded. "It's what *we* have."

"But when you add sex to it, you're talking life partner stuff here, and that's what I want you to be careful about."

They were sitting on the back of the boat, drinking a thick, dark, sweet Mexican liqueur after dinner, looking at the stars, listening to a mariachi band playing at one of the marina restaurants. "Would you trust him?" She turned to Skeet. "I mean, what's your intuition about him?"

"I liked him, you know that."

She did. Then she got even more honest. "This isn't about Ben, really. This is about us. We've always been the best thing for each other."

He smiled. "I know that. Why are you telling me this."

"The problem is, we limit each other ultimately, and that's just not good."

"Limit how?"

"We'll never be free for someone else if we stay roommates."

"But we're emotionally tied. You want to break that too?"

"No," she said, and meant it. "I love you."

"So you feel you can't pursue your relationship with him living with me?"

"I don't know. I feel weird."

He asked the big question. "Are you trying to tell me there is more to your feelings for me?"

She stood up, and the boat rocked in the quest water of the protected marina. "No, silly. You know that. I just feel like we're in this—what? I'm almost afraid to leave it's so comfortable."

"Jesus, Judy," he said, his anger rising, "I thought what we have is good."

She apologized. "I didn't mean it to sound the way it did. I just want to really marry someone I'm wildly in love with and have kids and all that stuff."

He stood up behind her. He wrapped his arms around her waist and put his head on her shoulder. "A long, long time ago, I said to you that I loved you so much that I wanted you to be happy, more than anything in the world. Remember?"

She nodded, clutching his hands on her stomach. "I remember."

"I meant that then, and that was when I was in love with you. Well, I mean it now as well. I just want to protect you from being hurt."

"I'm a big girl. I have to make my own mistakes, if this is one."

He kissed her cheek. "Judy, do me this one favor, give it a little more time."

She hesitated. "I don't know."

"Give it time," he whispered in her ear, touching it with his lips. "It's only a new flame that's started burning, wait a while and see if it cooks, you know?"

She giggled. "Chef talk?"

"I'm serious. If it does, when you are sure, one-hundred-percent sure, then go for it. Move out and risk that dream. But be sure this isn't another Kyle first."

"God," she said, dreamily, "why do you have to be agreeable? That's why it's so easy to love you."

He kissed her cheek. "I love you too."

She turned her head, wrapped her arms around him and they held each other for several minutes. "Judy, Judy," he whispered, "I haven't felt this close to you in so long."

"Skeet," she whispered, carried away by the feelings, the comfort of his gentle but manly touch, the familiarity. This was her best friend in the world. "I'm going to sleep. Good night."

He nodded. "I'm not."

"What are you going to do?"

With a sly smile, he said, "I think I'm going over to the Giggling Marlin, where it is noisy, where everyone is drunk, and where, I'm sure, I can get laid."

She laughed and disappeared down into the teak-lined salon. "Just don't drag her back here and rock the boat. I get seasick, remember?"

Chapter Seventeen

The woman who came to the door of the nondescript frame house looked fearful and tired. "Who are you?"

Annie Chestnut made up a name. "Sylvia Kathawa."

"I don't know you."

Annie knew she'd get the door slammed in her puss if she told the truth, so she became a storyteller again. "You a religious woman?"

"First Rockford Baptist Church," the woman said proudly, "if that's any of your business."

"Sister Hulsebus, I'm with the Christian Woman's Federation," Annie lied. "I'd like to talk to you about helping spread the word about our volunteer work."

The woman squinted, looked suspicious. "I don't have time."

Annie softly said, "You're hurting. I can tell."

Mrs. Hulsebus seemed taken aback at that, but relented. "Yes."

"I lost my little girl," Annie said, almost tearfully.

"About a year ago; seems like yesterday. The work of the church has helped me stay with Jesus."

"Praise Jesus," the woman said, and held the door open. "Come have some coffee."

"Obliged," Annie said, entering the house. Step one, accomplished. Step two was going to be the hard part.

Annie *oohed* and *raahed* about the decor, which was missing only a painting of Christ on black velvet to be perfectly complete. There was a lot of Elvis tchotchkes, even an Elvis clock on the wall, the early Elvis, not the bloated old Elvis.

"I'm from down Memphis way, originally," the skinny woman said, putting a spoonful of Folger's instant into two teacups. "Elvis was my man."

"Saw him in Vegas," Annie said, which was true.

"That there's a terrible place."

"Was then. Now it's Disneyland. He was fat. But great."

"That he was, the greatest. I don't think him as ever being fat. He was just bigger than life."

Annie felt like gagging. "He was the King." She glanced at pictures on the walls of a good looking, blond boy, photos ranging from about age ten through his late twenties. Annie recognized him, though she'd only gotten a glimpse of Kyle once when he picked Judy up at her house, shortly after Annie had moved to Palm Springs. One photo was taken at a swimming pool—she loved the tight trunks, the incredible lanky physique—that she was sure was the pool at the Grand Champions Resort in Palm Desert. "This your boy?" she asked softly.

The water kettle whistled. "My Kyle."

"How long ago did you lose him?"

"How'd you know that?"

"It's in your eyes."

"Two years June twentieth. Like yesterday."

"I understand," Annie said.

"By the way," the woman said after pouring boiling water into the cups, "I'm Deidre."

"Sylvia."

"Howdy, Sylvia. Well, here, best I can do." She poured coffee that smelled like it had been sitting there for days. "Cream?"

"Sure." Annie never took cream or milk but she figured she had to disguise this taste somehow. Deidre poured a good quarter cup of heavy cream into her cup. Annie stopped her as she was about to do the same to hers. "Just a smidgeon."

They ate stale Oreo cookies and talked about their losses, Deidre's Kyle and Sylvia's "Heather" (she didn't know where *that* came from), and before long Deirdre got into the story of what had happened to her boy. "He spent almost two years in the desert out there. Grew up shoveling snow here in Rockford; guess that's why he liked hot dry weather. I visited him once, took the bus out. Stopped in Vegas on the way, but it's a terrible place."

"Yes, you said."

"I'm not a gambler."

Annie pressed. "What happened to Kyle's father?"

"Run off. Before Kyle was born. He was just a boy."

"I see."

"I was young then, too; we all were." She looked up at a photo. "First went to Texas, but hated the humidity. He wanted arid land. Loved Palm Springs. I think Kyle's heart was always in Rockford, though. Mothers know those kinds of things."

Annie doubted that, but said, "It was home." Rockford seemed like a pretty decent city. "So how did he die?"

"They found him in the Arizona desert."

"Arizona?"

"He didn't say he was leaving, never mentioned he was moving on. I'd just talked to him a week before they found him. But there he was, in the desert."

"What killed him?"

Deidre took a deep breath. "Drugs."

Annie took a deep breath. Did that mean sacred datura?

The woman's voice was wracked by pain. "They said it was something strange, wouldn't tell me exactly at first, said it was something exotic."

"Exotic?" Annie asked.

"That's the word they used. Said it was seldom seen these days, something the Indians used to use for rituals. Big white flower apparently. I heard that kids sometimes still die from it if they find it growing in the desert and put it in their mouths."

"They tell you the name?" Annie inquired.

"Yes, but I don't recall. Jimsing or something like that. No, I'm mixing it up with ginseng."

Annie wished she had a book on poisonous desert plants. But then she remembered that time, when she first moved into the house and Judy brought Juan over to give her an estimate on landscaping, Juan had pointed out a creeping vine, dark green in color, with huge pure white blooms that he warned her to stay away from. Poison, he had said. "How had he ingested it?"

"Said he ate it. Cop told me that. I hit him. I told them my boy didn't do drugs."

But he had. Annie had checked with former co-workers at the Hyatt. He'd done just about every drug you could imagine. But no one could imagine poison plants. Just like Norman. Just like Troy. Craig. There was another thing Annie was wondering. "Why didn't anyone in Palm Springs ever hear about his death?"

The woman shrugged. "How would I know what they heard?" Then she sounded suspicious again. "How would you know? Why would you care?"

Annie gave a look that said she suddenly realized she'd overstayed her welcome. "Where in Arizona was he found?"

"Wait a minute," Deidre said slowly, looking

Annie up and down, "why did you ask that question?"

"Phoenix? Tucson? Sedona?"

The woman looked stunned. She'd figured it out. "You're that nosy writer who called me, aren't you?"

Annie knew she couldn't keep pretending. "Yes. I'm Annie Chestnut, and I'm sorry for this sham, but you would not have talked to me otherwise."

"How dare you come into my house!"

"I want to help you. I think your son might have been murdered." She didn't know why she said it, she wasn't even thinking it. A drug addict dead of a massive overdose out in the desert, what was to wonder? But she was talking like Dick would, doing what he would do, and so she said it again. "You too think someone killed your boy, don't you?"

"Yes!" The woman's tired eyes went wide with anger. "Somebody fed him full of that poison and left him to die out there. Yes, ma'am. Somebody killed my boy. But they don't listen to me. I'm just the hysterical mom."

Annie said, "I believe you. I honestly do. Someone just did it again to a young man named Troy Skinner, and he has a mother somewhere grieving as well. Where did they find Kyle?"

The woman had calmed down again. "Phoenix, or Scottsdale, really. All his stuff was in his Jeep, so I think maybe he was going to look for a new job at one of those fancy hotels there."

"Why did he leave a good job at the Hyatt in Palm Desert if he loved it there so much?"

Mrs. Hulsebus said, "A girl."

"Girl?"

"Some girl he was in love with. It tormented him. He said he knew she would never be his. I think that's what made him move on."

"I wonder," Annie said, "if that's what got him killed."

Back inside the rental car, Annie kicked herself. Why the hell had she said that? Christ Almighty, she was talking about her best friend! Judy had nothing to do with the man's death, she didn't even *know* he was dead. But, boy, wasn't it perfect for Dick? A string of dead men, a beautiful young woman who was a kind of black widow spider.

Driving to the Borders bookstore on State Street, Annie thought it through. Craig Castle falls in love with Judy, turns up dead of a "suicide" by a poisonous plant—after something happened that scared him and changed him. Kyle Hulsebus, drug addict with a nice pair of Speedos, falls in love with Judy and ends up DOA in the Scottsdale hospital of an overdose of some other beautiful plant he ate. These guys sure liked their desert foliage. Norman Lempke, famed octogenarian architect, falls in love with Judy (or is perceived by the killer to have had something going on with Judy) and is hacked to death in cold blood—only after somebody tried to get him to drink coyote melon, another desert killer. Sacred datura, which killed Kyle, shows up in the body of a waiter from Fancies, who everyone knew had a crush on Judy, dead in a sweat house. Consistent modi operandi? At least an interesting pattern.

The hastily printed sign in the window read ROCKFORD BORDERS BOOKS BIDS WELCOME TO THE ONE AND ONLY ANNIE CHESTNUT, but short notice notwithstanding, they were lined up as usual when she walked into the store. A well-coifed woman named Darlene told Annie she wanted her to return soon to do one of her women's club lectures, and Annie said she'd be delighted. Jean Casper asked her to sign a book to her husband, Bob, who was her "biggest fan." Bill Bersted, next in line with all seven of her books in his arms, made *his* claim to being just that, while a brassy gal who pushed her way to the front of the line said her name was Maxine, and they were all wrong, *she* was Annie's biggest fan. "Fight over it," Annie ordered, delighted. She signed countless books, the names running together—JudyDavidDebbieIrish PearlJimBarbPaulineKaraMartyBobJean, and someone's beagle named Butch. At the end of the line stood two old friends from Annie's Texas days. "My God, Jeb and Sally Kresge," Annie gasped. "What the hell are you doing here?"

"We moved to Belvidere," Sally said. "Right up the road. Jeb was born there."

"Back to my roots." Jeb smiled a boyish grin.

"Better roots than Texas."

"Your ex still in prison down there?" Jeb asked.

"Better be, or I'm not gonna live long," Annie answered. "Hey, got time for dinner?

"Because I want to talk about plants."

Nestled into a booth in the corner of Genghis Khan restaurant, being fawned over by the owners because they were her "biggest" fans, Annie listened as Sally and Jeb Kresge talked about poisonous plants. Jeb was a pharmacist who had done his Ph.D. work in herbal medicine and Chinese cures, and Sally was an emergency room nurse who specialized in poisons. Annie remembered they were both avid gardeners. "Ever heard of coyote melon?" she asked.

"Whoa," Jeb said. "Dissolving organs."

"Lethal," Sally agreed.

Annie nodded. "How about sacred datura?"

Jeb scratched his head. "Hmmm."

Sally said, "That's the one with the seeds, I think. Yes, ants are attracted to it because it discards this sticky, hard-shelled seed. It's found all throughout the Southwest. We saw it often in Texas. Kids mostly would find the seeds sticking to them and they'd lick them off. Lost one doing that, actually. It's a horrible death."

"How so?"

"Starts with pain and stomach cramps," Sally said, "extreme dehydration, very ugly. 'Course, the right dose will just stop your heart."

Annie suddenly didn't feel very hungry. "Okay, here's another one. I don't know the correct name, but it sounds something like ginseng."

"Jimson," Jeb said. "Jimsonweed."

"Final answer?" Annie joked.

Jeb said, "I'll bet that's what you mean. *Datura meteloides.* Also called Thorn-Apple. Beautiful and deadly."

"White flowers?"

Jeb nodded. "Pretty, but creepy."

Sally knew it too. "It's a vine, kind of clings to the ground."

Annie said, "Yeah, had it in my yard."

"I think the Indians used that one in ancient ceremonies. If done sparingly, I think I recall, it'll make you hallucinate. Sorta like opium in that way. Extremely addictive, does what you used to see in old Charlie Chan movies, you're completely stoned all the time. I think the Indians liked that part."

Annie asked, "Could someone maybe play around with it, like the Indians did, to hallucinate and get high, and maybe get really stoned and eat some thinking they were gonna get higher?"

Jeb looked unsure. "I suppose you could get so stoned that you don't know what you're doing."

Sally disagreed. "I think that's completely unlikely. You know it's poison. I don't even think anyone today knows how to make the kind of drug that the Indians made from it."

Annie squirmed. "My God, I feel like we're talking about my life in the seventies."

"I can send you a book on all those plants and more," Jeb offered. "Fascinating stuff."

She handed him her card. "Thanks."

"Why did you want to know?" Jeb asked. "New book?"

"More like an old story," Annie said, "that I'm going back to."

Chapter Eighteen

Judy worked in Cabo San Lucas for about another full week, trying to redo her design for the outdoor seating. The patio just wasn't going to work the way she'd designed it the first time, for she hadn't counted on the roof supports, and Spanish tile, because it was so heavy, required more support than she'd anticipated. She had to move the fountain and the arbor to make room for the overhang of the roof, which the workers had extended three feet longer than the plans stated, and it seemed to Skeet, after much thought, that the kitchen was too small as well. It had to be enlarged without intruding on the restaurant, for fewer tables meant less profit.

She talked to Ben by phone every night, and longed to see him again. The weekend was coming, so she booked a flight to San Diego the next day. Knowing she would see Ben again took the edge off. When Skeet asked if she wanted to "do the town tonight," she said sure.

At Cabo Wabo, they had two double margaritas, which loosened them up and make them hungry.

After a delicious dinner at El Galeon, across from the marina, they sat on the outside terrace overlooking the water, from which they could see Skeet's boat. Judy was amazed how many million-dollar–plus yachts floated silently in the harbor. It looked like Monte Carlo.

After dinner, they walked around the waterfront Plaza Bonita, where Judy got lost in Cartes, the interior design store with an array of hand-painted pottery and tableware. She fell in love with a set of silver chargers with a double rope design on their rim, but decided not to buy them because they'd only sit in a cupboard. "Oh, get them anyway," Skeet said.

"We'd need a new table. They're too big for ours." Their house in Palm Springs was only sixteen hundred square feet, and most of that was kitchen/family room. The formal dining area was cramped.

Skeet bought them despite her protests. "We'll have a bigger place one day," he said, "or you and Ben will, with all the kids you're planning to drop. We'll take eight."

"Skeet, four is enough. I don't want *that* many kids."

"Eight."

She acted upset, but was really thrilled. She was beginning to loosen up. It was like old times. She'd talked about Ben all through dinner, and Skeet was interested, supportive, kind. They strolled up Boulevard Marine, looking into the shops, saying hello to the times-share hawkers, most of whom Skeet knew, feeling part of the rowdy nightlife. "Hard to believe," he said, "this is the same dirty fishing town, full of foul-smelling canneries, that I discovered back when we were in college."

"Now it's a land of shopportunities." She giggled, drooling over a silver necklace in a window.

"Come on," he said, pulling her in the other direction. "Chargers are one thing, heavy silver strands are another."

She laughed, and they crossed the street. They walked, talked, ate ice cream cones, laughed, and relaxed. Then Judy looked at the time. "I've got an early flight. You taking me?"

"Sure."

"Maybe we'd better get back to the boat."

"We've got one more thing to do first."

"Huh?"

"That surprise I told you about."

She brightened. "Hey, I forgot about that. Yes, you told me. So?"

"So, come on." He led her to the marina parking lot, where they got into his Jeep.

"Where are we going?" she asked, fastening her seat belt with the chargers balanced on her knees.

"Up the road a piece. . . ."

"Well?" Skeet said, turning off the ignition. "What do you think?"

She was staring straight ahead, her mouth open in shock, wonder. She could not find words. She unfastened her seat belt as Skeet took the chargers from her, and she stepped out, all while keeping her eyes fixed on the structure before them. It was white, all white, and in the light of the full moon, it glowed like a star that had come to rest on the earth. "My God," was all she could say as she started toward it.

The house was her dream house. She'd played for years with a design for the "house on the cliff" she would build one day, for some client if not herself. Now it was built, finished, on a cliff overlooking the Gulf of Cortez. Skeet pushed open the big carved Mexican door and clicked on the lights. "Had to wait till today to get the electricity permanently hooked up."

What she saw made her weak in the knees. It was the room she'd envisioned time and time again, in sketches and in her dreams. Three walls of glass faced her as she entered, with a magnificent fireplace in the middle of them, ocean views all around. To the right was the kitchen and outdoor dining room surrounded by a wall painted a deep sunflower yellow, with a bird-of-paradise plant rising from a huge pink pot spotlighted in the corner. On an old wooden table, set with wonderful mismatched Mexican chairs, Skeet put the chargers on top of colorful cloth place mats. "That's why you bought them!" Judy was in shock.

Skeet had made her design dream come true. He'd done everything down to the last detail. The two upstairs bedrooms, with their lavish baths, their little

Greek island windows copied after a place on Mykonos Judy had once fallen in love with, everything was just as she'd seen in her mind's eye.

They sat on the patio chairs outside the living room, feeling the night breeze, watching a cruise ship slowly heading for the marina.

Skeet looked up at the rocky hillside. "I was thinking, we're getting older, neither of us seems to be very lucky in love, I figured we'd have a retirement house, or a getaway, or something like that."

"It's overwhelming. I'm touched, deeply touched. It's beautiful."

"You designed it, I just had it built."

"Without me knowing! Wow."

"I was gonna wait for the next time you're down, got stuff to do yet, but you just might run off with Benny and never come back, so I figured I'd show you now."

She reached out and took his hand.

"You just give it some time, like I said yesterday. If you live here one day, great. If not, well, it's a monument to your talent. Hell, I'm sure as hell gonna live here."

She stood up. "I want to stay the night."

"All I've got is a cot upstairs, a bar of soap, it's not really habitable yet."

"I don't care. I have to spend the night." She turned to him, pulled him close to her. "See, I always dreamed what it would be like waking up to the sun streaming in through all those little windows. I've got to do it, Skeet."

He nodded. "There's a couple of blankets in the back of the Jeep. I can use those."

She smiled.

He started toward the vehicle. "Skeet," she called.

He turned. "Yes?"

"Thank you." Her voice was filled with honest emotion. "Thank you so much."

"I love you, roommate. No matter what."

It was just as Judy had hoped, like waking up on an island in your dreams, at one with the sea that stretched out in a blue haze before her. It was the most magical sight she'd ever seen. She got up with the sun, tiptoed down the stairs so as not to wake Skeet, and went to the kitchen. She'd spotted a coffeemaker there last night, found the beans in the freezer, made a pot as she studied the details, the recessed niches for statues and art and pottery, as she ran her fingers over the glass block wall that ran behind the countertop. She ran her toes over the whitewashed saltillo tile floor. She found a mug in a cabinet, filled it to the brim, and went outside. There she spied something she'd missed the night before.

On the hillside above the house, about thirty feet up, was a little building that looked like a pump house for a well. She wondered what it was, so she put her shoes on and set off to find out. As she reached it, she saw that there was a little tower on it that she'd not been able to see from below, a spire really, with a cross on top. The building was a chapel. There were two stained-glass windows, one on either side, and the door looked like it had been copied (or stolen) from an old Catholic church somewhere. Skeet had been raised Catholic, but had never practiced, at least not as far as she knew. How odd.

But how delightful. It was the perfect complement to the stark, modern newness of the house, this ancient-looking miniature church. It seemed as though it had always been on this hill, though she was certain it went up when the house had. She was dying to see inside, but the door was locked. She shook and pushed, but it would not budge.

"It's a sin to break into the house of God!" a voice shouted from below. Skeet was standing there, hair a mess from sleeping on the floor on only a blanket, coffee in hand as well, smiling. "Not finished yet."

"I love it!" Judy called down, then she went back down herself.

"I thought it was a cute touch."

"What's inside?"

"Nothing yet."

"What's going to be inside?"

He shrugged. "A shrine, I think."

"To?"

"Hmmm. How about you?"

She laughed. "I think the house counts as that already. You know what you should do with it? Turn it into one of those sweat houses you and Ben talked about. You guys can hole up in there and beat yourself with palm fronds or whatever macho stuff you do in there, and I'll sit by the pool waiting with the iced tea."

"Hey, not a bad idea," he said. "Not bad at all."

Chapter Nineteen

Juan walked around Judy's kitchen. He'd finished in the yard, but he could not bring himself to leave. He was nervous, although it was not from fear that someone would catch him in there. He knew Skeet and Judy were in Mexico for several days at least. His agitated state came from the frustration that he could have anything he wanted of hers—all he had to do was steal it—but never her.

He went to the extra bedroom that she used as an office. He sat in her swivel chair, incongruous for the type of house this was, but certainly comfy nonetheless. He looked in the desk drawers. Folders, sketches, old letters, clippings. There was a note from the recently deceased architect telling her he "looked forward to meeting again and really discussing the project." Another, deep under a bunch of TWA Aviators mileage statements, from Kyle. It had been written on the back of a Julie's Hallmark bag, apparently left on her car where she might find it. He sounded desperate. "S: Can't stand it. Have to wear a long tank at the pool cause people will see I'm thinking about you. Found your car in the lot here. Don't go home after the dentist. Let me massage your gums. Meet me at my place. K."

Juan felt enraged, but excited at the same time. He wanted more than anything in the world to make love to Judy, but could only accomplish that vicariously through the men who were lucky enough to share her bed. Craig. Skeet. Kyle. Norman? Troy? Ben?

He found a photo of Judy standing on a beach—he guessed it was Hawaii because they were under a coconut palm—with Craig. She looked so different, for it had been taken many years before. He hardly knew her then. They looked stoned. He had known Craig well at that time, knew all about Craig's passion for drugs and hallucinogens. Juan was certain he would have ruined Judy's life had he lived. He crushed the picture in his hand, not really realizing his emotion, and tossed it angrily back into the drawer.

In a file cabinet behind the door to the room, he found an envelope, sealed, addressed to Kyle, but obviously never sent. He opened it. And read it:

Dear Kyle,
I don't know how to answer you other than to tell you I'm not ready to make any more commitment than I have made to you. I've never felt so good about myself, and you do that for me. You want to know if it's all about sex, well, yes, it is, and more. The glow seems

to last forever, and when it dies, you light it again. I can't give you the answers you seem to need right now, and I'm in no way ready to even think about starting something permanent. Let's just enjoy this now, with no expectations for the future, but open to all possibilities, okay? Can't wait to see you tomorrow night as usual.

xxx Judy

Juan saw the date was close to the day Kyle had disappeared from Palm Springs, so she'd never gotten to send it. He laughed. Too bad. He must have known anyway that she would never be his. Just as she'd never be Juan's. That was clear. Then he found a Christmas card. "From your favorite Fancies waiter, happy holidays! Troy Skinner." His blood surged through his veins. A boy. A damned kid. Not him.

The frustration led him to her bedroom. Night was coming fast. He knew, had she been here, that she would shower or pamper herself in the tub, and then slip into a very sheer nightgown, the same soft yellow one she always wore. Then once in bed, she'd pull the fluffy down comforter high to her neck. He'd watched from outside many times. Skeet would return late from the restaurant, make his way to his own room, but she wouldn't even know it. She slept very soundly.

Tonight, Juan found himself doing the same. He stripped off his clothes and left them piled where he dropped them, on her bedroom floor. The water and bubbles in the tub relaxed him, the aroma of lavender made him smile as he put his head back and dreamed of her, and dreaming of her made the tip of his erect penis poke up out of the water.

When he had dried himself with the towel she always used, he found the yellow nightgown she wore, and he slipped it over his head. It was a tight fit, and for a moment he thought he'd have to remove it because he was afraid his arm muscles would force the seams apart. But it held. Tightly, as he thought of it clinging to her.

He swung his feet up onto the mattress, then pulled the comforter to his chin. He basked in a rich and powerful place that sent him far beyond the pleasure of the priest, into another realm that was solitary and satisfying. Yet it wasn't her. It was only *of* her.

Judy flew back to California the next morning, and she and Ben decided to spend the weekend in Palm Springs. Skeet offered to stay at his studio in the restaurant so they could feel free to "do the smoochies," as he joked. She took Ben to the Desert Museum for the first time, and that night Annie joined them out at the cinemas on Dinah Shore Drive for a movie and popcorn. On Saturday, they hiked Tahquitz Canyon, and this time made love at the side of a running stream, under the shade of two ancient palm trees. Sunday came too fast, and Ben was distraught that he had to leave. Judy promised at dinner that night at Fancies just before Ben left to come down to San Diego the following weekend.

"But it's your birthday," Skeet reminded her.

"Yes. So?"

He was forced to tell her. "I'm throwing you a party. No surprise anymore, but it's set in stone."

Ben brightened. "I can come back up. If I'm invited."

Skeet laughed. "Second guest of honor." Then he had an idea. "Hey, wanna do the sweat house thing that afternoon? Party's not till eight."

Ben looked enthused. "Where? The one I know about in San Diego County?"

Skeet shivered. He thought of Troy. "I'm never going there."

"I'm sorry. Right." Ben looked sheepish.

"I think they closed it anyhow," Skeet said. "There's one up near Joshua Tree, Yucca Valley actually, went there once. It's still used quite often, you hear about it now and then. Troy told me about it, in fact."

Judy was curious. "You knew of his interest in that stuff?"

"Only slightly. He said he was getting into Indian rituals. I asked why. He said for his 'spiritual' side."

"So," Ben asked, "who's gonna do this? Just the two of us?"

Skeet shook his head. "No, we'll put together some guys. I'll hunt down someone who really knows what he's doing. This stuff is beyond my expertise. Neither of us wants to end up like Troy."

Ben said, "Where's Craig Castle when we need him?" He turned to Judy when he realized how he sounded. "I didn't mean to be insensitive."

"No," she answered, "Craig was the best, he did know all that stuff. Personally, I think it's all pretty stupid."

Ben winked at Skeet. "Not if we come back more enlightened and thoughtful human beings, right, Skeeter?"

"Right on, man."

She finished her wine. "You just better not be late for my party."

Ben smiled. "We'll bring you gifts from the Indian spirits."

"Only gift I want," Judy said, "is for you both to come back sober."

Ben drove up late the next Friday night, and Skeet showed up at the house for breakfast around ten the next morning. He told them that he had gotten a few buddies together, and that he'd located a real Indian by the unlikely name of Elvis Silva, a young and hip descendant from the Cupeno band, whose great grandfather, Francisco, had been one of the most famous tellers of the Indian legends and stories. Annie spied them drinking coffee out on the patio and joined them. "You gotta be kidding," she said when she heard what the guys were planning to do that afternoon.

"It's about balls," Judy joked.

"Don't you have enough?" Annie asked Skeet.

"Honey, *you* should be going," he told her.

Half an hour later, Juan showed up. He tipped his wide-brimmed hat to all of them, and then just stood there. "Join us for coffee," Skeet offered, "we'll be leaving in less than an hour."

Judy gave Skeet a confused glance. "Juan did the yard yesterday."

"I'm going to the sweat house, Miss Judy," Juan explained. "Mr. Skeeter invited me."

Annie's mouth dropped open, but she said not another word. Her speculation was just too tenuous to voice. She only hoped what they were doing wasn't a big mistake.

The sweat house near Yucca Valley was very different from the one in which Troy Skinner had died. Slightly larger, it was dug deeper into the ground, making it almost subterranean. The roof was domed, made of clay and palm leaves piled onto a wooden frame, with a hole in the center, directly over the firepit, which was deep and large. This one was built to last.

Elvis Silva had told Skeet that his grandfather had built the original one in this place, but that subsequent generations had improved it to become the solid structure it was today. Outside was the traditional tile platform on which to lie to cool off, and nearby was a stream, flowing from the mountains in the distance, where one could dip into the icy-cold water to relieve the heat. Elvis had called Skeet's cell phone to say that he had been delayed, that they should start the fire without him, he was on his way. Ben worried that would make them late for Judy's birthday party, but Skeet assured him it wouldn't matter. The party would go long into the night. Skeet, Ben, Juan, and two other young men, Scott and Gordon, killed time talking just outside the house while the fire they had built warmed the inside.

When Elvis showed up finally, the heat had already dissipated some, and they added more wood to the fire and waited. They sat on the bank of the stream and talked.

"Were women ever involved?" Ben wondered.

Elvis nodded. "Among the Yurok and other northwestern California people, shamans were almost always women. They went through training in which they had to dance, fast, and devote themselves to ritual until eventually, in a dream or trance, they attained a vision."

"What kind?" Skeet inquired.

"An ally would appear."

Scott said, "A person?"

"The ghost of a dead person," Elvis said with a nod. "Or a monster, or animal spirit."

Gordon said, "Wasn't pain involved?"

"Pain was an object, a physical manifestation of power," Elvis recited. "In the weeks following the vision, she had to struggle to gain control over the pain, to swallow it and regurgitate it. Once done, she could summon it when needed and draw power from her dream ally."

"I recall," Skeet said, "a story where a woman became a doctor in that way. She danced in a sweat house for five days and had a craving for crab meat, found a claw on the seashore, got sick from it, and it led to pain that led to her becoming a healer."

Elvis nodded. "There are many such stories. Gentlemen, are you ready? I think it is hot enough."

They began to take off their clothing. When Ben and Elvis stripped bare-naked, Gordon, the youngest, looked surprised. "All the way?"

"However you feel most comfortable," Elvis assured him, "but the Indian way is to free the spirits in your nakedness." Gordon stripped nude like the others. They piled their clothing outside the house, leaving shoes, cell phones, everything worldly out there. They entered the sweat house the way they had come into the world, bare, unadorned, vulnerable.

Inside, the room was blazing. It was hotter than any sauna Ben had ever been in. Juan gasped as the heat overwhelmed him. They took their places on the rough, warm stone floor around the fire, and Elvis told stories of Indian bravery, magic, and inspiration. Also stories that made them laugh. It was a comfortable, strangely energetic bonding they began to feel as they each told of their secret fears and dreams. Skeet admitted he feared loss. Scott admitted his greatest fantasy was a night with Britney Spears. Juan longed for the serenity of the Venezuelan mountains, to be lost in the jungle forever. Elvis hoped to become a real doctor one day, for already he could cure rattlesnake bites and heal cuts. Gordon wanted to be as good as his older brother, whose shadow he'd grown up in. Ben, even though he was an expert swimmer, admitted that he'd always had a fear of water. Water reminded Skeet that Juan had brought bottles of it. Juan said he had set them in the stream to keep cold. Skeet volunteered to fetch them, quickly returned, and handed a bottle to Juan, who passed it to Ben, who handed it to Scott, who was at the far side, and then Ben kept the next one, and then Juan. Skeet turned and handed one to Elvis, one to Gordon, and opened the last one for himself. They gratefully replaced some of the water they were losing in perspiration. Elvis threw sage leaves onto the glowing coals, and the room filled with a magnificent scent.

Everyone was gulping their water bottles but Ben. He could not get the plastic safety seal off his cap. He finally broke it with his teeth. Then he took a sip and felt the cooling liquid quench his thirst. A second later, he gasped and fell backward, his eyes opening wide as a gurgling sound came from his lips. The men froze.

It looked like he was dead.

* * *

When the men had not returned at six as promised, Judy called Skeet's cell phone, but only got the voice message. She left one, saying she was about to dress for the party, that all the food had arrived on time, and she hoped they'd had a good afternoon—but where were they? At seven, she began to get nervous. When Annie showed up at 7:30, Annie got nervous. But they told themselves not to worry. There were any number of reasons the guys could have been delayed. Esther and Henry agreed when they arrived, and told Judy she should just start enjoying herself. Ben and Skeet would be walking through the door any minute—sweaty, perhaps, but just fine. "Guys do this thing out in the desert all the time," her father assured her.

The party started clicking at about 8:15, when everyone seemed to arrive at once. Every friend she had in the desert seemed to be there—Selma Sherman, Tori and her family, the Larsens, the Weinerts, everyone from the restaurant, even crazy Mrs. Hennessy and her friend Tom Denny from Newport. Judy's pals from Gold's were there, and Jay and Kevin from Total Health Care, where she went for just that. Her dear buddy Kervin Satterwhite had returned from a year in London, and Judy felt that was birthday gift enough. Skeet had baked a gorgeous cake, but by nine he and Ben had still not shown up. Judy and Annie left several messages for Skeet, Ben, and Juan, but none had been returned. At 9:30, because everyone could feel Judy's tenseness and worry, Carey Gold sat down at the piano and started a songfest, which buoyed spirits for ten minutes, until the front door opened and Skeet rushed in, followed by a uniformed highway patrol officer. The music died. All heads turned toward the door. Judy rushed to Skeet. "What?" she said in a panicked voice. "Where's Ben?"

"Judy," Skeet said with visible emotion, "I don't know how to say this." He glanced up at Annie, then the others, and looked back into Judy's eyes. "It's Ben."

Chapter Twenty

Judy, Skeet, and Annie spent the night in Desert Hospital, just outside the Intensive Care Unit, where Ben was in a coma. The doctors had determined that he'd been poisoned by the bottle of water he was drinking in the sweat house, a bottle of crystal-clear water that had been contaminated with coyote melon.

The police had questioned Skeet and Juan at the scene, and again later, at length, as well as Elvis Silva and the other men who'd participated. The men told the police that there had been no hint of anything that could possibly go wrong, and that Indian plant-extract rituals were not even discussed. This was a simple bonding experience between males, in the fashion of the men of the Cupeno tribe. Bottled water was simply there to replenish the liquid they were sweating off.

But who had brought the water?

Juan.

He had been grilled long into the night. He had bought the water, at Skeet's request, at a convenience store on the way out of Palm Springs. He had not removed any of the plastic safety bands over the pop caps. He had placed the bottles, still in the plastic grocery bag, in the stream. It was Skeet who had handed them out arbitrarily among the men. "I just brought the bag inside," Skeet explained emphatically. "We all grabbed one. I mean, I just passed them to the guys."

Juan said, "You gave me one, I passed it to Ben, who passed it to Scott. You gave me another, and I passed it to Ben. I kept the next one you gave me."

Skeet nodded. "I handed one to Elvis, one to Gordon, who were on the other side of me, and then took the last one for myself. It could have been any of us who drank the one that Ben drank."

Annie and the cops checked the twenty-four–hour convenience store, and were told that the bottles had been purchased from the actual shipping cases that they had set up on display. The owner and clerk were shocked at what had happened.

Sitting in the hospital the following morning, waiting for an update on Ben's condition, Annie saw a nurse walk by with a hypodermic needle in her hand. "A syringe," Annie said, the truth suddenly dawning on her.

"What?" Judy asked.

"That's how the extract could have gotten into the bottle with the safety seal still on it. A syringe."

"But who did it?" Skeet asked. "And was it meant for Ben?"

No one could answer that.

They kept a vigil until noon, when the doctors told Judy that Ben had opened his eyes. The drug seemed to be wearing off. "There's a kind of paralysis that comes with this type of poisoning," the doctor explained, "and it appears to be a coma, but it really isn't."

Annie nodded. "That's probably what the Indians liked about it."

The doctor continued. "When this happens, we just have to make sure the heart keeps pumping and lungs keep breathing and it wears away. I think that's what occurred here. You can see him now, but don't wear him out."

Judy rushed to Ben's side with tears streaming down her face. "God, I'm glad you're alive!"

"Whoa," he said, weakly, "I'm not ready to check out."

"Hey, amigo," Skeet said.

"So," Annie added, "you dudes over this Iron John stuff now?"

"What happened?" Ben asked, confused.

"You drank coyote melon," Judy explained.

Ben looked perplexed.

After Judy explained, Annie asked Ben the same questions she'd asked Skeet and Juan and the others, and the answers were the same. No one knew how or when the plant extract got into the bottle, and no one could say for whom it was meant. Possibly it was meant for no one in particular. Possibly some nut was just poisoning people for the fun of it.

But Annie doubted that.

She doubted it so much, she boarded a flight to Phoenix late that very afternoon.

That afternoon, Annie found herself in a Chevy Blazer, holding on for dear life in the passenger seat, as Detective Peter White drove over rocks and gullies, arroyos that had been formed as water cut into the sloping mounds of sand. White was the Scottsdale detective who'd headed the investigation into the death of Kyle Hulsebus. He laughed at her discomfort. "You never got off-road?"

"Christ," Annie said, "I thought Scottsdale was like La Quinta, manicured and full of brand-new, smoothly paved streets."

"Thank God some of this is left."

Where they ended up—the spot where Kyle's body was found—surprised Annie. Yes, it was in the middle of nowhere, in the forbidding terrain of the Arizona desert, but so was all of Scottsdale. What shocked her was that the crime scene turned out to be only feet from a walled compound enclosing a million-dollar estate. "I thought we were gonna be on the moonscape, and here we're next to Mar Lago."

"The Rupp property." White nodded toward the wall. "Raymond Rupp, big industrialist, some kind of machinery, don't ask me what."

"Can't believe the victim was found this close to

a house." Annie looked back the way they'd come, up a dirt path. "What's this road for?"

"Service. Underground telephone, cable, water, sewers. Used it building the place too, I assume."

"Where was Kyle's truck found?"

" 'Bout a quarter mile back."

"Signs of a scuffle getting him to where he died? Tire tracks?"

"Listen, it doesn't take more than one person to ingest Thorn-Apple."

"Humor me."

The big man shrugged and lit a cigarette. "We had a storm before we found him. Footprints, anything and everything, were washed away by the downpour."

Annie pondered. "If he was killed, would—?"

"Killed?" The man looked surprised. "Addict's overdose, pure and simple."

"Humor me some more," she continued. "If someone killed him, they could have come from the Rupp place, over the wall, covered their tracks, and jumped back over."

The man nodded. He blew out a thin line of smoke. It was an interesting theory, appealed to the investigator in him. But he didn't buy it. "They got angry mutts back there, security, all the usual stuff that goes with a place like that. They're never there anyhow, which makes them guard it even more."

"Or," Annie pointed out, "makes it easier for someone who knows the security to get in and out."

"If you say so."

"What do you know about desert plants?" Annie asked.

"A fair amount. I know that Thorn-Apple kills."

"It plentiful?"

He stomped the cigarette into the sand and pointed toward the wall. "See there?" She saw a fairly large spread of rich green leaves on the ground, sprinkled with brilliant white flowers, stamens to the sun. They looked completely harmless. "That's it," he said.

Annie walked over to the plants and crouched. She remembered that she'd found them growing in her yard when she bought the house in Palm Springs. Juan had told her what it was. "You know," she said after she'd studied them a while, "from over there they look gorgeous, like lilies or something. But when you get close, they're scary. The texture of the leaves, the perfection of the flower, there's something creepy about it."

"It's a weed, that's why," the cop said.

"No, on a different level. I know why the Indians felt so strongly about it, why it was so important to them. It's amazing." She moved her fingers to the blossom nearest her, was about to touch it, but thought better of it.

"Good idea," White said, "stay away. Even a drop of the juice from it can cause disorientation."

Annie drove back to the station with the man, made copies of the records on the short investigation into the death of this "drifter," and accepted a ride from the detective back to the airport. "Sorry we couldn't help you more," he said as she got out of the Blazer.

"I think I got more than I was expecting," Annie said, and waved good-bye.

Inside, she had a beer while waiting for her delayed flight to Palm Springs. She dialed her cell phone. "Selma?" she asked, hearing the familiar voice. "Annie."

"Hi."

"I'm in Phoenix, stuck a while. America West seems to be east somewhere. I got a question."

"Shoot."

"Something is gnawing at me. Remember the poop sheet on Juan Torres? There was an offense in Arizona."

"Yes."

"Remember what city?"

"Hmmm. Seems to me," Selma said, giving it thought, "it was Scottsdale."

Ben quickly recovered, spent a night with Judy, and returned to San Diego, where his students awaited him and couldn't wait to hear about his brush with death.

The next night, Ben called as usual, but he sounded anything but happy. "What's wrong?"

"Some . . . problems."

"Problems?"

"At school."

"Oh." She'd never heard him sound like this before. It was like all the life had been drained from his voice. "Anything you want to talk about?"

He didn't answer. There was a long pause. Again, unlike him.

Judy jumped in again. "Okay, listen, I have those days too, work stuff gets you down. If you don't want to talk about it, we won't talk about it. Just know I'm always here."

"I do."

But she heard some kind of fear in his throat. "Ben, you sure you're okay?"

"It's just some heavy stuff."

"I love you."

He brightened. "I love you too. Listen, I think I can pry a few days off and come up in a week or two."

"I'd love it. Or I'll come down."

"It's a plan."

At midnight, Judy was in the former third bedroom that they'd turned into a cozy office/den when she heard the front door open. She set her book in her lap, expecting Skeet to walk in, but it was Annie instead. "Where have you been?"

"Illinois, Arizona, Phoenix airport forever, then Cathedral Canyon Country Club to see Selma, all for the same reason."

Judy didn't know what to make of that. "For what?"

"To find out who killed Norman. And maybe all the rest of them."

Judy was befuddled. "Huh?"

Annie was apprehensive about sharing what she knew with Judy, but if Judy was the object of some person's obsession, then who better to answer questions that could shed light on the story than Judy herself? "Go with a what-if for a minute, okay?"

Judy nodded. "What if what?"

"What if some guy wanted you all for himself, but never could really approach you?"

"Like in his mind?"

"Right."

"What's this got to do with anything?"

"What if Norman was killed because the guy perceived Norman getting too close to you?"

Judy turned white. "You're kidding."

"What if Kyle Hulsebus was killed for the same reason? The waiter too."

"Kyle? Killed?"

Annie nodded. "I saw where they found him. In the Arizona desert. I knew he was dead because I visited his mother."

The book slid from Judy's lap to the floor. "Kyle really is dead? Him too?"

Annie told her everything she knew about Kyle. Judy was shocked, and saddened, but she did admit that he had done drugs. It was one of the problems with their affair, he was often too stoned to perform. He kept wanting her to leave Skeet for him, and she wouldn't do it, so she thought he just moved on. But the death by Jimson or Thorn-Apple stunned her. "He never mentioned any interest in plants or stuff like that. That was Craig's thing, not Kyle's."

"Plants weren't Norman's thing either, if I recall."

"Jesus, Annie."

"What if these guys were all murdered by the same man? Troy as well. And the attempt on Ben."

Judy looked chilled, despite the embers glowing warmly in the fireplace. "Now you're really scaring me."

"I know this is like Desert Dick dicking around," Annie apologized, "but I gotta wonder, what if in this pattern the common denominator is you?"

"My God." Judy could feel goose bumps covering her whole body. "Somebody killed them because they were too close to me?"

"Yes."

Judy shook her head and laughed out loud. "Troy and I weren't close."

"It's in the perception. He had a crush on you."

Judy blinked. "God, who?"

Annie took a deep breath. "Juan."

Judy felt the breath go out of her for a moment, then she grinned. "That's nuts."

"He feels close to you but can't communicate it, has a passion for you yet isn't self-confident enough to tell you. I think he might be so sick as to eliminate any man he perceives as a threat."

"Oh, puh-leez." Judy drew her feet up under her. "You're writing fiction again."

"Juan has an unhealthy obsession with you. He brought the water to the sweat house. He could have been in San Diego County the night Troy died. He—"

"We all know Juan likes me, but to jump to—"

"He steals your underwear."

Judy gasped. "What?"

"He writes about you. Has pictures of you. Your toothbrush. He took your bikini top from out by the pool the other day. I witnessed it."

"How do you know all this?"

"I've been in his house. The boy's got a problem."

Judy got up. "I'm not going to listen to this. This is just too out there."

Annie followed her into the kitchen. "His shack is filled with books on plants, on Indian rituals and medicine, and he's a goddamned gardener! He warned me away from Jimsonweed the first day I met him. And he's a got a violent side, been arrested several times, and he's a liar."

Judy whirled around. "Why is he a liar? I think you hate him for whatever that was all about in the restaurant parking lot."

"That was about my suspicions. Shit, I should have dug a little deeper before I told you any of this."

"I'll say." Judy started unloading the dishwasher. "It's preposterous. It's upsetting. It's stupid anyway, Juan couldn't have known Craig all that long ago."

"It was only ten years ago," Annie reminded her. "He's been in this country for twelve years. And he was old enough to kill when he arrived."

Judy slammed two pans into a cabinet, nervously started putting the coffee mugs away. "Boy, you know a lot about him. How much of it have you 'written'? How much is fiction?"

"Why defend him so? He's not your brother."

"He is a decent person."

"So was that clown who murdered all those boys in Chicago. What a wonderful man! You hear it about every serial killer."

"Juan's no serial killer. Those deaths don't connect because of me." She squeezed the Tupperware bowl she'd just pulled from the dishwasher so tightly it started to crack. "I'm not the reason they died!"

"Honey," Annie informed her, "those dishes are dirty."

Judy looked down to see chunks of leftovers in the Tupperware. The coffee mugs were covered with encrusted brown spots. She didn't know what she was doing. She closed the dishwasher and rinsed her hands. "I don't think you have anything but a wacky theory."

"Maybe. But maybe not." Annie sat at the island. "I did learn one thing tonight that prompted me to come here. Selma learned about a conviction Juan had in Arizona."

"Arizona?"

"Yeah, Arizona, where Kyle died."

"What was it?"

"Possession. Served a little time, first offense. More interesting was where he worked when he was in Arizona."

"Where?" Judy asked, drying her hands so hard it looked like she was trying to rub her skin off.

"Big steel magnate named Rupp."

"So?" It meant nothing to Judy.

"So Kyle Hulsebus's body was found about twenty feet from the back wall of the Rupp estate in Scottsdale."

Judy gulped.

Skeet walked in. Within seconds, he'd joined the discussion. At first he was on Judy's side, believing this was preposterous, defending Juan. But the fact of Kyle's body having been discovered, of all places almost on the property Juan had once tended, was too pat to write off as coincidence. When Annie zeroed in on the night of Norman's murder, Skeet sent a shiver through all of them when he went over what he knew about that evening.

He realized that he had no idea where Juan really was from about nine in the evening, after he finished his meal at Fancies Beverly Hills, till the next morning, when Juan drove the truck with the table back to the desert. Skeet returned to the apartment at about two a.m., where he saw Juan asleep in the guest room. Skeet reluctantly surmised that Juan *could have* gone down to the marina, killed Norman, and driven back to the apartment before Skeet got there. He could have parked his truck in a convenient place on the street so as to then use the "sprinkler in the window" story to explain away the wet seat. "Come to think of it," Skeet said, "he never reacted to Norman's death much. He had met him too."

Annie perked up. "He had?"

"Yes," Judy explained, "when Norman came out for a few days. He missed the water," she remembered fondly, "and kept saying it was too damned hot."

"How did they get along?"

"Norman complimented Juan on his artistry," Skeet recalled.

"Did Juan know Kyle?" Annie asked both of them.

"Of course," Skeet answered.

"They went out drinking together a few times," Judy admitted, which was news even to Skeet. "We ran into Juan on El Paseo one night, and he joined us for dinner at Locanda Toscana."

"They get along?"

"It seemed like it. They were about the same age, both sort of loners. They were desert rats and had stuff in common."

"Drugs?" Annie asked.

Judy shook her head. "Not Juan. In fact, I think that's why they didn't really become buddies. After they knocked around together a couple of times, Kyle told me he was tired of Juan getting smashed on two drinks, and Juan didn't like Kyle's doing coke."

"Did Juan know Troy?"

"In passing, they could have," Skeet said. "Juan was often at the restaurant. Troy talked about an 'instructor.' Guess it could have been Juan." Skeet shook his head. "Oh, it's just nuts."

Judy recalled, "Juan was in the yard one morning that Troy brought dishes over to taste. Right after Norman died."

Annie asked, "Ever hear any of them talk about Jimsonweed?"

"What?" Skeet said.

"Never mind. How about opium?"

Skeet reacted. "Opium? I'm curious. Why?"

"Report on Craig's death indicates they found a fair amount of Chinese opium in his place after he died."

"It happened *before* he died, about a week before," Judy said. "He was scared to death, could barely tell me. He wanted no one to know, because it could have ruined his career—I mean, a professor being charged with possession, that can really screw up your life."

"The opium?"

Judy nodded. "He'd gone to China. I wanted to go with him, but had to work. My first project with Charlie Trotter in Chicago, I couldn't turn it down. When he got back, he was very agitated and upset. Said someone set him up. Someone had mailed him, from his hotel, on the last day he was in Shanghai, a parcel filled with lacquered Chinese boxes. Of course, it looked like he'd sent it to himself."

"What was inside?" Skeet asked.

"Incense, herbal medicines. But more. Bear's claw and something they make from the gall bladder, other animals as well, all from endangered species, all very illegal."

"I knew that's why you believe he killed himself," Skeet said to Judy, "the trouble he was in was overwhelming. But where does opium come into play?"

"It was in one of the boxes as well."

Annie got herself a beer. "Either Craig was moonlighting as an importer, or someone really set out to destroy him." She popped the cap. "You know, opium comes from poppies, another flower, another plant you could call dangerous, I guess." She took a slug of the Anchor Steam. "Anyone else want one?"

Skeet ignored her. "Something just dawned on me. If this nut—I still can't believe it's our Juan—is bumping off all the guys he thinks Judy loved, then I'm fucking next."

"No," Judy said, paralyzed with fear suddenly. "He, whoever he is, would have killed you a long time ago. You're no threat for some reason. No, if he's murdering the guys I love, that water last Saturday was meant for Ben. Ben is next."

Dear Diary:

He used opium many times. The first time was when he returned from a conference at Berkeley. He had gone to Chinatown, to an old dealer there who was said to have the finest opium China had to offer. Someone said it had actually come from Burma. It did not matter to him. It was good.

It was very much like being in the sweat house, he said, the high was so much like the old Indian plant extracts. That was his quest, to relive that experience and gain on it. Never satisfied with the knowledge he got, each time had to be more intense, more exotic, pushed finally to the very edge. He was not Indian. He did not understand.

He would have died anyway, had I not killed him. He would have done himself in, for the addict is never satisfied, he always longs for more. And he would have died in the very same way, trying to reach the place of supreme wisdom, as the Indians had, with the help of natural potions, our forefathers' medicines.

I only helped him get there sooner.

His was a long, excruciating death, worse even than Kyle's out in the desert.

But it saved Judy.

Chapter Twenty-one

Ben hopped a commuter flight to Palm Springs the following Friday night, and Judy drove him directly form the airport to Korakia Pensione, her favorite place to stay in the desert. He'd sounded distant all week long, bothered by the pressures and problems at school, but kept telling her not to worry, it would work out. She didn't press, instead made him look forward to a relaxing, loving weekend in an idyllic place.

He got more than he'd bargained for. As they turned onto Patencio Road, Ben heard music, Latin salsa strains that stirred the soul. It was coming from inside Korakia's front courtyard, across the street from where Judy parked. He could see what looked like a million twinkling lights and burning candles everywhere, a band set up in the corner of the patio, and people dancing through the leafy green of a grapefruit tree. Judy took his hand as they crossed the street. "Doug is giving a party tonight."

"Doug?"

"Doug Smith, the owner, and a fascinating man."

"Yeah, I think Skeet mentioned him at Passover."

Indeed, the minute they pushed open the big, rusted steel gate, Doug, an affable man with spirit and zest for life, hurried to Judy and hugged her. He greeted Ben with a firm handshake and a warm welcome. "You've got the Nash House, if that's okay."

Judy explained to Ben, "It's the old Mediterranean villa across the street that once belonged to J. Carol Nash and is now part of the hotel."

"Give me the keys to the car," Doug said, "Melissa will take your things inside and start the fireplace."

Judy handed them over. "Who's the group?" The music was infectious.

"Pink Martini, they're called, from Portland. That's China Forbes singing. Amazing, huh?"

The singer was performing a haunting rendition of "Que Sera, Sera." "She's wonderful," Judy remarked.

"Wow," Ben said. Looking around, he drank in the place. "Moorish? Moroccan?"

Doug said, "It was built by Scottish painter Gordon Courts, who tried to recreate his earlier life in Tangier."

"Korakia means 'crows' in Greek, right?" Ben asked.

Doug was impressed. "First time I can recall that I didn't need to answer that question."

"Doug owned a café in Greece before this," Judy said. "Watering hole for Mick Jagger and Jackie O."

"And next," Doug offered with enthusiasm, "is

Havana, and I don't care who comes. Whenever I can do it, I'm buying a hotel there. That's where I really want to live."

Ben and Judy settled into taverna-style chairs on the stone patio, listened to the fabulous band, and held hands. Jennifer, a dark-haired beauty, poured them some good Greek retsina, and they enjoyed the music in the lush tranquility. Pink Martini did "Amado Mio," and they got up and danced, half-tango, half-samba, smiling every moment. The band did "Never on Sunday" and they danced slowly. They kissed before the song ended, and Judy took his hand and let him through the keyhole arch and carved Islamic double doors into another world.

They stopped in front of a roaring outdoor fireplace, looking down at the black-tile crow at the bottom of the dagger-shaped swimming pool, glistening in the night, and they felt a stillness that detached them from the rest of the world. Intimacy rushed through them like a powerful potion, calming and securing them in their love. They held one another and felt they were the only two people in the world. In the air, the strains of "Andalucia" echoed against the mountains.

The Nash House was a suite of five rooms they never wanted to leave. It had high wood-beamed ceilings and a massive fireplace. There was a sun porch, dining room, secluded patio, full kitchen, and, in the bathroom, a bathtub made of the same granite desert rocks as the walls and floors of the villa. They slept in each other's arms in the hand-carved four-poster bed, surrounded by Oriental carpets, turn-of-the-century Italian tables, chairs from Afghanistan, pillows from Macedonia, and a Thai sofa. It was the most romantic night, Ben said, of his life.

In the morning, they ate breakfast in the courtyard where they'd enjoyed Pink Martini, feeling the rays of the morning desert sun, surrounded by citrus and olive trees, date palms and bougainvillea. Donatella Versace and two bodyguards were eating scrambled eggs with chives and toast to the left of them, while on the right Susan Sarandon was conversing with Andy Garcia, who looked like he was still asleep. "How'd we ever wangle a room here?" Ben joked.

"Pays to know the owner," Judy joked right back.

After breakfast, they sat on the swing under an old lemon tree, and shared minted iced tea. Judy tried to get Ben to talk about the trouble down in San Diego. "Problems with students? Faculty? Too much work? Some kid bring a gun to class?"

"Hey, I said it isn't that big a deal, just the shit you go through, you know. I want to talk about happy things. Like our future. I want to be with you more than I can say."

She smiled and took his hand. "I've gotten a real scare," she admitted. "Not so happy here."

"How so?"

She told him about Annie's suspicions of Juan. That Annie felt Judy might link the motivations. Ben was fascinated, and surprisingly interested in the details, grilling her on every aspect of the drugs, of Craig's search for Indian hallucinogens, about the opium, Troy's crush, Kyle's addictive behavior. When she asked him why, he said he was just curious. "Like hell," she challenged. "I know you better than that, even in this short time. There's something you're not telling me."

"That's my problem at school."

Her heart skipped a beat. "What?"

"Drugs."

"Whose drugs?" she gasped. "What? Explain!"

"A few weeks ago, I get a call from this parent who wants to know if their kid was making up a story, like if the boy was mad at me or something, or did I really provide drugs to kids?"

"Jesus."

Ben nodded. "Well, I know the student, and no, there's no bad blood between us, so I told the father it was ludicrous, and then talked to the boy about it. He would only say that 'someone told him' that I sold drugs."

"Who?"

Ben shrugged. "Wouldn't say. I wrote it off as ridiculous. Somebody was mad at me for flunking them on a paper or something and got their revenge making accusations."

"But that wasn't the end of it?" Judy surmised.

"Then the shit hit the fan." Ben took a long sip of his tea. He played with the sprig of mint in the glass. He was obviously troubled. "The parents of a girl I have in two classes found a discarded printed e-mail note telling her where to go to get drugs at school: from Mr. Spiegel. They went to the principal, who wrote it off as a prank."

"Same kid probably."

Ben nodded. "That's what I thought. Then there was an e-mail all about me, a guy who taught a course in Indian studies, 'experimenting' with dangerous drugs in a sweat house. And the article from the *Desert Sun* about me almost croaking of poison plants in the sweat house. Shortly after that, the enterprising parents of that girl's best friend, parents who, unlike most, are computer literate, start doing a search about Mr. Spiegel. Apparently, the rumor wouldn't die, or it was being spread some more. They found that I'd been a drug addict, had been arrested in Malaysia, was thrown out of that country for that reason."

Judy was aghast. "That's preposterous."

"No," he said calmly, "that part is true."

She blinked. "True?"

"I got very fucked up on drugs in the Peace Corps. It's the reason I went to Paris to work in a bookstore. I was burned out, had to get my life back together."

She had no idea.

"I was arrested in Kuala Lumpur for possession, paid this shady lawyer every dime I had saved to get the charges dropped on the agreement that I leave the country forever."

"I'm speechless," she said softly.

"Man, the Information Age, huh?" He drank again. "Someone is trying to jeopardize my career."

"No," she said softly, "someone is trying to destroy you."

"I don't buy it," Annie said to Ben at lunchtime. He and Judy were sitting at Annie's kitchen table, eating donuts, which were the healthiest item in Annie's pantry, and drinking coffee. Annie bit into a chocolate one. "God, what this town needs is a good Krispy Kreme store."

"I agree," Ben said.

"It's too slick, too sophisticated for some enterprising student to have pulled off." She chewed the donut like it was a hard bagel.

Judy offered, "But any bright kid with a computer could have learned about his past."

"Yeah," Annie said, "I guess, but the point is, someone hates you."

"That's comforting," Ben said.

Judy told Annie, "We figured it was good sharing this with you because you might tell Ben what to do next."

"It's what the person who's out to get you will do next that I'm worried about," Annie answered.

"What do you think?" Judy asked her friend.

"Speaking as a writer," Annie offered to Ben, "and going on the stuff I've already learned, the stuff I assume she told you . . ."

Judy nodded. "I did."

Annie stared at Ben. "Well, the question then is, who perceives you as a threat?"

"Juan might," Judy answered, "but I just don't believe Juan could do this."

"Jesus," Annie said, "I just remembered something. I still have the cushion from his truck seat."

"Skeet," Ben said soberly. "He might find me threatening. Hell, he's the one who handed out the bottles."

"Randomly," Judy reminded him. "You said so yourself."

"Sort of."

"He's no killer either." Judy was firm. "That's nuts."

Ben tried to make a point. "Some people aren't what they appear to be."

Judy was hurt. "Ben, you can't think that about Skeet."

Ben shrugged. "Sorry."

Annie extended the thought. "In a novel, someone like Skeet would be too easy, too pat. It has to be someone more like the gardener, who keeps his passion secret but palpably fears his love is going to be 'taken' from him by the other, more gregarious man."

"Me?" Ben asked.

"You," Judy assured him.

"And Troy. And Norman. And Kyle. And Craig." Annie looked perplexed. "I have a question, Ben.

What kind of drugs did you get caught with in Malaysia?"

"Thai weed."

"No opium?"

"No way."

"No poison plants?"

Ben smiled. "I almost died from one. No, thanks."

Judy and Ben returned to Korakia and spent three hours at the pool. A woman was busy doing a charcoal sketch near the rock fireplace. A Disney executive was carrying on what seemed like ten conversations at once, albeit quietly, on three different cell phones. A girl was reading a potboiler, while another was reading Sartre. Ben fell asleep and slumbered for almost an hour.

When he woke, Judy was gone. He found her in the room, washing her hair in the rock-walled shower. He stripped off his bathing suit and joined her, soaping her hair, letting her do the same to him, then washing each other's bodies from head to toe with the bubbles and foam, and making love standing there with the aid of the slippery lather. Afterward, they basked in the glow of dusk over the mountains till they got hungry and walked to dinner at the old Las Casuelas.

When they went back to the hotel, he started painting, illustrating the Missy Potato stories, and Judy worked on sketches for her new Restaurant Associates project. Ben felt all the fears of what was going on back in San Diego fall far behind him. This was heaven. Secluded, romantic, and inspiring.

They didn't know that Juan was watching them through one of the windowpanes.

"Sandy," Annie said to the perky guard at the Cathedral Canyon Country Club West Gate, "I'm here to see Selma again. She leave a pass?"

"She forgets to call," the woman in the uniform said. "Go on in, honey."

"Thanks." Annie piloted the big Caddy to Calle Loreto, then turned right. Selma was out in front of her house, on her knees cutting roses. "For me?" Annie asked as she got out of the car.

"What you bringing me in return?" Selma joked.

Annie handed her a plastic bag filled with what looked like the stuffing of a pillow.

Selma gestured with her garden shears. "What's this?"

"Seat cushion."

"Sweet of you."

Annie smiled. "For the lab. Let me know if there's salt water in it, okay?"

"Salt water? That's all? No sweat, no blood?"

"Salt water, baby, that's it." Annie helped herself to the bouquet of bright roses from Selma's arm. "Hey, thanks. Great tradeoff, I must say."

Selma shook her head as Annie headed back toward her barge. "I'll give you the results at the gym," Selma teased.

"Bitch," Annie hissed, getting back into the car. "But hurry, okay? I got a feeling a very nice guy is being targeted as the next one to go."

"Who?"

"Just get the results and leave the details to me."

"Where have you been?" Skeet asked when Judy showed up at the house the next morning.

"Ben's in town."

"How are you and Ben doing?"

"I'm worried about him."

He looked concerned. "Why?"

She didn't answer, didn't want to go into the whole explanation. Instead she got to what was really on her mind. "Skeet, you've known Juan as long as I have, and you even know him better. Is there any chance that what Annie is dreaming could be true?"

He shook his head. "I swear, I've been asking myself the same thing. Last night on the plane, I really couldn't shake it."

"Plane?"

"Oh, I ran up to San Francisco; dinner with Alice."

"Waters?"

"What other Alice would I go to San Francisco for?"

"Sorry."

He listed his suspicions. "I can't help but think how odd it is that Kyle was found where Juan had worked. And that Juan's truck was seen leaving the marina after the murder. And the wet seat. And that he was alone at the time of the murder. And all that stuff about plants. And he brought the water to the sweat house. It gives me the creeps."

Annie waltzed in on that line. "That's nothing. I got more. Ready for this? I just got a call. Our friend Juan lied about something else as well. Judy, remember when I asked where his family was and you said all his other sisters are in Carcas? They're not. One is in Shanghai. In prison there, as a matter of fact."

Judy gasped. "Prison?"

"How'd you find this?" Skeet asked.

"Internet, took me all goddamned night, almost. She's in prison with her Chinese husband, a slick gangster she married to get her out of the poverty of South America."

"What are they in jail for?" Skeet asked.

"Drug smuggling."

Judy felt her stomach turn. "I have a feeling you're going to tell us *what* drug."

Skeet nodded. "And that it isn't marijuana."

"That's right. Opium."

But it proved nothing. It just connected more of the dots. It raised suspicion, but the evidence was circumstantial at best; "out there," as Judy put it: incomplete and inconclusive. When Judy and Annie drove over to Korakia together to fill Ben in on the news, they found Ben painting out by the fountain near the pool. Annie told him she'd spent a good part of the night looking into his problem with his school situation. He was eager to know if she learned anything.

"You had a teaching assistant named Alex Keaton?"

Ben reacted with wide eyes. "How'd you learn that?"

"Anything's possible," Annie assured him.

"I was instrumental in having him fired because I learned he was doing crystal meth."

"And he's got a brother named Oliver?" Annie questioned.

"He was arrested about six months back. Dealing. Didn't serve any time, though. Rich family."

"But if you blew the whistle," Annie surmised, "alerting the San Diego authorities to a user, and he lost his job because of you, and then ultimately his brother gets caught as well, you really don't think they'll be sending you Christmas cards, now, do you?"

Ben looked shocked. "They did it?"

"Wouldn't surprise me."

"My God. What can I do about it?"

"Prove it," Annie said. "Of course, we don't want to get into trouble like that beautiful paragon of American virtue Linda Tripp did, we don't want wiretapping charges hounding us. So I talked to a private dick I once met at a convention who works out of Oceanside. He's going to do some fancy computer surveillance for me."

"You'll find out if the Keaton brothers really did it?"

She shook her head. "We have to wait for the next shoe to drop. But it will, that's for sure."

Judy, who'd listened silently to all this, looked very relieved. "Then this has nothing to do with me? Nothing to do with Norman, Kyle, Troy, or Craig?"

"Hope not," Annie said.

Judy closed her eyes. "Then you're not being hounded because of me."

Ben took her hand and squeezed it. "For you, I could deal with it. But these punks back home, that really pisses me off."

"Good!" Annie exclaimed. "That's a healthy place to be when you're being made to be the victim."

She left Judy there with Ben and returned home to write. When she pulled in to her driveway, there was Juan's truck in front of Judy's house. And Juan himself shooting daggers through her as he stood holding a blower, sending bougainvillea leaves—almost with delightful scorn—over into Annie's yard.

She eyed him back, a challenging look that communicated *I'm onto you.*

Fuck you, lady, his look sent back.

Annie watched Juan from a window for half an hour, trying to put the pieces together, and then gave up staring and went back to her computer. But the sight of the same screen she'd been staring at all night long made her head hurt. She closed her eyes, leaned back in her comfy leather armchair, and fell asleep in seconds.

* * *

Ben and Judy enjoyed an exhibit at the Desert Museum, then had crisp salads and iced coffee at California Pizza Kitchen. They started talking about what Ben was going to do for the summer, when school was out—which was not that far off. "I'm thinking about spending the summer here."

She brightened with enthusiasm. "I love it. Everyone is gone, that's what makes it so special, no blue-haired old ladies in Cadillacs they can't see over the hood of, no lines in the stores, no waiting for the movies. It's hot, but the humidity, except when storms come up from Mexico, is low, so it doesn't feel as bad as it does back East. I'll be working on Fancies Los Cabos a lot, I think, so we'll go down there and play. Ever been?"

"Nope."

"It's a great place."

"But we won't be staying in that villa Skeet built you."

She agreed. "No, we won't."

He smiled. "I'd hoped to go to Argentina. But I don't think I can afford it. And I wouldn't want to go without you now."

"Oh, I'd love that," she said exuberantly. "Maybe on our—" She stopped herself, not daring to say the word she was thinking. "On our first vacation together."

But he knew what she wanted to say. "Honeymoon?"

She looked dreamy.

Ben reached into his backpack. "I brought this with me this trip, and I've been trying to figure out the right time to give it to you. I reached for it about ten times at Korakia, but I always think the next moment is going to be the better one. So I've decided to give it to you now, in what is possibly the most unromantic spot in the desert."

"What?" She watched him fish out a ring box.

"It's from my heart."

Judy took the box from his shaking hand. She opened it and found a simple, exquisite diamond ring. "Oh, Ben."

"This is a dumb place to do this," he said, looking around the busy patio, seeing the shoppers walking up and down the street.

She was paying no attention to them. "Oh, my," she said as she slipped the ring onto her finger.

"I had it sized from another one when you were sleeping one night."

"It's just beautiful."

"So are you," he whispered, taking her hand. "So, Judy Sussman, will you marry me?"

"Yes, Ben, I will."

He leaned back in his chair. "Didn't know that was going to be so difficult to do!"

"I'm overwhelmed," she said, staring at the diamond.

"I know it's fast. We haven't known each other that long."

"Oh, but we have. We've known each other a lifetime but just didn't realize it," she answered, then bent forward and kissed him. "Argentina for the honeymoon. I've got a ton of TWA miles. We can fly nonstop LAX to San Juan, then take a partner down to Buenos Aires."

"I've got enough saved for the hotel," Ben said.

"It's a deal." She lifted her iced tea. "Or maybe a cruise."

"I love you," Ben said, clicking his glass to hers.

She suddenly grinned mischievously. "I want to elope."

He laughed out loud. "Your mom would die."

"Honest, I don't want to wait. I don't want a big dragged-out formal affair."

Ben shook his head. "I don't either, but your family would never forgive you. Only child, remember?"

She took a deep breath. "And a girl yet. How about your family?"

"I don't think they'd like the elopement idea either. How about if we just did it real soon?"

"Yes!"

"When?"

"June," she said, "a June bride, right after school's out for you."

"That's only a little more than two weeks away."

She loved it. "Yes!" It was a pact.

"Want company?" They both turned. It was her mother. Esther and Henry were standing there, arms loaded with bags.

Ben stood. "Hi, welcome," he said, pulling out a

chair at their table for Esther. Henry went around to the other empty one. "What are you two doing? Buying out the city?"

"Not a dime," Esther said proudly, piling the bags on the ground. "Collecting donations for AIDS Assistance League. I'm chairing their gala."

"Good for you," Judy said.

"Which reminds me," Esther said to her daughter, "you've got a sketch Norman did of the Santa Monica building. The one in color. It's signed. Do you think you'd want to part with it?"

Judy looked unsure, for it meant something to her.

"It would bring in a lot of money," Ben said.

"Thank you," Esther said to him with a nod. "Judy, come on, you have others."

Judy agreed. "Sure. Norman would have liked that."

Esther laughed. "That stingy old goat? Sat on the board of every charity know to man, but give himself? It was only right he left everything to an animal shelter, makes up for his past sins."

Judy said, "Why don't you donate a painting, Ben?"

Esther loved it. "That would be terrific."

"Done," Ben said, pleased.

"Ben," Henry Sussman said, changing the subject, "how long you in town?"

"One more day. Just a weekend jaunt."

"Join us for dinner tonight."

Esther threw him a look. "I'm not in the mood to cook."

"We'll go to the Ritz Carlton."

Esther and Henry ordered iced teas from the waiter, and when he walked away, Esther said, "Okay, you two, what's new?"

"Oh, boy," Ben said.

"You want the good news or the bad news first?"

"Good news first always," Esther answered.

Judy merely held up her hand. "Look."

"Oh!" Esther exclaimed so loudly half the patio turned to her. "Oh, my God! I didn't notice, I didn't see!" She looked at Ben. He nodded with a smile at her approval. "Oh, I'm so happy for you both!"

Henry, with the reaction of a typical father to his only girl, gave Judy a look that asked, are you sure about this? She nodded. He turned to Ben, extended his hand, and said, "Welcome to the family, son."

They talked for a few minutes about their engagement, Judy and Ben agreeing they wanted to be married as soon as possible, Esther already thinking about which rabbi, which hotel, how big, until Judy said she and Ben would decide all that. "Mother of the bride syndrome," Esther sighed, "what can I say?"

"We are planning to be married as soon as school is finished for Ben."

Esther nodded. "And when is that?"

"Little over two weeks."

Esther looked like she had been slapped. "You must be kidding."

Ben took Judy's hand. "We decided we want to do this as fast as we can."

"That won't even give me time to get my hair done," Esther moaned. "Henry, talk them out of this."

Henry said, "I rather like the idea, if you want to know the truth."

"Second weekend in June," Judy said firmly.

"Right," Ben agreed, figuring the less planning and fussing the better.

"So," Henry piped in, "what was this bad news you mentioned?"

"You asked for it," Judy warned them, and then started to tell them everything they knew about Annie's suspicions of Juan.

When Judy pulled up to her house two hours later, Juan was still working in the yard. Neither of them had thought about or prepared for the meeting. How would she react to Juan the next time she saw him? On one hand, she was as suspicious as Annie. On the other, he'd never done anything but treat her with respect and admiration.

"Buenas tardes," Juan said warmly.

But she could not mask her reaction. She now saw Juan in a different light. Even though she said, "Afternoon, Juan," her voice quavered.

"What's wrong, Miss Judy?"

"Nothing."

"I did something?"

"No. It's just me." She tried to smile, but she had never been good at masking her feelings. She was thinking of what Annie said about stealing her underwear. She thought of him falling asleep looking at a photograph of her. She saw him looking strange that morning she'd found the truck seat wet—or was it only now in retrospect that she was noticing that?

"It's her, isn't it?" he said.

She focused, pulling her mind back to the moment. "Who?"

"Her." He gestured toward Annie, who could be seen watching them from the window of her office. "She poisoned your mind against me."

Amazing choice of words, Judy thought. She gave Annie a little wave, but Annie didn't respond. "Annie is my dearest friend," Judy said, trying to make him understand that she would indeed listen to Annie if she had a problem with Juan.

"Fat bitch, she hates me," he said. "I'm sorry for speaking so about your friend. She is very evil. I do not like her."

"She's a private investigator," Judy said in an apologetic tone. "She has to follow her hunches, even if she is wrong."

He spat toward Annie's property. "She has hurt my good name."

"Juan," Judy said, "calm down."

He glared at Annie till she pulled the window curtain. "She will destroy my future here," he predicted. "Our friendship."

Judy thought, yes, that is most likely true. But she wasn't willing yet to end that relationship. She hoped Annie's hunches *were* wrong, dead wrong. "Everything is going to be fine, Juan. Now, excuse me, I have to go inside."

About twenty minutes later, as she finished washing her hair in the kitchen sink, a quirk of hers when she didn't want to shower for the second time in a day, she found Juan standing about four feet from her. She jumped. "Christ!"

"Sorry, Miss Judy," he said, removing his floppy-brimmed sun hat. He held seven tall roses whose buds were just about to open in his hand. "First blooms from the new plants on the south side."

She caught her breath. Wrapping her head in a towel that she fashioned into a turban, she took the roses from Juan with a nod, plopped them into a drinking glass and ran some water into it.

He stood there, watching. When it was obvious she was not going to say anything more, he took a step backward, put his hat back on, and said, "Adios, then."

When he got to the door, her voice stopped him. "Juan, I think from now on, whenever you want to come inside, you should knock."

"Oh?" It caught him by surprise.

"Yes, it would just be right, don't you think?"

No, it was clear from his face, he didn't think. But

he nodded. Then, as he left, he gave Annie's house a look of anger, knowing that he'd been right, she was going to ruin things with Judy, everything.

Henry and Esther Sussman had an argument when Judy phoned them to say that Skeet wouldn't let them go to the Ritz Carlton for dinner. He insisted they all come to Fancies. He was going to give them a proper engagement party and he wouldn't take no for an answer. Esther didn't want to do it, she was "tired" of Fancies already, but Henry won out. If Skeet wanted to help them celebrate in style, they should let him do it.

So to Fancies they went. And the evening turned out to be delightful. Skeet gave them the best table in the house, poured the finest merlot he had in the well-stocked cellar, and made a gracious toast. "I want my best friend, my soul mate, on this earth to be happy, and I think she's going to be very happy with Ben." They all smiled and drank the wine.

But then, just before the salads were served, Ben said to the waitress, "I know this sounds silly, and everyone forgive me for being so gauche, but could I have some ice? I sometimes like to put it in my red wine."

Judy froze, but wasn't exactly sure why. It rang a bell, but she couldn't place where or when. All she knew was that it bothered her.

Chapter Twenty-two

While the Sussman party was dining in Palm Springs, Annie Chestnut was sneaking around Juan Torres's little house in Cathedral City. She had followed him when he left Judy's place that afternoon to another client's, where he worked for about an hour, and then home. She waited down the street, at the corner as she'd done before, until he departed again. This time she followed him. He took Date Palm Drive to Dinah Shore, turned right, drove all the way past Mission Hills Country Club to the movie theaters out near the Home Depot store. When she saw him purchase a ticket and enter the theater, she knew she had, for sure, two hours. It would take her fifteen minutes to get back to his house, but it would take him that time to return as well.

She picked the lock in less than a minute, and went directly to the first bookshelf. There they were, all the books on poison and medicinal plants. One of them was the exact one that Jeb Kresge had sent Annie. There was a book on Cahuilla Indian medicine that had been well read. She pulled it from the shelf and saw that a page had been dog-eared. On that page: Jimsonweed.

She walked to his bedroom. She hadn't looked under the bed the first time, and was glad she did now. Boxes holding about twenty yellow pads filled with his handwriting sat in the dust underneath. She withdrew one and hurried through it. Poems to Judy. Musings on Judy's beauty. A whole page on how to protect Judy—from what? Unimaginable monsters? The night? She couldn't tell. She scanned line after line, on page after page, and then bingo: *Kyle*. Pages and pages, some dated roughly when Judy and Kyle were having their affair, on Kyle. Nothing particularly hateful, but they weren't fan letters. Again, worry for Judy seemed to be the theme. He'd protect her? Ah, Annie thought, from Kyle.

In the next box, she found some kind of loony writings about a girl named April Rose—was that made up?—and it seemed as though he forgot about Judy for about a month as he raged on and on about the gorgeous, attractive, angelic April Rose. Then it abruptly ended. She surmised that Daniel Heiss, whoever *he* was, had stolen the heart of this newly beloved, and left his heart pining again for Judy. It went on and on.

Annie tired of it, worried about the time, then tried the third box. This one was the oldest, and the name Craig Castle blinked like neon in the dim bed-stand light before her. Again and again, Craig Castle appeared, and it seemed as though Juan had known him but hadn't yet learned Judy's name! Could it be possible that Juan actually met Judy because of Craig? There were all kinds of references to Craig and their "spiritual quest." But they had to have known each other ten years ago, and no one was talking about "spirituality" then. Perhaps, she thought, he meant it in the Indian sense of the word.

Craig and Juan. It tweaked her imagination. This was no simple gardener, this was his cover. This was a guy who had been on the fringe of Judy's life for more than ten years, and she never knew it. He'd had some kind of relationship with her drug-addict college-professor lover. She'd never considered that, had wondered how in the world Juan could have been connected to Judy so long before he lived in the desert, but he would have been in this country already—she saw the date, perfect—and these papers answered that.

A line caught Annie's attention: *"I long for her, the gorgeous flower, the beautiful morning poppy blooming in the sun, the flower that Craig loved."* Poppies. Opium. Annie cringed. The bad poetry reminded her of when she was young and read Rod McKuen.

She slid the boxes back under the bed.

Then she checked the bathroom. Sure enough, in a drawer, a bag of BC Ultra-Fine II insulin syringes. Capable of penetrating a plastic water bottle without a trace, except under the scrutiny of a police lab, which concurred with Annie's theory that the poison had been injected into the water bottle by a syringe the exact size—8mm, 3/10 cc—of the bag she was looking at.

The computer was her next stop. She had less than an hour left. She had to find something more conclusive, not just boyish yearnings for a girl he couldn't have. The computer was in sleep mode, just like last time, and again she needed a password. She had thought about this. What did people usually use? A number, probably, which was usually some derivative of their birth date, social security number, ATM code, or license plate. Or they used a word. A word that would be so easy no one would guess it. She guessed. *Flower.* No go. *Juan Torres.* Nope. She tried just plain *Juan,* just *Torres,* then *Flowers, Cactus*: nothing. Then she tried *Gardener.* It didn't work. But it felt right to her. She shortened it to *Garden.* And she was in.

She hurried through Windows Explorer until she located the titles of his documents. A lot of shit on gardening, she thought, and clients. Then she saw a file called "nlempke.doc" and looked into it, her heart racing. It surprised her. It was a letter, unfinished, that he'd written to Norman reminding him that he'd liked Juan's work when he saw it at Judy and Skeet's, and that he would like the opportunity to do the same for him sometime. She saw that he couldn't spell worth a damn (and obviously hadn't put it through Spell Check), but the letter was certainly not suspect by any means.

Another file was called "hulsebus.doc." She looked

inside and found a letter he'd sent to Kyle, apologizing for the fight they'd had, but warning him strongly that Judy didn't deserve to be "lied to, and the drugs you do, man, are gonna catch up to you." Strange.

Nothing about Craig Castle, at least nothing she could find. Nothing about Troy Skinner.

But there was a document called "poppy.doc." She opened it and punched in a search for the name "Craig Castle." And found it. "Amazing about Craig Castle re opium." Annie's heart was in her throat. She punched in "Rupp." Sure enough, pages on someone named David—she guessed a son of the family—who was involved with his sister, Robin, it seemed, in the opium-smuggling scheme. So was Juan really the gardener out there in Scottsdale? Or was he involved with the Rupp kids in the smuggling? If he was, he could have had access to opium with which to frame Craig. This was finally making sense.

But Annie's fertile brain stopped charging as she saw, in the reflection of the screen in front of her, the image not only of her face, but of one directly behind her. She gasped, her fingers freezing on the keys, as she felt the hand on the back of her neck. Juan said, "Don't move a fucking inch, fat lady, or I'll kill you."

Annie thought it was best to believe him.

But she wasn't about to give up without a fight. "So, didn't like the film?"

"No."

"There is incriminating stuff here."

"Up yours," he said. "You're in big trouble. *Me entiendes?*"

"Me?"

"Break in my truck, break in my house. Why do you hate me?"

"I'm investigating crimes I think you know something about."

"You crazy—"

She turned slightly and saw that he had a piece of steel in his hand, something he had probably picked up in the yard. She didn't let it frighten her. "You want to confess?"

He laughed.

She tried to get her purse, which she'd set on the floor, closer to her reach. It was open wide at the top. Her gun would be easy to grab if she could find the chance.

But she had a surprise coming. Before she could say another word, two uniformed men entered the room, two Cathedral City cops with guns draw on her. "We'll take over now," the one cop said to Juan, who immediately dropped the piece of iron.

"Holy shit," Annie said, more stunned at the turn of events than worried how she'd get out of this pickle. "Now I'm really confused."

It took hours, but Annie talked her way out of trouble. She had been trespassing, yes, digging into someone's privacy without permission, but the lieutenant knew Selma and gave Annie the benefit of the doubt. The man talked with Juan for a long time as well, convincing him not to press charges, for which he'd get Annie's promise to stay away from him. Annie did have good reason to suspect Juan, and she made a convincing case why the police should consider him a suspect. The lieutenant elicited her promise to get what she knew to Tom Sparks at the LAPD.

"Harry's a good man," Selma said when she came to fetch Annie at the Cathedral City police station, adding, "but he could have busted you. *Should* have busted you."

"Thanks."

"You probably fed him a good line of crap."

Annie said, "Your being his neighbor helped a little too." She scratched her head uncomfortably. "Juan seemed more agreeable than I'd figure for someone with lots to hide."

"What the hell did you take that chance for?" Selma asked, driving Annie to her car, which was still parked down the street from Juan's house. "Why not get a warrant?"

"Don't have enough evidence to warrant one. Like my pun?"

"Stinks." Selma turned onto Highway 111. "You didn't find anything useful?"

"Yes, but I didn't have enough time. There are ties to everything, everyone, all the murders." Annie shook her head. "But why would he call the cops? Why would he risk getting arrested himself? That's what I don't get."

"Either he didn't do it or he doesn't think you can pin it on him."

Annie shrugged as she saw her car sitting there in the dark. "I don't know what to believe. The lieutenant didn't think I had enough for them to pull him in."

"Well," Selma said, parking behind Annie's finned wonder, "you do now." She handed Annie a slip of paper. "Lab report. Salt water on that seat stuffing, no doubt about it."

Dear Diary:

I am the shaman and I am the chosen poisoner.

His death was not peaceful. I learned he was in Arizona at the Rupp Compound. I knew who had sent him there. It was the right place to go when you were in trouble. I understood he was in very bad shape.

David said all he talked about was Judy, how he should never have left, how he was going to clean up his act, how he was going back for her. Robin said he was doing cocaine day and night and she wanted him out of there.

The Rupps were gone when I arrived. In fact, they never knew I had even come for him. Which was perfect, as it turned out. He was in worse shape than I had suspected, and thus had little fear of me, or any great suspicion or distrust of my helping him. It was relatively easy to get him to go "out into the desert," where we would visit the sweat house and purge ourselves of the poisons. He actually believed there was a sweat house nearby. He would have believed anything. I told him I knew he loved Judy and was going to help him go back and declare that love. He was naive. His trust was there.

We sat in the sand near his truck at midnight. It was cool. Still. He was getting anxious. He wanted the sweat house, the experience I had promised. I told him first he must take the shaman's liquor, the dream drug, to put him into receivership of knowledge, to empty his heart and allow it to fill again. He was so stoned, he would have believed anything. I gave him a full dropper of dreamweed on his tongue. He rolled over and over in the sand, gasping, trying to scream, but no cry would come. He tried to get up and was paralyzed, and he said he saw bears. He was not Indian. It was hallucination.

Then he crawled to his dinner in the sand. He died in anguish. I have written of his death already. His pain was great. He deserved every moment of it, and I knew this, and I wept for him. The poisoner weeps for his victim. No one misses him more.

Chapter Twenty-three

Ben and Judy, slathered with suntan oil, sat on matching chaises on the Sussman patio, overlooking one of the rich green fairways of The Reserve. Judy was tense, and Ben was well aware of it. After some small talk that neither of them had any enthusiasm for, he reached over, took her hand, and said, "What is it?"

She took a deep breath and adjusted her bikini top. "Something you said."

"Now we're getting someplace." He sat up, put his feet down on the hot patio decking, and faced her. "Tell me."

"You said you sometimes put ice in red wine."

"Yes."

"Ben!" Her eyes flashed.

"What? I know it's strange, but don't condemn me for it."

"It came to me this morning. I heard that about you from someone else."

He shrugged. "Huh?"

"Joan, the waitress, the woman in the airport that day. The one who said she knew you."

He blinked. "That woman moving to La Jolla? On American that day?"

"Yes. She said you're the guy who always put ice in his red wine."

"Lots of people do that."

She was startled. "Nobody I know has ever done that. Maybe with white, but never red."

"Well, it's a coincidence."

"Ben, come on, if you were here before, why not tell me? I mean, how many times have people said they thought they recognized you?"

Before he could say another word, Esther Sussman appeared, in a tizzy. "The Ingleside Inn, the Ritz, the Renaissance Esmerelda, and the Marriott are all booked for June," she announced. "Bighorn Country Club has an opening, but I'm not sure that's the right place." Then Esther had a thought. "Hmmm, how about here?"

Ben looked at Judy. Judy looked at Ben. The Reserve? Together they said, "No way." Judy put her sunglasses on, and hand in hand, they jumped into the pool.

Esther shrugged and went back inside.

Ben paddled the short distance toward his future bride and took her hand in the water. "It's coincidence, Judy. Why would I lie to you?"

"Dennis at the gym recognized you, too."

Ben shook his head.

Judy lifted her dark sunglasses and nodded. "Let's forget it."

"No. If you think—"

"It's over and done with. I trust you." Judy changed the subject. "I never liked big hotel weddings."

"Your mother obviously doesn't know that."

"She was married at the King Edward in Toronto. Mom was Canadian."

"I have an opinion."

She smiled. "Which is?"

"Tell your mom what *you* want."

She said nothing, considering the idea.

"Which is?" he prompted.

She looked desolate. "I don't know. I'm not sure. I never gave it much thought 'cause I never thought it would happen."

"Never subscribed to *Brides Magazine,* huh?"

She laughed as an idea came to her. "How about the top of the tram?"

He blinked. "Wow."

"I'm kidding."

"I like that."

"Ben, I'm joking."

"Think about it, it's meaningful because it's where we met. It's easy for everyone to get to, just a short ride in a tram car. It overlooks the world, so the view at night must be spectacular. And there's a restaurant up there, it'll hold a lot of people."

The idea was catching on. "We could have a sundown ceremony," she said, "so it could be on a Saturday."

Ben nodded. "It would be dark by the time we had the reception." The idea had real legs now. "I wonder if anyone's ever done that up there?"

"Oh, Ben, it could be so cool!"

"Middle of June? Cool?"

"It will be up there," Judy assured him. "And so what if it's hot? It's *our* wedding."

"Right on."

Esther came back outside. "Kay Pitts has offered her fabulous house at the Vintage Club! It's almost twenty thousand square feet—it's divine."

Judy yelled, "It's horrible! I adore Kay and Don, but their airport hangar is sterile, tacky, and frightening."

Esther slumped into one of the patio chairs. "Maybe Rancho La Quinta."

"We decided where we're doing it."

Esther looked down at them in the water. She could read in their faces that she wasn't going to like this. "Oh, don't tell me."

"The top of the tram."

"Oy." Esther looked like someone had just doused her with ice water.

"Where we met," Ben added.

"Oh, my God," Esther muttered, "you're serious."

Judy flipped off her raft and swam as close to her mother as she could. "Mom, you can do everything, find me the dress, fill the place with any flowers you want, decorate, plan, invite, it's all yours. But that's where we're doing it."

"If," Esther barked back, "they'll even let you get married up there."

Ben swam over to Judy. He put his arm around her in the water. "We'll persuade them," he said. "Besides, this way my mom and sisters can scratch the tram off their 'to do' list when they come out here for the wedding. We'll kill two birds with one stone."

"If it doesn't kill me first," Esther moaned.

Judy smiled. "It'll be wonderful, Mom. Unique. No one will ever forget it."

"Hmmm," Ben murmured, "one problem. I think my Aunt Sadie is afraid of heights."

Even Esther laughed. Then she stood up. "Okay, I'm calling the tram, going to check this out before we send out invitations and Dramamine. Hopefully they'll say no."

Ben followed Judy out of the pool, each grabbed a towel and dried off, then helped themselves to the pitcher of iced tea that Esther had put out for them earlier. "What time's your flight?" she asked him.

"Four."

"Mine's at eight, through Phoenix, last one down to Cabo for the night. Skeet always takes it."

"You're going together this time?" he inquired.

"Yes. We need to work together on the building down there. I've put it off for too long. I wish you could go with me."

"Me too. My heart will be there."

"What are you going to do next weekend?"

"Don't know yet. Probably have a long talk with

Mom, tell her our plans." Then concern came over his face. "What about all this stuff Annie's brought up? About Juan."

Judy shrugged. "I don't like to think about it because it gives me the creeps. I keep hoping she won't tell us more until she really knows for certain, or someone makes an arrest. There is nothing I can do anyway, so why live in fear?"

Ben feared for her, and he told her so as she kissed him good-bye at the curb at the airport. "I want you to be careful," he made her promise, "and listen to Annie. She knows a lot more about this than we do."

"A lot more than I want to."

She didn't strike him as a girl who practiced denial, but he understood her desire about this. He knew it would be difficult for her to distrust Juan until she knew something for certain, and he also was sure that she wanted not to feel blame even in a roundabout way for the deaths of the men who had, to some extent, loved her.

She was having the same thought all the way back to the house, and it worried her. Ben and Skeet were close to her, and someone had tried to kill one or both of them. She was mad at Annie. Why had she told them this stuff? Now Judy completely distrusted Juan, even felt afraid of him, and that wasn't fair. She tried to get it out of her mind. On the corner of Sunrise and Tahquitz, she dialed Skeet at the restaurant from her cell phone. "Hi."

"Hi," he said. "Packed?"

"Going home to do just that."

"You picking me up?"

"Sure," she said, "better to leave just one car at the airport."

"Ben gone?"

"Just saw him off."

"Listen, be prepared. Don't bring a bag you'll need to check. There's a storm headed for Baja, and for all we know, we might get stuck in Phoenix tonight."

"That might be nice. Haven't been there in a while." Then she thought about Annie telling her where Kyle's body had been found, and that Juan had worked near there, and she rethought it. "Actually, I'll pray the storm passes."

"Me too, or at least holds off. I need to get the boat out of the water."

"Can't you have someone do that for you?"

"Yeah, but I'm never sure. Mexico, you know?"

She was approaching Indian Avenue. "See you at when? Seven?"

"Sure, we've got boarding passes already. Bye—oh, Judy? Bring me the khaki cargo shorts I got at the Cabazon Mall. They're still in the bag in the bedroom."

"Okay. I'm almost home, bye."

"Later."

As she drove up to the house, she shivered again. Juan's truck was parked out front.

She drove into the garage, noticing him waving to

her from near the clumped palms, and she nodded politely in his direction. She immediately pressed the visor button to close the door after she'd driven in. It was the first time in years she hadn't entered the house through the front door. In fact, she didn't even know if the back door to the garage worked—no one ever used it. It did, she learned, after she moved rakes and loose saltillo pavers and an old laundry basket to get to it.

She had avoided talking to Juan, and she bet he knew it. She opened the shutters of the little guest bedroom just a crack and peeked out the window, and saw that he had an odd look on his face, one of hurt, with a mix of underlying anger. Suddenly he was looking her way. She flipped them shut. Had he seen her spying on him?

She went into her bedroom, pulled out her carry-on bag, and began to pack for Cabo. She didn't need much, she realized, a couple of lightweight outfits, bright blouses and long skirts, shorts, tees, tanks, bathing suit, and her vitamins, her herbs. She was about to zip the suitcase closed when she remembered Skeet had asked for his new shorts. She looked on the chair in his bedroom, but there was no bag there, only clothes piled up for the dry cleaner. She opened his closet. There were three unopened bags lying on top of his shoes. One was a Gap bag with a baseball cap in it, which she thought cute and tossed into her suitcase. The other was the J. Crew bag from the outlet mall near Cabazon, the one he'd asked her about, containing a pair of khaki cargo shorts. The other bag had the name Jordan's printed on it. Where in the hell was a store called Jordan's? She looked inside. Ralph Lauren Polo undershorts, package of three low-rise white briefs, size thirty-two, with the plastic torn and one missing. She tossed it back into the closet and forgot about it.

She wheeled the bag into the foyer and stood it near the door, against the wonderful convent table. She had not gotten the mail, but didn't want to venture out at the risk of having to speak to Juan. But she wanted to see if anything important had come before flying to Cabo. She looked out the door. Juan's truck was still there, but he wasn't. Thinking he was around back, she hurried out to the street and opened the mailbox. As she scooped the items into her arms, she noticed that there was a car parked in Annie's driveway, a nondescript tan Ford Crown Victoria, which she immediately knew was an unmarked police car.

When she got back into the house, as she was sorting the mail there in the foyer, she heard a rap on the glass of one of the French doors in the kitchen. She figured it was Juan. Or was it? Could be Annie and the cops. She had to see. She walked into the kitchen and wished she hadn't. It was Juan. She opened the door, but stood there to make sure he knew he wasn't welcome to come in. "Yes, Juan?"

He was agitated, shaking. "I did not do the things she thinks."

"Juan, I don't know anything about it," she said. It was a lie, and it was also the truth.

"They are at her house. Los Angeles detectives, I know. She wants to destroy me."

"She wants to track down a murderer," Judy said.

"Miss Judy, you like me. Your mama likes me. I have been with you a long time now, we are close."

"We aren't close, Juan. But yes, you've been with us all a very long time."

"Stop her!" he pleaded.

"There's no way I can do that," she argued. "Juan, I don't believe the accusations. But I'm not a detective, I'm not an investigator."

"Or a writer," he snapped, glancing toward the writer's house. "She makes up things, always making up things. She doesn't know where books stop and lives she can hurt begin."

Judy wanted to agree, but she didn't dare. She was confused. "I don't know what to think, Juan."

He looked at her with deep conviction. "I did not do these things. Tell me you believe me that I did not do this."

"I . . ." Her voice started the sentence, but her emotions wouldn't let her finish it. "Juan, I just don't know. I don't know anything."

"No one defends me."

"Juan, I *can't* defend you. I'm sorry. There is too much evidence."

"Evidence?" He swore so fast in Spanish that all

she could make out was that he was calling Annie a nosy cunt. She'd never seen this side of him.

"I don't know, assumptions maybe, but they are chilling." She tried to be strong. "And I know how you feel about me. But considering what I know, I think it best that you no longer work here."

Juan blinked. She as easily could have punched him in the stomach. "You firing me too?" he gasped.

"I'm sorry, Juan. I'll tell my mother what happened, and I think it's best you stop working there as well."

He trembled. His eyes, she thought, were going to fill with tears, but instead he seemed to breathe fire. He took a step backward, rage overwhelming the hurt he felt at her rejection, and spat at her feet. She cried out, shocked, and then he disappeared around the house.

Judy pulled herself together, wiped her sandal, closed the door. She got herself a bottle of water out of the refrigerator. That shook her even more. She grabbed a Snapple instead.

A few moments later, when she hadn't heard Juan's truck start, she wondered what he was doing. She set the Snapple bottle down and was about to move toward the foyer when she was startled to see Juan rush through the backyard, leap over the spa, climb up the rocks behind it, and disappear over the stucco wall, into Mrs. Hennessy's yard.

Judy rushed to the front yard. She knew immediately what had made him run. The two detectives were closing the doors of his truck; they'd been searching it. She watched them move toward their car, where Annie was already in the backseat, get in, and start it. Only then did she realize she should be telling them that Juan had fled. They probably thought he was still working in Judy's backyard.

But she was too late. They were driving off down the street before she could reach them, and it was useless, all her waving wasn't going to get them to notice.

She didn't know what to do. Call the police? But they *were* the police. Where had they gone? To Juan's, of course. She was sure of that. And that's where Juan probably had gone as well. She called Annie, left a message about what she'd seen, telling her she could reach her in Cabo. Then she paced the house nervously until it was time to pick up Skeet and catch the plane.

When she arrived at the restaurant, though, Skeet was not standing out front as she was sure he would be. The parking lot was filled with the vehicles of early diners, but one stood out, a tan Crown Victoria parked in one of the four handicapped spaces. The police and Annie were there, she saw the moment she entered, talking to Skeet. "Here she is," Skeet said to them. "Honey, they want to talk to you too."

"Were you just at home?" Annie asked. "Didn't see the car."

"I closed the garage door," Judy said. "I saw you drive off. I thought you were going to Juan's."

"Wanted to ask a few questions here first," one of the two detectives said.

"This is my friend Tom Sparks," Annie said, "and this is his associate, Tom Solberg, of the LAPD. They want to talk to you about Juan."

"He's gone."

They all looked at her. "Gone?" Sparks said.

"Gone. If you had gone to his place when you drove off, you might have gotten him. He fled."

"Fled?" Solberg said.

"Through my backyard," Judy explained, "about two hours ago."

"Shit," Annie muttered. "Shit."

Dear Diary:

The wild bear crashes through the forest. Hunted, he rages from one side of the canyon to the other, seeing refuge, safety. When he has found water, he drinks, but the arrow that comes so very close to his hide tells him there is no safety even in drinking. He runs for the higher ground.

The hunters are there too, and soon he is trapped. He roars an almighty warning, but these Indians are fearless. The bear is meat, sustenance, strength. The bear is sacred in some Indian cultures, but here it means nothing. These are not Cahuilla hunters.

The bear is wounded, arrows piercing his thick skin. He leaves a trail of red where he hurries over the rock, where he runs to the other rim of the canyon. There, more hunters, white men with guns, more deadly than those from which he just escaped. Shots ring out. The bear falls. It is over. Even running to another country does not help save him. There are hunters everywhere.

There is no safety for the bear except with Cahuilla. He would have been safe with me.

Chapter Twenty-four

Nestled in the rich comfort of the Gulfstream V, which Skeet managed to find for them after the two flights that connected to Cabo that evening were already gone, Judy felt drained. "All those questions."

"They were at it with me for over an hour before you arrived. I knew we weren't going anyplace."

"What do you think happened to Juan?" she asked.

"I don't know," Skeet said.

"If he did 'do these things,' as he put it," Judy says, "then we're in danger until he's caught."

"They can't arrest him yet. They only want him for questioning."

Judy folded her arms. It was all so upsetting, but in a curious way, almost as if the pieces didn't fit. "When I fired Juan earlier," she said, "something occurred to me. You were the one that found him initially. I was thinking Mom and Dad did, but you brought him to them."

He nodded. "I got to know him through Craig."

She was stunned. "Juan? Through Craig?"

"Yes. Craig introduced me to him. He was just a kid, hardly spoke English, fooled around with grass for a while—that's how he knew Craig—but got his shit together. He came to the desert with me and Craig for the first time. We did a sweat house thing together. He was just a boy then."

"My God, I never knew any of this. Craig connects everyone, you, Ben, and now Juan!"

"Juan was a good gardener, young and enterprising. He moved to Palm Springs. I told him to go work for your parents. When I bought the house here, I hired him."

"My mom told me you'd found him at the unemployment office, looking for day work."

He looked puzzled. "I must have said that not wanting to give them the wrong impression, about the drugs. They knew about Craig by that point."

She understood. "Guilt by association." Judy heard the roar of the little jets, and then felt the surge as they floated into the sky. "I just hadn't realized you knew him that long."

"He was really good, knew his stuff. I told him he should start a business, none of this day-labor crap. Your father hired him and he bought himself a truck."

"Don't mention his truck."

Skeet smiled. "Sorry. Jesus, I don't know if I believe all this, you know?"

Judy agreed. "I do know." The steward asked what they would like to drink. Judy said she would prefer white wine, Skeet nodded the same. "Still I get shivers."

"Annie said he wrote some pretty sick stuff about you."

"And the drug stuff fits, his knowledge of plants and Indian lore. He once loaned me a book on the Cahuilla tribe that was fascinating."

Skeet nodded. "Holding him for questioning would at least mean he's in custody. They'd know where he was. God, for all we know, he's stowed away in here."

"I assure you both," the steward interjected, "that is not the case."

The plane they were flying belonged to a Denver businessman who came to the desert regularly and dined with his wife at Fancies whenever he was in town. He'd always asked Skeet what he could do for him. Tonight the answer to that question came when Skeet realized there were no more flights, that the hurricane was moving closer to Cabo, meaning tomorrow's commercial flights could well be canceled, and that the wealthy man from Denver was at that moment sinking his chops into a thick grilled porterhouse steak.

The cops had made them accompany them to Juan's. First they checked to see if his truck was still on the street in front of Judy and Skeet's, and it was. Judy was confident they would find him in his little house in Cathedral City, scared to death. But when they arrived, they saw that he'd definitely been there but was most definitely gone. The things of importance were missing: his computer, the boxes under the bed, the pictures of Judy, her undergarments, the syringes, everything that had made him look guilty. He'd left his clothes, and certainly all his hundreds of books, behind. On a piece of white computer paper he'd scrawled in big block letters "I DID NOT DO THESE THINGS."

The police were sure he had. After setting in motion a call to the local law enforcement departments to pick Juan Torres up for questioning, Sparks and Solberg grilled Skeet and Judy on everything they knew, suspected, or even imagined about Juan Torres's involvement in the murder of Norman Lempke and the possible murders of Craig Castle, Troy Skinner, and Kyle Hulsebus. When Skeet told of the night of Norman's murder, it was clear that he had no idea where Juan was at the time of the killing, and that the story about a sprinkler wetting his truck seat was really pretty silly. Especially now that a lab had determined that the water had come from the ocean.

"But where did he go?" Judy asked, sipping her wine. "How did he get away without his truck?"

Skeet shrugged. "Might not have gone far."

"With all that stuff?"

"You have a point. They'll find him, wherever he is. Maybe at his sister's in Hemet, that would be my guess." He'd told the cops that.

She felt chilled again. "If I were him, I'd have gone to the other sister in Todo Santos."

He took her hand, seeing she was frightened. "Hey, don't worry. If he's in Mexico, they'll find him there. And you've got me to protect you."

"I'm more worried for you." Her voice was sober and deep. "He won't kill me. He's after Ben and maybe you too. If he's in Mexico, we shouldn't be going. He might just want to kill you."

"May I offer you some light fare?" the steward interrupted, unveiling a tray filled with cheeses, spreads, nuts, celery sticks, chopped liver, and radishes.

Judy tried the chopped liver. "Mit schmaltz," she said, surprised, and loving it. "Almost as good as Mom makes."

"I'll stick with the cheese," Skeet said, helping himself to a big chunk of Maytag blue.

"Hey," Judy said, trying to change the subject, "where is a store called Jordan's?"

"Huh?"

"A bag in your closet. Jordan's, you got underwear there. It's vaguely familiar."

"Yeah, San Francisco maybe? Don't recall." He bit down on the cheese, obviously approving. "Food fits the plane. When I'm rich, I'm going to have one of these."

"You're already rich."

"Honey," he said, looking around the plane's opulent interior, "not rich enough."

Then she pulled a novel from her bag and found

her place, laying the bookmark on the table before them. Skeet picked it up. "What the hell is this?"

She laughed. "A photo of Ben."

"I can see that."

"I stole it from his apartment. I liked it."

"That's the old hot dog place on Highway 111."

She froze. "What?"

Skeet was examining the photo. "Yeah, right across from Maria's restaurant down there in Cath City. It was so popular, then it moved down to Indio, but who in hell is going to drive all the way to Indio for a hot dog?"

"This photo was taken in *Palm Springs*?" She almost gasped.

"Sure. I remember that place well."

Softly she muttered, "So he has been there before."

"What?"

"Skeet, something's wrong. Very wrong." She told him about the guy at the gym who recognized Ben, about the woman boarding the plane that day who thought she knew Ben and said he was the guy who put ice in his red wine, and that Ben denied it. "But *he* said it just the other night in Fancies, and now he claims it's a coincidence."

It was all Skeet needed. "Honey, I've kept my mouth shut. I've let Annie be the sleuth, and she's probably right about Juan. But I always suspected Ben."

Judy choked on her wine. "Suspected him of what?"

"You know."

"I suspect he's a liar. What are you talking about?"

"The killer."

"Jesus, Skeet!"

"Calm down. This is before Annie told us everything about Juan. Just hear me out. Ben comes out of nowhere, sweeps you off your feet, he's suddenly marrying you, while guys who find you attractive are dying all around."

"Ben's no murderer."

Skeet thought for a moment. "What's her name?"

"Whose name?"

"This woman who recognized him."

"Joan Jordano."

"Have her number?" He didn't wait for her to answer. "Never mind, I can get it from information." He picked up the phone and dialed. "Spell it." She did. When he got Joan, he handed the phone to Judy.

"Joan, this is Judy Sussman. We saw each other in the airport that day?"

"Yeah, sugar, how are you?"

"Joan, be straight with me. The man I was with, Ben Spiegel, did you really know him? I mean, were you sure that was the same guy you said put ice in his red wine?"

Joan was silent.

"Joan?" Judy looked at Skeet, her face starting to show her upset, as if she knew what was coming.

"Yes," Joan said, "and he's gonna hate me for telling you. He stopped by my seat and asked me not to let you know, said it would really mess things up or something like that. But you're my friend, not him. Sorry, honey."

Judy's stomach turned over. "It's okay." She bit her lip. "Listen, did he come in often? I mean, how well did you know him?"

"He kissed me once in the parking lot when we were closing."

Judy's heart sank.

When she told Skeet what the woman said, he took her hand and said he was really sorry. "Trust is everything."

It was. And it was diminishing. Because now she knew that Ben had been lying about having been in Palm Springs before. And, if he could do that, what else could he lie to her about?

The storm hovered off the Baja Peninsula for two days, drenching Cabo in rain, but Skeet had time to safely store the boat on land. He introduced Judy to three Mexican boys she hadn't met on her previous visit, boys who had been helping him ever since he bought the building in which to put the restaurant, Tomas, Manuel, and Pedro. His "banditos," he called them, and she thought the title fit.

"Thugs," she assessed.

"They're just kids who've had a hard life," he protested.

"I sure wouldn't want to meet them on a dark street."

"That's why I've got them working for me, teaching them how to make a legitimate living."

"They worked on the villa too?"

"Yes."

Judy and Skeet were staying at the villa. She took the downstairs guest bedroom, far from the upstairs master where Skeet slept. But she would not be able to sleep till she talked to Ben about why he'd lied. She called him that first night there. She tried to attack the subject of having been in the desert before, but the connection was crackling because of the storm. She confronted him. She told him about taking the photo from his apartment, and that she knew where it had been taken. She knew he lied to her when he told her he had never been to Palm Springs before. Why?

Skeet found her out on the covered terrace, listening to the rain. "What did he say?"

"The connection died."

"Did you tell him you knew?"

"Yes, and he was starting to answer. He said he could explain, and that was the last word I heard."

"You okay?"

She laughed sarcastically. "Fine, other than my fiancé lies to me, and we have a hurricane approaching."

"What else is going on in your head?" Skeet asked gently. He knew her.

"This house. It's so incredible to me, touches me so deeply that this is the dream I designed again and again over the years. I mean, version after version. And that I'll never live here."

"Oh, come on."

"Well, I won't."

"You want me to sell it to Mr. and Mrs. Benjamin Spiegel, fine."

"Stop, Skeet." She got up from the chair and walked to the edge of the covered part of the terrace. She put her hand out and felt the rain. "It's warm." Then she added, "*If* there's going to be a wedding."

Her cell phone jingled. She grabbed it. "Ben?"

"Yes, we got cut off. I can barely hear you."

"Talk to me, Ben, please!"

Skeet took a step away.

Ben said, "I did lie, I admit it. I lied because I fell in love with you the moment I set eyes on you. It was the only way to see you again. And I felt like such a heel, I didn't know how to get out of it."

"But—"

"Judy, I love you. This has been killing me. I know it was wrong and I—"

The connection died again. This time for good.

She told Skeet what Ben just said.

"Do you believe him?"

"I do."

"Because you really do or because you want to?"

She didn't even blink. "Because I do."

He shook his head.

"Skeet, don't do this to me!"

He shrugged, seeing she would not budge.

"Okay," he said, "then enough of that. We go on from here."

"We planned the wedding. Second week of June."

"That's like tomorrow!"

She smiled proudly. "Yes, and it's driving my mother nuts. And we're doing it at the tram."

"The what?"

She laughed. "I suppose everyone will say that. The top of the Palm Springs Aerial Tramway."

The idea took him a minute, but it appealed to his sense of the theatrical. "Cool. Very cool. Where you met, significant."

"Will you do the food?"

"That fast?"

"I've seen you pull together brunch for two hundred overnight."

He laughed, then walked up to her and put his arms around her waist from behind. "Honey, I'm going to make you the cake of your dreams, the food of your life. It's going to be so special that every detail will be etched into your mind forever."

Judy's cell phone rang early the next morning. She sat up, thinking the sound was thunder at first, for the rain was beating against the guest room windows with real force. But the sound that had made her rise was the annoying metallic beep-ring of her Nokia. "Hello?"

"Sleepy?"

"Ben!"

"I woke you."

"It's all right. Can you hear me okay?"

"I said, did I wake you?"

She knew he couldn't hear. It sounded like sparks were bouncing off the satellite. "Ben?"

"Judy, you there? I feel so bad about what I did, I can't tell you. I didn't sleep all night!"

"Let me try calling you back on the house phone." She didn't know why she even bothered saying it. She clicked off the cell and picked up the receiver lying on the floor next to the bed, then punched in Ben's number. It took a while, and there was terrible noise on this line as well, but finally he picked up. "Hello?"

"Can you hear me this time?"

"Judy. Is it the storm?"

"Yes. It's pretty bad." Palm fronds were whipping against the stucco. "I'm amazed this line is working."

"Judy, do you forgive me?"

"Yes, of course, I understand. Just don't ever lie to me again, Ben, about anything."

"Never, I promise."

She could hear the concern in his voice. "What else is wrong?" She could feel it.

"Someone sent e-mails to the parents of every child in my school—every damn one—about the drug arrest."

"Oh, no."

"There are rumors flying."

"Were the e-mails anonymous?"

"No. They're signed 'A concerned parent.' "

"Bullshit." She was emphatic.

The line crackled, went dead, but came back again. "Someone really wants to hurt me. Any word on Juan?"

"I haven't heard anything from Annie."

"I'm off to school."

"How are the kids treating you? This affecting them?"

"Judy, I can't hear you suddenly—you still there?"

"Ben?"

"Judy?"

It was no use. The line went dead. She set the receiver down and sat up. The wind was rattling the windows now. She could smell coffee. That meant Skeet was already up, so she slipped into a robe that had been folded on the bed along with fresh white towels, and made her way into the kitchen.

Skeet sat in boxer shorts at the table. He'd already poured her a mug. She joined him without a word. She sipped. It was strong, gave her energy. Then she said, "Phone went out for good this time, I think."

"It was working?" He looked amazed. "Mexican phones don't work on a good day."

"Ben apologized."

"Good." He gestured to a box of Mexican church candles. "Ready for the blackout as well."

She couldn't even respond before the lights went out. She started laughing. "Got matches?"

He flipped the cap of a lighter and ignited one of the tall beeswax candles. "More romantic at least."

She eyed him.

"Didn't mean that kind of romantic." He leaned back. "We may be trapped here a while. Got to make the best of it, but there's not much going on. Christ, even Scrabble is on the boat."

"Where's your computer?"

"Didn't bring it."

"The one you keep down here, stupid."

He shrugged. "On the boat as well."

"Wonderful." She looked in the refrigerator for something to eat, choosing half a papaya that had already been cut and seeded. The reddish-pink flesh looked delicious. "I could sing."

"Just eat," he said.

And she did.

"How's Ben, other than remorseful?"

"Not good. More problems." She took a bite of the papaya and then told him about the e-mails that someone had been sending.

He said, "You think he could be making himself look like the victim for some reason?"

"Come on, Skeet."

"So it's Juan?"

"That's what I'm wondering."

He got up and rinsed his mug in the sink. "Cops should pick them both up. Give them both the third degree."

"Come on," she shouted, "Ben didn't poison himself in the sweat house!"

"Why not?" Skeet shot back. "If he knows about that kind of stuff—and he told you he teaches Indian shit—why wouldn't he know just how much plant juice to use to make himself look poisoned, but only be sick for a day and stay very much alive?"

"That's just nuts."

"Or it was meant for me and he goofed."

"Skeet!"

He shrugged. "I wonder if Annie's learned anything."

She looked out at the raging storm. "We're going to be the last to find out." She walked to the window, and shivered at the sight of the dark, howling wet wind.

They couldn't imagine who would be calling at two in the morning.

Esther thought it might be Judy, and said so as she sat up. Henry fumbled for the light next to his side of the bed. Once he found it and turned it on, he grabbed first the phone, then his glasses, and said, "Judy?"

"No, Mr. Sussman, it's Ben."

"Ben?" Henry looked at the clock.

Esther shouted, "Ben?" at Henry. "What's wrong? What's happened?"

Henry put his hand up to shush his wife. "Ben,

please call me Henry, and tell me what's wrong? I can hear it in your voice."

"I couldn't get through to Judy," Ben said.

"The storm."

"Yes. And I didn't want to call my mom, because of her heart."

Henry's skipped a beat. He tried not to alarm Esther, but the look on his face had already panicked her. She gasped, "Oh, my God."

"Ben," Henry said, "I'm glad you called us. Please tell us what happened."

"I've been arrested."

The word hit him with such unexpected force that it barely registered at first. He might have expected Ben to say he was sick or he was hurt. "Arrested?" he finally said.

Esther gasped again. "Arrested? Who? Ben?"

Ben continued, softly, "I'm in jail. I get one call, just like in the movies, and it had to be to someone who might know how to help me."

"Ben," Henry said, as warmly, fatherly, and full of support as he could make his voice sound, "tell me what happened."

"I came home tonight, after school and dinner with another teacher, to find my apartment trashed. Destroyed."

Esther, who was now pacing nervously in her nightgown, interrupted. "What's he saying? Why that look?"

"Ben, hold on," Henry said, and cupped the phone.

"You're not helping anything standing there like that," he snapped at his wife. "Please, let Ben talk."

Ben talked. "The door had been broken down. I thought I'd been robbed. But when I got closer, I saw that there were two men standing inside. They were wearing suits. Two others had come from somewhere behind me, they were just suddenly there."

Henry asked, "Who were they?"

"Detectives," Ben said.

Henry looked startled. "Detectives?"

"They said they found drugs in my apartment."

"What kind of drugs?" Henry asked as his wife stood there gaping.

"Opium."

Chapter Twenty-five

The full force of the hurricane swept the Baja Peninsula that night. The relentless winds pounded the landscape with rain as if the sea was being picked up and hurled onto land. Judy and Skeet watched two recently planted palms get uprooted and vanish down the muddy hillside. A construction shed that still stood near the side of the house just disappeared, along with everything in it. Skeet seemed most worried about the little chapel, watching it again and again from the house. But it seemed to be secure—or perhaps blessed. It was made of stucco over concrete block, and that was a pretty worthy opponent for the wind's fury. Judy ran around the house putting towels under windows or sliders, mopping up water that inevitably found its way inside. Skeet taped a window when it cracked after being hit by flying debris to prevent if from eventually shattering.

There was no electricity, so there was no television, no radio, nothing at all. Skeet knew he should have bought a generator just to play it safe, but hadn't. There was enough food to get by, but by morning they were going stir crazy. Lack of sleep—who could sleep through the howling?—made them irritable and short with one another. When a few hundred pounds of mud made its way like molten lava onto the back terrace and threatened the doors there, they grabbed shovels and valiantly attempted to stop the creeping gook. They were covered in it themselves by the time they finished, only to learn the water had stopped running. They walked out into the rain, which was dangerous with all the debris in the air and the sheer force of the wind. But they held tightly to concrete pillars and stood there long enough to wash off the reddish, clinging mud.

They dried themselves and lit a fire in the living room fireplace, which was a mistake because there was no draft through the chimney. They had to douse the wood with bottled water to put it out to keep from asphyxiating. It worsened the mood. But the candles gave the place a warm glow, and Judy moved three of them together so she could read the novel she'd brought with her.

When her head started to hurt, she slid down on the chaise, put the book on her chest, and closed her eyes. A sudden thud against the window made her look up to see what might have hit it. She screamed, "Skeet!"

Skeet ran in from the kitchen. "What?"

"A man! Someone's out there!" She had seen the figure of a man move by the glass, close enough to it to rub up against it. She had been so startled, she hadn't been able to tell who it was or even if she'd really seen him.

Skeet didn't believe her. "Yeah, right."

"Go look!"

"You crazy?"

She rushed to the doors, looked out, then grabbed a candle and motioned for him to follow her to the windows at the side of the house, in the direction she'd seen the man move. She looked out the window and saw him again. "There!" She saw someone duck from behind a pillar and disappear into the darkness.

Skeet thought he saw something as well, though he wasn't certain it was a human being. He opened the window to see better and called out, but it was pitch-black and of course no one answered. He then ran around to the slider, went outside, and called out. But there was no response.

"Maybe there will be footprints," she said.

"In all that water?" He shook his head. "Christ, you really think someone was here?"

"Yes. I saw him. It was a man, all right."

He bit his lip. Then he said what she was already thinking. "Juan."

"See him again?" Judy asked Skeet after she'd woken from an hour's sleep. It was four in the morning.

He shook his head. "Nothing. Shadows playing tricks on me, that's all."

"I feel safe with you."

He nodded, took her hand. "I've always got a good knife. J.W. says you need a gun down here. Maybe he's right."

She looked out the glass pane herself. She couldn't see a thing. "It's pitch-black."

"I know."

"You should get some sleep."

"Can't." He turned away from the window. "Hey, I think I have a deck of cards."

"Yuck," she said, "you know I hate cards."

But she played anyway, for two hours, until they both heard, all at once like a shower being turned off, the relentless pounding rain lessening. The storm was letting up. She looked out where they'd shoveled the mud, and sure enough, the water was coming down with much less force. She could actually see the bougainvillea branches, stripped of all leaves, at the end of the terrace. The pool looked like it was filled with dirt soup. "I think it's over."

"I wonder what happened to the restaurant," Skeet voiced.

"The whole town might be under water." They were high on the hill, but Cabo was right there at water level, and flooding was common. She looked out the back windows, seeing it getting lighter now that the sun was up, somewhere behind the swirling, gray clouds. She looked at the chapel. "Looks like Our Lady of Guadalupe saved it."

"It's a special place."

Then she noticed it, the wire. "Skeet?"

"Huh?"

"That a phone line leading into the chapel?"

He looked at her as if she were nuts. "What?" He walked over and stood at the window as well.

She pointed to the line that ran to a pole where the other telephone line hooked to the house. The pole had held up through the storm; the lines were all secure. "Why a phone in there? You've got your cell anyway."

"Like having one in the bathroom," he joked.

"Gimme a break."

He gave he a stupid look. "It's electricity, dummy. Comes off the same pole."

She blinked. "I thought you ran it underground."

"For the house," he explained. "The chapel was an afterthought."

"Ah."

An hour later, the rain stopped. Skeet went outside to inspect the damage, while Judy put the wet towels and rags into the dryer. From the little window of the laundry room, she saw an odd thing. Skeet moved up the muddy slope to the chapel and tried the door. She thought he was going inside, but it looked like he was making sure it was locked tight.

And she thought that was very strange.

Annie listened to the details of Ben's incredible story of the discovery of his ransacked apartment, his arrest, his having to spend the night in jail, and

Henry's arranging bail for him. She was stunned. "And Judy doesn't know?" she asked.

"Phone lines are out. Apparently the storm really took a toll," he responded. "I'm home now, got the Weather Channel on."

"You gonna be okay?"

"Yes." He cleared his throat and tried to make light. "I may not have a job, but I'll be fine. Hell, really basically a week to go."

"We are sure Juan went down there. But Judy's with Skeet. She'll be fine."

Then Ben said an odd thing. "Does Skeet really like me?"

"Come again?"

He held back. "Never mind."

"No, tell me. Say it."

"No, it's a silly thought." He said no more, other than good-bye, and asked her to let him know the minute she heard from Judy.

When she hung up, she realized he'd asked about Skeet liking him because he was having suspicions about him. Which were understandable, but ridiculous. Skeet had been her friend for years. She liked him. She was a good judge of character. Utterly ridiculous. Hell, Skeet was probably having suspicions about Ben.

She wanted to help Ben find out who'd done this to him, and to save him from what was coming next. She put in a call to the guy in Oceanside, left a message, made herself a ham sandwich, and carried it out to the pool. She listened to updates on the storm in Cabo on the radio. Then the phone rang.

The man in Oceanside said, "The e-mails that all those parents got about his drug bust and all that, they didn't come from Ben's computer."

"Aha!" But she already was sure of that.

"But neither did they come from Cathedral City."

"Oh." She sounded surprised, but deep inside she really wasn't. "Where did they come from "

"Untraceable computer south of the border."

"Mexico?"

"Mexico," the man assured her.

Annie shivered, because she hadn't expected that. "Mexico. That's where we assumed Juan went."

"They apparently can't find the actual computer, like they did back with the I Love You virus last year in the Philippines, but in Mexico they can tell which ISP they went out on. Trouble is, Mexico is still the new frontier when it comes to the Net."

"Thanks, babe," Annie said, "and keep me informed."

"Sure will."

She knew someone who lived in Mexico. An idea which had been floating in a sea of denial in the back of Annie's head could no longer be ignored. She got up and walked into Judy's yard, found the spare key under the third terra-cotta pot to the right, and let herself in.

She felt like an assassin, slinking around, looking at everything through careful, suspicious eyes. She had felt at home here for years, and now she was an intruder.

Finally, in Skeet's closet, she found an item of interest. In a pair of freshly laundered, folded jeans, she saw a little bump where the pocket was. She ran her hand over it and guessed it might be a little rock. But it turned out to be a piece of thick paper that had been balled up and washed and bleached, and she managed to open and flatten it out. It was a Skywest Airlines boarding pass from San Jose Del Cabo for McCloy, S. The date was hard to read. April something. It looked like a "4." If it was the fourteenth, that was just two days before Easter, the night Passover began. The night Troy died. What really bothered her was the destination. The bleached airport code looked like SAT. Which would be San Antonio, Texas. But it could have been SAN. San Diego.

No way. She immediately thought no one would be so dumb as to fly in their own name if they were going to murder someone in a sweat house, but then she recalled that the new airline regulations had changed all that. There really wasn't any other way, unless you assumed another identity and got a driver's license or birth certificate to back it up.

She slid the boarding pass into her pocket and left.

The electricity started up that afternoon. Without warning, Judy heard the refrigerator suddenly kick in. "Skeet!" she cried out, "I think it's on!"

He was outside, working with Tomas and Pedro,

who had somehow managed to get up the hill in a beater of an old Chevy truck that was covered with mud from roof to wheels. They were digging out, lifting oozing soil by the shovelful, tossing it away from the house, clearing the patio.

The water had started shortly before the power, but it initially ran brown and dirty. Judy opened the taps for half an hour before it cleared, but when it did, the water looked clean enough to use. "Boil it first," Skeet warned. "This is Mexico, after all." They always drank bottled water, but they wanted their cooking and bathing water to be safe as well.

An hour after the power returned, Skeet left the boys digging and took a long hot shower. Dressed in clean clothes and shaved for the first time in three days, he cooked up bacon for BLTs, along with some rice and beans. Judy tossed a salad, and they ate in the sublimely air-conditioned dining room. Everything was just fine. Now all they needed was for the phones to work.

Judy drifted off to sleep while reading at about eleven. She'd not slept well since arriving here, so this was comalike. With Skeet and "the boys" she felt safe, and the world was calm and quiet. She had nothing to wake up for. She thought of Ben and pictured herself in a white dress, on her father's arm, with Ben waiting under the canopy at the end of the aisle. . . .

Annie drove to Fancies. It was a busy night, and Anna the hostess seemed harried. Good, Annie thought, she won't be suspicious. "Howdy," Annie said to her. "I'm doing a writing project for Skeet, a brochure for the new place down in Cabo."

"Ah," Anna said with a smile, crossing off names on a seating plan. "Cómo está?"

"Fine, gracias. He said I'd find some stuff he typed upstairs in his office."

"Sí," she said, and withdrew a key as the phone rang again. "Fancies Palm Springs, hold please." She handed the key to Annie. "You need I show you where?"

"Been in there before," Annie said, which was a lie.

But Anna certainly believed it. Annie went upstairs, found Skeet's office in a flash, and let herself in. This was going to be more of a challenge than she'd thought, because the room was filled with files and papers and cabinets. His desk was heaped with magazines, floor plans, seating plans, newspapers, and cookbooks. Annie sat in his chair and turned on the computer. It booted, and Windows flashed to life, then she opened WordPerfect. She opened the list of documents and found all were called "DIARY." Some had numbers, some had dates, some had a mix of both, but none could be accessed because she needed a password. She tried guessing, but she soon realized how lucky she'd been with Juan's computer, for nothing worked here.

Anna popped in with a beer. "I think you like," she said.

"I like very much," Annie answered, "gracias. You Mexican?"

"Oh, no, not very much," Anna replied. "I am coming from Argentina."

"Classy spitfire with bad English, it's pretty charming," Annie said. She knew that was precisely why Skeet had hired her. She was amusing, but she had elegance.

"Very good cooking book," she said, patting the cookbook on the top of the pile on the desk.

Annie saw it was one of Alice Waters's Chez Panisse cookbooks. "I'm sure," Annie said. "Don't know much about it myself. Never read a recipe in my life."

"She is Mister Sketer's good friend, he say she give him this personally when he see her in San Francisco a week ago."

Annie opened it to read the inscription. There was none. On the back, she saw the Barnes & Noble sticker still attached. She then thumbed the pages. Deep inside, near the back, was a receipt. The book had been purchased at the Barnes & Noble at Horton Plaza in San Diego, not in San Francisco. On the day Skeet said he'd been in Berkeley.

"I bringing you food?"

Annie looked up. "No, thanks. You know who you remind me of? Charo."

"No comprende," Anna said.

"Cugat's wife?"

"Ah, Coogie!" Anna's buzzer buzzed so loudly it

looked like she'd just experienced an electrical shock. "I have call, hope it is Meester Skeeter, I worry about storming."

Annie worried about the storm too, but hoped it was not him calling. When Anna left, she locked the door. And went back to the computer. There were five documents that intrigued her because they had numbers after them that meant something to her, but she couldn't put her finger on it:

DIARY 9–4–92
DIARY 7–2-00
DIARY 3–27–01
DIARY 4–14–01
DIARY 5–05–01

Dates that she knew, but why? The fourteenth of April, the day Troy died. Judy's birthday stood out, May fifth, the same day Ben was poisoned in the sweat house. 3–27–01. March 27, this year. My God! The day Norman was killed, yes. What were the other dates? Kyle's death? Craig's death? She felt a pallor overpowering over her rosy cheeks, and downed the beer in one long slug. Another document that intrigued her was "SHAMAN.DOC," but she couldn't open it to read the contents.

She went through every paper in the room, but found nothing more. She got up, let herself out, and returned the key to Anna, who was welcoming customers. The restaurant was filling with the sound of conversation, tinkling wineglasses, the roar of the moneyed crowd. Anna suggested she stay for dinner.

Dinner? Annie wanted to throw up. But she didn't want to leave a stone unturned. She knew that Skeet had a little desk in the corner of the kitchen, and she wanted to see it. "How about a doggie bag? Something I can take home to microwave."

Anna sneered. "Microwave, no! But sí, we giving you," she said, motioning furiously to a dark and oddly handsome busboy. In Spanish, she ordered him to load Annie up with "dinner to go."

Annie followed the busboy to the kitchen, where the pastry chef was rolling soft white dough balls and dabbing bits of melted chocolate and coconut in the centers. A cook with gloves to his elbows like a surgeon, sporting a hair net like a helmet, was making salads. The man she assumed was Skeet's second in command was doing a balancing act with two skillets, steak on the grill, and a whole fish poaching in what looked like old bathwater topped with ten thousand bay leaves. She made her way over to Skeet's desk and managed to flip up the pages of a pad and saw several notations, but nothing she was interested in—until she came to the word *Juan*. It was written several times on one page. That was all.

"Ma'am," the busboy asked, "what kind of salad dressing?"

Annie turned to answer him but didn't, for something caught her eye. The wooden wall there, right over the busboy's buff shoulder, was fashioned from the same paneling Skeet had done the dining room here in. The dark wood, however, had holes in it.

Small, sliver-like holes. Annie walked up closer and peered at them. The busboy again inquired about her salad dressing and she muttered, "Blue cheese." The holes were ragged, harsh. Someone had rammed something sharp into the wood again and again. "What are these?" she asked the busboy.

"Oh," he said with a laugh, "the boss, he like to show off."

The main chef gave him a sour look.

"Nothing bad, I mean," the boy corrected himself, having read the look.

"Show off how?" Annie asked, pretending to be amused.

"He toss the knives," the boy explained.

Annie felt her stomach tighten.

"By the handle," the boy continued, obviously in awe of such a trick, "but the tip, it stick in the wall."

The pastry chef grunted. "Like in the circus."

"This place *is* a circus," the other chef said, shaking a skillet as if he were stabbing a stick to protect himself from a mad dog.

"The boss is very good, very very good," the handsome busboy said. "Throw from over there and it stay in the wall." He pointed to five feet away.

"Grandfather was a butcher," the pastry chef added. "I guess he learned from him."

The busboy put Annie's food into a designer shopping bag complete with fabric handle, with "Fancies" written on the side, and smiled. She thanked him and looked at the wall one more time, recalling where she had seen the very same thing. On the teak wall in Norman Lempke's boat. A hole where a knife tip had penetrated from being tossed, hard, from about five feet away.

It was enough to make her sweat.

She was so panicked that when she set the food bag on the trunk of the Cadillac so she could get her keys out of her purse, she forgot it was there, and drove off with it still standing in the spot she'd put it. It fell off as she rounded the corner, and another car swerved but couldn't avoid crushing the carton of penne with garlic and basil to a pulpy mess. All the way home, Annie let her mind go where she hadn't allowed it to wander before. How could she have been so blind? He was her friend, she'd known him a long time, she was a great judge of character. Yeah, like she'd been with her former husband. Shit.

All this time they'd thought it was Juan. But Juan was being set up by Skeet. Of course he'd put suspicion on Juan by admitting, reluctantly—which was brilliant—how Juan actually was alone that night. Skeet had taken Juan's truck after Juan had parked it in front of Skeet's apartment in Beverly Hills. He'd driven it to the ocean, gotten it wet when he swam back after killing Norman, and then parked it where the sprinklers were on, opening the windows, letting Juan discover it—and think he himself had caused it—in the morning. Pretty clever. But how did Skeet know Juan wouldn't find out? Were they in on this together? No. Annie was positive that Juan must have been drunk for Skeet to risk taking the truck. Drunk enough to be knocked out. Hell, perhaps Skeet knocked him out himself.

When she got home, Scout seemed as interested in dinner as she had been, lying morosely at the back door. "I feel just like you look," Annie said.

She thought about things. How Skeet admitted getting the water bottles from the stream. How Ben had said Skeet passed the water bottles out. Gave one to Juan, who passed it to Ben, who passed it to the guy on the end. Then the next one went to Ben, Skeet knew that, he knew who would end up with it. The syringes in Juan's house could have been for plant propagation, or maybe the bastard was secretly a diabetic for all she knew. Skeet could easily have had syringes as well. Anyone could get hold of them.

She turned on the TV and the Weather Channel told her all of Baja was mopping up. There were pictures of mud slides that looked just like Malibu when it periodically washed into the ocean, and a report that phones, electricity, and water were slowly being restored, but that it would take time. Time she didn't have. Judy was trapped down there with a killer. The man who had killed all her lovers, and was probably planning on killing her fiancé.

She picked up the phone and started dialing. But she stopped herself. "Cell phone, cell phone," she said, nervously, "you stupid ass." She knew Skeet never used Judy's mobile unit. She listened for the message, and then left one that she was certain would scare Judy, send her for a loop, but might in fact save her life.

But it wasn't all she could do. Or should do. She needed to get this man as well. Her evidence was slim, so she couldn't turn to Tom Sparks. She could and would do this alone.

She packed a small suitcase and found a map in a drawer in her office. She spread it out, smoothed it with her hands, and studied it, gauging the distance and the time. She looked at her watch. She wished she hadn't had that beer. In the bathroom, she found some speed that had been left over from nights on deadline, and swallowed a couple capsules. Then she hurried into the kitchen, grabbed some cans of dog food from a cabinet, some doggie biscuits, a sack of dry food, and said, "Hey, Scout!"

He sat up, ears perked, tail wagging.

"Wanna find yourself a hot chihuahua down in Mexico? And maybe save someone's life?"

She also took her gun.

Chapter Twenty-six

About two in the morning, when dreams of Ben had dissolved into a deep and peaceful sleep, Judy opened her eyes. She felt an odd sensation: edgy, off. At first, trying to register what it was, she thought perhaps she was dreaming that Juan was outside, wanting to kill Skeet. But she shrugged that off. It was more that something wasn't right, something was out of kilter. She went downstairs to find the two workers lying in their underwear on the living room floor. They startled her at first, but she quickly realized that of course Skeet's men were going to stay the night. She walked into the kitchen, without turning any lights on, and looked out the window.

It was a moonlit night. The moon wasn't full, but there was enough light to cast shadows. She saw the shadow that the chapel cast down the hillside. The cross at the top looked enormous now, like some giant X marking the space just outside the kitchen door. Her eyes followed the dark image up the hill to the building itself, which was less white now and more spotted with mud from the storm. But what drew her attention was the light on inside the little structure. And the shadow of someone inside was clear in the window.

Skeet? What was he doing in there at this hour? She was curious, and unsure. The line leading to it was obviously the power, just as he'd said, because the light was clear. Or was it? It seemed to flicker. Was the power going out again? She turned on a black iron lamp set on the kitchen table. The light did not flicker at all. She looked at the chapel again and then guessed it was candlelight. Was that why he'd supplied the house with that stash of Catholic church candles? For his own little chapel?

But why? What was he doing in there? Praying? She laughed at the notion. Skeet, praying. Fat chance. He'd been raised Catholic, she knew, but had never, in her recollection, practiced. He was drawn to the spectacle of the Catholic Church, the ritual, the exotic theater of it, as most lapsed Catholics were. But to set up a little chapel to Saint Whoever and light candles in the middle of the night and pray, that was beyond the realm of possibility.

Then she had a wild thought. She'd believed that line was a telephone wire, not electricity. If it was for power, why was he burning candles? What if she had been right? What if the phones were working? She turned to the other wall of the kitchen and lifted the one hanging there. She expected the hollow silence that she'd gotten each time she'd tried to use any of the phones in the past few days. But this time she got a tone—not a dial tone or a busy signal. But it was a tone of some kind. A kind that she'd heard before.

She hung up the extension when she figured out what it sounded like. A computer. When she was on-line and picked up an extension, this was the steady metallic tone she heard. Could Skeet be on-line in the chapel? It didn't make sense. He said his computer was on the boat. Why would he have it in the chapel?

She stepped outside. It was warmer than she imagined. She started climbing toward the light in the tiny chapel window, finding the earth was still too wet for anything to settle. Almost there, she held back from her desire to knock on the door. Instead, she went to the side and tried to get up on her tiptoes to peek through the small window. She couldn't reach it.

She spied an old sawhorse sitting nearby. She could see it in the moonlight, encrusted with stucco, and figured it must have been used as the workmen stuccoed the exterior of the chapel. She dragged it over and positioned it, but as she tried to climb up on it, one leg slid in the mud, and she collapsed to the earth, slamming against the side of the chapel.

Skeet was outside in a second. "What the hell?" He saw her, helped her up. "My God, I thought it was Juan!"

She didn't know what to say. So she kept quiet. Her leg hurt like crazy, and she'd really banged her hip hard. It was going to be black and blue tomorrow.

"What were you doing?"

"I was trying to figure out who was in there and what he was doing."

"Boss?" The voice came from below.

Judy and Skeet looked down to see one of the boys who'd been fast asleep on the living room floor standing in his undershorts with a rifle in his hand. "Okay, Tomas, it's all right."

"Jesus," Judy gasped.

"Go back to bed," Skeet ordered the boy. The other one had shown up in the background. "You too, Pedro."

"Sí, boss."

"Buenas noches."

Skeet turned from Judy and went around to the front of the small building. When she got there, he was locking the door. "What are you doing?" she asked.

"I'm done."

"Done what?"

"Writing."

"What?"

"A cookbook."

"So you do have a computer in there."

He nodded sheepishly. "True."

"Why were you untruthful?"

"Because I was afraid you'd laugh."

"Why would I laugh? I've often said you should write one."

"Because it's on Indian recipes. Cactus, mesquite."

She blinked. "Coyote melon?"

He seemed startled. "That isn't funny."

"Were you on the Net?"

"Huh?" He looked dumbfounded.

"I picked up the phone and got a tone."

"There's no phone line in there. . . ." He was already hurrying down the rocky, wet hillside. "But if the phone is making a sound, then we might be in business."

But it wasn't. It was completely dead again.

They both went to sleep.

But this time it was restless for Judy. She tossed and turned for hours, uneasy that Skeet had lied to her. Finally, at ten in the morning, she fell into a deep slumber. She awoke to Skeet's touch at three in the afternoon. "Honey," he said gently, "you gonna sleep all day?"

She realized what time it was and sat up. "My God." She stretched and yawned. "It's like someone gave me a Halcion."

"We cleared most of the mud away. They say the coast road will open tomorrow, at least one lane. A few houses washed clear down to the ocean."

"Phones?"

He nodded. "Working, but intermittently. Seems no one can call in, but I've gotten a few out. It's very iffy."

"I'm gonna try my cell."

"I'll make you some breakfast," Skeet said, and left.

She stood up, went into the bathroom to brush her teeth, then tried her cell phone. It seemed to be working. She tried to call Ben, but it wouldn't go through. On the second attempt, it died altogether. As she ate, she kept trying the house line, but when she finally got a dial tone and started dialing a number, it disconnected. In the early evening, when she was beginning to go stir crazy being trapped in the house, she tried it again, but again there was no way to get a call through. She gave her cell phone another shot, and though she was unable to make a call, she was able to punch in her code and retrieve her messages.

There were several, which had piled up over the past few days. The first was from Ben, prior to her storm and his own, saying he loved her. Then Kervin, her mother, someone selling Internet access, her mother again and again (a total of eight times), and finally Annie. Her voice sounded different. Frightened. Urgent. The message: *"Judy, get out of Mexico, Ben needs you. He's in trouble. If you get this message, please, understand what I'm saying, get out of there now. Go to Ben. I love you, this is Annie."*

"Is the airport open?" Judy asked Skeet.

He shook his head. "Maybe tomorrow, I heard."

She looked panicked.

"What's wrong?"

"Something's happened to Ben. Annie left a message that sounded crazed, like she was holding back. She just said I had to go to Ben."

Skeet's eyes widened. "I'm sorry. Christ, I wonder what's wrong?"

Judy suddenly looked as though she was going to cry. He put his arm around her. "I've got to get out of here," she said, her voice quavering.

"It's going to be okay, honey," Skeet said, strong, controlled, supportive, his arms holding her in the same way. "It'll be fine. The wedding will happen as planned."

"I've got to get out, Skeet," she said, feeling imprisoned. "I have to get to San Diego. *Now*."

The airport, which had sustained only minimal damage, reopened the next morning, but the coast road was still under water in places, and mud slides had continued to prevent the safe travel of vehicles. By that time Judy was truly panic-stricken. She still could not get a call through to Ben, or to Annie, or to her mother and father. Nothing worked but local numbers. Skeet brought his computer into the house, where he tried to hook up to his Internet service provider, but the connection would fail each time. In desperation Skeet called J.W., who called a friend who owned a 120-foot yacht, which he'd just sailed back to Cabo from up the Sea of Cortez, where they had taken it to wait out the storm. "He got a chopper on that tub?" Skeet asked.

"Helicopter? Sure."

"We would like to use it."

An hour later, Judy was being flown over the coast road, over San Jose Del Cabo, to the airport, where she would make the last flight out tonight.

About ten kilometers from the Los Cabos air field, a big pink Cadillac was parked in the muddy soil in front of an open-air taco stand. As Annie sat at one of the little tables, feeding herself a pollo taco and a beef tamale to Scout, she heard the sound of a helicopter and looked up. She thought it was probably surveying storm damage, which the taco stand proprietor told her was "very much bad" on the corridor road. Or perhaps it was flying out someone who had been injured in the mud slides. In any case, she paid it little attention. All she cared about was getting to Judy before it was too late.

The man had been right, the coast road was worse than "very much bad," it was completely closed. She had no choice but to wait, along with buses of tourists who'd arrived today, thinking the storm was over and they'd go on with their vacations, all grousing about being held up. Wait, she thought, till they find their hotels destroyed. She slept in the car for a few hours as night descended over the landscape. Around midnight, a man from what she assumed was the highway department told them the road would open "mañana." She put the top up and slept some more.

At daybreak, she joined the caravan of trucks, automobiles, vans, and creaking, rusted "Chebbies," following a police vehicle and huge dump truck outfitted with a snow plow for mud, and headed for Cabo San Lucas. They had to take turns, in groups of ten vehicles, traveling east and west, stopping every so often to let the opposing traffic crawl through, then continuing on at their own snail's pace on the treacherous road. They traversed gullies, arroyos, washed-out bridges, and packed mud. They saw huge billboards, advertising hotels and the idyllic lifestyle of the area, torn in half, ripped to shreds by the wind. Telephone and power poles had been snapped like matchsticks, and at times they had to drive so slowly that Annie felt they weren't even moving. The procession got to Cabo San Lucas in seven hours, a trip that should have taken no more than one.

It wasn't hard, once there, to find out where Skeet's new house was. Everyone knew him, everyone was aware of his wonderful new villa. "Sí," a woman on the street with two children clinging to her skirt said, "his girlfriend, she is with him there too." Annie drove to the house.

But she did not drive up the driveway. She doubted she could have anyway, without chains for the mud. She continued past it about a quarter of a mile, and then parked the car well into the brush. She made sure the windows were all open five inches for Scout to breathe, for she couldn't risk taking him with her. The sun was out, but it wasn't very hot, just muggy and heavy. It was already four in the afternoon. Annie got out, took her gun from her purse, and tucked it into her pants, under her top, and started walking.

She didn't dare go up the drive, but how else to get up there? She walked half a mile, surveying the area to see how in the hell to get up there without being seen. The hill was wet and muddy, but a lot of the terrain was solid rock, which gave her a footing. She decided to climb up from the left side of the house, coming upon it from the back, almost directly alongside a little building that looked like a chapel. Out of breath, feeling her heart was going to give out from the climb, she took a moment to calm down. She was actually uphill of the house, and looked down from a clear vantage point. No one seemed to be around but two Mexican boys who were piling debris into a beat-up old truck. There was no sign of Skeet, no sign of Judy. The boys seemed to be alone.

They finished loading the truck. One of them, without turning away, decided to take a piss on the back truck tire, while the other started up the hill, heading, it seemed, straight at her. She was so surprised by the first one opening his pants so nonchalantly that by the time she ducked, she feared she'd been seen. But she heard nothing, and nothing happened. When she lifted her head again, the boy was coming from the chapel, and she thought she heard him say something.

Yes, he was talking, but to the boy who'd finished

peeing, not anyone in the small building. They laughed about something and then got into the truck, started it, and slid down the slippery hillside. She was glad she hadn't parked anywhere nearby.

She waited a while. There wasn't a sound. Obviously, Judy and Skeet were not here. But that could be good. Hopefully, Judy had gotten her message and had gotten the hell out. She worried that Skeet would overhear it. That's why she told Judy to go to Ben, to get her worried enough to hurry to the safety of Ben's arms, where she surely would not take Skeet along. Annie wanted Skeet here, where she could get him herself.

But first she needed proof. She had circumstantial evidence, but she needed more. This was the best place to start. So she moved cautiously down the wet, rocky hillside toward the house. Her tennis shoes oozed with mud. She reached out and touched the back of the white stucco chapel with her hands, and then rounded the corner, peering down at the house. Suddenly it occurred to her that there could be someone in the chapel. Skeet might be there, that could have been why the boy had gone to the structure before driving away. She pulled her gun. Then she made her way around the corner of the building and saw that the door was ajar. She lifted the gun in front of her, looked through the slight opening of the door, but didn't see movement inside. Step by careful step, she moved closer to the door, put her right toe against it, and pulled it all the way open with her foot. Then she put the gun down, for no one was in there—but what she saw there took her breath away. She stepped forward, aghast. Then she stepped inside, her mouth open in wonder and horror.

The walls of the tiny structure were papered with a kind of collage of black-and-white photographs of Indians. Indians at work, hunting, playing with children, building adobe dwellings on the desert floor, building brush houses in the mountains, photographs of Indian schoolchildren and proud parents, shamans, and chiefs. Annie saw that most of them had been ripped from books, and almost all had text under them explaining the year they were taken, and the significance. She eyed one in particular. The text said: "Maria Los Angeles, 1899. Maria works on a coiled basket. A bundle of deer grass rests in her lap."

What troubled Annie was that Maria's face had been replaced in the photo with Judy's.

On all of them, the women had invariably been doctored to become Judy. Likewise, most of the shaman photos now had Skeet's face. Under a photo of shaman Skeet McCloy atop a rock in Palm Springs's Chino Canyon, there was a quote: "They would say we were related to the bears. They would say that when you looked at him and he was still dancing, all of a sudden you would see a bear. —Alvino Siva." There were pictures of the Indian bird singers, and all those faces were now Skeet's as well.

Did he fancy himself some kind of Indian? Annie

took her eyes from the walls and let them fall on the little altar, over which sat not a crucifix as she'd expected, but a color photo of a petroglyph made from maze stone. She knew they were found in Baja as well as Southern California's Sonoran desert, but as she looked closely, she saw this was the Hemet Maze Stone, the finest example of Indian rock art that existed. On the table beneath sat candles that had been burned almost completely. And there was an opened laptop computer. With a phone line plugged into the modem jack.

Annie sat down and hit the space bar. The screen flickered and came alive. On it was an unfinished document:

> *. . . I will sing the birdsongs after her wedding, the songs that tell of a great journey, the journey we will make together once she has seen her error in judgment. I understand. I will not hold it against her, for she has not yet learned what I have learned. They knew about everything, my Indians, about the stars, about the world. Deep, deep things. She will join me in the birdsongs, as women before hesitated to do. She will join me in spirit that has been joined for many many moons anyway. . . . I am poisoner shaman of my tribe. I weep for my victims.*

Annie looked to the right. There was a book there, an oversized paperback. She turned it over and saw the cover. *The Heart Is Fire*. She knew this book, she had a copy of it herself. It was a first-person record of the history of the Cahuilla Indians. She opened it and almost every page had been marked, highlighted, and photos had been cut from it. They were now on the wall. The quotes were in his diary. Did he believe himself to be Indian? Was that why he had used plant poisons? He saw himself as some shaman? Was he joking? Or was he just plain mad?

Annie didn't get time to answer that question in her mind, for all at once she felt someone press a gun into the small of her back, accompanied by two words: "Drop that."

She did.

Chapter Twenty-seven

"It's been four days," Judy said to Ben, suddenly looking up from the *New York Times,* "and still nothing." Her voice was edgy with frustration and sadness. Annie had been missing since Ben had talked to her the night of the hurricane. Her car had been found, two days later, abandoned at the end of a sand-swept, seldom-used road where people dumped old sofas and car batteries, about forty kilometers north of Todo Santos. It was assumed she had gone there in pursuit of Juan. But no one knew anything for sure. There were no fingerprints on the car but her own. Dried blood had been found on the steering wheel, driver's seat, and floor, which testing proved to be Annie's. There was no sign of Scout.

Judy and Ben sat on the private patio of the Havana Suite at Korakia, surrounded by a primitive stone wall covered in bougainvillea, which had dropped petals all around, as if someone had strewn roses at their feet. They had rented the suite of rooms the day they returned to the desert. In just a few more days they would be married, and, as her mother pointed out, it didn't look right living with another man right until your wedding day. Besides, Ben had ordered it.

He now had a distrust of Skeet that wouldn't die. Ever since his talk with Annie, he had the gnawing feeling that Skeet had something to do with everything that had happened. He had not a shred of evidence on which to base his suspicion; it just rose from his gut. It was also a bone of contention between him and Judy, and after bringing it up three times and being shot down on each try, he dropped it. He had looked suspicious himself, he realized, because of his lies.

Ben sat with his face into the midday sun. He and Judy were going to look for a house together, and he was seriously considering moving to the desert to teach there. Start fresh, with a whole new challenge. Too much damage had been done back in San Diego, whether he was innocent or not.

Ben tried to put his growing fears about Skeet and worry for Annie out of his mind. School was out, and he was free, and he was in love. No matter how hard he tried, those happy thoughts did not overcome his unease. "Anything more from Mexico?"

"Mexican police are watching Juan's sister, but she's led them to nothing. The husband hasn't been around. Probably off on another toot."

"Huh?"

"He's apparently a notorious drunk. Juan mentioned it to me once."

Juan, still only Juan. Ben had wondered ever since that last contact with Annie why the police didn't consider that Skeet lived down that way. Annie could have gone to Mexico to find Judy, warn her, protect her—or to get Skeet.

Skeet had returned from Baja to find the Sussmans, Judy, and Ben dining at Fancies. He joined them for dessert. The discussion revolved around the missing Annie—everyone had a theory of why she went to Mexico. Ben's was the only one that hinted at Skeet. But he had nothing concrete to go on, and couldn't accuse him outright without some kind of proof.

At Korakia later that night, Ben tried to tell Judy what he suspected. That Skeet was really in love with her. That he had long feared her abandoning him. That he was a control freak who feared losing his power over her. Judy refused to hear any more, then got angry when Ben pressed. So he backed off.

The next morning, she shared something with him that made him even more suspicious, even though he didn't reveal that to her. She told him about thinking Skeet had a phone line in the little chapel, and how strange it was that he was writing in there. Plus, he wouldn't let her inside. That made Ben more convinced he was on the right track.

"Ben?"

He opened his eyes and looked over at Judy. She had folded the *Times* open to the crossword puzzle on the table, but she was sitting with her arms crossed. "Do you think we should postpone?"

"The wedding?" Then it dawned on him. Annie and Kervin were going to stand up for Judy. Annie might not be there. "I guess I just expected she'd turn up before we had to make that decision."

"You think she's dead, don't you?"

He shrugged. "I want her to be fine. But I'll be honest. I'm afraid of what might have happened to her. Look what happened to the others."

Judy clenched her lips, then let out a sigh. "I suppose we have to go on."

He reached over and offered his hand. "We do. Too late to cancel anyhow."

She took his strong hand and held it tightly, and Ben felt her sadness immediately run through his fingers.

Then her cell phone rang. "Hello?"

"Miss Judy?"

Judy's eyes widened. "Juan!"

"My God," Ben said, jumping up.

"Miss Judy, I have to tell you—"

"Juan, where are you?" she shouted. "What happened to Annie, do you know?"

He wasn't listening, he was talking. "It is Mr. Skeeter, Judy, it's Skeet!"

"What are you saying?" she gasped.

"Don't trust him!" And the phone went dead.

"Damn!" she shouted. "Hello?"

Ben said, "He probably feared he was being traced. What did he say?"

She looked shocked. "He said it's Skeet. Don't trust him."

Ben felt validated. But he only asked, "Nothing about Annie?"

She shook her head and slumped into a chair. "No. He just sounded wildly upset. He said, 'It is Mr. Skeeter, Judy, it's Skeet.' "

"Jesus."

Skeet sat in their living room. *His* living room now. His and his alone, never again to be Judy's. It was a room they seldom used over the years, even though it was perhaps the most charming, comfortable, and warm space in the old house. They always congregated in the kitchen. But then, wasn't that the way in most houses? He wished he'd knocked out the wall separating the two rooms. He could still do that. But what for? He would never share this house with her again. There would be no parties, no quiet winter nights reading near the fire, no summer evenings lounging in the pool, nothing.

He got up and tried to do some work. He studied the wedding catering plan. Appetizers at the bottom of the tram, champagne for the journey up to the top of the mountain, then the full buffet dinner in the clouds. What a silly idea. Had to be Ben's. Where they met, how sweet.

Tomorrow was the rehearsal. He hadn't been up the tram in years, and it was time he got a feeling for the equipment he'd need, what would work the best. They'd told him they had a commercial range up there, but he might have to bring one up. Decor was all taken care of by Judy and Esther. He wrote "kosher?" in the margin of the menu. This was going to be a Jewish affair, and undoubtedly some guests kept kosher. He'd talk to Esther about it. Maybe, just for fun, he'd grind a little ham into the chopped liver. The schmaltz would cover the flavor, and he'd get a good laugh. Christ, he needed one. He was worried to death.

Annie. The nosy bitch's body had never been found. Why? They'd left her there, in the car, bleeding to death. The car was discovered exactly where they'd left it, but she and the dog were gone. It hadn't occurred to Skeet about the dog until he returned to Palm Springs and saw one of Scout's gnawed tennis balls lying in Annie's deserted yard. Where the hell had the dog gone? Under the car was his guess, where he'd die of starvation and dehydration. Instead, they were both missing. Of course, what worried him was the fact that because no body had been found, woman or dog or both could still be alive. The dog couldn't talk. But the woman could. And with her big mouth, she certainly would.

All because Judy had abandoned him for Ben. It was almost unbearable, this solitude, this knowing she would never be back. That she would be joined to him by marriage was completely unthinkable. That would mean losing her forever. Unless, of course, there was nobody to marry.

The poisoner shaman would see to it.

He looked at the seating chart and put an X over the chair that said "Groom."

In the tramway parking lot, Skeet saw Esther and Judy drive in. The first thing Judy said when they got out of the car was that Juan called. "Juan?" Skeet said, shocked. "From where? Did they get him?"

"No. I don't know. He was crazed."

"What did he say?"

"He said not to trust you."

Skeet blinked. "Me?" he laughed, then looked at Esther.

Esther Sussman gave him a blank stare. This was no ally. "We're going to be late."

They went up to the tram reception area. Raffie, an African-American girl with dazzling eyes who said she'd moved there from Hawaii, greeted them, then said in a rehearsed voice that sounded more like the narrator of a travel piece, "The Aerial Tramway represents a virtual miracle in engineering and construction. Considered one of the world's major attractions, it extends from the desert floor to more than a mile above into the high wilderness forests. Vistas of both the desert and mountain areas are opened to view. Within a few minutes, passengers ascend from temperatures of desert heat to the coolness of alpine mountains."

Esther glanced at Judy, and Judy glanced at Skeet, who said, "This isn't our first time."

Judy added, just so the guide would be sure, "That's why we wanted the wedding here."

Skeet said, "Did you tell the police about Juan's call? Could they trace it?"

Judy shook her head. "I didn't know what to think."

"Well, then," the girl said bouncily, "let's go on up, shall we?" They followed her. They were eager to run through all the plans before the others showed up for the actual rehearsal.

In the new revolving gondola, which had been reserved for just the four of them and a male operator, the girl continued her spiel, but told them a few facts they hadn't known. Francis Crocker conceived the tramway in 1932, when Palm Springs was just a hundred people, one café, one grocery store, one drugstore, and one small bank branch.

"Crocker Bank, I'm sure," Skeet said with a nod to Esther.

"The telephone company was in someone's house," Raffie continued, "and there was no air conditioning."

Judy couldn't even imagine.

"Crocker chose Chino Canyon, where we are now beginning our ascent." The gondola was moving free of the platform, starting on its way up, moving farther and farther from the rocky soil, hanging in the air. "We are leaving the Valley Station, at an altitude of 2,643 feet, and it will take us fifteen minutes to reach the Mountain Station, at 8,516 feet. There are a total of five towers supporting four steel track cables, as well as four for hauling, two auxiliary cables, and a communications cable. We have two cars, built in Switzerland, one ascending, one descending, which and carry eighty passengers each, plus one operator."

Judy rolled her eyes. She had heard all this the day she had met Ben.

Esther groaned. She started to talk to Skeet about the gondola, how to disguise it, how she planned to decorate it so it looked special, romantic, almost like a fairy-tale carriage. But Skeet, who claimed he'd never heard the history of the tram, asked the girl to tell them more.

"Since you are talking about the gondolas," the girl continued in her programmed voice, "they were just replaced this last year. The lower portion revolves now to give you a sweeping view. This is a double reverse tramway, for each car stays on one pair of track cables moving up and down without turning around."

"Each car counterbalances the other," Skeet said.

She smiled. "Right. In other words, the car coming down helps pull the ascending car up."

Judy looked at Skeet suspiciously. "Why do you care about this stuff?"

"It's interesting." He peered up at the cable above them. "The track cables are tensioned by counterweights?"

"Yes," the girl bubbled, seemingly impressed.

"Counterweights at the Valley Station weighing a total of 166 tons."

"They're gonna need it for Anita Olken's husband," Esther quipped.

At the center point, the descending cable car passed them, filled with tourists taking pictures. As they neared the top, they saw that the snow looked so much more plentiful than it did from the vantage point of Palm Springs, down at sea level, almost ten thousand feet below. Judy felt a secret thrill when she saw the telescope where she had first met Ben, and a big smile crossed her face.

Esther and Skeet talked wedding. He wanted to do one thing, she had planned something different; they finally compromised. She had her heart set on the ceremony being near the windows, but he told her the tables could go nowhere else but that spot. The girl from the tramway thought the guests might enjoy seeing the promotional film, *Crocker's Dream*, on the history of the tramway, but Esther assured her they would not.

After an hour of putting the pieces together, they all felt satisfied, and prepared to leave. Unlike coming up, however, they descended with a group of tourists. As they stood in line to board the gondola, Skeet had an idea. "Why don't you and Ben plan to leave alone from here, like we came up?"

"How do you mean?" Judy asked.

"Go off on the honeymoon from here. Get everyone out here on the platform to throw rice and wave."

Esther loved it. "Like your father and I did. We left in an old Packard with Molsen beer cans dragging behind."

Judy laughed, but liked the idea immensely. "I think that would be great."

"Where are you going, if I can ask?" Skeet said.

"You can't," Judy said, adding, "we want it to be completely private."

As they descended, Skeet stood near the girl from the tramway and asked her, "On hot days, what happens to the cables? Don't they expand?"

The girl nodded. "The concrete counterweights at the bottom compensate for any stretch or contraction in the cable. The cables expand as much as eight feet on a day like today."

"So one can be totally empty and one totally full and still there would be no danger?" Skeet asked.

"None at all."

He said nothing more.

"I can't help her," the older, grizzled man shouted in fury at the younger man standing next to the cot. He put his parched lips to the tequila bottle, finished it, and tossed it against the wall. It bounced when it hit the floor of the cabin, then rolled to a stop at the foot of the cot on which the woman was lying. "Praise Jesus, I can do nothing."

Juan sucked in his breath to keep from shouting

back, got up, and walked out, slamming the door. The sun hit his face like a blast furnace. He could smell the sea, even though he couldn't see it. The Pacific was down under the cliffs, beating away at the rocks.

Juan had gone to Skeet's house during the storm. He had watched them through the windows. He was sure that Judy had seen him, but he knew they could not find him, for the storm was too menacing. He'd never left. When the sun shone again, he had been hiding on a service road to one of the rich country clubs that had gone up along the coast. He was staying in the van that he'd bought the day he leaped the fence in Palm Springs, the day he'd withdrawn all his money at the bank and fled before they got him. He knew that Skeet had framed him, that his only chance was to get him first.

He'd gone to his sister's, but only for an hour, knowing that would be the first place they would look. It was too obvious. He sought out Skeet's villa. He'd watched the goings-on in the chapel, he'd seen Judy distraught, wanting to get out, and finally felt his heart soar as she was able to do so. And then the fat detective showed up.

That he had not counted on. She snuck up to the chapel, watching two of the three Mexican boys Skeet used for henchmen, and then her stupid curiosity got her caught. He had a good vantage point from the top of the hill, above where Annie had climbed.

Clearly, they were going to take her someplace from which she'd never return.

He followed. He kept his distance, but since there were few roads to take once they left Cabo on the way to Todo Santos, he felt secure in the knowledge that he would not lose them. He almost missed the tracks in the road where they'd turned toward the interior away from the ocean, but once he realized it, he managed to park the van and walk the entire way to where they finally shot her.

It had shocked him. He had never seen a murder before in real life. Skeet had poked a gun in her back at the chapel, and then the boys had shown up, covering her with their pistols. Skeet sat in the front seat with Annie, while one of the thugs held a gun to the back of her head from the rear seat. The other boy followed them in the pickup truck. When Juan came upon the scene out in the arroyo, they were taunting Annie, who was still sitting behind the wheel, though the car had come to a stop, its wheels dug deep into the soft sand.

The first shots were at the dog, just to scare him, it seemed to Juan. He jumped, barked, the dirt exploded under him. Then he ran and the boy shot again, but if he was trying to hit him, he missed. Annie screamed, and they all looked at her, at which time the dog, frightened to death, scurried under the protection of the big old Cadillac.

Then as Annie pleaded for her life, Skeet took a gun from the uglier of the two henchmen, coldly lifted it, and shot her. It surprised Juan. He thought he would poison her. Her mouth gaped open in disbelief, and then her head fell forward against the steering wheel. There was an eerie silence. Skeet, moving a few feet back, shouted, "I am the shaman!" and shot her again, this time from behind, probably to make sure she was dead. Then, whooping and hollering, the boys followed Skeet to the truck, and they drove off.

Juan ran to the Cadillac. The wheels were stuck in the sand, so he knew he could not drive her away. Blood seemed to be everywhere, and he expected Annie to be dead. But she spoke to him the moment she realized someone was there. "Thinks he's a goddamned Indian," she mumbled. Even dying, she could make people laugh. But Juan didn't laugh. The front door of the car had been left open, and he knelt there, lifting her head back, realizing she was conscious. "Annie! Annie!" he shouted, not wanting to let her go under.

Her head fell backward, and she gurgled, blood coming to her lips. "Scout," she said softly.

"Scout's okay, he's not hurt," Juan said, "but you are going to die if we don't get help." Against everything he'd been told—don't ever move an injured person, call for help!—he reached into the car and started to pull her out. Almost on cue, perhaps from having heard his name, Scout crawled out from under the car, whimpering. Juan lifted Annie and supported her with his shoulder, pulling her left arm up over it. He felt she weighed five hundred pounds. He was quickly covered with her blood.

But he dragged her, slowly, toward a spot where he was sure he could drive the van to without fear that the wheels would sink into the sand. He laid her down on the ground, promising that he'd be back, but he knew she had already slipped into unconsciousness. Scout sat next to her as he hurried away, wagging his tail in fear.

When Juan returned minutes later with the van, he had a terrible time getting her into the back, but because he had a mattress in there to sleep on, it helped prevent further trauma to her. He used towels to try to stop the bleeding at the hole in her shoulder and the gaping hole in her back. Then he scooped Scout up, tossed him in the front with him, and drove like a madman.

There was no hospital nearby, so he drove to the only doctor he knew and could trust: his own brother-in-law. Hector was standing outside the local bar where he conducted most office hours, a bottle of beer in his hand. Juan drove up, whistled to him, ordered him to get in, and, when he did, whisked him off without explanation. Scout climbed into the older man's lap.

After explaining what had just happened, they drove to Hector's seldom-used clinic office, where they picked up medical supplies. Stopping to buy him some tequila to get through this, Juan drove to a secluded shack that he had remembered his sister said she used to go to when Hector was on a rampage.

Hector did what he could. Bolstered by the ever-diminishing contents of the first bottle of tequila, he worked by candlelight, with Juan as his nurse, performing surgery to remove the bullets that had brought her so close to death. A lung had collapsed, there was great bleeding, and she had gone into shock. But she held on, hovering in that netherworld between light and darkness.

Scout ran up to Juan holding a wet piece of mesquite in his mouth. Juan groaned. He'd been playing games with the dog since the day they bandaged Annie up and got her temperature down. Juan kicked at the stick with his foot, but the dog just pushed it back with a whimper. Juan took it and tossed it. Scout skipped after it, ferociously digging it from the dirt, and returned with saliva and sand all over his furry face. Juan brushed him off. Then Scout's ears perked. What did he hear? A car in the distance?

No, it was something in the cabin. He raced to the door, yapping, yelping, his tail wagging. He wondered what the hell was going on, was he hungry? Juan got up and opened the door.

Hector was kneeling next to the cot, talking to Annie. It was Annie's voice that Scout had heard. The dog rushed in and leaped with all fours up on top of her stomach, knocking the breath out of her. Hector admonished him, pulling him off, and the dog ran around in circles in happy delirium. "Juan," Hector said, "your lady friend, she wake for you."

Juan walked over to her. His eyes met hers, which were clear now, not faded and fuzzy as they'd been when he rescued her from the Cadillac. When she focused on him, she whispered, "You!"

"Me," he fairly boasted.

Annie was in shock. She tried to look around, assess the situation, but it was clear she didn't have any of the pieces of the puzzle. "Jesus Christ," she said. Then she eyed Juan again. "What the hell are you doing here?"

"I saved your life, you fat bitch," he snapped back softly.

She looked at Hector. "Who the hell are you?"

"The doctor he give no credit," Hector answered.

She closed her eyes. She took a few deep breaths. Then she opened them again and said, "Skeet . . ." It was coming back to her. The car. The guns. The drive. The boys. The shots. "Oh, God," she moaned.

"We saved your lousy life," Juan said, "so now maybe you'll believe me."

Hector wiped her brow with a cloth. "You have damage lung, but it getting better. I leave one piece of bullet in shoulder, not harm coming, lose too much blood taking out. You live on fluid. You lose much weight."

"I knew I'd find some good in all this," Annie quipped. She coughed, and pain creased her face. "Jesus."

"Hurting," Hector said, "I know. But it gets better. Here." He gave her a slug of tequila from the new bottle he'd opened.

She gasped, then licked her lips. "Never tasted so good." She let her arm swing down to the floor, where she rustled Scout's fur. "Where the hell are we?"

"I'll explain everything," Juan said, "but you better know I am on your side. I am your friend."

"Well," she said, "I do owe you some seat padding."

"You owe me more than that."

She smiled, and he smiled back.

"You're a sick fucker," she said, eye to eye, "you know that?"

He looked shamed. But he said nothing.

"Now," she said, "what's happened to Judy?"

Night was setting over the California desert. It was almost nine, and overhead lay a blanket of purple and pink, with streaks of orange, tangerine really, fading fast to darkness. The still night air, even at this hour at ninety-two degrees, magnified the quiet, gentle peace of Chino Canyon. The wedding rehearsal was over. When the last cars left the Valley Station parking lot, the silence was punctuated only by the pounding of Skeet's rapidly beating heart.

He was sitting in his car, looking up. He could still see the cables against the sky. In a moment, they would be gone, black lines fading and melding into the inky backdrop.

He pulled out a cigarette and lit it. He looked fascinated, eager. He was talking to himself, had been talking to himself since they came down from the mountaintop hours ago. The idea had come to him on the way down with Esther and Judy and the guide, and it wouldn't leave his mind.

A Winston between his lips, he grabbed his cell phone. He had to think hard to remember the number, but after one misdialed call, he got it. Tomas answered, in Spanish. "Amigo!" Skeet said.

"Sí, boss," the voice said, with obvious pleasure, "buenas noches."

"Amigo," Skeet repeated, "I need you boys up here tonight."

"No, boss," Tomas answered.

"Tonight!" He was emphatic. "I can't do this alone."

"Sí, boss. My brother in San Diego," the boy bragged, "he get us there mañana."

"It's gonna be dangerous," Skeet warned.

Skeet heard Tomas repeat that to someone in the background. Then he heard laughter. "With so much danger, boss," Tomas said, "we go pray in chapel first." And more laughter.

Skeet told Tomas where to have his brother bring them. Then he hung up. He pulled the cigarette from his lips and tossed it out the car window. Then he looked up at the blackness, knowing the cable was virtually overhead.

Annie used the cell phone that Juan had brought her. She dialed Judy. She thought she was calling her cell phone, but she had mixed the numbers up in her head and didn't even realize it when she heard Judy's message, which was different on the home machine from that on the cell line. She left a message with a considerable amount of panic in her voice: "Honey, it's Annie, I'm okay. Skeet left me for dead in the desert. You and Ben get away from Skeet, hear? It's been Skeet all along, as crazy as that sounds. I love you, girlfriend. Bye."

When Skeet walked into the house a few minutes later, he saw the light blinking, and he played the message.

His face drained of blood.

And then, shaking with fury, he erased the message. He knew what he was going to do.

Dear Diary:

There is an Indian story of a shaman who rides to the top of San Jacinto Mountain on the wings of a gentle bird. At the top, the shaman drinks from the melting snow, eats the piñon, sleeps in the forest. He ages, but grows younger as he releases all power to the wind.

Beneath is a man who has shamed the tribe. The shaman sends for him, the bird flies down to pick him up, lets him ride on his wing in the same way. But halfway there is a loud noise. Guns have come into existence by this time, and the bird has been shot by a hunter. The wings no longer flutter, and the bird—and the bad man—drop to the rocky canyon below.

The shaman can save them both. He saves the bird, brings the bird back to life. The bird teaches the shaman new birdsongs to sing the future generations.

The songs are of bad men and how they die. The songs teach us never to hurt, never to shame, always to love. It was an easier time before the white man's guns and pollution and these computers. There were rules then. There are no rules now. Everything is about balance.

The shaman does not save the bad man.

The bad men must die.

Chapter Twenty-eight

On Saturday morning, Hector opened the creaking gate so Juan could drive the van behind the shack. It was still dark, only a few candles burning inside the shack. The patient was doing better. "She eat," Hector said to Juan as he stepped from the van, "like a pig, she eat."

Quiere volver a engordar. Juan laughed and hurried into the building. Annie indeed was doing better. She was sitting up, Scout in her lap.

She looked relieved. "I was a little worried I was going to be here alone with Dr. Feelgood here for the rest of my life. Did you get Tom Sparks?"

"Sí. He'll be waiting for us at the L.A. airport when we arrive."

"You know what?" she said, looking at her wristwatch lying on a table. "My watch is dead. I don't even know what day it is."

"Saturday, June twelfth."

Panic filled her face. She grabbed hold of the chair Juan was sitting in to steady herself. Scout looked up, sensing fear. "Christ! Saturday. The wedding is tonight!"

They hurried out to the van, and Juan headed off in the growing dawn light. When they reached the road for Los Cabos, Annie said, "Listen, tell me how you met Skeet?"

"I met him through Craig Castle."

She was surprised. "How'd you know him?"

"Bought drugs from him when I was seventeen. In L.A. I was curious. Never got into it."

"Why the needles in your place?"

He looked trapped. And embarrassed. "My dick."

"Pardon me?"

"Caverject. Makes you hard. Harder. Surprised you didn't find *that*."

"Jesus," she said, "sorry I asked. You sure got problems."

"None of your business, lady."

"Yeah, yeah. Tell me about Skeet and Craig."

"Well, Skeet shows up one day at Craig's and we got to shooting the breeze. He's asking me what I do and I tell him nothing much, I'm from Venezuela, I work on gardens, I'm learning English. He calls himself a 'desert rat,' starts telling me about Indians and herbs and history. He loved the history of cowboys, of Indians. He says he wants to live in Palm Springs someday when he is rich and famous."

"Don't we all."

Juan stepped on the gas, sending the truck surging forward. "He has this passion for native desert plants, very curious about this kind of thing, wants to experience and experiment with what the Indians ate and drank and used as medicine."

"You two go to the desert together back then?"

He nodded. "Many times, camping overnight."

"Ever know Ben back then?"

"No. I have a book on Indian medicine and rituals, and once Craig and I built ourselves a sweat house. First time I did that, like the Indians did, naked, free. We took peyote and drank cactus tea and tried many different Indian drugs. It was a powerful experience."

"Get sick?"

"Got wise. We saw visions, apparitions, ghosts."

"Have some tequila with your poison as well?"

He laughed. "Tequila is made from agave, a desert plant."

She felt a pain in her side, irritated by the bad road. "Wish I had some now. Tell me, you guys ever try Jimsonweed? I mean, I know Kyle ended up eating it. How about you?"

"Yes. Skeet said we were braves. We were to recreate the ceremony of the elders, and the shaman prepared the potion for us."

"The shaman being Skeet?"

"Yes. He brewed a tea from it, had me put a finger in it and lick that, only a drop to me, to initiate me, he said. I got very very sick."

"That powerful, huh?"

"I fell into a Teddy Bear Cholla."

"What's that?"

"A cactus. The joints break off easily. The spines sting. You need to use pliers to pull them out. I still have scars."

"How about Craig? How'd that stuff affect him?"

"He had hallucinations. And convulsions. It is very powerful. I think he liked it. He always wanted to 'push the envelope,' as they say."

"Pushed the envelope till it killed him." She adjusted her bra straps. She caught him looking. "How about Kyle?"

"I was jealous," Juan admitted. "I knew him. I disliked him. Not good enough for Judy."

"Another drug addict."

"I sent him to the Rupp place when he told me he was splitting. I knew they could get him a job. I don't know how Skeet found him."

"I guess Skeet counted on the fact that both guys were users, so their deaths would be blamed on their addiction."

"Even Troy looked like an overdose. Poor trusting kid."

"Jealous shaman. A madman, as it turns out."

She shifted uncomfortably. Her wounds were really hurting. "Hey, you gonna promise me you'll get some therapy? You're a good kid, but all that shit you wrote, that obsession, that's not healthy. It almost got you arrested for murder. You hear me?"

He nodded, saying nothing more.

* * *

In Palm Springs, Kervin Satterwhite, who, as Judy's other bridesmaid was now thrust into the position of matron of honor, was hosting a brunch for the couple at her glorious house in the Movie Colony. After cocktails around the pool, the guests ate outside in the palapa, feasting on delicious Mexican specialties created by Carmen, the youngest and most attractive Mexican chef in the valley. Conspicuous in his absence, Judy noticed, was Skeet.

When the guests had all left, Kervin and her husband, George, talked with Judy and Ben about the wedding details. Judy had left it up to Kervin to choose her own dress, especially since this was an overnight decision. Kervin showed them the perfect, understated but hip, soft green sheath that she'd found at Carol Dean on El Paseo. Judy told her she was wearing her mother's dress.

"Damn," Ben suddenly said, "gotta remember to pick up the tux for Garry." Garry Dougvillo had been his buddy since high school, and was flying in from Wisconsin to be his best man.

"Desert Tux Rental?" George asked.

Ben nodded. "I brought mine from San Diego. Had a big sale at Jordan's last year and I've never worn it. Never thought I'd be buying it for my own wedding."

They all laughed.

All but Judy. "Where?"

Ben turned to her. "What, honey?"

"Where did you buy it?"

"Jordan's. Old San Diego store."

Judy swallowed. "Is Jordan's a May Company store?"

"Don't think so," Ben said.

George, who was a savvy businessman, said, "Nope. Last of the independents."

When Ben left to get the tuxedo, Judy drove to the restaurant. Skeet wasn't there, either.

"Anna," she said when she stepped inside, "I need to ask you something."

"Ah, the brushing bride!"

"Anna, did Skeet fly to San Diego a few weeks ago?"

She shrugged.

"Anna, you know everything he does. I've asked you so many times, the dumbest things, and you always know because you always have to be in touch with him."

"The cell phone should be surgically attached to my arm."

Judy laughed. "Maybe one day we'll just have them implanted in our brains. Anna, was he in San Diego?"

"He say I should tell San Francisco. Go see Miss Waters in Berkeley. But I no lie to you, Miss Judy."

"I see." Judy hid the churning she felt in her stomach.

Anna reacted with a smile. "Mr. Ben is coming from there, yes?"

"Yes," Judy replied. "So Skeet was in San Diego. . . ." She moved through the restaurant before Anna could say another word, and she went on talking even though there was no one to hear her. "At least for a few hours. At least for enough time to put drugs in someone's apartment."

She went up to Skeet's office. She didn't know why, didn't know what she was looking for. She sat at his desk and tried to process what she had just been told, Ben's fears, the message from Juan warning her about Skeet. It wasn't possible, there had to be some mistake. Then she knew it was not, for amid the clutter on the desk was an Avis car rental folder, which she opened.

He'd been in San Diego another time she hadn't known about. He'd rented a car there on April fourteenth, a one-way rental, drop-off location—Palm Springs. The day he showed up at her parents' house for Passover. He'd flown to San Diego from Cabo, rented the car, killed Troy in the sweat house near San Diego, spent the night there, and returned to Palm Springs the next afternoon, turning the car back in at the airport. Skeet was the "instructor" Troy was studying with. Troy had kept that a secret, probably at Skeet's request. Part of the ritual. No wonder Skeet had tried to instigate suspicion of Ben. Ben may have been a liar, but he was no killer. Skeet was the killer.

When she got back to her car, she tried to drive but couldn't. She pulled over to the side of Ramon Road and cried. She felt herself coming apart. Once the tears were finished, when the emotion was all out of her, she continued back to Korakia. She rushed back into the room. At the sound of the door, Ben turned around. A plastic-enclosed tuxedo lay on the bed. "What's going on?"

She ran to him and clutched him. "Hold me, just hold me," she said, trembling, until the firmness of his arms around her made her feel safe.

Annie collapsed getting off the plane at LAX, and Tom Sparks had her rushed to the nearby Centinella Hospital. They put her through tests most of the afternoon, and the doctor said she had to stay a couple of days at least. Tom Sparks said he was heading to Palm Springs. There he'd be joining a stake-out by local law enforcement.

The minute Tom left the hospital, Annie made Juan sneak her out. She wasn't going to miss the wedding for a damned bullet wound. And besides, Skeet hadn't been caught yet, and Judy didn't know, and she wanted to be the person to tell her. She was off to the desert as well, driven by her personal chauffeur, her new friend Juan.

Judy already knew, though. She told Ben that she'd driven to the restaurant and learned that Skeet had indeed been to San Diego just before Ben was arrested for possession. All Ben's suspicions came to the surface, and together they pretty much outlined what had happened. They called the police, only to learn that the police already knew. They'd been searching for Skeeter McCloy since the night before, but he had vanished. His computer had been found, however, and it had already produced a crazy scenario of diary letters written as if by someone who believed himself to be an Indian.

Judy had Ben drive her to Loran Loran in Palm Desert to get her hair made up. Judy asked Loran herself for just a simple styling that would make the beautiful headpiece from her mother's wedding ensemble, with a small lace veil, stand out.

"An angel," Selma Sherman, who also happened to be there, gushed, "you're going to look like an angel."

Loran said, "I think she looks pretty much like Judy to me." Which is exactly what Judy wanted.

Suddenly, another voice boomed over all of the buzz. "What the hell's going on in here? What you bitches cackling about?"

The words stunned Judy. Not the words themselves, but the voice that spoke them. She turned. No one had seen the person come in. The place was buzzing so with coffee, curlers, dryers, gossip, that no one had noticed. But even Selma, whose back was to the door, heard the voice, the unmistakable, rough, tough, wonderful voice of Annie Chestnut. "Oh, God!" Judy screamed, jumping out of the chair, practically knocking Selma over. "Annie!"

Annie wrapped her arms around her. "Honey,

honey," she said softly, and soon they were both crying.

"Speak of the wonderful devil!" Esther said, getting up from under a dryer.

Selma glowed. "Doesn't this beat all? Hey, Lazarus, where you been?"

Annie looked at them and said, "Little vacation in Cabo. Nobody's writing my obituary just yet." She turned to Judy. "You got my message?"

Judy looked perplexed. "What message? Only Juan called."

Annie explained she called and told her she was alive and that it was Skeet. "I left it on the cell."

Judy shook her head. "No, you didn't." Then it occurred to her. "You sure you didn't dial the home number? If you did, Skeet got the message."

Annie realized that's what had happened. "That's why they can't find him. I tipped him off myself, damnit!"

Selma said, "That's all we've been talking about. Skeet was on the news this morning. Manhunt!"

"How did you survive?" Judy asked Annie.

"Juan."

Judy gasped. "Juan?"

"But they found the car, bullet holes, blood," Esther said.

Annie shushed them with her hands. "Everyone, back to your stations."

A hairdresser rushed to her with clippers in hand. "Sit right here, darling," he said.

"Okay," Annie began. "I made that miserable drive to Cabo only to find the place half washed into the sea. I must have just missed you, Judy."

"Skeet got me a helicopter out."

"My God, that was *you* above me!"

"Annie, what *happened*?"

She began to tell them.

In a tacky Indio motel, where he had put the boys from Mexico, Skeet went over the final plan in detail. Did they understand?

"Sí, boss," Pedro said.

"Oh, understanding very much!"

"Boom!" Manuel laughed.

Skeet shook his head. "No boom unless necessary. Don't go off half-cocked."

"Sí, boss," Manuel apologized.

"Ready to go?"

Tomas, who was lying on the ratty bed in only his undershorts, said, "Where, boss?"

"We are going into the canyon."

The boys looked perplexed. "Tram canyon?"

"No, Palm Canyon. You boys have a mission, the braves must be brave. I am your shaman, sent to guide you and give you knowledge. We will go up the canyon, where we will be given courage and strength, where our ancestors will provide us with the courage necessary to carry out our task."

The boys glanced at one another. They'd heard this kind of thing before, and they weren't real thrilled with it. Manuel said, "Boss, why not just snatch her? Taking her away, before the marriage, you know?"

Skeet let a strange smile creep over his face. "No, she must have freedom. I gave my word to her a very long time ago, and I am a man of my word. In that freedom, with that freedom, she remains mine. To put her in a cage would be to destroy everything."

Tomas looked at the other two. He pulled himself out of bed and reached for his fatigue shorts. "We going up the canyon, compadres, up the fucking canyon."

"There is a dream elixir you will taste," Skeet said, "that will enable you and enoble you to do your best tonight."

Pedro said, "I think maybe I'd rather have a Corona."

"Come," Skeet said, "my boys, my braves, we don't have much time."

The tram cars started filling up at six o'clock, and by seven the last car filled with guests had risen to the top. The temperature on the desert floor was 110 degrees, while at the top it was only 76. The Mountain Station had been transformed from a fairly tacky tourist hut into a beautiful, shimmering, candle-filled room that held what seemed like thousands of white flowers, from roses to desert blooms, white linens and sparkling silver, and a wedding cake that took people's breath away. Skeet's people had done a fine job, and Esther's overall plan was magnificent. The rabbi had arrived. Now all they needed was a bride and groom.

Down at the Valley Station, Ben's cell phone rang inside the breast pocket of his tuxedo. "Last gasp," he answered.

"We're ready up here, son," Henry said.

"Coming right up, Dad," Ben said with affection. He put the phone back in his pocket and turned to Garry, who was trying to figure out how to keep the tux pants he'd rented from dragging on the floor—they only had his waist size with a thirty-six-inch inseam, and Garry needed a thirty-two at most. There hadn't been time for alterations.

They stepped into the gondola, and the operator closed the doors. "Ready?" the boy asked.

"For the ride?" Ben responded. "Yes. For the vows, I'm not sure." Ben saw a roll of gaffers' tape that someone had left after they had decorated the Valley Station platform for the wedding. Together, the guys "shortened" the best man's pants by folding the material under and taping it inside the leg.

"Wow," Garry said as they started to ascend the mountain. "This is incredible."

"Wait," Ben said, "you haven't seen nothing yet."

Had Ben looked down at that point he would have seen a young Mexican standing near a truck in the parking lot, just feet from a policeman on stake-out, making sure Skeet didn't do something before the ceremony. Tom Sparks, who was already at the top, figured he was long gone, that he'd run when he was sure everyone knew the truth, but it was best to play it safe.

When Ben and Garry reached the Mountain Station, the crowd greeted the groom and best man with applause. Esther gave Ben a kiss and warmly hugged his best friend. Ben was getting nervous, and the collection of black-tied men and bejeweled women in this newly transformed, elegant setting all gathered because of him and Judy gave him the willies. Garry patted him on the back. "I went through this once. Gail felt the same way. It's normal."

Ben swallowed hard. "I can't really believe it. Me, the old bachelor." He saw his mother talking to his Aunt Sadie out on the platform where he'd first met his bride, helping her look through the very telescope they'd looked through. "Sure wish Dad could have lived long enough to see this."

Garry said, "He's watching. Probably pretty closely, 'cause this place is a lot nearer to heaven than I ever thought I'd get."

Ben smiled. Then he warmly touched his friend's shoulder. "I never told you this, but you wrote me the best sentiment in that sympathy card you sent when Dad died. You wrote, 'He was a wonderful man, and the best thing about him was he gave me you.' "

"Be happy," Garry said.

"Okay," Esther groaned, "cue the bride."

Henry stepped out to the gondola, turned on his

cell phone again, and said, "Send her up." Had he paid attention, he would have seen a Mexican laborer standing near the back of the building.

Kervin was adjusting Judy's headpiece when the call came. Annie was adjusting her girdle. She had lost enough weight almost dying that the only possible dress for the wedding hung from her shoulders like a shroud. They'd dug through her closet after the hairdressers, but found nothing suitable. The only thing that fit her, a polyester slinky number she'd brought with her from Texas, just wasn't going to work.

Kervin took her to Saks, where they'd found an outfit, but the dress was a wee bit tight—thus the girdle. "I can't breathe," she moaned.

"You'd better breathe," Judy said, "at least till after the ceremony, then you can expire."

"Oh, shit," Annie said, "you're not getting rid of me now. Anyhow, I got me a doctor down in Todo Santos who's gonna keep me alive forever. Or pickled."

"Ready?" Kervin asked. Judy nodded. "You look gorgeous."

When they reached the top, and she got off the tram car with the help of her two bridesmaids, Judy was radiant. Annie and Kervin fixed her, fluffed her, and then gave the signal, and at 7:43 the music began. Kervin took the bouquet handed her and made the walk down the aisle to Garry and Ben, and then turned and waited for Annie.

Annie sparkled. Her hair was a little overdone, but then she wouldn't have been Annie without a little Texas still showing. Her dress was dark blue, elegant but not too sophisticated, just the right blend of formal yet soft and pretty. She had a smile on her face a mile wide, for she'd survived, she'd made it, and nothing now was going to stop her dear friend from becoming Mrs. Ben Spiegel. She took her place next to Kervin, Garry, and Ben, and turned and saw Judy appear in the doorway. She looked radiant in her mother's soft, antique satin gown. Her eyes were wide and the smile crossing her lips came from her heart. She started to walk to the strains of the wedding march, on her beloved father's arm.

At the chuppa, the rabbi gave a short but quite impassioned lesson about love and friendship, about equality in a marriage, not power or control, and wished them a long and healthy life together. They were honored and applauded, and then everyone breathed a sigh of relief, for everyone there had had the same fears, that Skeet McCloy wasn't going to let this happen. But it had. Tom was right, he was long gone.

They sat down to dinner. "What happened to Juan?" Judy asked Annie.

Annie shrugged. "Dunno. Last time I saw him was when he dropped me off. He went home, I assumed.

I called him to invite him, like you told me to, but no answer."

"I think," Ben offered, "this would be difficult on him."

Judy nodded. "It's probably best. I did want to thank him, though, for what he did."

Annie lifted a glass of champagne. "To Juan."

Everyone at the table toasted and drank.

From that moment on, it was nothing but fun. The food was delicious, although Judy found it uncomfortable that they were eating Fancies catered food after they'd learned Skeet was really a madman. Ben did his best to take her mind off it, and when they started dancing—when Pink Martini started to play "Brazil"—the mood took off, and everyone had the time of their lives. Esther and Henry couldn't have been happier, nor prouder.

At ten, Judy and Ben were ready to leave. They had a flight out early the next morning, and wanted to be rested. They started saying their good-byes, while Henry and Garry, at Ben's insistence, piled the tram car with gifts. "We're riding down alone," he said, "no sense not taking advantage of the space." The table designated for gifts seemed ready to collapse. They took as many as they could. The operator closed the door and the gondola started to move. Everyone threw rice and waved and wished them a happy, long life together.

Halfway down, Ben turned to Judy and kissed her tenderly. "I love you, you know," he wanted to assure her. "It's no different now than it was hours ago."

"Did you think it would be?"

"I wondered," he tried to explain, "if maybe it would break the spell."

"Oh, don't use that word, it's too shamanlike right now."

He smiled and hugged her.

"I love you too," she said, "more than ever."

And then, suddenly, without warning, with a jerk that caused even the tram car operator to gasp, the gondola stopped. The cables had tightened and stopped. The car was frozen in midair, motionless once the swinging had stopped. "What happened?" Ben asked.

"I don't really know," the operator said. He grabbed his walkie-talkie and tried to get the Valley Station, but there was no answer. Then the walkie-talkie went dead.

"Electricity?" Judy offered.

They looked down. No, the lights were on above and below, and in the tram car. "This is very strange," the operator said. "This has never happened." He tried the controls, but nothing made a difference. They were simply frozen there.

Ben's cell phone rang. He had forgotten it was even in his tuxedo pocket. "Hello?"

"Ah, the happy groom," the voice said.

A shiver crawled up Ben's spine. "Who is this?"

"Who do you think it is?"

Ben looked at Judy. She said, "Oh, my God. Skeet?"

"This is the shaman," the voice said. "I'm watching you from above. And I have the power below. You are in my control now."

"What?"

"You heard me."

"Your *control*?"

"There's nothing you can do but obey me."

"Are you mad?" Ben shouted. "What do you want? What do you think you are going to do to us up here?"

Skeet laughed. "Madness is all in perception. But perceive this: The counterweights have enough explosives rigged to them to blow them off the face of the earth."

Skeet was ranting loudly enough that both Judy and the operator could hear him, and they looked panicked.

Skeet continued. "There are two of my boys at the bottom who know to set the charge should anyone try to interfere with this. There is a man at the top who will blow the cable apart should something happen down at the bottom. I am watching from the clouds."

"You're in the clouds, all right, you fucking lunatic!" Ben shouted in rage.

"You do what I want, she does not get hurt."

Judy grabbed the phone. "Skeet! Please, don't do this, please. . . ."

"It's up to Ben," Skeet hissed. "It's up to your husband."

Ben took the phone back. "What? How is it up to me?"

"Do you love her?" Skeet asked.

"Of course I love her."

"How much?"

"More than my life."

"Good. *Then step out of the car.*"

Chapter Twenty-nine

Ben gasped. Suddenly, the gondola glowed. They were bathed in light from below. On the phone, Skeet was talking loudly enough for everyone in the gondola to hear. "I want everyone to see you die, so I had the boys rig a little candlepower for the occasion."

Judy cupped her mouth with her hand. She froze in fear.

"You're crazy!" Ben said.

"Skeet, no!" Judy cried. "You can't do this."

But Skeet's voice cackled with nutty firmness. "If you really love her, Ben, and really don't want her to be hurt, just step out of the car."

Ben looked down. And his stomach turned. "Go to hell."

"You've got ten minutes to make up your mind. If you don't answer when I call, you'll all fall to your deaths." Skeet clicked off.

Within five minutes, the police had surrounded the Valley Station and were discussing their options. In that same time, everyone up at the Mountain Station had learned what was happening, and they all stood outside on the deck overlooking the city with their eyes fixed on the cable car, halfway down the mountain, bathed in a bright spotlight.

Henry tried to put his wife's fears at ease by promising her nothing would happen to Judy and Ben, for no one yet understood what was going on, but when Garry walked over to the big steel structures that held the cables in place, he saw a Hispanic man dressed in jeans and a work shirt holding a gun. "No one comes near," he said, "or I blow the cable in a million strands, comprende?"

It wasn't until Ben called up to Henry on the cell phone that the wedding guests realized what had happened. Henry reacted like everyone else to Skeet's impossible demand: He's crazy! Yes, Annie said, he is, and that was why they had to take this seriously.

In the gondola, Ben's phone rang again. "Yes."

This time it was the police. "Tom Sparks, LAPD, here, Ben. Talked to the men down at the bottom. They say these guys are terrorists ready to die for Allah, if you know what I mean."

"For their shaman, you mean."

Judy grabbed the phone. "What can you do? Where *is* Skeet?"

"We'd grab him if we knew," Tom said. "Did he give you a clue?"

"He said he was watching from the 'the clouds.' "

"Up here?" Tom said.

"Maybe a helicopter?" Annie suggested, standing next to him.

Ben took the phone back from Judy and said to Tom, "I'm going to hang up. He said he'd call back in ten minutes. I'll stall him."

"Yes, exactly," Tom insisted.

"Don't worry, I'm not about to get out of this car till it's on the ground." Ben took Judy's hand.

She asked the gondola operator, "Anything you can think of?"

The frightened boy shook his head, then said, "To think I did this tonight just 'cause they are paying overtime. Jesus."

Ben's phone rang. "Skeet?"

"Said your final farewell?"

"No."

"Our Indian forefathers—"

Ben shouted, "You're no fucking Indian! You're a mockery, an insult to all Indians. You're white trash from Los Angeles!"

"Our forefathers," Skeet continued calmly, "believed some men were destined to be poisoners. A man's father, when he begins to make him a poisoner shaman, places a crystal in his left hand. He has to eat the root of a poison plant. He takes his son into the brush where he shoots porcupine quills at a feather."

Ben cupped the Nokia with his hand, telling Judy, "He's babbling."

"Good, it gives Tom time."

Skeet continued, "After poisoning and killing someone, he cries for the man more than anyone, he grieves for the one he has killed. I will grieve for you, Ben, as I grieved for Kyle and Troy, Craig and Norman."

"My God. What crap."

"There are mystical visions and ecstatic experiences associated with this," Skeet said seriously. "Do not mock me."

"I'll mock you, you asshole, for you are a mockery—a mockery of a human being, a mockery of Indians, using their words and traditions to justify your own fucked behavior."

"Step out of the car, Ben. And nothing will happen to Judy."

Judy shouted, "And what will you do? Take me away again to that prison in Cabo? Lock me in your little shrine to the Indian princess? Skeet, you're sick, you need help!"

"If he really loves you, Judy, tell him to step out of the car. And you can go on alone. I will never harm you, never possess your freedom. The shaman wants only to rid the world of the spirits of those who would taint you."

"Ben is a good man. I love him! He won't 'taint' me."

"Judy," Ben said, "you're trying to talk sense here. It can't be done."

She clenched her fists and clung to him. Ben pressed the button to cut Skeet off. The phone rang immediately. "Ben, it's Tom. We think he's up here somewhere. Don't know how he got here, for no one took him up in a cable car, but the signal from his phone is coming from the top of the mountain. I want to find him and get him and let his buddies know it's over."

"They might still go ahead with it. The Indian braves pleasing their shaman." It was a wild guess on Ben's part, with no clue how close he was to the truth.

"Stall, stall," Tom said. "We need time."

Yet no one could find Skeet. The police SWAT team hesitated to attack the Valley Station, for the two thugs down there had taken three workers and one limousine chauffeur hostage, and to storm the place certainly meant risking their lives. At the top, there were no cops but Tom, and he could not risk going after the boy in the work shirt without assurance that the explosives wouldn't be set off. They were stymied, as frozen in time and space as the cable car.

Every time Skeet called Ben, Ben tried to talk him down, tried to reason with him, tried to humor him. He knew it was pointless, but he figured that not speaking to him at all might frustrate him to the point where he'd kill them both. And he did believe Skeet when he said he didn't want to harm Judy, only Ben. It made his skin crawl how much he believed him.

The phone rang again. This time it was Esther Sussman. "Honey," she said to Judy, "are you okay?"

"Mom, yes, oh, Mom!" Judy felt her heart breaking.

"I've got an idea. Ben, you listening?"

Ben placed his ear to the phone. "An idea?"

"This is almost as crazy as what Skeet is demanding, but hear me out. . . ."

Juan knew that he was close. He had come from Idylwild, the back way, through the trees and the trails, to watch the wedding through the windows. He knew he would have been welcome as a guest—hell, he'd been a hero—but he had to do it this way. His love for Judy would never diminish, but it would have to remain a love that burned from afar. That he watched her be married from afar seemed fitting.

But then he'd seen Skeet. Moving, fast, through the trees. The night was falling, it was getting dark by that time, but he was sure who he'd glimpsed. He knew Skeet was moving toward the Mountain Station, and Juan feared that he was going to stop the wedding.

But Skeet never showed up at the building. Juan watched the wedding proceed without any problem, and then from the trees, he'd sadly watched Judy and Ben descend amid all the rice and loving wishes. He knew Skeet was still up there. And he was puzzled why he'd done nothing.

Now he knew what had come to pass. He'd seen the wedding guests peering down the mountain from the deck. He heard their panicked voices. And he was on a desperate search for Skeeter McCloy, to stop this before someone got hurt. He heard the snap of a twig, then Skeet's voice on the phone. He was closer to the edge, close to the cables. Suddenly Juan could see down, see the little glowing cage that held Judy and Ben. But he couldn't figure out exactly where Skeet was.

"Ben?" Skeet said.

"Yes."

"Ben, it's time. We don't have all night."

"Why not?"

"Ben, this isn't going to change. If it goes on forever, I'll just have the boys blow up the cable. Judy, tell him to take that little walk, okay? Sophie's choice. It's you, Ben, or both of you. Don't be selfish, Benji. Don't take her with you."

Skeet heard Judy cry, "He means it, Ben."

"What do you mean he means it?" Ben shouted at her.

"He's crazy! He is going to kill all three of us!"

Ben said, "So it's better only I die?"

"I didn't say that."

Skeet heard the cable car operator say, "Man, I'm not gonna check out just 'cause you don't want to, man!"

"Screw you too," Ben yelled.

Skeet liked this. This was exactly what he wanted. He didn't have to say a word. He perched atop a boulder and looked down and waited. He knew what was going to happen.

"I'm not playing into his insanity," Ben shouted.

"I don't want to die!" Judy yelled.

"Me too, lady!" the operator yelled.

"Judy, stop it!" Ben sounded hysterical. "Damn you, kid, get your fucking hands off me!"

Skeet heard noise, a scuffle, he could see the cable car swinging. He heard the loud gasps from the guests as they watched through the telescopes and with their own eyes. Skeet heard Judy suddenly screaming—

And then he saw the most unimaginable sight in the world. It was as if it were a vision induced by the dreamweed, a nightmare of petrifying proportions. The door on the cable car, Skeet saw through his binoculars, opened. But Ben did not step out.

Judy did.

Ben's scream could be heard echoing through Chino Canyon, his terror crying out in a guttural, heartrending wail of incomprehensible pain.

Skeet's binoculars followed the descent of his beloved Judy, a vision in white in her bridal gown, with the veil still attached to her head, blowing in the wind, as the weight of her body propelled her faster and faster down through the beam of light that was shining on the car, to her death on the jagged hot rocks of the canyon five thousand feet below.

Chapter Thirty

Skeet's own cry of pain was overshadowed by the screams from all the guests at the Mountain Station. They too were witness to the unbelievable incident, and their collective shock bathed the mountain in grief. On the phone, Skeet heard Ben crying, "Judy! Judy! Judy, what have I done? Oh, my God, oh, my God."

Juan had heard Skeet's scream. He was only twenty feet away, perched atop a boulder, holding his binoculars in one hand, teetering, it seemed, in shock. As Juan withdrew his gun from his pocket, Skeet clicked the phone off, stopping Ben's regrets, and dialed again. He said, "Tomas, go—"

Juan fired, stopping his voice in mid-sentence, the bullet entering just over his right eye, shattering his brain. Then he toppled into the darkness below. The shaman was gone.

The Mexican at the cable wheels looked over toward where the gunshot came from just long enough to be distracted. Tom Sparks, Garry Dougvillo, and three other men in tuxedos attacked him. He was apprehended.

"Boss? Boss?" Tomas shouted into the phone. "Boss, what we doing?"

The cops overtook him and Manuel as well, and when they had figured the shaman had gone to his great reward, they were not willing to join him for that great fire in the sky just yet. They surrendered without incident, and the hostages were released. And the car was now on its way down.

But there was the body of the bride to deal with.

Tom Sparks and Annie found Juan sitting atop the boulder where Skeet had fallen. Juan was weeping. Annie knelt down and comforted him. "Well, I wondered where you'd vanished to."

"I killed him."

"Yes. Good."

"Judy is dead."

"I don't think so."

"I should have found him faster." Juan was lost in recrimination.

Annie shook him. "She's *not* dead!"

"What?" He blinked through his tears.

"She's not dead. Judy is as alive as you and I."

As the car began to move, Judy got up from the floor in her underwear and Ben held her tight. "It's over," he said. "You okay?"

She clung to him. "Fine, I'm just fine.

"You sounded really believable," she told him.

"Yeah, well, it wasn't hard."

"Man," the gondola operator said, "what a night. You guys are good."

"You did a pretty convincing job yourself," Ben assured him.

Esther's idea that they pack as many wedding gifts as they could into Judy's dress had worked. The gaffers' tape that Ben and Garry had used on Garry's pants was still in that gondola, so they were able to bind the gifts, some opened, some still in boxes, to the inside of the dress so that it had seemed to Skeet, who they gambled was far enough away, that it was really Judy who had fallen from the car in her fight with Ben.

When they stepped off the car at the Valley Station, a cop offered her his shirt. Ben put his arm around her and said, "It's finally, really over." And she kissed him.

It turned out not to be the wedding night they had planned. They spent most of it being grilled by the police, tying up the loose ends, trying to understand it all, and with Annie and Juan's help, they did. Judy hugged Juan when Annie and Tom Sparks brought him in, grateful to him because he had saved not only Annie's life, but hers and Ben's and the cable car operator's as well.

Late that night, as the family and Annie gathered at the Sussman house, Esther asked, "Did he really believe himself to be some kind of shaman?"

"Apparently," Ben said.

"I think back," Judy offered, "and realize he was always fascinated with the desert, with its history, with Indian life. He served desert foods in the restaurant, barrel cactus tea sometimes, chayote. He had taken classes on Indian history, but of course this was all so long ago that I had forgotten. Now it all comes back in living color."

"Fitting," Annie growled, "he died up there with his Indian legends."

"I have to say," Ben's sister Julie said, "talk about performance art! Oh, too cool, you guys. I wish I had it on tape."

"Hey," Ben said to Annie, "I forgot to ask. Did they have enough explosives to really break the cable?"

Annie soberly replied, "Enough to bring down the entire mountain."

Esther looked at her daughter, her head resting on Ben's shoulder on the sofa. "You two still leaving in the morning?"

They nodded. "Nothing's stopping us now," Ben said.

"And the cruise ship leaves Miami on time," Judy said. "We want to be on it."

"South America," Esther said to Henry, "how come we never went there? Oh, Buenos Aires."

Henry said, "It's the Antarctica part that I like. Boy, you're going to have a ball."

"Juan gave me the name of several restaurants in Caracas," Judy said, "while we were hanging around the police station. It's going to be great. It's our second port."

"God," Esther said, "be with you both."

Judy and Ben smiled.

Epilogue

Caracas, Venezuela
Five Days Later

When the mighty ship had been secured in the harbor at the port of La Guaira, Venezuela, Ben and Judy disembarked and went by cab over the mountain to Caracas, to the Hotel Avila, which Juan said was the most charming and his favorite there. It turned out to be true. Formerly the Rockefeller Estate, it was located in a rich suburb, surrounded by gardens and so bedecked with flowers and vines that they gratefully forget that they were in a sprawling, overbuilt, crime-ridden South American city. Their room had a balcony with a view of the mountains, a breathtaking sight blanketed in jungle green, reminding them very much of Palm Springs with Mount San Jacinto standing guard. But that memory was harmed now by the recent terror on that same mountain, so they put it out of their minds.

They went shopping in the old town for two hours, and then decided to have lunch and consult their guidebooks to learn which of the sights, churches, museums, and monuments they would visit that afternoon. It was a sunny, breezy day, and they wanted to eat outdoors. Judy pulled out the list of places Juan had provided, and remembered which one was outside for sure. They set off to find it.

They took a metro to the Plaza Altamira station, then walked to the Centro Plaza shopping center. Juan said it was three blocks up from the center, on Eduardo Street. He didn't, of course, know the exact address. They walked three blocks up the street, looked around, but they did not find the restaurant they were looking for. Oh, there were several to choose from, for this was the Altamira restaurant sector, but Judy had had her heart set on the charming place Juan had described, with fresh tortillas like he used to buy from a tortilla factory as a kid. Ben saw an English-speaking tour group walking behind a stout woman with a cane. He said to Judy, "I'm going to ask her."

Judy said, "There's a cop, I'll try my Spanish out on him, he might know better."

Ben went toward the group leader, and spoke with her, to no avail.

Judy went toward the corner, where the cop was directing the impossible traffic. Ben noticed her out of the corner of his eye, gesturing wildly. Her Spanish must not work here as well as it had in Palm Springs, he figured.

When he finished thanking the woman, who lifted her cane and led the charge of the group up the street, he turned and walked to the corner. Judy was no longer with the policeman. He looked around, suspecting to find her right next to him. But she was nowhere to be seen.

He waited patiently for a moment, then began to wonder. He spoke to the cop, who didn't understand a thing he was asking. "The woman you just spoke to," he shouted over the roar of the cars, "which direction did she go?" He pointed, gestured, pantomimed, but the cop just kept saying, "No comprende, señor."

Mystified, he returned to the curb and waited.

And waited.

And waited.

20 July
The Interior, Venezuela
Dear Diary,

I have not been to this region since I was a boy and we went to visit the cousins. I visit my relatives again now, and they are welcoming us to their lives. They understand everything. They will help. They are family.

It will take her time, that's all. Time to adjust, time to get used to it, time to see the truth about love and open her wounded heart. She speaks fairly good Spanish already, so she can talk to the relatives and feel she is part of the family. She will always be treated with honor and respect.

The money I saved from working those years in Palm Springs will get us through for a very long time. It is less expensive here, in Venezuela, and certainly a lot more inexpensive to live in the mountains here than in a city like Caracas. I go there from time to time, to buy her things, anything she wishes, anything she desires, and for my own needs if she will not meet them. I understand this will take her time. I'm prepared to visit the priest until she is ready.

Very compelling to me now is my long-ignored Indian culture and traditions here in the mountains, very much like the Cahuilla traditions and legends and birdsongs. I see plants on my morning hikes through the rain forest and I wonder about them, what do they do medicinally, can they alter consciousness, do they make you dream? I want to learn more. I am starting a diary about it all. I am perhaps sounding like Skeet. But I am not Skeet.

I am not crazy.

I am not the madman.

Thom Racina's Web site:

You're invited to visit the author on the web at www.thomracina.com, where you can learn more about him, his books, and his career writing daytime television, as well as sign his guestbook and e-mail him your thoughts and opinions.